Also by the Author

The Erin O'Reilly Mysteries
Black Velvet
Irish Car Bomb
White Russian
Double Scotch
Manhattan
Black Magic
Death By Chocolate
Massacre
Flashback
First Love
High Stakes
Aquarium
The Devil You Know
Hair of the Dog
Punch Drunk
Bossa Nova
Blackout (coming soon)

Fathers
A Modern Christmas Story

The Clarion Chronicles
Ember of Dreams

Bossa Nova

The Erin O'Reilly Mysteries
Book Sixteen

Steven Henry

Clickworks Press • Baltimore, MD

First publication: Clickworks Press, 2022
Release: CWP-EOR16-INT-P.IS-1.0

Ebook ISBN: 978-1-943383-91-7
Paperback ISBN: 978-1-943383-92-4
Hardcover ISBN: 978-1-943383-93-1

For Mark, the most positive
(and toughest) guy I've ever known.

We've got a bonus story for you!

We're so grateful for the love and support you've shown for Erin and Rolf. As a special thank you, we want to give you a free bonus story starring Ian Thompson, Carlyle's bodyguard.

Keep reading after Bossa Nova to enjoy

Saline Solution

An Ian Thompson Story

Can two broken people make one another whole?

Bossa Nova

Pour ¾ oz. dark rum, ¼ oz. apricot brandy, ¼ oz. Galliano herbal liqueur, 5 oz. pineapple juice, and ½ oz. lemon juice into a cocktail shaker half-filled with ice cubes. Shake well and strain into a hurricane glass. Garnish with pineapple fruit flag and serve.

Chapter 1

"Brethren," Father Byrne said. "Let us acknowledge our sins, and so prepare ourselves to celebrate the sacred mysteries."

In the moment of silence that followed, Erin O'Reilly shot a sidelong glance at the people in the pew beside her. To her right was her boyfriend, Morton Carlyle, head bowed, wearing his Sunday best. On his other side sat Ian Thompson with the blonde woman, Cassie Jordan, who'd accompanied them to Mass. Cassie's six-year-old son Ben, already restless, dangled his feet aimlessly and fidgeted. Erin couldn't see Ian's gun, but she knew he was carrying one, even inside the church. She did see his cane, leaning against the pew between him and Carlyle. Ian was too young to be hauling one of those around, but his leg was still weak from a bullet he'd taken in a gunfight three months ago.

Carlyle started in on the Penitential Act. Erin, caught a little off the mark, came in just behind him. "I confess to almighty God," they said, "and to you, my brothers and sisters, that I have greatly sinned, in my thoughts and in my words, in what I have done and in what I have failed to do."

Ian, Cassie, and Ben didn't join in. Erin wasn't sure, but she thought Cassie was some sort of Protestant. This might be her first Mass. Ben certainly hadn't gone to Catholic Sunday School.

And as for Ian, Erin had no idea what he believed these days.

Mechanically, Erin struck her breast with one hand, the way she'd been taught, saying in unison with Carlyle, "Through my fault, through my fault, through my most grievous fault."

Erin believed in God, but she wasn't always so sure about the Catholic Church. She'd been raised in it, sure, by good Catholic parents, but she was a little too independent-minded to be completely comfortable with the canned responses. She'd learned to be distrustful of unthinking obedience, and as an adult, she hadn't been the most regular attendee at Mass.

"Therefore," she parroted, "I ask blessed Mary ever-virgin, all the angels and saints, and you, my brothers and sisters, to pray for me to the Lord our God."

Did intercession really work? Was Heaven structured the same as the NYPD, or a Mafia family, with a strict hierarchy, in which you had to work through your commanding officer, and he through his, all the way up the line to the Police Commissioner, or the Godfather, or God Himself?

She hid a smile at the sacrilegious thought. That was probably the sort of thing she ought to tell the priest in Confession. *Bless me, Father, for I have sinned. I have compared the Almighty to a Mob boss.* They said priests had heard it all, but she'd bet Father Byrne hadn't heard that one.

The priest was talking again, giving absolution. Erin obediently said "Amen," along with the rest of the congregation, and just like that, she was right with the Lord, at least for the moment. If the church blew up, or a gang of mobsters burst in and machine-gunned them, or a meteor hit New York City, she ought to go straight to Heaven.

There'd be plenty of opportunities to commit sins later on, but right now, spiritually speaking, Erin O'Reilly was good to go. She supposed that was one less thing to worry about.

* * *

"Why aren't we eating at the Corner?" Erin asked. They were out on the street in front of the church, watching the parishioners scattering at the end of the service.

"It's good to get away every now and again," Carlyle said. "Besides, it's Ms. Jordan's first meeting with us. I'd no wish to intimidate her in my own domain."

"You sound like some sort of medieval nobleman," Cassie said, smiling. "Ian's told me a little about you, but he specifically said I shouldn't be scared of you."

"Did he?" Carlyle's eyebrows went up. "Well, darling, I'd hate to make the lad a liar. He's right. You needn't be frightened of me."

"We should get off the street, sir," Ian said quietly. He seemed calm, but his eyes were darting around and Erin knew he was considering possible ambush sites or sniper positions.

Cassie slipped a hand into Ian's. "Relax," she said softly. "It's fine. Where are we going, Mr. Carlyle?"

"I've a fine place in mind, just down the street," he said. "Italian. I hope that'll serve?"

"Everybody likes Italian food," Erin said. "How about you, Ben? You like spaghetti?"

"I like spaghetti," the boy said.

"I rest my case," she said.

"Perhaps I ought to give Marian the sack and hire an Italian cook for the Corner," Carlyle said thoughtfully.

"If you want your pub to turn into a Mafia hangout," Erin said.

"That's a bit of a stereotype," Cassie said.

"You ever heard of the IACRL?" Erin asked.

Cassie shook her head.

"That's the Italian-American Civil Rights League," Erin

explained. "It was founded back in the Seventies by a guy named Joseph Colombo. Its purpose was to fight ethnic stereotyping of Italian-Americans as mobsters. Know what the funny thing was?"

Cassie looked blank, but Carlyle smiled knowingly.

"Joseph Colombo was a member of the Mafia himself," he said. "During one of the League's rallies, he was shot and nearly killed in a failed Mob hit."

"Oh," Cassie said. "Well, you still can't say all Italians are mobsters. That'd be like saying all the Irish are drunks."

Erin opened her mouth. Then she looked at Carlyle and closed it again. Both of them started laughing.

"Sir, please," Ian said.

"Very well, lad," Carlyle said. "Let's be moving. We'll talk more once we're safely indoors."

The restaurant was only a couple of blocks away, close enough that it was quicker to walk than to manage the Manhattan traffic. Erin watched Ian's movements. He still had a slight hitch in his stride, but he covered it well.

Ian had recently rejoined Erin for their customary morning runs, though he moved slower than before. Erin kept an eye on her own speed, knowing the former Marine might push himself too hard to keep up if she let him. It was on one of their recent jogs that she'd learned about Cassie Jordan. The news that Ian Thompson had a girlfriend had stunned her. Her detective's instincts had run parallel to her friendly curiosity and she'd immediately tried to extract more information from him. Ian, true to form, hadn't been talkative on the subject. All she knew was that he'd met Cassie while doing physical rehab for the multiple gunshot wounds he'd sustained protecting Erin's family three months ago and that she had a son from a previous marriage.

That had been plenty to pique Carlyle's interest once he

found out. He'd insisted on meeting the young lady in question and had invited them to join him for Sunday Mass, followed by a midday dinner, his treat. And so they found themselves going into a very nice Italian restaurant on a cool September day.

Carlyle had made a reservation and their table was waiting. Once they were seated with their menus in front of them, Carlyle started in on Cassie with his Irish charm.

"Ms. Jordan, your lad here hasn't exactly been forthcoming on how the two of you came to be acquainted. I understand you're a nurse with the Veterans' Hospital?"

"That's right," Cassie said. "I work with wounded veterans on their rehab. That's how we met."

"You were his nurse?"

She nodded. "It isn't every day we get a guy in who's been punched full of holes *after* he got his discharge. I was curious and we got to talking. Then he saved Ben's life."

"What?" Erin exclaimed. "You're kidding!"

"It wasn't a big deal," Ian said. "She's exaggerating."

"The gate on the playground fence at Ben's daycare had a faulty latch," Cassie said. "Ben saw me coming to pick him up and came running out. Ian happened to be walking his dog and he ran into the street. He kept Ben from getting hit by a car."

"That's exactly what I'd expect Ian to do," Erin said.

"Anybody would've done it," Ian said.

"That's not true and you know it," Cassie said. "There must've been fifty people on that sidewalk and you're the only one who moved fast enough."

"That's just training and reflexes," he said.

"Lad, there's such a thing as too much modesty," Carlyle said. "But I can take a hint and change the subject if you'd rather. How's the dog treating you?"

The dog had been Erin's idea. She'd felt that as Ian recovered, an animal companion might be therapeutic. She'd practically dragged him to the animal shelter, where he'd found the most disheveled, scraggly-looking stray in the place. He'd adopted the animal on the spot, named her Miri, and taken her home.

"She's a good girl," Ian said.

"She's cute, in a weird way," Erin said. "But I do think if you put her next to Rolf, they look like 'before' and 'after' pictures on a PSA about canine drug use."

"Miri's never used meth," Ian said. Then he admitted, "She does kind of look like it, though."

"Ian speaks very highly of you, Mr. Carlyle," Cassie said. "From the sound of it, you stepped in as his mentor when he was young."

"Rather like a godfather, I suppose," Carlyle said. "The lad had lost his mum at an early age and his da wasn't holding up his end of things. I did what I could."

"It's hard being a single parent," Cassie agreed, ruffling her son's hair and smiling down at him. "Ben and I had some tough times when his dad didn't come home."

"He was in the Corps, too," Ian said. "KIA."

"I'm sorry for your troubles," Carlyle said to Cassie.

"Dean was a Marine," she said. "We always knew it was dangerous. I guess we never thought it'd happen to us, you know?"

Carlyle's phone vibrated. "My apologies," he said, taking it out and glancing at the screen. He frowned. "I'd best take this. It won't be but a moment."

He stood up and walked away from the table. Cassie looked at Erin.

"So, how did you and Mr. Carlyle meet?" she asked.

"Through work," Erin said.

"And you're with the police?"

"Detective. Major Crimes."

Cassie nodded. "And so you met because...?"

"Oh, he was a murder suspect," Erin said brightly.

Cassie blinked. "You're joking," she said, a little uncertainly.

"Don't worry, he didn't do it," Erin said.

"She's joking," Cassie insisted.

Ian shook his head. "Afraid not," he said. "I told you. Mr. Carlyle deals with some complicated people."

"Oh." Cassie looked like someone who'd just picked up a rock, found a bunch of bugs crawling around under it, and was wishing she'd left it on the ground. "Do you know what you want, Ben?"

"Spaghetti," Ben said in tones of certainty.

"Women like a man who knows what he wants," Erin said, grinning at the kid.

Carlyle returned to the table and slid back into his seat. "I'm sorry for the interruption," he said.

"Anything important?" Erin asked.

"Hard to say," he replied. "I just heard from a lad up in Otisville."

Cassie looked mystified, but the name told Erin what she needed to know. Otisville was the site of one of the medium-security Federal prisons in New York.

"Who do we know up there?" she asked.

"Old Man Acerbo's been a resident for the past few years," Carlyle said.

Vittorio Acerbo was the titular head of the Lucarelli Mafia family. He'd been rounded up along with the heads of the other major Mafia clans in the mid-Nineties and was serving a long stint for racketeering.

"How's our friend Acerbo these days?" Erin asked, mostly just making conversation. Then she saw the look in Carlyle's eyes.

"He's been better," Carlyle said. "He's departed Otisville,

leaving his mortal remains behind."

"He's dead?" Erin hissed, pitching her voice low so as not to alarm Ben. Cassie was watching the exchange, her eyes growing slightly wider.

Carlyle nodded. "Aye. He's a goner."

"So who's in charge now?"

"You know that as well as I do." Carlyle's face was grim. "Vincenzo Moreno."

The waitress had come to take their order, but suddenly, Erin had lost her appetite.

Chapter 2

"I'll have the fettuccini Alfredo," Cassie said. She nodded to Ben. "And he'd like the spaghetti with meatballs, child portion."

"And for you, ma'am?" the waitress asked Erin.

Erin had no idea what she wanted. "I'll get the same as him," she said.

"Children's size?" the waitress asked.

"No. Normal size."

As the rest of them ordered, Erin tried to bring her mind back to what she was supposed to be thinking about. This was the closest thing Ian could get to bringing his girl to meet the parents. They should be concentrating on Cassie, getting to know her. The nurse seemed like a nice enough woman. She was obviously pleasant, intelligent, and easy on the eyes. And Ian, despite his continued hypervigilance, was calmer around her. He even seemed happy. Erin glanced at him with a smile.

The smile fell off her face. Ian was paying no attention whatsoever to the waitress, or to his girlfriend. He was focused on something across the room. His eyes narrowed. Suddenly, with no warning whatsoever, he jumped to his feet. His chair tumbled backward. His coat was already open. His right hand dove inside. By the time it came out again, gripping his nine-millimeter Beretta, he was stepping around the back of Cassie's chair, shielding her with his body.

"Get down!" he shouted.

Erin had started moving in reaction to Ian, her police instincts kicking in, but she'd been a little sluggish. Before she could do anything, he was already up. She'd learned to trust Ian's awareness. She wasted no time asking for an explanation. Instead, she ducked, pulled up her right pants leg, and whipped out the snub-nosed .38 she always carried, on duty or off.

Someone screamed. Across the room, Erin saw a waiter running toward the kitchen and a man springing after him. In the man's hand was the sort of shape every cop learned to recognize.

"Gun!" Erin shouted. Then she followed up with, "NYPD! Everybody down!"

The gunman fired. Blood blossomed on the upper back of the waiter's white jacket, but the man kept running, flinging himself through the swinging doors and out of sight. Erin drew a bead on the shooter. However, the other restaurant patrons had now had time to realize they were witnessing a shooting and were panicking. Several civilians rushed across her line of fire.

She caught a quick glimpse of the shooter as he pursued the fleeing waiter. It was hard to tell what was going on. The dining room had turned into instant bedlam. Maybe twenty percent of the customers were being sensible and either hitting the floor or sitting very still. Everyone else was running, shouting, or both. She saw several cell phones being held next to diners' heads, so at least she could safely assume backup would be on the way as soon as Dispatch got the calls.

"Stay with them," Erin told Ian as she started for the kitchen.

He nodded, holding his pistol in a two-handed Weaver stance. "Go," he said, not bothering to look at her or the rest of their party. His attention was solely on the chaos across the room.

Cassie, Erin noted approvingly out of the corner of her eye, had gathered Ben into her arms and dropped under the table. Carlyle was crouched beside them. They ought to be okay. This had the looks of a personal attack, not a terrorist incident or a mass shooting.

As Erin ran against the flow of terrified New Yorkers, she saw a man slumped over a table. Blood was pouring out of him. Another man, beside him, had grabbed a white cloth napkin and was holding it against the wounded man's neck. The napkin was already turning bright red.

She hesitated an instant, torn between two duties. But as long as there was an active shooter, her priority was to neutralize him. Other cops would be on site momentarily and could help administer first aid. She rushed into the kitchen, hearing two more gunshots as she ran.

Erin shouldered through the double-hinged doors and saw half a dozen cooks and wait staff, all looking stunned and frightened. She also saw a blood trail on the black-and-white checkerboard floor tiles. The irregular pattern of red spatter led straight through the kitchen and out the back door. She saw no sign of the gunman. Assuming he was chasing the man he'd shot, she followed the blood.

With a pang, she wished she hadn't left Rolf at home. Her K-9 partner was at his best in pursuit situations. He could have already caught up with the shooter and tackled him. But Rolf was lounging around the bedroom with one of his chew-toys, so Erin had to rely on her own two feet.

The door led her into a service hallway at the back of the restaurant. A bloody smear on the back door drew her to it. She went out in a rush, revolver at the ready, and saw an empty alley. The blood trail ended so abruptly that she knew the guy had to have gotten into a car, which had driven off.

Why would a waiter have a car waiting for him? And what had happened to the gunman? Erin stood frozen for a moment, perplexed. Something was going on that she didn't yet understand. But she could hear sirens and knew more cops were on their way. It was pointless to run down the alley and out into the street on the off-chance of snagging the shooter. Better to go back in and see what she could do for the victim who was still in the dining room.

She stepped back into the service corridor and nearly ran into a man in a black suit who had just emerged from another door. With a flash of recognition, she saw it was the guy who'd been chasing the waiter.

"Hands!" she shouted, throwing her gun in line and taking aim at his center of mass.

"Whoa, lady," the man said, showing two empty hands. "I don't know what you think is going on..."

"NYPD Major Crimes, asshole," she snapped. "Face the wall. Now!"

"I didn't do nothing," he protested, but he obeyed.

"Bullshit. I watched you shoot a guy less than two minutes ago!"

"Oh. Sounds like I'm in some trouble," he said, sounding less than concerned. "So you've got this guy you say I shot, and the gun you say I shot him with?"

Erin was reaching for her handcuffs when she remembered she was wearing her Sunday church clothes which did not, in fact, include a set of bracelets. She cursed silently and frisked the man anyway. She didn't find a gun on him, but she did find an empty holster on his belt.

"Care to explain this?" she demanded.

"Fashion accessory," he said. "All the cool kids are carrying them."

"Where's the gun?"

"What gun?"

"The gun you were carrying."

"I don't know what you're talking about."

"I'm talking about the holster you're wearing, for the gun I saw you use to shoot a man in the back! I'm talking about the gunpowder residue you've got on your hands and clothes."

"That's all circumstantial," he said glibly.

"What's your name? Or is that circumstantial, too?"

"Frank Vanzano, ma'am."

"Well, Frank Vanzano, you're under arrest for attempted murder, reckless endangerment, and illegal possession and discharge of a firearm. I've got a suspicion you know your rights, and this isn't the first time you've gone through this, but I'm going to read them to you anyway."

"You do what you gotta do, lady," Vanzano said. He'd been amped up when she'd first run into him, but now he just seemed bored.

The kitchen door flew open and a pair of uniformed officers burst through. Erin held up her hands, but made sure to step back from Vanzano and keep an eye on him.

"O'Reilly, Major Crimes!" she shouted, letting her revolver dangle from one finger by the trigger guard. The last thing she wanted was to get popped by an overeager rookie. She saw Vanzano tense for a moment, but the gunman decided against making a run for it.

"Where's your shield, ma'am?" one of the officers demanded.

"Pocket," she said. "I'm taking it out now."

She eased her gold detective's shield out slowly and showed it to them.

"And who's this mope?" the other cop asked, indicating Vanzano.

"He's the one who started shooting," she said. "We've got one casualty in the dining room and one who ran out the back."

"The guy in the dining room wasn't shot," the uniform said.

"He wasn't?" Erin hadn't expected that.

"No, ma'am. Somebody slit his throat. The knife was right there on the table next to him."

"Is he dead?"

"Don't know."

"Shit," Vanzano said.

"You know the victim?" Erin asked.

"I got nothing to say to you, lady. I want my phone call and my lawyer."

"Can you guys take custody?" she asked the uniforms.

"Copy that, Detective," the first cop said, pulling out his cuffs. Vanzano rolled his eyes and gave the ceiling a long-suffering look as the steel bracelets clicked shut around his wrists.

"Take him to the Eightball," she said. Then she slipped her .38 back into her ankle holster and headed back to the dining room.

The restaurant was louder and only slightly less panicked than it'd been when she'd left. Several uniformed officers were trying to restore order, but the patrons weren't making it easy for them. No paramedics had arrived yet, and Erin saw a couple of cops at the table with the wounded man. The guy who'd been holding the napkin against the other man's throat was now standing to one side with yet another cop talking to him. She noted that man was also in handcuffs.

Carlyle, Ian, Cassie, and Ben were still at their table. They were standing now. Cassie was holding Ben in her arms. Ian no longer had his gun out, which was a good thing, considering how many law-enforcement officers were present. His left hand was resting on Cassie's shoulder in what was probably meant to be a comforting gesture, but his body language was fully activated and alert and his right hand remained empty and ready.

Erin clipped her shield to her belt so it was obvious. She crossed the room to rejoin her dinner companions.

"It's over now," she said to Cassie. "Nobody else is going to get hurt."

"What happened?" Cassie's voice was sharp with agitation and fear.

"Mob hit," Ian said. In contrast to her tone, he sounded perfectly calm.

Cassie looked from Ian to Erin. "Is he serious?"

"Usually," Erin said. "I think he's got a sense of humor, but it's pretty well camouflaged."

"But was it? A mob hit?"

"I don't know yet. And I need to get to work now, sorry. I have to duck out on dinner."

"Mommy," Ben said.

"What is it, honey?" Cassie asked.

"You're squeezing me."

"Sorry." Cassie loosened her grip a little, but Erin had the feeling she'd have to break the other woman's fingers if she wanted to get her to let go of her son just then.

Carlyle stepped forward. "Erin must be about her duties," he said. "Why don't the rest of us go back to the Corner? I've rather lost my taste for Italian cuisine."

"I'll see you later," Erin said. "Nice to meet you, Cassie. Ben. I wish it was under better circumstances. But this is my job."

"I'm familiar with the aftermath of violence," Cassie said. "I'm just not used to watching it happen. I'd like to get my boy out of here, if I can."

"Look for one of the sergeants," she said. "Give him your statement, then you should be good to go. And don't worry about Ben. Do you know what's going on, kiddo?"

Ben shook his head. Erin ruffled his hair and smiled at him. She gave Carlyle a quick kiss on the cheek and watched them go. She felt relieved. Something awful had happened, but the people she cared about had only been on the edge of it and it hadn't had anything to do with them. Now all she had to do was her job.

She approached the blood-soaked table, trying to get a picture of what had happened. The cops who had been trying to perform first aid had given up. The man at the table was obviously dead. His throat had been opened from ear to ear.

"He's gone?" Erin asked rhetorically.

"Bled out," one of the uniforms said. "Looks like they got him in both carotids, jugular, and windpipe. Straight across, one and done. Hell of a cut to make with a steak knife."

"That's the knife?" she asked, pointing to the table. A knife, identical to the ones at the other place settings, lay in a pool of blood.

"Looks like it," the cop said. "But you're the detective, so what do I know?"

Erin bent her knees to peer into the dead man's face. She saw a man who was older than he had first appeared. His eyes had crow's feet around them and his cheeks were lined and weathered. His receding hair had definitely gotten a black dye-job. She could see hints of gray around the roots. He was wearing a very expensive black pinstriped suit with a crimson necktie and matching pocket square. He also had a red carnation pinned to his coat. In short, he was the spitting image of a movie Mafia don.

"Who's this guy?" she asked, cocking a thumb at the handcuffed man.

"Martin Stracchi, according to his driver's license," another cop said, holding up the man's wallet. "Native of Manhattan. We got an address in Little Italy. Oh, and he was carrying this," he pointed to a black automatic pistol near the edge of the table, "and this," moving his finger to indicate a switchblade knife next to the gun.

"You got a permit for that gun, Mr. Stracchi?" Erin asked.

Stracchi glowered at her and shifted his shoulders, trying to get more comfortable in the handcuffs. His hands and the sleeves of his shirt were soaked with the dead man's blood.

"Doesn't matter," she added. "You'll have a record, won't you, Mr. Stracchi? And a convicted felon doesn't get a New York gun permit. Plus, that's an illegal knife. We're definitely going to have some questions to ask you."

"Detective?"

Erin turned to see a Patrol Sergeant. "What is it, Sarge?"

"This your case?"

"I guess so."

"You guess? What're you doing here, if you don't mind my asking?"

"I was trying to eat Sunday dinner. Now I'm working a homicide."

"Oh. Was wondering how a gold shield got here so fast. That's some crazy response time."

"I was here before it happened. But I didn't see much. I suppose Major Crimes will end up playing tug-of-war with the Organized Crime Task Force, and maybe the Feebies."

The Sergeant sighed. "The only thing better than a bureaucracy is more than one. Better you than me, Detective. What do you need my guys to do?"

"Get statements from the rest of the customers," she said. "But none of them are suspects. Put out a BOLO for a guy in a white waiter's jacket and black slacks, GSW in the upper back or shoulder. He's about average height, dark hair, either white or Mediterranean complexion. And I want to talk to the manager."

The manager was a tall, graying, dignified Italian gentleman with a neat little mustache. His name was Giovanni. For a man whose restaurant had just hosted a brutal murder, he was remarkably composed. Erin met with him in his office, a dark-paneled room furnished with a heavy desk and a couple of maroon leather chairs.

"It looks like one of your waiters killed one of your customers," Erin said, not bothering with preliminaries.

"Yes, it does appear that way," Giovanni said. "It's very odd. Mr. Luna never gave any signs of abnormal behavior. This is the first time he's done anything of the sort."

Erin gave him an odd look. "I would hope so," she said. "What did you say his name was?"

"Alphonse Luna," the manager said.

"And how long has Mr. Luna been working for you?"

"Six months, give or take. I can give you the exact date of hire once I check my records. But he's been a model employee."

"What about the dead man?"

"He was not an employee," Giovanni said.

"I know that." Erin took a deep breath. "I mean, had he been in here before?"

"Oh yes. Mr. Rossi has been coming to Andolini's every Sunday for years."

That made sense. If the victim had made a habit of coming here, it would have made him vulnerable to a planned attack.

"The curious thing is," Giovanni continued, "Mr. Luna served Mr. Rossi on many occasions. They were on quite friendly terms."

"Did they have some sort of argument?" she asked.

"No, not that I heard."

"I'll need your information for Mr. Luna. Address, phone number, emergency contacts, all of it."

"Of course, Detective. Anything I can do to help."

Erin stepped out of the manager's office and fished out her phone. It was time to bring the rest of the gang on board.

Lieutenant Webb didn't answer until the fourth ring. Then, instead of his usual terse "Webb," he said, "This better be important, O'Reilly."

"Why don't you decide, sir?" she replied, nettled. After all, her day off had also been spoiled. "I was sitting down to a nice Sunday dinner at Andolini's Restaurant when one of the waiters decided to slit a customer's throat."

There was a short pause. "So, you witnessed a murder?" Webb asked.

"Yes, sir."

"And you know who did it."

"Pretty sure, sir."

"So this is open-and-shut."

"I'm not so sure about that, sir."

"Explain."

"The suspect escaped. He's injured, but he's in the wind. And he had a getaway car, which means there's probably an accomplice. Plus, our victim had a pair of bodyguards carrying illegal guns, and if they don't have records, I'll eat my own shield. Which means—"

"Organized crime hit," Webb sighed. "Yeah, I copy. Andolini's, you said?"

"Yes, sir."

"I'll be there in thirty. Call Neshenko, would you?"

"Will do."

Chapter 3

"Yeah?"

The voice on the phone was slurred almost to the point of unintelligibility. Erin took a second to double-check that she'd called the correct number.

"Vic?" she asked. "That you?"

The answer was something that sounded sort of like Russian, if the guy speaking it was talking with a mouthful of cotton balls.

She tried again. "Vic! It's Erin!"

"Whaddaya want?" he mumbled.

"I want my Major Crimes squad. Get to Andolini's Restaurant. Manhattan. Forthwith."

"Why?"

"Why do you think? We've got a body."

Vic muttered something. Erin didn't speak Russian, but it sounded like swear words. Then again, Vic could make almost anything sound like cursing.

"Vic?"

"What?" He sounded a little more awake now, but grumpier. "Not so loud!"

"Are you drunk?"

"What if I am? I'm off duty."

"First off, no, you're not. Because you've just been called in. Second, it's noon on a Sunday. You know who gets drunk at that time of day?"

"Is this some sort of trick question?"

"Drunks, Vic. That's who."

"Erin, aren't those always the people who get drunk?"

That silenced her for a few seconds.

"Whatever," she finally said. "Just drag your sorry ass down here ASAP. And for God's sake take a cab if you're too drunk to drive."

Erin hung up, wondering what was wrong with everybody. Then she went around the restaurant asking whether anyone had seen anything that would help. What she got was pretty much what she already knew. Cops loved the idea of an eyewitness who'd seen the whole thing happen, but in this case, it was surprisingly little help. But then, she recalled a previous case where several hundred eyewitnesses had watched a murder happen, and they'd still ended up tying themselves in knots trying to solve it.

"I watched it happen," a breathless woman told her earnestly. "The waiter walked up to the table and took their orders. Then he just picked up the knife, right off the placemat, and whoosh! Cut right across! Like he was opening a letter! Then he ran away and that other man jumped up and pulled out a gun! And he shot him! The man in the suit, I mean, shot the waiter. Not the other way round. But he kept running! The waiter, not the other man. Well, the other man ran, too, after him. They both ran through that door."

"Thanks for your help, ma'am," Erin sighed. The murder was only a few minutes old and they had a positive ID on the killer. She should be happy, but she was thinking about the phone call

Carlyle had gotten right before Mr. Rossi had choked on his steak knife and ruined his fancy suit. It might be a coincidence, but Erin didn't believe in coincidence. Not when it came to homicide.

Webb and Vic still hadn't turned up when she finished canvassing the witnesses, so she borrowed the use of a Patrol car's computer and looked up the four names she had. While she was doing that, someone knocked on the squad car's window. She looked up to see Webb and Vic. Webb looked about like he usually did, which was to say tired and exasperated. Vic looked bad. His eyes were bloodshot, his hair sticking out at odd angles, and his shirt looked like he'd slept in it.

Erin rolled down the window. "Thanks for coming so fast," she said.

"I'd have been here sooner, but I ended up playing chauffeur," Webb said, giving Vic a sour look.

"Don't look at me," Vic said. "I didn't kill anybody. It's not my fault our day off got spoiled. How come you didn't kick this over to the boys in Homicide?"

"Because she doesn't dodge responsibility," Webb answered for her. "What've you got on our victim, O'Reilly?"

"Stefano Rossi," she said. "He's a *capo* in the Lucarellis."

Vic whistled. "A made guy," he said, looking a little more alert. "Whacking him is a big deal. Don't you have to get permission or something?"

"You're supposed to," Webb said. "But then, you're not supposed to kill people in the first place. Somebody's always forgetting the rule book."

"But the Lucarellis are gonna come gunning for the guy who killed him," Vic persisted. "That's how it works."

"They'll have an easy time finding him, I think," Erin said. "Our suspect, Alphonse Luna, is one of their soldiers."

"Wait a second," Webb said. "You're telling me this Mafia bigwig got done in by one of his own guys?"

"That's how it works," Erin said, echoing Vic. "It's actually more likely than being killed by a member of one of the other families. That would be a declaration of war. This is more like a headcount reduction. Did you hear about Old Man Acerbo?"

"Isn't he serving about a hundred years upstate?" Vic asked.

"He had a life sentence," she said. "That sentence is up as of this morning."

"Natural causes, or homicide?" Webb asked sharply.

"My source thinks he was murdered," she said.

"Confirm that."

"I can call them," she said. "But he died in a Federal facility. That's not our jurisdiction."

"It may not be our jurisdiction, but if there's a mob war starting in our city, it's going to be our problem," Webb said. "Whether the FBI gets involved or not."

"They will," Vic gloomily predicted. "Goddamn Feebies can't keep their hands out of the cookie jar."

"In this analogy, are mobsters cookies?" Erin asked. She got out of the squad car so she didn't have to keep cranking her neck sideways to talk to the other detectives.

"Yeah," he said. "And I'm not talking chocolate chip, either. The shitty oatmeal raisin kind."

"I hate those," Erin said.

"Everybody hates them," Vic said.

"So where's our suspect?" Webb asked in an effort to steer the conversation back to murder.

"On the run," she said. "He's got a bullet in the back, so he may not get far. I've got a BOLO out."

"Okay," Webb said. "Let's find out where a wounded Lucarelli would go to get a GSW treated off the books.

Neshenko, work your SNEU contacts. They've been hitting the Lucarellis."

Vic grunted noncommittally. "You think they're gonna know anything about street docs? They're narcotics hounds."

"I don't know, Neshenko," Webb said in tones of weary exasperation. "Will you just ask them?"

Vic sighed. "Yes, sir."

Erin shot him a look. One of Vic's contacts with the Street Narcotics Enforcement Unit was Zofia Piekarski, a petite blonde firecracker of an officer he'd been seeing for several months. Vic should have been glad of the chance to work with her. Erin's intuition nudged her something was going on there. It could wait.

"O'Reilly," Webb said, turning his attention to her. "Any point in bringing your K-9 here?"

"I don't think so, sir. The blood trail ended abruptly. Luna got to a vehicle. I've got an address for him."

"Pick up your dog and get an ESU team. Then get over to his place and knock the door down. I'll have the warrant ready by the time you get there."

"How come Erin gets to kick in doors?" Vic demanded.

"Because you're either sick, hung-over, or drunk off your ass," Webb said. "And in none of those cases does it make sense for you to be serving a warrant."

"You really think Luna will be there?" Erin asked.

"Probably not. But he may have gone back. Maybe you can pick up his trail. Do I have to do all the thinking for this squad?"

"Only on our off-days, sir," she said, which earned her a weary, cynical smile.

"Anything else I should know?" Webb asked.

"We've got both Rossi's bodyguards in custody," she said. "One of them is on his way to the Eightball, the other one's still inside."

"They'll be useless," he said. "But I'll take a run at them anyway. I hate Mob hits."

Erin was inclined to agree. The whole point of an underworld assassination was to make it clinical and professional. Usually the killer had no personal beef with the victim. He was just carrying out an assignment. It made it extremely difficult to know why the man had been killed, or who had ordered the killing, unless they could catch the hitman and flip him to give up his boss. And that was iffy, since everybody knew what happened to snitches. Even these days, with most of the really big old-school mafiosi doing hard time, the low-level gangsters were more scared of their bosses than they were of anything the New York legal system could throw at them.

"We oughta reinstitute the electric chair," Vic grumbled, as if reading her thoughts. "Put the fear of God and lightning back into these bastards."

"It didn't work back then," Webb said. "You know the definition of insanity?"

"I think it's in my job description," Vic said.

"Don't you have a phone call to make?" Webb suggested.

Vic walked away, muttering darkly to himself.

"Sir," Erin said.

"What now, O'Reilly?"

"Something going on with you and Vic?"

"I have no idea what's going on with Neshenko," Webb said. "And I don't care. I look at his life and I think of those slow-motion crash-test dummy videos. It's ugly, but maybe the rest of us can learn from it. As for me, I was in the middle of talking to my ex-wife when you called, if you must know."

"Didn't she go back to Los Angeles after that thing with the real-estate agent?"

"No, the other ex-wife. The first one."

"Oh."

"Our daughter, the older one, wants a car."

"Does she have a license?"

"You think that's the point?" He rubbed the bridge of his nose. "I could swear she's still in the third grade. It really sneaks up on you, the way they grow up, especially if you're living apart. You know how dangerous driving is. Next thing you know, she'll be interested in boys. Then she'll be going off to college. I was in the middle of a delicate negotiation, trying to talk Susan around, when you interrupted the call."

"Sorry, sir. And I hate to break it to you, but I was interested in boys way before I turned sixteen. If it's any consolation, I was in the middle of a conversation about how Italians aren't all Mafia goons when one of them cut another wide open."

Webb chuckled. "Really?"

"Really."

"So I guess this screwed up everyone's day."

"Particularly the dead guy's. I'd better get going. I'll pick up Rolf on the way and call you when we're ready for the warrant for Luna."

* * *

Ian had driven the others in Carlyle's Mercedes, so Erin was stranded. She took a cab back to the Barley Corner. Carlyle's pub really did feel like home now. The rough Irishmen who filled the place every evening were on friendly terms with her, even though—and maybe because—she'd blown away the O'Malley family's chief enforcer in a vicious close-quarters fight back in June. Mickey Connor had definitely had it coming, and any woman who could take him down was not to be trifled with.

Erin's conscience bothered her when she remembered a good many of these guys were going to go to prison because of her, assuming everything went according to plan. She and Carlyle had been amassing evidence for months, forwarding it to Lieutenant Phil Stachowski's files. They had wiretaps, recorded conversations, names, dates, and crimes. All they needed to put the final nails in Evan O'Malley's coffin was his ledger. Carlyle knew some of Evan's financial records, but they needed all of them in order to make a clean sweep of the O'Malleys. And so far, they didn't have the ledger, didn't even know where it was.

That wasn't her greatest worry with the O'Malleys. Neither was the fact of Carlyle's undercover work, though that was a constant source of raw material for her nightmares. The O'Malleys liked her, trusted her as far as they'd ever trust a cop. And that was the worst part. She'd killed a man and accepted Evan's money for doing it. And that meant, sooner or later, he'd expect her to do it again.

That would just become so much more evidence against him, she knew. But once she got the order, it meant they'd need to shut things down. Immediately, whether they were ready or not. Because Erin was never going to kill for the Irish Mob.

It must be these Mafia hits working on her subconscious, she thought as she opened the Corner's door. She was getting gloomy and pessimistic and that was bad. Pessimists made mistakes because they expected to fail.

The pub wasn't terribly crowded now that the Sunday brunch crowd had come and gone. Erin saw Carlyle at the bar, but she didn't see Ian, Cassie, or Ben. They must have already eaten while she'd been busy at Andolini's. But she did see one face she wasn't keen on. The man was playing darts. As she watched, he threw a perfect bulls-eye. He did it casually, almost carelessly, like he did most things.

"Corky," she growled.

As if he'd heard her, James Corcoran turned toward the door. The red-headed Irishman saw Erin and his eyes slid away from her. Those eyes held none of their customary sparkle. Without looking at her again, he sidled into a booth and sat down.

Erin wanted to go over there and shake him until his teeth rattled. She wanted to punch his lights out. She wanted to scream at him. It had been three months since his canoodling with her sister-in-law had drawn Michelle O'Reilly into Mickey Connor's orbit. That had resulted in Michelle's abduction and Mickey's death, along with the deaths and injuries of several other people, including two police officers and Corky himself.

Ever since then, Corky had been avoiding Erin. He still came to the Corner, but aimed for times when she was likely to be at work. When their paths crossed, he got out of her way. He'd been uncharacteristically subdued, like a whipped puppy. Either he was afraid of her, or wrestling with his own guilt. Either way, she was out of patience with him.

Carlyle, ever the gentleman, was on his feet to greet her. A shadow of concern crossed his face when he saw her looking at Corky. Rather than wait for her to come to him, he crossed the room.

"All's well?" he asked quietly.

"Do you know Stefano Rossi?" she asked, pulling her gaze away from Corky's booth.

"I've heard of him, aye. Lucarelli captain, I believe."

"Not anymore. He's the guy who got his throat slit."

"I see."

"Can you find out anything from your guy up in Otisville about Acerbo?"

Carlyle drew her off to one side of the room. "My lad's a prison guard," he said. "What is it you're needing to know?"

"I need to know who killed Acerbo."

"Can't you get that through proper channels?"

"Probably. But your guy got the word to you fast. If Lucarellis are getting whacked, more of them may be on the chopping block. We need to move on this."

"I'll ask him. What's your next play?"

"I'm taking Rolf and trying to run down the hitman. Is Cassie okay? I hope she isn't too freaked out."

"She's a tough one, I'm thinking. Apparently her husband was a Marine. Poor blighter was killed in Iraq a few years back. She's no stranger to hardship."

"I meant about Ian. The way he whipped out his gun. Some women might find that disturbing."

"The lad makes no secret of who he is. Remember, she helped him through his recovery. She knows what he's capable of. Besides, his first impulse was to protect her. In my experience, a lass takes kindly to that manner of thing."

"I guess. Speaking of protecting women, what's *he* doing here?" Erin cocked her head in the direction of Corky's booth.

"He's a paying customer, Erin. And he's my friend."

"You know what he did."

Carlyle raised his hands, palms outward. "Don't do this, darling."

"Do what?"

"Force me into this position."

"And just what position is that?" she demanded.

"Don't ask a lad to stand between his colleen and his mate. He'll wind up defending each against the other. In the end they'll both be angry with him."

Erin put her hands on her hips. "Don't tell me you're on his side!"

"If you want me to admit he acted rashly, I'm the first to agree with you," Carlyle said. "But he'd no notion anyone would get hurt."

"He tried to screw my brother's wife!" she hissed.

"I'm not excusing him," he said hastily. "But he's very sorry and he'd like to make amends."

"And just how does he plan to do that? He hasn't exactly been falling over himself apologizing."

"The lad's ashamed of himself."

"Corky's never been ashamed of anything in his life!"

Erin said it loudly, not really caring who overheard. She saw Corky's head poke out of the booth in response. She spun away from Carlyle, moving too quickly for him to get in the way, and stalked toward the booth.

"Yeah, you!" she snapped. "How many women have you slept with? How many men have you killed?"

"Erin," Carlyle said. "This isn't the place for this." He shot a meaningful look at the few other patrons, who took his hint and became suddenly very interested in the TV screens.

She ignored him, continuing her advance on Corky, who was sitting very still, watching her. "And how many friends have you gotten killed? Yeah, you always walk away, you and your goddamn luck of the friggin' Irish! When did you ever look back? When did you care what you left behind?"

She was right up next to the table now, an anger she'd hardly realized was in her pouring out in a flood, the accumulation of three months' brooding. She leaned in, glaring at him, daring him to say one word, just one word in his own defense.

"Anything else you'd like to say?" Corky asked softly. His eyes were bright now, but to Erin's astonishment they were shining with unshed tears.

Erin couldn't stop now that she'd started. She'd temporarily lost control of her tongue. "You tried to break my family, Corky," she went on relentlessly. "Shelley's still having nightmares. My brother's miserable, thinks the whole thing is his fault because he wasn't there to protect her. Mickey came after their kids. Don't you get it? They could've *died!* And Ian practically did! He's your best friend's son in all but name and he nearly got killed protecting my family! And now you're sitting there, wallowing in self-pity like that makes things any better. That's just as much bullshit as pretending it doesn't matter. It's all just a way for you to duck responsibility, like you've been doing your whole life! You're still just the same little boy you've always been. When are you going to man the hell up and deal with your shit?"

"You're right," Corky said.

"And you can't just go on—" Erin continued, unprepared for agreement. She paused, partly to catch her breath, partly out of belated surprise at how tamely Corky had taken her outburst.

"You're right," Corky said again. "I've done something terrible and I'd best pay for it. I owe you and your family. What can I do?"

"This isn't a negotiation!" she said.

"Then why are you standing here?" Carlyle asked. "What is it you want of the lad?"

"I want him to understand!"

"I rather think he does."

Corky stood up. "Will that be all, Erin?" he asked.

Feeling a little deflated, Erin bit her tongue and nodded.

"If there's anything you're needing, anything at all," Corky said, "it's yours for the asking. And that goes for Michelle or your brother, too."

He walked past Erin and out of the Corner without another word.

"I'll be damned," Erin said, mostly to herself. "I think he really does feel bad." She'd never seen Corky so subdued.

Carlyle nodded. "Try not to hate him, darling."

She sighed. "I don't. Not really. But he's so... frustrating!"

"I've known him a sight longer than you, Erin. As God's my witness, I know. But his heart's in the right place. When the chips are down, he's a good lad to have at your side."

"Maybe, but I think I'd rather have Rolf," she said. "And I'd better go up and fetch him. Shit! Luna could be out there right now, running. I've wasted too much time already. I've got to go."

"Good luck, darling." He gave her a quick kiss on the cheek. "And do be careful. These Italian lads can get a bit rough."

"Nothing compared with the Irish," she replied.

Chapter 4

Rolf knew Erin had been having fun without him. The German Shepherd smelled the residual adrenaline on her and read the tension in her body language. He wagged his tail and jumped back and forth, crouching low with his paws extended, telling her he was ready to get in the game.

The K-9 had only recently gotten a clean bill of health from his vet. In the tussle with Mickey Connor, Rolf had broken three ribs and received a nasty concussion. The ribs had taken almost twelve weeks to fully heal. Erin hadn't had the heart to leave him at home all that time, but he'd been stuck on limited duty, which mostly meant moping around the Major Crimes office. He hadn't bitten a single criminal, nor even chased one, in three months. At least the damage had been all internal, needing no stitches, so he'd been spared the supreme indignity of the plastic "cone of shame."

"All right, kiddo," Erin said, getting his leash off the coat rack. "Ready to be real police again?"

Rolf was ready. He was the readiest dog in the five boroughs. Or he thought so, until he saw his partner getting out his K-9 body armor. Then he discovered he could be that little bit readier. He went up on his hind feet and spun in a tight circle, pawing the air and barking sharply.

Erin felt her anger at Corky melting away at the sight of the badass Shepherd acting like an exuberant puppy. "Okay, okay," she said. "But you've got to hold still so I can get this on you. *Steh! Bleib!*"

Rolf immediately stood perfectly still except for his tail, which kept sweeping the floor with great enthusiasm. Erin strapped on his vest, clipped his leash to his collar, and headed out.

* * *

Alphonse Luna's address was in Little Italy, which came as no surprise to Erin. It was a brick apartment building, slightly dilapidated. Erin had called ESU ahead of time and she saw the massive, intimidating silhouette of their Lenco Bearcat idling just up the street. She unloaded Rolf from her Charger and hurried over to the armored car.

"Hey Parker," she said. "How's your weekend going?" She knew the ESU A-team, having worked with them in the past. Parker was an old friend of Vic's from his ESU days.

"Typical sleepy Sunday," he said, racking the charging handle on his AR-15. "You know, have dinner with the missus, take a nap on the couch, kick in some doors, dodge bullets. Same shit, different day."

"What're we looking at here?" the commander, Lieutenant Lewis, asked.

"The suspect cut a man's throat earlier today," Erin said. "He's been shot in the back, but I don't know how bad he's hurt. He's a Mafia foot-soldier, so we have to assume he's got a gun. He may or may not be alone in there. Hell, he may not be there at all, but we've got to look. Do we have eyes on the exits?"

"Twig's in position," Lewis said, pointing to a rooftop opposite the apartment. Twig was the unit's sniper. "And Hopper's covering the fire escape in back."

"Sounds good," Erin said. "How do you guys want to play this?"

"Standard entry," Lewis said. "We'll stack up in the hallway. Carnes will make entry. Parker behind him, then you with your K-9, the rest of us on your six. Doesn't sound like a barricade situation, so we'll do this one by the numbers. Anyone else live here?"

"Not that I know of."

"Okay, people," Lewis said, making a circle in the air with his forefinger. "Let's get this done. Clean, hard, and everybody goes home when it's over. You get me?"

"Copy that, sir," several voices chorused.

The ESU team moved into the apartment with quick, cool professionalism. Erin always felt a slight shiver of admiration whenever she watched them work. They moved like a military unit, complete with heavy body armor, helmets, and assault gear. She was very glad they were on her side. She was wearing her own vest, but detectives didn't typically wear heavy tactical helmets, and since she had to handle Rolf with one hand, she held her pistol instead of the ESU boys' automatic rifles. She felt a little underequipped.

They called the elevators down to the ground floor and locked them in place. Then they went up the stairs to the third floor, rifles at their shoulders, ready for anything. They saw nobody on the way up. The team deployed into the upstairs hallway and lined up along the wall next to unit 301. Carnes, the biggest, strongest guy on the team, carried a sledgehammer in addition to his weapons. He glanced at his commander, waiting for his cue.

Lewis nodded once.

Carnes thumped the door with a fist almost as big as Erin's head. "NYPD!" he shouted. "Open up!"

There was a brief, tense silence. Then Lewis nodded again.

Carnes swung his sledgehammer in a sideways arc. The door practically exploded inward. Wood splinters spun in all directions. It sounded like the impact of a cannonball. At this point, some tactical teams would have thrown in a flashbang grenade to stun and disorient anybody inside, but New York had forbidden such tactics after a couple of fatal incidents with the supposedly nonlethal devices. Of course, the assault rifles the ESU guys carried were still totally fine. That was bureaucracy for you, Erin thought as Parker sprang through the door, rifle poised.

Erin went in hard on his heels, Rolf straining at his leash. Parker was moving to the left, so Erin went right, getting out of the bottleneck in the doorway and clearing the living room. She checked her corners, exactly the way she'd been trained, looking for movement or human-shaped figures, seeing neither.

"Clear!" Parker barked. He was standing in a little kitchenette, also deserted.

Erin saw a short hallway with doors on either side, presumably leading to the bedroom and bathroom. She pointed down the hall and held up two fingers.

Carnes and Lewis rushed past her and split up, one going through each door in unison. Erin followed them, but she already knew this would be a washout. No way had Luna come back here. Sometimes you could feel when a perp was gone, and Luna was well and truly gone.

"NYPD! Hands! Let me see your hands!"

Erin felt a fresh jolt of energy run up her spine. Lewis had gone left and he was shouting at someone. She hurried to the doorway and narrowly avoided colliding with Carnes, who was on his way out of the bathroom.

There was a splintering crash from the bedroom. Erin got to the doorway just in time to see Lewis reel backward and slam into the wall. The remnants of a bedside lamp spread around him in a blizzard of broken glass and ceramic. Lewis hadn't dropped his gun, but he had his hands in front of his face and wasn't pointing the weapon anywhere useful.

Erin caught a glimpse of a small, slender figure scrabbling at a nightstand. She registered it as a woman just as the suspect snatched up something else and threw it at her. With peculiar clarity, Erin identified it as a cut-glass ashtray. It tumbled lazily toward her, shedding a comet-trail of ashes and cigarette butts.

Erin had killed men in gunfights, had even shot a woman once. Technically, this woman was assaulting police officers. Erin could legally shoot her. But she made the split-second decision not to. An ashtray might hurt, but it wouldn't kill her. She swung a hand and batted it aside at the last moment. The tray struck the doorframe and shattered.

"NYPD!" Erin yelled, hoping to get through to the woman by force of repetition. Rolf tugged eagerly at the leash. The fight was on, he knew it, and he wanted a piece of the action.

The woman either didn't hear or didn't care. She went for the next thing on the nightstand, which proved to be a digital alarm clock/radio. She hurled it at Erin. It made it halfway before running out of power cord and falling abruptly to the bedroom floor.

"That's enough of that!" Erin said sharply. "Ma'am, put your hands in the air! I've got a K-9 here and—"

That was all she got out before the woman pulled the cord out of the wall socket, jerked the alarm clock back toward her, and swung the cord in a tight, vicious arc. The clock/radio whistled toward Erin, making an orbit around the other woman.

Erin ducked. She'd had enough of this bullshit. "*Fass!*" she said and let go of Rolf.

The K-9 went in low and fast, springing up onto the bed far too quickly for his target to attack him, or even to dodge. The woman went down with Rolf's teeth around her arm. The clock/radio, out of control, smashed into a dresser and came apart. Broken bits of plastic and the electronic guts of the device joined the broken glass and pottery already littering the floor.

"Clear," Erin said, kneeling on the bed next to the downed woman and snapping a cuff onto one wrist. "Rolf, *pust!*"

The K-9 let go of the woman and sat back, tongue hanging out in a broad, panting grin. He was happier than he'd been in months.

"What the hell happened, sir?" Carnes asked.

"I'm fine," Lewis grunted, wiping blood off his face with the back of one hand. He had several small cuts on his cheeks. "She threw a lamp at me. You believe that? A damn lamp?"

"I've seen you take down stone-cold killers," Carnes said with a laugh. "And some chick takes you out with a piece of bedroom furniture!"

Erin had to lean in and bring some pressure to bear on her captive, who was struggling and spitting profanity. She looked to be a young woman, probably no older than twenty. Despite her skinny frame, she had a wiry strength. Erin had dealt with muscle-bound drunks who didn't fight half so hard.

"Take it easy," she said through clenched teeth. "I don't want to hurt you. Where's Alphonse Luna?"

"Kiss my ass, *puttana!*" the woman spat.

"You know the great thing about this job?" Erin asked Carnes and Lewis as she finished securing the woman.

"Enlighten us, Detective," Carnes said, grinning.

"The opportunities for higher education," she said.

"And what opportunities are those?" Carnes asked, playing along.

"I can say 'bitch' in three different languages."

"Well, it's 'bitch' in English," Carnes said. "And I guess '*puttana*' in Italian."

"'*Suka*' in Russian," Erin added.

"And '*perra*' in Spanish," Lewis added. "So now you know four."

"Yeah," Erin said. "Funny thing is, I've got a German dog, but I don't know the German insult."

"Always good to have more to learn," Carnes said.

* * *

The young woman's student visa indicated her name was Ariana Ricci. She was nineteen years old and was enrolled at NYU. Her place of birth was listed as Palermo, Sicily. Erin, after checking her over and finding no significant injuries, had seated her on the couch in the living room. Now, while the ESU team combed the apartment for clues as to Luna's whereabouts, Ricci sat trading glares with Erin. Rolf was lying on the carpet, paws wrapped around his special rubber Kong ball, chewing and slobbering, happy in the knowledge that he was a very good boy.

"Where's Alphonse Luna?" Erin demanded.

"I do not have to answer your questions!" Ricci spat.

"Oh? And why is that?"

"I am Italian! Not American! I have diplomatic immunity!"

Erin blinked. "Ms. Ricci, in order to claim diplomatic immunity, you have to be a diplomat. And you're not. You may be an Italian national, but while you're in America, you're subject to American laws."

"I demand to talk to my embassy!"

Erin sighed. "New York doesn't have embassies. Those are in Washington. Did you mean the consulate?"

"Yes!"

"You have the right to notify your consulate that you are being detained. But you're still under arrest. Now, where is Alphonse Luna?"

"I do not know!"

"Your English is very good. How long have you been in this country?" Erin already knew the answer from looking at the student visa, but she found that getting a suspect to answer a question, any question, was always a good starting point. Once they began talking, they were likelier to keep talking. It was an inertia thing.

"A year." Ricci was sulking now, her lower lip sticking out in a pout. "When my father learns how you have treated me, you will be in big trouble!"

"Who is your father?" Erin asked.

"Alessandro Ricci." The girl said it proudly, like it should mean something.

"Never heard of him."

"He is a big man," Ricci said. "He sells wine from Sicily. Very good wine, very expensive. He has powerful friends. You will be sorry your dog attacked his girl. He will have your dog shot." She gave Rolf a baleful look. The K-9, unimpressed, ignored her and continued gnawing his toy. He'd been shot before.

"That would be a class A misdemeanor," Erin said, holding onto her temper. "Then we'd arrest him, too, and he'd go to jail for at least a year."

"Nobody arrests Alessandro Ricci!"

"First time for everything."

"He knows people!"

"What people?"

Ricci's mouth snapped abruptly shut. She stared defiantly at Erin.

"What's Daddy going to say when he hears you've been screwing around with a Mafia goon?" Erin asked.

"I do not know what you are talking about!"

"Alphonse Luna," Erin said patiently. "He's a murderer. If you're protecting him, you're abetting him. That's a crime."

"Bedding him is not against the law!" Ricci protested. "I am of age! I can bed whoever I want!"

"Abetting," Erin repeated. "Not bedding. It means helping him."

"Helping the man you love is no crime!"

"That depends on the man. When did you last see him?"

"How do you know I know him at all?"

"You were in his bedroom, in his bed," Erin said reasonably. "Not wearing very much. Now, when did you see him?"

"This morning," Ricci said sulkily.

"When?"

"When he left for work. About ten o'clock. He works the lunchtime shift."

"At Andolini's Restaurant?"

"Yes."

"If Alphonse got hurt, where would he go?"

Ricci blinked, and for the first time she looked surprised and worried. "What? Alfie is hurt?"

"He's been shot," Erin said, sensing weakness. "I'm afraid he may be badly injured. That's why we need to find him. He's in trouble."

Ricci bit her lip and hugged her own elbows. "You are not lying to me?" she asked. "Trying to trick me?"

"Look in my eyes," Erin said. "I saw the bullet hit him. I know he's hurt. Help me help him. His life is in danger. Think about it; if I'm lying, he wouldn't need medical help, so he won't be there anyway."

Ricci hesitated. Erin waited, letting her see the earnestness in her face.

"Once before, he was hurt," Ricci said at last. "He called me and told me to pick him up. But he was not at a doctor. And he may not have gone there again."

"I understand," Erin said. "Where was he?"

"A hospital for animals."

"A veterinarian? Which one?"

Ricci shook her head. "I think the name was South Manhattan, but maybe not. I was upset. I do not remember."

Erin jumped to her feet. Rolf, catching her movement and sudden energy, sprang up, his toy still protruding from the side of his mouth.

"Lieutenant!" she called.

Lewis came out of the bedroom. "What's up, Detective?" he asked. The rest of the ESU team drifted over to see what was going on.

"South Manhattan Animal Hospital," she said. "We need to move. Can we get a couple uniforms here to keep track of Ms. Ricci?"

"Sure thing," he said.

"Great," Carnes said. "Just great. A friggin' veterinarian?"

"I thought you liked knocking down doors," she said.

"Not into vet offices," he said. "Last time that happened, I got bit on the leg."

"By a Chihuahua," Parker said with a wicked gleam in his eye. "I saw it happen. There's Carnes, hopping around on one foot, this tiny little dog, it's gotta be two pounds, max, hanging off him. He's wearing full tac gear and the smallest dog you've ever seen is kicking his ass."

"Hey, those things are vicious," Carnes said. "And it bit me in a real tender spot. Wanna see the scar?"

"Only if you buy me dinner first," Erin said.

Chapter 5

"Raiding a veterinarian is a new one for us," Erin said as the ESU team clambered out of their Bearcat for the second time that day. She'd called Judge Ferris to ask for the new warrant on the way. The judge hadn't disappointed her, sending the paperwork to her onboard computer. Now she, Rolf, and the team were ready to go another round. She had her Glock in one hand, Rolf's leash wrapped around her opposite wrist, and a paper bag containing Alphonse's sock in that hand.

"You've really never done this before?" Parker asked. "I'd say your partner's a natural for this line of work."

"Yeah," Carnes added. "Might be some fine bitches in there for him to hit on."

"Rolf's a professional," Erin said.

Rolf chose that moment to cock a leg on the corner of the building. Sensing all eyes on him, he tilted his head and looked quizzically at the humans.

"Y'know, if I did that on the clock, I'd get a rip from the Lieutenant," Parker said.

"Okay, knock off the grab-ass, gentlemen," Lewis said. "You know the drill. We may have unsecured animals in there, so watch yourselves. I know the Chihuahua story is funny, but it's a lot less funny if you're taking fire with a dog chewing your ankle."

"Or if a teenager's beating your head in with a lamp," Parker said. But he stopped smiling and put on his game face as the unit lined up against the brickwork outside the vet clinic's front door.

ESU believed in the doctrine of overwhelming force. Go in heavy, show the other guy you were ready and willing to hit him harder than he could ever hit you, and you might not need to hit anybody. Thus the military-style gear, the Stormtrooper helmets, the black-and-navy uniforms. They were scary sons of bitches and they knew it.

It was a Sunday, but South Manhattan Animal Hospital was an emergency clinic, so the doors were unlocked. The ESU team burst in, guns at their shoulders, shouting all the usual things.

"NYPD! Don't move! Hands where I can see them!"

They were prepared for desperate, wounded, heavily-armed mobsters. What they got instead was a middle-aged female vet tech and a little old lady holding a Bichon Frise on her lap. Both women looked Italian, but other than that, they were two of the least Mafia-looking people Erin had ever seen. The vet tech, sitting behind the front counter, froze. Then she slowly lifted her hands to show they were empty. The old woman kept her hands around her dog, which immediately began barking at Rolf. The bark was high-pitched, penetrating, and absolutely relentless.

Lieutenant Lewis crossed the room quickly, indicating with hand gestures that two of his team should secure the women. Erin followed Lewis, opening the paper bag and taking out a dirty men's sock she'd acquired at Luna's apartment.

"*Such*," she said to Rolf, holding the sock in front of his snout. The Bichon kept yapping away, but Rolf ignored it, focusing all his attention on the sock. His nostrils twitched as he committed the smell of the man who'd worn it to memory. Then, as Erin had instructed him, he started his search, sniffing the air, filtering out the scents of all the other dogs and people who'd been there.

It must be a tricky job, Erin thought. An emergency vet's waiting room was so full of the smells of frightened animals, blood, and illness, even her own pitifully inadequate nose could catch some of the odors. And on top of that were the distractions of the shouting ESU team and that damn little white-haired dog. But Rolf seemed to have no trouble at all sorting through the other input and finding that one special smell he'd been ordered to track. Less than five seconds after Erin had shown him the sock, the K-9 was pulling toward the back of the clinic.

"He's here, sir," Erin said as Lewis reached for the doorknob.

"You can't go back there!" the vet tech protested.

"I've got a warrant that says we can," Erin said, pulling out the folded piece of paper and slapping it down on the counter as she went by. "Where's Luna?"

The woman said nothing.

Lewis, Parker, and Erin stacked up at the door. Rolf whined quietly and pulled. The smell of the man led through the door. He didn't understand why the humans didn't do their magic trick with the doorknob and open it already. K-9s could be patient, but not when they were in the hunt.

"Ready?" Lewis asked quietly.

"Yes, sir," Parker and Erin said.

Lewis flung the door open. All three officers aimed their guns into what proved to be an empty hallway with a row of doors that presumably led to examining rooms. Behind them, the Bichon kept barking.

"And that," Erin said in an undertone, "is why we don't use those little brats as K-9s."

"Violates the Eighth Amendment?" Parker guessed. "Cruel and unusual?"

"No, we'd shoot them ourselves."

Rolf snuffled at the first door, then moved on to the second. He scratched at the bottom of that door and whined. Erin nodded to Lewis. He and Parker moved up to the door.

"Alphonse Luna!" Lewis shouted through the door. "This is the NYPD! We're coming in, and I'd better see your hands when we do, or you're gonna get shot!" He paused, then added, "Again!"

Parker took hold of the doorknob and wrenched the door open. This was the most dangerous moment. If Luna had a gun, and decided to make a last stand, Parker was liable to take at least one bullet. Maybe his vest would protect him and maybe not.

Parker lunged into the room and sidestepped out of the doorway. Lewis and Erin were right on his heels. The examination room was small, very crowded for the five people and one dog who found themselves squeezed into it. A bearded man in a white lab coat stood against the far wall, hands raised. On the examining table sat a wounded man. He'd taken off his waiter's jacket and shirt and was sitting bare-chested. Surgical gauze was wrapped around his body, but Erin saw blood soaking through it on his upper shoulder, just below and to one side of his neck.

The injured man smiled shakily and showed a pair of empty hands. His olive complexion had a greenish-gray undertone to it and his hands trembled.

"You're not gonna believe me," he said. "But I sure am glad to see you fellas."

"Alphonse Luna?" Erin asked. She'd only seen him from the back as he'd fled the restaurant, but she'd gotten a good look at his mugshot afterward. This ID was a formality.

"Yes, ma'am," he said. "And I don't wanna impose, but could you maybe get me to a doctor? A real doctor, I mean. This guy here, he means well, but he don't know shit."

"Mr. Luna," the vet said. "As I was trying to tell you, you've got a bullet lodged in your brachial artery. If I try to remove it, you'll begin to bleed heavily and probably die. I can treat moderate injuries, but you need a trauma surgeon."

"You're also under arrest," Lewis said.

"Yeah, I figured," Luna said. "And I'm gonna want my lawyer, obviously. But a doctor first, okay? I'm hurting here. You really want me to die on you?"

Lewis was already keying his radio. "We've got two in custody," he said. "One serious GSW. We need a bus to South Manhattan Animal Hospital, forthwith."

"You carrying any weapons?" Parker asked Luna.

The wounded man shook his head. "Look, I ain't gonna cause trouble," he said. "Do you have to cuff me?"

Parker glanced at Lewis, who shook his head. Given the nature of the injury, that made sense. Hollywood would have you believe a gunshot wound to the shoulder was a minor thing; heroes in movies got shot there all the time and just kept going. But Erin knew better. Any bullet wound was a serious matter, and important stuff ran through the shoulder, including the top of the lung and, as the vet had said, the brachial artery. If you severed any major artery, your life was in immediate danger. From the sound of it, the bullet in Luna's shoulder was like the little Dutch boy's finger in the dike. Pull it out and there'd be a flood. And if they wrenched his arm around, they might dislodge the bullet by accident and kill their prisoner.

"Tell you what," Parker said. "I'll just clip your left wrist to me. That way I'll be able to keep an eye on you and nobody gets hurt."

"It's nice dealing with polite cops," Luna said. "I won't forget this, buddy."

"I'm not your buddy," Parker said. "I just don't want to kill you if I don't have to." He unslung his AR-15 and handed it to Lewis. Then his took out his pistol and handed it over, too. That was something else the movies got wrong, often with hilariously violent results. A cop in close proximity to a prisoner was never supposed to have a gun on him. That way, if Luna made a break for freedom, at least he couldn't get his hands on a police weapon.

"Excuse me, officers," the vet said. "I think I misheard you. You said something about two people in custody."

"You heard right," Erin said. "You're under arrest, too."

"For what?"

"Violation of New York Penal Code 265.25," she said. "Failure to report a gunshot wound is a Class A misdemeanor, which you know perfectly well." Every medical professional in the state was familiar with that particular statute.

"That only holds true if the doctor has correctly diagnosed the injury," the vet argued. "I was still making my diagnosis."

"You said he had a bullet in his shoulder," she reminded him. "Sounds like you knew it was a GSW. And I'm guessing this isn't the first bullet wound you've treated for the Lucarellis."

"I have no idea what you're talking about and I don't like what you're insinuating," the vet replied. Beside him, Parker snapped a cuff around Luna's left wrist and clicked the other bracelet around his own right arm.

"Of course you don't," Erin said, hauling out her own cuffs. "Face the wall. Pay attention, now; I'm about to read your rights. These go for you too, Mr. Luna."

After she'd finished Mirandizing the two men, the officers marched them out to the waiting room. The Bichon, upon seeing Rolf again, immediately increased the volume and frequency of its barking. Rolf remained aloof and unconcerned. All he wanted was his reward toy.

"We'll take a seat here and wait for the bus," Parker said, steering Luna and himself to a pair of unoccupied chairs as far from the old lady and her noisy companion as possible. Luna sat down very gingerly.

"And I'll take this mope out to the Cat," Lewis said, indicating the vet.

Erin's phone buzzed. She took it out and saw Webb's name on the screen.

"Good timing, sir," she said. "We've got our shooter."

"Great work, O'Reilly," Webb said. "Any trouble?"

"Not really, sir. He's hurt worse than I thought. He didn't resist. We're waiting on a bus to take him to Bellevue. He knows the drill. He asked for a lawyer before we even got around to Mirandizing him."

"That shouldn't matter," Webb said. "CSU found a gun at the restaurant. What is that God-awful racket?"

"Little yappy dog," she said. "We're at a vet clinic."

"Mob doctor?" Webb guessed.

"Yeah. We arrested him, too, while we were at it."

"Good. Anyway, the gun was in a can of bleach in a maintenance closet. I'm guessing the bodyguard who shot your boy dumped it there."

"In bleach?" Erin frowned. "CSU won't be able to get much evidence off that."

"But they can run ballistics," Webb said. "I don't suppose Luna's still got the bullet?"

"It's in his shoulder. But it's going to take a pretty dicey surgery to get it out."

"Good thing you know a pretty good surgeon," Webb deadpanned, referring to Erin's brother, Sean Junior.

"Vanzano must have dropped the gun in the bleach while I was in the alley," she said. "I should've been quicker."

"It made sense thinking he'd gone out the back," Webb said. "Anyway, that's half of why I'm calling."

"What's the other half, sir?"

"It's good you nailed this guy so fast. We've got another one."

"Another body?" Erin's heart sank. "Who's the new stiff?"

"Ever heard of Wonderboy Crea?"

"No."

"Labor racketeer for the Lucarellis. Somebody shot him on his front porch when he went out to get the morning paper. He was wearing a bathrobe and fuzzy slippers when they found him."

"So he's dead?"

"If he wasn't, they wouldn't have sent it to us. Patrol got the call a couple hours ago, but it took a while to get kicked up the ladder. How soon can you get down to Queens?"

"Just a second," she said, hurrying outside with Rolf and waving to Lewis. "Lieutenant, do you need me for anything else here?"

"No, Detective, we can handle it," Lewis said.

She nodded her thanks. "On my way," she said into the phone.

"Okay, swing back by Andolini's first," Webb said. "Pick up Neshenko. He's sobered up and he's getting restless."

"Copy that, sir. Where am I going in Queens?"

"I'll text you the address. Units from the 116 are on site. That's your old precinct, isn't it?"

"Yes, sir."

"You'll be talking to a couple of Homicide boys. Maybe you know them."

Erin felt a sudden sensation of impending, inevitable doom. She closed her eyes. "It wouldn't be two guys named Lyons and Spinelli by any chance, would it?"

"Oh, good. You do know them."

"Yeah. I know them. See you in a few." She hung up the phone and put it in her pocket. Maybe it wouldn't be so bad running into Lyons and Spinelli again, she thought. Maybe they'd forgotten all the ways she'd stepped on their toes during the art heist investigation that had earned her a detective's gold shield.

And while she was wishing, maybe she should stop on the way and buy a lottery ticket. It had about as much chance of coming up good.

Chapter 6

"Feeling any better?" Erin asked.

Vic muttered a profanity.

"You didn't miss much," she said. "Except maybe the part where the perp's girlfriend broke a lamp over Lieutenant Lewis's head."

"Feels like she did it to me," he groaned. He put an arm over his face and slumped down in the Charger's passenger seat. "Can you do me a favor and turn down the sun?"

"I'm sorry?"

"If you can't do that, then take out your gun and shoot me in the head."

"Jesus, Vic, you really did a number on yourself." Erin steered them toward Long Island and kept her eyes on the road. "What the hell happened?"

"Not really sure. When the phone rang, I was lying on my couch with two empty vodka bottles on the floor."

"Two bottles? Vic, are you trying to kill yourself? Because there's cheaper and easier ways to do it."

"Nah, one of them was mostly empty already. I think. What day is it?"

"Sunday."

"Oh. What week?"

Erin let that one hang in the air while she did some thinking.

"This is about Zofia," she said after a few minutes.

"Says who?" Vic growled.

"I'm a detective, remember? This is what I do." Erin held up a finger. "First item: you're drunk on a Sunday morning."

"I drink a lot. And I was off duty."

"I've never seen you drunk that early in the day." She shook her head and held up another finger. "Second item: you don't want to talk to her."

"I never said that."

"You didn't need to. I saw your face when Webb told you to talk to SNEU."

"You're obnoxious, you know that?" Vic rubbed his face.

"I've got older brothers," she reminded him. "I have years of practice."

"Okay, okay. Here's how it is. I thought things were going great, you know?"

Erin nodded.

"Of course, with me working days and her on nights, we hardly ever saw each other," he said. "But that was okay. It made things more... uh, energetic when we did."

She took a hand off the steering wheel to hold it up warningly. "Vic, I really don't need to hear about that part."

"And it was casual," he continued. "No pressure or anything. But lately she's been dropping ultimatums. Is that the right word?"

"I don't know, Vic, because I don't know what you're talking about yet."

"All this stuff about wondering where we're going as a couple, and is this all we want out of life, and all this emotional bullshit. What I like about Zofia is that she isn't like that, you know? She's not all sappy. She never wants me to buy her flowers, but she's been talking about this Colt Delta Elite she's been looking at, and I thought that'd make a good Christmas present."

"I can't think of a better way to celebrate the birth of Jesus than with the gift of a handgun," Erin said, straight-faced. "You two really are made for each other."

"I think she's thinking *commitment*." Vic said it in a hushed voice, as if he was talking about sex in Sunday school.

"Well, how do you feel about it?" Erin had been seeing a police psychiatrist for several months to help her work through her PTSD. Some of his diplomatic interviewing style had rubbed off on her. Spend too much time around psych guys and you'd always end up talking like them.

"I dunno," Vic said, in a classic Vic response.

"You like her, don't you?"

"Of course I do!"

"Do you love her?"

"Did you handle your brothers this way?"

"All the time, especially in high school."

"I dunno," he said again. "But that's not the point."

"What's the point?"

"The point is, she's an action junkie and I'm a screwup. I thought we were just having fun. But now she's given me a deadline. I've got a month."

"To do what?"

"To figure out what I want."

"That's what she said?"

"Pretty much. There might've been more swearing involved. And she threw a sofa cushion at me. So maybe you're right, I didn't miss much skipping out on that raid. If I want some crazy chick chucking things at my head, all I have to do is go home."

"Why do you think she gave you a time limit?"

Vic shrugged. "How the hell am I supposed to know that? She said something about needing to do something drastic or I'd never get my ass in gear. I guess some guys work better under time pressure."

"Do you know what you're going to do?"

"No. That's why I got drunk. I think. I'm a little fuzzy on the timeline."

"Well, Vic, I don't know that I'm the one you should talk to about relationship advice."

"I don't want your advice! I don't even want to be talking about this! You're the one who brought it up!"

"Okay, okay. Sorry I asked. But at least you've got a few weeks to think things over."

"You think that makes it better? Now I gotta go around with this thing hanging over me all the time! It's like there's a contract out on me and wiseguys are gonna start taking potshots."

Erin managed to hide her smile. "I don't think it's quite as bad as that, Vic. She didn't break up with you, did she? You're not going to have to resort to one-night stands."

"No. I do have one idea, though."

"What's that?"

"We stop talking about my love life and do some police work. What do you have on this latest body?"

"Nothing, except that he checked out on his own front porch in his slippers."

"At least he died comfortable. Dress shoes will wreck your feet."

"You're going to complain to a woman about uncomfortable dress shoes? Really? It must be so hard being you."

* * *

The scene of the shooting was a pleasant little house on 69th Avenue in the Fresh Meadows neighborhood of Erin's old stomping grounds. The house was brick on the ground floor, white wood siding upstairs. The lawn was neatly mowed and well-kept. Except for the pair of Patrol cars and the CSU van, it might have been any middle-class house in America.

Erin, Vic, and Rolf got out of the Charger and approached the scene. Erin was trying to suppress the butterflies in her stomach. She didn't like the thought of running into her old nemeses from Homicide again. Vic was fighting nausea and a hangover. Rolf pranced along with his head and tail held high, eager to go to work.

There they were: big, burly Lyons, and the little weasel Spinelli with his ridiculous pencil mustache. The Homicide detectives were talking to a CSU guy. Erin squared her shoulders and walked straight at them.

Lyons saw them first. The big detective did a classic double-take. Then the surprise fell off his face, replaced by an ugly glower.

Vic, sizing up the other man at once, returned the glare with interest. He'd been pissed off all day and had finally found a suitable target for his irritation.

Lyons elbowed Spinelli, cutting him off mid-sentence. "Look what we got here," he said.

"O'Reilly," Spinelli said, looking at her like she was something he'd just picked out of his nose. "I thought we got rid of you."

"*Detective* O'Reilly," Erin said, angling her hip slightly to call attention to the gold shield on her belt. "Detective Second Grade. You still just a Third Grade, Spinelli?"

"You guys from Major Crimes?" Lyons demanded.

"That's right," Erin said. "This is Vic Neshenko. Vic, this is Lyons and Spinelli."

"Pleasure," Vic said, meaning the opposite.

The four detectives stood staring at one another for several seconds.

"Okay, I get it," Erin said. "You want to prove you're the big dogs. I know you're still pissed about what happened last year. Thing is, I don't care what you think of me. What I care about is the Job. You don't have to like me, I don't have to like you. But we do have to cooperate."

"Oh, so now you want to cooperate with us?" Spinelli retorted. "I thought you had to do our job for us. You remember her saying that to us?"

"Yeah, I remember," Lyons said darkly.

"Who are these two pencil-dicks?" Vic asked Erin in a stage whisper. Erin was trying to stay professional. Vic apparently felt no such compunction.

"We have a history," she said. "Obviously. But the thing about the past is, it's in the past. Can we move forward, please?"

"If it'll move you on back to Manhattan," Spinelli said. "And out of our hair."

"Wonderboy Crea," she prompted.

"William 'Wonderboy' Crea," Spinelli said. "What do you want to know about him, besides the fact that he's dead?"

"Name like that, you know he's connected," Lyons said. "They shoulda called him 'Wonderbread.' Pasty-faced guy, soft around the middle. Not young, neither. Musta been fifty if he was a day. Dyed his hair or he'd have been gray. Boy my ass."

"What happened?" Erin asked.

"According to his old lady, he went out to get the paper," Spinelli said. "She was in the kitchen making breakfast. She heard four or five gunshots. One of 'em came through the front picture window and she hit the floor. She's scared, but not hurt."

He pointed toward the house. Erin saw that the big plate-glass window was indeed shattered.

"Anyone else in the house?" she asked.

"Two daughters," Lyons said. "College kids, both of 'em. Home for family dinner. Real sweet. Like a Sicilian Hallmark card."

"Where are the women now?"

"Inside." Lyons sneered. "Crying, probably."

"Sensitivity training just bounced right off you, didn't it," Vic said. "Those kids in there lost their dad. You think they ought to be turning cartwheels or what?"

"Daddy was a Mob boss," Lyons retorted. "You want me to get all broke up about him getting popped?"

"I'd like to talk to them," Erin said.

"What for?" Spinelli asked. "We already got their statement. I'll forward it to you, as a *courtesy*."

"I'd like to get it straight from the source," she said, stepping around Spinelli toward the house.

He stepped with her, staying in front of her. "Why's that? You think we didn't ask the right questions? You still trying to teach us how to do our job? I've been a detective six years. And I earned my shield the right way. I didn't have it handed to me under the table."

"I've fought for everything I've ever gotten on the Job," she said, moving to the side again. "And I never asked for the gold shield, but now that I've got it, I'm damn well going to make sure I deserve it."

Spinelli matched her movement, as if they were rehearsing a dance routine. "And how come Major Crimes is swiping this case out from under us?" he demanded. "It's just a homicide, straight-up gangland murder."

"It wasn't my idea," she said, wondering how much trouble she'd get in if she picked the little weasel up by the collar and chucked him into one of the Crea rosebushes. "But he's the third Lucarelli mobster to get whacked this morning. That makes it a pattern, and that makes it a Major Crimes problem."

"I got a procedural question," Vic said. "It's probably in the Patrol Guide, but I haven't read the Patrol Guide. Who's got time to read all those pages, anyway?"

"Your procedural question?" she prompted.

"Can we arrest other cops for obstruction?"

"That's not going to happen," Erin said, keeping her eyes on Spinelli and her voice level. "Because we're all on the same team here."

"Fine," Spinelli said, throwing his hands in the air. "Go on, double-check all our work. Hell, triple-check it if it gets you off. Turns out I get paid either way. And they're not going to tell you anything anyway."

"Nobody saw nothing," Lyons added.

"Then it'll be a quick conversation," Erin said, walking up to the house and ringing the doorbell.

A petite Italian woman answered the door. She was about twenty and would have been pretty if she hadn't been crying in her mascara, which made unsightly black smudges under her eyes. She was holding a crumpled wad of tissues in one hand.

"What do you want?" the young woman asked, in classic Long Island style.

"My name is Erin O'Reilly," Erin said, holding up her shield. "I'm a detective. This is Vic Neshenko and Rolf, my K-9. I'd like to ask you and your mom a few questions."

The other woman thought about it for a second. She looked down at Rolf, who cocked his head up at her, his long ears tilting comically to one side.

"Okay," she said, stepping back from the door. "C'mon in. Ma and Gabby are in the kitchen."

Erin wiped her feet on the mat on the way in. Little gestures often paid large dividends in goodwill. She was glad the witnesses were female. If Crea had had sons instead, they might have been more steeped in the Mafia culture of *omerta*, the code of silence. She thought she had a better chance of getting through to women.

The kitchen was at the back of the house. The place was clean and well-kept, nothing indicating a Mob associate had lived there. A fire had been burning in the living room fireplace, but had subsided into glowing embers. An early autumn chill ghosted through the broken front window. The kitchen was strewn with the ingredients of a big, hearty breakfast no one would ever eat. It looked like Mrs. Crea had been in the process of making omelets. Apparently the family had liked peppers; a cutting board was covered with neatly diced green, red, and orange bits.

An older woman was seated on a tall wooden stool. Another young woman, strongly resembling the first one, had an arm around the other woman's shoulders. The younger one had tears in her eyes, but her mother was serious and stoic.

"Hey Ma," the first woman said. "It's a couple more cops."

The older woman stared at Erin and Vic with dark, unreadable eyes. "You got names?" she asked in a strong Brooklyn accent.

Erin introduced them. Vic, as if to make up for nearly picking a fight with Lyons and Spinelli, was very polite, keeping his hands clasped in front of him and even trying to look pleasant. The expression didn't look right on his face, probably on account of his twice-broken nose.

"You sound like you're from around here," Mrs. Crea said.

"That's right, ma'am," Erin said. "I was born in Queens, just down the road a ways. I grew up here."

"What about the big guy?"

"Brighton Beach, ma'am," Vic said. "Little Odessa."

"That's all right, then." Mrs. Crea stood up. "Call me Emilia. Welcome to my home. This is Gabriella and Giana, but they go by Gabby and Jenny. I'll get you a cup of coffee." She pronounced it *caw-fee.*

"Thank you, ma'am," Erin said. Her mother was the same way. Put Mary O'Reilly in the middle of a family crisis and her first impulse was to cook something. She was only surprised Emilia Crea hadn't finished the omelets.

While the older woman busied herself getting the coffee, Giana got down on one knee in front of Rolf. "Is it okay if I pet him?" she asked.

"Sure," Erin said. "Rolf, *sitz Bleib.*"

"What's that mean?"

"It means 'sit' and 'stay,'" Erin explained. "Rolf was trained in Germany, so German is his first language."

Giana stroked Rolf's head. The Shepherd submitted to the attention with his usual aloof grace.

"Here you go." Emilia handed Vic and Erin steaming cups of dark, strong coffee. "What can I do for you?"

"I'd like you to tell me what happened this morning," Erin said.

"We already told those other guys," Emilia said. "They was kinda rude. Didn't want my coffee, like they were too good for it or something."

"Forget about those guys," Erin said. "I just want to help."

"I didn't see nothing," Emilia said. "I was in the kitchen, and it don't look out on the front lawn. All I can see is the back. I was making breakfast and Willy, I hear him come downstairs. He always likes to read the Sunday paper in his easy chair. So I hear him go outside. Then there's some shooting and the window busts open."

"How many shots?" Erin asked.

"Five."

"Could you tell if it was more than one gun?"

"It was one," Giana said. She was sitting on the kitchen floor now, an arm around Rolf. Rolf gave Erin a look, checking whether it was okay for him to be cuddling with a witness at an active crime scene.

"How could you tell?" Erin asked.

"I was in the living room," Giana said. "I heard this *pop-pop* and I started to go to the window to see what was going on. Then there was *pop-pop-pop* and the window shattered. Two shots, then three more, and they all sounded the same."

"Did you see the shooter?" Erin asked.

Giana shook her head. "When the window broke, I got down flat on the floor. They told us in school, if we're ever in a shooting, lie down flat. So that's what I did. Then I heard a car driving away."

"Did you see the car?"

"No. I stayed down. Then Gabby came downstairs to see what had happened. She looked out the window by the front door and started screaming. She ran outside, so I got up and went after her."

Gabriella shuddered and wiped her eyes. "I saw... Dad," she whispered. "Lying on the grass."

"On the grass?" Erin repeated. "Not the sidewalk or the porch?"

"The newspaper didn't make it onto the porch," Giana explained. "It was in the middle of the lawn. It's still there, I think."

"Did you hear a car drive up?" Erin asked. "Before the shooting?"

Giana shook her head.

"This is important, Jenny," Erin said. "Did you happen to see a car parked on the street? Either on your side or across the way? Maybe a car that wasn't usually there?"

Giana thought about it. "I think there was a car on the other side," she said. "In front of the Fergusons. But they have a garage. Besides, they drive an Odyssey. You know, a minivan. And this was a sedan."

"Make and model?" Erin asked without much hope.

"Black," Giana said with a helpless shrug. "Maybe a Toyota or a Honda. I don't know."

"How's your coffee?" Emilia asked.

"Very good, thanks," Erin said.

"You've got a really nice dog," Giana said, stroking Rolf's fur. "He's a good boy."

"Yes he is," Erin said. "Emilia, can you think of anyone who had any reason to want to hurt your husband? What did he do for a living?"

"He was a garbage man," Emilia said.

Memory jolted Erin. She thought of some things she'd heard about the infamous Garbage War between the Mafia and the Irish Mob.

"How long was he in that business?" she asked, keeping a poker face.

"All the time I knew him. We was married twenty-five years."

"Did he ever know a guy called Lorenzo Bianchi?" It was a guess, but Erin thought it was a good one.

"Yeah, Lorenzo was, like, his mentor," Emilia said. "But he couldn't have done nothing to hurt Willy. They was always good friends. And besides, Lorenzo died last year. Terrible thing. Overdosed on his heart meds, right after Valentine's Day."

"Yeah," Erin said. "I know." Lorenzo had been murdered, poisoned with his own medication. Erin knew that because she'd helped solve that case.

Erin produced one of her cards and handed it to Emilia. "If any of you think of anything else, please let me know," she said. "You can call me anytime. And thanks for your help."

"My husband never hurt nobody," Emilia said, shaking her head. "I know he was mixed up with some rough guys, but he never woulda hurt a fly."

Chapter 7

Erin, Vic, and Rolf left Lyons and Spinelli with the CSU team to collect what physical evidence they could. The body had already been picked up by the coroner's van and taken to the morgue, so there wasn't much else for the detectives to do. Erin told Spinelli to knock on doors in the neighborhood and find out whether anyone remembered anything about a black sedan.

"It'll be stolen," she said to Vic once they were in her Charger and headed back to Manhattan. "That's if they get plates, which they won't. And the best description we can hope for is a couple of Italian guys."

"I was wondering why you gave the job to those two losers," Vic said. "You just wanted to keep them out of our hair, didn't you?"

"And where they couldn't do much damage," she agreed. "Sorry you got dragged into that. I've got a history with them."

"I figured. I've only known them for ten minutes and I feel like I've got a history with them, too. What'd they do to you?"

"Botched that art heist, then blamed me and tried to get me thrown off the Force."

Vic grinned. "I bet it really burned them when you got promoted instead. Good call with the dog, by the way."

"Anything to get the witnesses talking, right?" Erin said. She reached back into Rolf's compartment and ruffled his fur. "He's trained in explosives, tracking, and apprehension. But I guess he makes a solid therapy dog, too."

"So what do you make of the hit?" Vic asked. "I mean, it was a hit, obviously."

"Definitely," she said. "And it was old-school professionals. Two of them."

"How do you figure?"

"With one shooter, there'd be a driver, too," she said. "But probably just the two guys. They knew our victim's routine. That means they're patient. They probably scoped him out over the past few weeks."

"Getting a guy when he's fetching the morning paper seems a little iffy to me," Vic said.

"How come?" Erin replied. "They know the guy steps out to get the paper. And they don't want to bust in and shoot up his house. That might mean the wife or daughters get shot. That's why I think these guys are pros. They set it up carefully and they didn't want to hit civilians."

"But what if the paperboy made a perfect shot and landed the paper right on the doormat?" Vic objected. "They wouldn't have time to set up a shot before he'd have the paper and be back inside, especially with handguns. Those things are iffy outside ten or fifteen yards unless you've got a real steady hand."

"I assume they were camped out on the street," she said. "They'd see the paper get delivered. What's to stop one of them getting out of the car and moving the paper out onto the lawn?"

"Oh." Vic blinked. "I feel kinda stupid when you put it that way."

"That doesn't tell us much," she said. "Not by itself. But together with Acerbo and Rossi getting killed, we've got a pattern. Can you take a look at the database and see if we've got any connections?"

"Of course there's a connection," he said. "They're all Lucarelli mopes."

"Yes, but there's a reason these particular Lucarelli mopes got killed."

"Okay, okay." Vic was typing and looking at the computer screen. "Let's see, Vittorio Acerbo is connected to everybody. No surprise there, he's head of the family. I got a list of *capos*. We've got Vincenzo Moreno, of course. Then there's Stefano Rossi, William Crea, Aniello Migliore, Joseph DiNapoli, Valentino Vitelli, and Matthew Madonna."

"And Acerbo, Rossi, and Crea are dead," Erin said. "That means the other five are suspects."

"Or targets," Vic said darkly.

* * *

Webb was at the whiteboard in the Major Crimes office when they arrived. He was working on a complicated diagram of the Lucarelli organization. Acerbo was at the top, with his captains in the next tier, followed by an impressive number of underlings, foot soldiers, and low-level earners. He'd divided the tree into sections labeled Drugs, Racketeering, Protection, and Prostitution. Acerbo, Rossi, and Crea's names had big red Xs drawn through them.

"Did you solve it yet?" he asked.

"No, sir," Erin said.

"Relax, O'Reilly. I was joking. We got lucky with Luna. If Rossi's bodyguard hadn't gotten a fluke shot and tagged him, he'd be in the wind too. Hitmen are always tricky."

"What do we know about the Acerbo murder, sir?" she asked.

"Not much," Webb admitted. "I called the prison and got shunted to some FBI dipstick special agent named Gucci or something."

"Like the fashion brand?" Vic asked.

"Maybe. Who he is doesn't matter. What matters is, he told me it was a Federal issue and to keep my New York nose out of it. Then he hung up."

"You should've told him you were from California," Vic suggested.

"He was right," Webb said, unamused. "The victim was a Federal prisoner, killed in a Federal penitentiary. Technically speaking, we can't do a thing about it, and we don't need to know anything."

"Except that Acerbo's lieutenants are getting popped all over the city!" Erin burst out. "You can't tell me it's a coincidence!"

He turned weary eyes toward her. "Of course it's not a coincidence. I agree with you. I'm on your side. But without a court order, I can't do anything but ask for information. They're under no obligation to supply it, and I think they've made it clear they're not going to."

"We could ask Judge Ferris," she said.

"Ferris loves sticking it to criminals," Vic said. "I don't think he wants to mix it up with the Feds."

"Is this just turf protection, sir?" Erin asked. "Or is something else going on?"

"Gucci knew something," Webb said thoughtfully. "Do either of you have anyone in the Bureau you can talk to?"

"Sorry, sir," Vic said. "I'm an asshole, but not a Federal asshole. I've got *some* standards."

Erin shook her head. "I might have something better, though," she said. "I know a guy who's got an inside man at the prison."

They looked at her. Neither one said Carlyle's name, but she could see it in their faces. After a moment, Webb nodded.

"That might help," he said. "In the meantime, I've got Patrol units shadowing the remaining Lucarelli captains."

"You put *protection details* on *the Mafia?!*" Vic was outraged and didn't care who knew it.

"They're citizens of New York," Webb reminded him. "Men whose lives are likely in danger."

"And we're putting cops right in the line of fire!" Vic retorted. "What if our guys start catching bullets?"

"That's the Job, Neshenko," Webb said coldly. "And it's entirely possible one of the men we're watching is behind the killings, so you can think of it as running surveillance on suspects if that makes you feel better."

"We oughta just let them kill each other," Vic muttered.

"While we're at it, why don't we repeal all our gun laws and just declare open season in the street?" Webb said. "Hell, why even bother with a police force? Because these bastards don't get to do this. Not in our town. You were talking about turf wars, O'Reilly? New York is our turf and we're going to defend it."

"Yeah," Vic said. "*Assault on Precinct 13* is one of my favorite movies. Say the word, I'm ready to rock and roll."

"Not what I meant, Neshenko."

"I'm going to go down to the morgue," Erin said. "Levine might have something useful for me. Vic, try not to shoot anybody while I'm gone."

"Okay," he said. "I'll wait till you get back."

* * *

Erin found Dr. Levine exactly where she expected; standing over a bullet-riddled corpse in the basement. The Medical Examiner was bent over the victim, a pair of forceps embedded in one of the holes in the man's chest. As Erin watched, Levine extracted a lump of metal and dropped it into a plastic tub.

"Hey, Doc," Erin said once Levine's tool was clear of the corpse. "Is that William Crea?"

"It was," Levine said. "Maybe it still is, mostly."

"What do you mean, mostly?"

Levine's eyes didn't leave her work. She began to fish around in another bullet hole. "It's difficult to say what's part of us and what's part of our environment. We're semipermeable membranes."

"Semi-what?" Erin hadn't paid as much attention as she should have during her high school biology class. It had been right after lunch and the teacher had been the most boring man she'd ever known.

"Semipermeable membranes," Levine repeated. "Our tissues take in some substances and screen others out. Meanwhile, we generate more of our own cells until we die. After death, as putrefaction sets in, our cellular matter begins to diffuse. At what point do we end and the world begin? That's arguably a philosophical question more than a forensic one, but there's overlap. I should do a paper on it."

"Good idea," Erin said. "Sorry to drag you down here on a Sunday."

Levine blinked and looked up for the first time. "Sorry? Why? Did you shoot him?"

"What? No!"

"Then why are you apologizing?"

"You must have had family stuff. Church, maybe."

"I'm Jewish."

"Oh, right." Erin felt like an idiot. She'd known that. "But you still probably had weekend plans."

"I'd rather be here," Levine said.

"That's good, I guess. So, this is the body that used to be William Crea?"

"That's what the coroner's team said when they dropped him off," she said. "He had no identification on him and I haven't run DNA or dental records. His clothing is over there."

Erin followed Levine's finger to a box containing a bathrobe, a pair of pajama pants, and a matched set of fleecy slippers. The bathrobe was pale blue, except in front. There it was deep, dark red.

"What can you tell me?" she asked.

"Male, Mediterranean ethnicity," Levine said. "Age between fifty and sixty-five. One hundred seventy-two centimeters tall. Weight approximately ninety kilograms."

"Can you give me that in feet and pounds?"

Levine sighed in exasperation. "Five feet eight inches, two hundred pounds. But that's a scientifically inconvenient and arbitrary set of measuring units."

It was Erin's turn to sigh. "Can I assume the bullets killed him?"

"Yes. Given the fatty tissue deposits, he probably had underlying issues with cholesterol and possible early-stage heart failure, but the bullets definitely accelerated the process of cardiac arrest. He was struck by three bullets. Two of these were survivable injuries, one just under the left clavicle and one in the lower left abdomen, but the third directly transected the heart. Death was almost instantaneous. No exit wounds, so all three bullets remained lodged in the victim's thorax and abdomen."

"Were they all from the same gun?"

"Impossible to tell at this point, and possibly impossible to determine at all. Two of the bullets struck bone, deformed, and tumbled, so ballistic analysis will be difficult. The bullet in the abdomen, however, is nearly perfect, so may be possible to match if the weapon can be recovered."

"We don't have the gun," Erin said, knowing the weapon that had been used was probably already at the bottom of the East River. If they wanted to find it they'd need a dredging team, a couple thousand metal detectors, a hundred years or so, and a whole lot of luck. "Anything else you can tell me?"

"He was shot from the front," Levine said. "The range was probably at least twenty meters. No powder tattooing around the wounds, and the lack of overpenetration suggests either underpowered cartridges or medium range. The weapon or weapons used were handguns or submachine-guns chambered for nine millimeter."

"The most common cartridge on the market," Erin observed. "Do you have Stefano Rossi in here, too?"

"Yes," Levine said. "I haven't performed a full autopsy on him yet, but external examination indicates a preliminary cause of death of traumatic laceration of the carotid artery, resulting in rapid exsanguination. Kerf marks indicate a serrated blade, probably along the lines of—"

"A steak knife," Erin interrupted.

"Yes, that would be consistent with the damage," Levine said.

"We know. We found the knife at the scene, covered with the victim's blood."

"That could be misdirection," Levine said, looking slightly annoyed.

"We've got eyewitnesses who watched it happen."

"Then what are you doing down here?"

Erin opened her mouth. Nothing came out.

"I'm busy," Levine said. "Go away."

"Copy that," Erin said. "I'll look for your report when it's ready."

Chapter 8

The Major Crimes office was on the second floor of the Precinct 8 station. The morgue was in the basement. Most people would have taken the elevator three floors, but a little of Ian Thompson's paranoia had rubbed off on Erin. Whenever she saw an elevator, she heard the former Marine say, "Ready-made kill-box." Then she was seized by a strong urge to take the stairs.

Accordingly, she heard the loud, angry voices echoing down the stairwell when she was on the landing between the first and second floors. So she wasn't taken completely by surprise to find Vic looming over a small, olive-skinned guy in a black suit. The two men were shouting at each other, their faces no more than six inches apart. Vic was twice the other guy's size, but the little guy wasn't giving an inch.

Webb was nowhere in sight. Rolf was sitting right where Erin had left him, next to her desk. The Shepherd was watching the argument with his head cocked, trying to puzzle out what was going on and whether he ought to do something about it. When the K-9 saw Erin come in, he wagged his tail and bobbed his head at her.

"You're interfering in a Federal investigation!" the little guy snapped.

"You're in New York City!" Vic retorted. "And these are New York homicides!"

"Last time I checked, New York was part of the United States!"

"And it's my job to uphold the law in New York!"

"Okay, then do your job! The law says Federal cases take precedence!"

"The Tenth Amendment to the Constitution says you have the right to screw yourself!"

"Oh, you want to bring the Constitution into it?" The little man's face had turned purple. "Article Six, Paragraph Two. That's the Supremacy Clause."

"I stopped believing in Santa Claus years ago!"

There was a momentary silence. The little guy blinked, suddenly confused by the sheer absurdity of what Vic had just said.

Erin cleared her throat. "I'm sorry," she said. "I didn't mean to interrupt any important police business. Or Christmas business, I guess. Where's Lieutenant Webb?"

"He went out for a smoke," Vic muttered. "He'll be back any minute."

Erin nodded. "I see. In that case, I'm the ranking detective in this office at the moment. Erin O'Reilly, Detective Second Grade. I assume you're with the FBI?"

The little man straightened the lapels on his suit and drew himself up to his full height, which was about the same as Erin's. "That's right, ma'am. Special Agent Freddy Giusto. I'm in charge of the investigation into the death of Vittorio Acerbo."

"Pleasure," Erin said, offering her hand.

Giusto shook with her, his handshake stiff and formal. Erin had taken him for a young man, but up close, she could see the lines around his eyes and guessed him to be in his early forties. He was clean-shaven, dark-eyed, his hair slicked down with gel. His suit was a little more expensive than was typical for a Fed. He was wearing a shoulder rig with what looked like a Glock 22 in it, the big brother to Erin's trusty Glock 18.

"I was just explaining to your colleague that Acerbo's death falls under Federal jurisdiction," Giusto said.

"I don't think there's any doubt about that," Erin said. "After all, he was killed in a Federal penitentiary while in Federal custody. What's the problem?"

"The problem is, I got a call from this office earlier today while I was handling that investigation," Giusto said. "Then I find out the NYPD is poking around the Lucarelli organization."

"That's our job!" Vic said loudly. "Since two of them got murdered this morning! That's two that we know about. There may have been more. And murder is a state crime, not a Federal one. Which is why—"

"Which is why I'm here," Giusto said, interrupting before Vic could get going again. "So our respective organizations don't get in one another's way. I can't share the details, for obvious reasons, but we've been looking into Acerbo and his people for quite some time. There's an ongoing investigation."

"How can we help?" Erin asked, making her voice as sweet and pleasant as possible. Inside, she was inclined to agree with Vic, but if she started yelling at the Feds, it would only make things worse.

"We'll take anything you've got on the other killings," Giusto said briskly. "Suspect descriptions, evidence from the scenes, that sort of thing."

"We've got more than suspects," Vic said. "We've got—"

Erin willed him to shut up. Somehow, in spite of his temper, Vic read the message in her eyes and cut himself off.

"You've got what?" Giusto asked.

"Some excellent leads," Erin said smoothly. "But we're not ready to share at this time. Obviously, we'd like to assist the FBI in any way possible to dismantle the Lucarellis' criminal organization. Do you have a card with your number, so we can keep in touch with you?"

"Sure." Giusto produced a card from his pocket and handed it over. "I appreciate this, Detective O'Reilly. We're all really on the same team here."

"Of course," she said. "And I'm sure you've got a lot on your plate with the Acerbo killing. The death of somebody that big in the Mafia will make all kinds of waves. We'll be in touch."

She and Giusto shook hands again. The FBI agent, oblivious to the idea of kill-boxes and the fact that he was only one floor above ground level, walked to the elevator and got in.

The moment the doors closed, Vic exploded.

"What the hell was that, Erin?" he demanded. "The goddamn Feebies walk right into our house. Our house, like they own the place! Even Webb said we're gonna defend our turf. And what do you do? You roll right over for them! He was full of shit, but if you'd kissed his ass any harder, you'd have sucked it right out of him!"

"You're smarter than this, Vic," she said, thinking, *this is why you're never going to make Lieutenant*. "This guy was in Otisville this morning. That's a ninety-minute drive, if you're lucky with traffic. He must've got on the road right away when he got our call. Who drives an hour and a half just to tell you to back off?"

"A guy who's pissed off, or a guy who's worried," Vic said. "But you didn't need to be such a pushover."

"I needed him off our backs," Erin said. "Why do you think I shut you up?"

"You didn't want me to tell him we had Luna in custody," Vic said. "But won't he find that out anyway?"

"Eventually, yeah." Erin turned over the card in her hand. "But I want to know more about Freddy Giusto before I go sharing all our secrets with him. We're not going to drop two homicide investigations just because an FBI agent asked us to."

"What do you think his game is?" Vic asked.

"I don't know," she said. "But until I do, I'm going to be really careful what I tell him."

"You're hanging out with gangsters too much," Vic said. "It's making you paranoid."

The elevator chimed. Both detectives looked toward it. Webb emerged from the car, wearing the contented expression of a man who'd just gotten his nicotine fix.

"Did I miss anything?" Webb asked.

Erin and Vic looked at each other.

"Hypothetically speaking, sir," she said slowly. "Would you want to know if one or more of the detectives in your unit was engaged in activities he or she had been warned against by a man purportedly acting in the interests of the Federal Bureau of Investigation?"

Webb's face clouded. "That would depend," he said. "Would these alleged activities involve anything illegal or immoral?"

"Absolutely not, sir. Hypothetically."

"And would these alleged activities fall within the normal purview of the NYPD's duties?"

"They would indeed, sir."

"Hypothetically," Vic added.

"Then I could see the value of maintaining a degree of distance and deniability," Webb said. "And I would have no need to know. Hypothetically, of course."

"In that case," Erin said, "you didn't miss anything."

"Oh, that's good," Webb said. He sat down at his desk, his face a bland mask of professional indifference. "Did Levine find anything interesting on the bodies?"

Erin told what little she knew about the victims. She and Vic updated the whiteboard with the information they'd gotten from the Crea family. Webb looked on, rubbing his chin and clearly already wanting another cigarette.

"We don't have much," he said when they finished and stood back. "Different MO on the hits."

"Acerbo's death was pretty similar to Rossi's, from what I hear," Erin said. "Stabbed in the prison cafeteria."

"I don't think that makes any difference," Vic said. "We already know it was three different killers. The method's not as important as the result."

"Vic's right," Erin said.

"Can I get a signed statement of you saying that?" Vic asked. "I think I'd like to frame it and hang it."

Erin rolled her eyes. "The point is, these were professional, coordinated hits. These were carefully planned ahead of time."

"I'll buy premeditation for the shooting in Queens," Webb said. "That was obviously an ambush. But the restaurant job? What sort of idiot hitman doesn't bring a weapon with him?"

Erin and Vic were both shaking their heads. They started talking over each other.

"He knew the routine and the bodyguards—" Vic said.

"Luna was inserted ahead of time—" Erin said.

"One at a time!" Webb said.

"I'd say 'ladies first,'" Vic said. "But in the absence of any, why don't you lead off, Erin?"

"Alphonse Luna is a Lucarelli foot soldier," Erin said. "So what the hell was he doing waiting tables? If you give a guy like that a side job as an income, it's some union make-work position where he doesn't even have to show up. According to the manager, Luna had been working there six months, and doing good work while he was there. That's long-term planning, sir."

"But was he inserted to kill Rossi specifically?" Webb asked.

"No way to tell," she said. "We can ask him, but I don't think he's going to spill."

"He's facing Murder One," Vic said. "That's a whole lot of years. He might crack."

"Murder Two, tops," Erin said. "We may know it was premeditated, but the DA will have trouble proving it. That's actually another reason to grab a knife off the table. His lawyer can always argue it was a spur-of-the-moment thing, or even temporary insanity."

"That's a good point," Webb said. "What were you going to say, Neshenko?"

"Good bodyguards can spot a gun under a guy's jacket," Webb said. "Or a knife up his sleeve. Rossi's guards were on the ball. They may not have been able to save him, but they tagged the guy who killed him. This was a great way to get close to Rossi, especially setting it up so far in advance. Luna just had to know Rossi liked to eat at that restaurant every Sunday."

"It was his routine," Erin agreed. "Routine makes it easy to get murdered."

"So you both think the hit on Rossi was set up half a year ago?" Webb asked.

"At least," Erin said. "Maybe longer."

"And a couple of guys camped out in front of Crea's house this morning, maybe overnight, to get him?"

Erin and Vic nodded.

"And then Acerbo gets shanked at the breakfast table," Webb finished. "On the plus side, that's probably all the bodies that are going to drop for the moment. Any other targets will either be running scared or laying low by now."

"Unless a couple more lowlifes got disappeared," Vic said. "Maybe they'll turn up in a few months in the Jersey swamps, or next time the Harbor Patrol drags the East River."

"I don't think so," Erin said. "None of these killings were secret. Two of them were extremely public. The killers want people to know these guys are dead."

"So why now?" Webb asked.

They looked at him. "What do you mean?" Vic asked.

"Let's assume you two are right," Webb said. "The bad guys have been setting this up for a while. Why not last week? Or next? What's going on in the underworld right now?"

Vic shrugged. "Beats me."

"So why don't you do what I asked you to do and talk to the people who are dealing with the Lucarellis?" Webb suggested.

Vic mumbled something.

"I can't hear you, Neshenko."

"Copy that, sir."

"O'Reilly, I can't believe I'm saying this," Webb said. "But you already know what I'm going to tell you."

"You want me to talk to my boyfriend, sir," Erin said, keeping her face carefully neutral.

"And anyone else who can tell me what the Lucarellis have going," Webb said. "Take a stick and poke the anthill. But use a long stick and stand back."

"Yes, sir," Erin said.

"I just realized I ordered both of you to pump your lovers for information," Webb sighed. "What a sorry excuse for proper procedure this is. Tell you what. Get out of here, talk to your significant others, go home. If you get anything pertinent, you can log it as overtime. Otherwise, it's a Sunday afternoon. You two are lucky enough to have personal lives. Take care of those. Go on, scram."

Chapter 9

Erin got back to the Barley Corner tired and ready for a drink. She gave Rolf a quick turn around the block, then went into the pub. It was a little early for supper, but her growling stomach reminded her that she'd skipped lunch, so she made for the bar. A juicy cheeseburger and a pint of Guinness would cheer her up.

She'd gotten about halfway across the room before she realized something was off. She'd been preoccupied with thoughts about the case and her own hunger, but something sent a tingle up her spine. She'd recognized a man at a side table and subconsciously identified him as dangerous. That was no great surprise; the Corner had plenty of clientele who qualified. After all, it was a Mob bar. But Erin knew to trust her gut when it whispered a warning.

She turned slowly, calmly, keeping her face nonchalant and her hand away from her gun. The last thing she wanted to do was provoke a shootout in Carlyle's pub.

It took her a second to place the man. He was Italian, in his mid-twenties, dressed in his Sunday best. The suit was a little flashy for Erin's taste, but well-tailored and expensive. The guy's features were smooth, clean-shaven, and handsome, except for the eyes. His eyes were cold and empty, reminding her uncomfortably of Mickey Connor in their lack of expression.

His name was Carlo. She didn't know his last name, but she knew he worked for Vincenzo Moreno. He was a muscle guy, a gunman. What the hell was he doing sitting calmly in an O'Malley pub, a glass of red wine in front of him, while Irish thugs watched a soccer game on the big-screen TV?

Carlo inclined his head in acknowledgment of Erin's look and raised his glass in a silent salute. Erin nodded once, curtly, and scanned the rest of the room for familiar faces. She saw one of Ian's guys by the far wall and relaxed slightly. There had been no attack on the Corner. Carlo must be here on business.

She twitched Rolf's leash and walked over to Ian's guy. This man, she recalled, was Kenneth Mason. Like all Ian's associates, he was former military. Mason had been a Marine, to judge from the anchor-and-globe tattoo peeking over the collar of his black button-down shirt. He was large, muscular, and taciturn, a man with a short haircut and puckered scars on both cheeks.

"Ma'am," Mason said, predictably.

"Hey, Marine," she said. "Ian around?"

"No, ma'am. He's off today. I've got the duty."

"Where's Carlyle?"

"In back." Mason tilted his head toward the meeting room.

"With whom?"

"Couple Italian guys."

Erin felt a thrill of alarm. "Any of our people in there with him?"

"It's a private meeting, ma'am, but old man O'Malley and the Snake are there."

"Evan's here, too?" Now Erin was really worried. Why hadn't she known this was happening? It must have been a last-minute thing, or Carlyle would have warned her. She hurried toward the back hallway. Private meeting or not, she needed to see what was going on.

She retained enough caution to knock. It was never a good idea to startle a room full of gangsters. She rapped three times on the door and waited. Rolf, picking up on her mood, stood beside her with his ears at full attention, nose thrust forward, tense and ready.

The door opened. Erin had to steel herself not to take a step back. Mason had warned her the Snake was present, but she hadn't yet gotten used to Mickey's replacement. Gordon Pritchard was a frightening man. He lacked Mickey's size, but he moved with a predator's quick, feral grace. His eyes' irises were so dark as to be nearly black and his voice was perpetually hoarse and rasping. But the most horrifying thing about him was the scars. One whole side of his face was a mass of poorly-healed burned tissue, and Carlyle had assured her the scars ran all the way down the right side of his body. He always wore a black leather glove on his right hand to cover up some of the telltales. The burns, Carlyle had told her, were a souvenir of Pritchard's youth as a pro-Republic teenager in Northern Ireland. During a particularly nasty incident between a crowd of protesters and the British military, Pritchard had tried to throw a homemade Molotov cocktail. A very unlucky rubber bullet had shattered the bottle in his hand, coating the young man with burning gasoline, resulting in ghastly scars and damaged vocal cords.

"Detective," Pritchard rasped.

"Afternoon," Erin said. "I'm looking for Cars."

Pritchard glanced over his shoulder. "It's O'Reilly," he said to someone in the room. "And her dog."

"Let her in," said a male voice she recognized as belonging to Evan O'Malley.

Pritchard shrugged slightly and stepped back, clearing the doorway. Erin walked in, Rolf at her hip. The room was dimly lit, a green baize card table at its center. Around the table sat Evan O'Malley, Carlyle, a gray-haired Italian man Erin didn't know, and Vincenzo Moreno, otherwise known as Vinnie the Oil Man.

Carlyle was already on his feet to welcome her. The old Italian was the second to rise, Evan and Vinnie right behind him. Carlyle smiled and motioned her in.

"Grand to see you, darling," he said. "Would you care for a drink? I've a bottle of Glen D here."

Erin's body reminded her again that she hadn't eaten since breakfast. It wasn't wise to drink on an empty stomach, particularly when you needed to keep your wits about you. But it was more important to blend in.

"Sure," she said. "Pour me a glass."

"You already know Mr. O'Malley," Carlyle said as he opened the bottle and poured. "And Mr. Pritchard. I believe you're acquainted with Mr. Moreno as well."

"We've met," Erin said, giving Vinnie a stiff nod.

"And this is Valentino Vitelli," Carlyle finished, indicating the older Italian.

Vitelli bowed in a formal, old-fashioned style and held out a hand. Erin reached out to shake. To her consternation, he bowed again over the hand and lightly kissed the back of it.

"*Bella signora*," he said. "I've heard so much about you. It is an honor."

"Thank you," Erin said, not knowing quite what else to say.

"Shall we?" Carlyle said, gesturing to the table. All of them sat down. Carlyle handed Erin her drink.

"Rolf, *sitz*," she said quietly. The K-9 settled on his haunches beside her chair. He was just tall enough so his eyes and ears poked over the tabletop.

"We're nearly done here, regardless," Carlyle said.

"I think we're all in agreement," Vinnie said. "It's much better to talk out our differences like reasonable men than to come to blows over trifling disagreements. I'm sure Miss O'Reilly agrees."

"Does this mean you boys are going to play nice?" Erin asked.

Everyone smiled except Pritchard, whose facial muscles were so damaged it might not be possible for him. Evan's smile was a chilly, artificial thing, but at least he was making the effort.

"You'll be pleased to hear our little spat with Mr. Moreno's organization is concluded," Evan said.

"I'm glad to hear it." Erin was surprised by everything in Evan's words, but she tried to hide it. The Lucarellis had been fighting with the O'Malleys for months, primarily over the distribution of narcotics on the Lower East Side. There had been bad blood, some of which had ended up staining the streets.

"One has to know when a war's over, darling," Carlyle said. "Else we'd always be fighting."

"Why now?" Erin asked, thinking of Webb's question.

"It's a fortunate confluence of events," Vinnie said. "Suffice it to say, there has been a recent realignment of certain elements which were previously obstructing negotiations. They do say every cloud has a silver lining."

Vitelli nodded. "A sad day, but a hopeful one," he said. "God rest his soul, but my dear friend Vittorio might have preferred a different resolution."

"We don't need to bore Miss O'Reilly with our maunderings," Vinnie said.

"Mr. Vitelli brings up a good point," Evan said. "Would you like any representatives of mine to be present at the funerals?"

"That might be a little premature," Vinnie said. "Some of my boys might get the wrong impression. We don't want any friction."

"Of course," Evan said. "Perhaps some gesture of condolence, then? A tasteful floral arrangement is, I think, traditional?"

"That would be appreciated," Vinnie said.

"Then that's settled," Evan said. He stood up again and extended his hand across the table. Vinnie shook with him. The two men smiled with the lower part of their faces.

The meeting broke up. Vinnie and Vitelli shook hands with all the Irishmen. Vitelli insisted on kissing Erin's hand once more.

"Mr. Carlyle is a very fortunate man," he said with a hint of wistfulness. "Ah, to be in his place, and twenty years younger."

"It was very nice meeting you, Mr. Vitelli," Erin said as diplomatically as she could.

"Give my regards to your lad," Carlyle added. "How old is he now?"

"Twenty-two," Vitelli said with a smile. "Time does hurry by. Good evening."

The Italians left the room. Pritchard followed them out. Erin had the feeling it was more to make sure they left peaceably than out of etiquette.

"Quite a day, Mr. Carlyle," Evan said softly.

"I hope you got a good deal," Erin dared to say.

Evan looked surprised and a little pleased. "I think we'll all come out of it well enough," he said. "But Miss O'Reilly, I hope your organization doesn't rock the boat too much. We're all in it together, after all, and the water can get very cold this time of year. I wish you a very pleasant evening."

Erin watched him go, feeling the heat of Carlyle's whiskey burning in her. She felt hollow and uneasy. And she still hadn't gotten her supper.

* * *

"Okay," Erin said. "What the hell is going on?"

They were upstairs in Carlyle's apartment, a reinforced steel door between them and the rest of New York. Erin had a bacon cheeseburger in her hands and a basket of fries and a pint of Guinness on the dining table. Rolf's nose was buried in his dog dish.

"It's something of a surprise to me as well," Carlyle said. "It seems our friend the Oil Man wanted to broker an agreement with Evan. War is bad for business, after all."

"Only some businesses," she said. "I don't think anybody ever went broke selling guns."

"Not in America," he said with a chuckle.

"So what's the arrangement?" she asked.

"The O'Malleys are getting out of the heroin trade."

"They're *what?*" Erin dropped the half-eaten burger. The patty bounced off her plate and stopped just short of the table edge, to the disappointment of Rolf, who had finished his own dinner and was watching with interest. He'd never beg for Erin's scraps, but if something hit the floor, he was ready to clean it up.

"It's true," Carlyle said. "I can't say I'm unhappy with that. Truth to tell, Evan's been making noises about it ever since Liam's misfortune."

Erin nodded. Carlyle was referring, with characteristic understatement, to the brutal shooting of Liam McIntyre, Evan's top narcotics guy. That hadn't been done by the Mafia, but it underscored the dangers of the drug trade.

"Evan says we can't compete with both the Italians and the South American lads," Carlyle went on. "He wants to consolidate the business, focus on other revenue sources. I understand a great deal of the impetus for the change comes from Kyle Finnegan."

"So the Irish give up something they wanted to get out of anyway," Erin said. "What do the O'Malleys get in return?"

"The Lucarellis stop fighting us over the labor rackets in Long Island," Carlyle said. "They become almost entirely dedicated to the heroin trade. And we stop killing one another."

Erin put a hand on his arm. "It's no coincidence, three Lucarelli big shots going down right before this talk," she said. "Do you think Acerbo would've nixed the deal if he'd still been alive?"

"Difficult to say," Carlyle said. "I've no real knowledge of that gang's inner workings. I'd always understood Vinnie was speaking for his boss, but now I'm wondering."

"You think someone made a power play," she said. "Alphonse Luna, the guy who killed Stefano Rossi, is a Lucarelli. Look, it's got to be either someone working inside the Mafia, or else Evan turned someone."

Carlyle nodded. "Evan's quite capable of that," he agreed. "And he certainly wanted the deal to go through. If he'd gotten word Acerbo was against it, he might have made that happen. I'm not the only one with contacts inside Otisville."

"Speaking of which, did you find out anything?" she asked. "We tried calling up there and an FBI agent slapped us down pretty hard."

"Did he, now?" Carlyle smiled thinly. "And would this Federal agent happen to have an Italian surname, by chance?"

"He did, now that you mention it," Erin said. "What are you implying?"

"It wouldn't be the first time an agent was swayed by an outside organization."

"This isn't the 1970s anymore," she said.

"So police corruption doesn't exist?" He raised an eyebrow.

"That's not what I mean! I mean... shit, maybe you're right. But even if you are, there's nothing I can do about it right now. What could your guy tell you?"

"The lad who did for Acerbo is a lifer by the name of Roy Aiello," Carlyle said. "You might know him as 'Icepick.'"

"Doesn't ring any bells."

"I thought it mightn't. He's been inside about as long as you've been a copper. Your da probably knows of him. He's an executioner for the Lucarellis. The lawyers pinned eight murders on him, but I've heard the total's closer to twenty. He's serving eight life sentences."

"At a Federal prison? For murder? That's a state charge."

"Aye, on account of the racketeering. He was part of the case that locked Acerbo away. That was around the time I came over from the old country. Made quite the stir on the street."

"Did he resent that? Being dragged down with Acerbo?"

"According to my lad, the two of them were old mates. Best of friends." Carlyle paused. "Up until Icepick opened Acerbo's throat, that is."

Erin shuddered. "I'll never get used to it," she said. "The way you guys betray each other."

"Aiello is old-school Mafia," Carlyle said. "He still believes in the code. He never tried to bargain for a lesser sentence, never turned on his lads. He'll kill one of them, but he'll never betray them to the law. And he's not one of ours. Erin, either he was working for himself, or someone else in the Lucarellis told him to kill Acerbo."

"So it's an internal coup," she said.

"Aye, that's my thinking."

"And Evan told me to let it go."

"Not in so many words, but aye, that's his meaning."

"Because of the peace agreement."

He nodded.

"Please tell me you got that conversation on tape," she said.

Carlyle grimaced. "They showed up unannounced," he said. "I hadn't my wire about me, and no time to fetch it."

"Damn," Erin said. "We could've gotten something on Vinnie. Do you think it was him? Or one of the others?"

Carlyle shrugged. "You'd need to ask them. Not that they'd tell you."

Erin thought about it, chewing morosely on some French fries. "So, all you can tell me is it was a Mob hit?"

"And you knew that already," he said.

"I'll be looking into all the Lucarelli lieutenants," she said. "Vinnie, that dirty old man Vitelli, and the whole rest of the crew."

"Evan said—" Carlyle began.

"I don't work for Evan!" she snapped.

"But you do, darling," he said gently. "You know that."

"No, I pretend to work for him. There's a difference!"

"And if you want to keep up the charade, you have to make allowances," he said. "You think I'm enjoying everything I have to do to keep up bloody appearances?"

Erin bit back an angry retort. "You're right," she said through gritted teeth. "I have to keep up appearances. But that doesn't mean I stop doing my job. It just means I have to look to Evan like I'm doing what he wants at the same time."

"Can you manage that?"

"Isn't that what you're doing?" she shot back.

"Every day, darling."

Chapter 10

Erin sat on the couch and stared at her phone. Her parents' number was on the screen, her thumb hovering over the green call button. Carlyle was downstairs, holding court at the bar. She wanted to talk to her dad. His lifetime of police experience might be able to shed some light on her current situation. But she wanted to get her thoughts straight before calling him.

Prior to the incident with Mickey Connor, she wouldn't have dreamed of dragging her father into this. Sean O'Reilly had known Erin was dating Carlyle, and though he hadn't exactly approved, he'd gradually gotten used to the idea of his only daughter seeing a mobster. Carlyle had worked his usual charm and Erin had dared to hope the two men might even become friends.

All that had changed when Michelle, Erin's sister-in-law, had been kidnapped and nearly murdered by another O'Malley associate. While the family was dealing with the immediate crisis, Sean had been a pillar of strength. But Erin still remembered the look in his eyes and the sound of his voice when he'd finally gotten her alone, after the immediate danger had passed. It had happened on the sidewalk just outside

Michelle and Sean Junior's brownstone, a few days after the bodies had finished falling.

"Erin," he said, laying a hand on her shoulder. "What are you doing?"

"I'm doing my job, dad," she said. "The Job."

"I'm not talking about the shooting," he said. "God knows the bastard had it coming. I'm talking about your boyfriend."

She felt a sinking feeling, coupled with a sense of inevitability. "What about him?" she asked quietly.

"You can love whoever you love," he said. "Old, young, rich, poor. Hell, you can love a goldfish if you want, and it'd be a part of the family."

"A wet, scaly part," she said, trying to lighten the tone.

Sean didn't laugh or even crack a smile. "But when your love life puts the rest of our family in danger, it's time to take a good long look at yourself."

Erin felt a flash of anger. She shrugged his hand away and glared at him. "Carlyle didn't make this happen," she said. "He hated Mickey as much as any of us did!"

"That's my point," Sean said. "If he hadn't brought his enemies into the family circle, Shelley would've been just fine."

"Shelley is fine!"

"Like hell she is!" Sean's mustache bristled angrily. "You know what this sort of thing does to people. She'll push it aside and try to go on with her life, but she'll never get over it. She'll be scarred for years, maybe forever. And it wasn't just her. The kids could've been killed, too! It's just dumb luck they weren't!"

"It was more than luck," Erin shot back. "Ian took bullets protecting them. And he was there because Carlyle told him to be! If you want to lay blame on him, then at least pretend to be fair!"

"None of that would've been necessary if he'd just steered clear of you in the first place! And you're still protecting him, after his goddamn stupid

street fight spilled over into your brother's house? Do you really believe his hands are clean? You're smarter than that, kiddo."

"You don't understand, Dad."

"I understand plenty. I understand I've got perspective on this, because I'm looking at it from the outside. You're on the inside looking out, and you're blinded by the way you feel about him!"

"I love him, Dad. Can you even admit it?"

"Okay, you love him. So what? You think love gives you a pass? Maybe it does, if you want to throw your own life away. But there's more lives than yours on the line."

"He's a good man."

"No, he's not! He's a career criminal who built bombs! He's killed men!"

"I've killed men!"

"That's different!"

"You're wrong about him," Erin said, speaking more quietly but with the same intensity.

"Oh? And just how am I wrong about him?" Sean huffed. "And you'd better have something good, because right now, if he shows up, I'm liable to break his face."

"It's... complicated," she said, aware of how lame it sounded.

"Erin, I raised you better than this," he said, making an effort to soften his tone. "This guy's no good for you, for any of us."

"He's..." she began. Then she choked off her words. She didn't have the right to tell him. Sean might think Carlyle was putting them all in danger, but revealing the truth about the Irishman had its own dangers.

"What?" Sean asked. His eyes, which had been angry, grew sharper and more thoughtful. He'd seen something in her face, heard some of her unsaid words. Now he was curious. Sean O'Reilly had been a career Patrolman, but he had a detective's brain.

She shook her head. "I'm sorry, Dad. I can't."

"Can't..." he repeated. His voice trailed off. There were several seconds of dead silence. Then Sean glanced up and down the street, making sure no one was close enough to hear them.

"He's a CI," Sean said very quietly. "An informant. You flipped him."

"He had a choice," she said. "After he got shot last year and IAB found out about us. He chose me."

"Can you tell me any details?"

"Dad, I can't even tell you what I just told you. This is super-secret stuff. There's not ten people in the whole world who know this. All I can say is, Carlyle's one of the good guys. He's on my side."

Sean ran a hand across his scalp, rubbing the bare skin where he'd once had hair. "Is this how he's planning to get out of the Life?" he asked. "For good?"

"Yeah."

"Risky. Dangerous."

"I know it is. So does he. But everything about the Life is dangerous. He likes to say there's a lot of young mobsters. Not so many his age."

That finally earned her a slight smile. "This Connor punk," he said. "Did he know?"

Erin shook her head. "He was trying to take over the O'Malleys. Carlyle was just in the way. They didn't like each other, but it wasn't anything personal."

"Just business?" Sean said, making the obligatory Godfather *reference.*

"Yeah. And Evan was pissed Mickey pulled family into it. He wanted to pay me for taking Mickey out, if you can believe it."

Sean raised his eyebrows. "So my daughter's taking Mob contracts now?"

"I had to take the money," she said. "Or he'd have been suspicious. I handed every cent over to my case officer."

"That's my girl," he said. "Look, kiddo, I didn't know. About him."

"You weren't supposed to. I shouldn't have told you. And you can't breathe one word of this. Not to anyone. Not even to Mom." Erin paused. "Especially not to Mom."

"She means well," Sean said, nodding. "But I wouldn't trust her to keep this quiet. She'll keep shameful secrets if she has to, but if it's something to be proud of, Mary can't help herself. But can you promise me, this won't involve the family again?"

Erin shrugged helplessly. "Evan's old-school," she said. "He'd never go after civilians. He's just like the Mafia that way. If he's going to take Carlyle out, he'll find a way to do it when nobody else is around."

* * *

Erin sat back on Carlyle's couch and dropped her phone to the coffee table. She didn't need to call her dad after all. Their conversation three months ago had told her where she needed to look.

"Maybe it's you, Vinnie," she said quietly. "Or your buddies. But it's sure as hell one of you."

She was sure it was just business. The Mafia's business might involve killing, but Erin O'Reilly's business was murder, too.

"Nothing personal, Vinnie," she whispered. "But I'm coming after you."

So instead of calling her father, she called Vic. After the first three rings, she wondered whether he'd pick up. But on the fifth ring, just as it was about to roll to voicemail, the call connected.

"Yeah?" he growled.

"Oh, good," she said. "I thought you were drunk. Or maybe dead."

"I wish."

"Which one?"

"Take your pick. What's up?"

"I need to talk to some Lucarellis."

"So what's stopping you?" he retorted. "You don't need my permission."

"No, but I need your help."

"Like hell you do. I don't hang with mob guys. That's more your thing, isn't it?"

Erin's mouth twisted and she gripped her phone a little tighter. "I get it, Vic. You're pissed at the world. But I need to get in touch with the Lucarelli *capos* and I thought Logan's SNEU squad could give me a hand. You're going to have to talk to Zofia sooner or later."

"Okay, in that case, I choose 'later.' I'm off the clock, Erin. You can call them. Logan likes you; you'll be fine without me."

"While you do what? Sulk and drink yourself stupid?"

"Wow. It's like you can read my mind. You got a problem with that, we can talk about it tomorrow. When I'm working." And Vic hung up.

"Sheesh," Erin muttered. But in spite of his surliness, Vic had a point. She didn't need him to be on board. She'd worked with Sergeant Logan's team several times and they'd always gotten on well with one another. She had Logan's number in her phone. SNEU tended to work nights, so they were probably on duty. Erin shrugged and called Logan.

After three rings, he answered with a terse, "Logan." He sounded out of breath. In the background were sounds of some sort of scuffle.

"O'Reilly here," she said. "Catch you at a bad time, Sarge?"

"What're you talking about?" he replied. "I'm having the time of my life out here. Just nailed a couple idiots we caught dealing out of a food truck. They made a break for it in the truck. Janovich did a perfect PIT maneuver, spun the bastards into a traffic light. Then these dumbasses jumped out and made a run for it. We just collared 'em. No sweat, Detective. Everything's under control."

"Great. I was hoping you could give me a hand with something, if you're not too busy."

"Can you come over to my office? I got kind of a full plate."

"Sure. Where are you?"

"Corner of Hester and Baxter in Little Italy. We'll be here for the next hour at least. You hungry?"

"You buying?" she volleyed back.

"Not exactly. Food truck has some pretty good meatball subs."

"I'll pass, but Rolf may want one."

"Copy that," Logan said. "But when you come, drive careful. It's an uncontrolled intersection. At least it is now."

* * *

Erin had to park two blocks from the scene, on account of the traffic jam Janovich had created. It was easy to find the SNEU squad, however. She and Rolf just had to follow the flashing lights and the cacophony of honking horns.

They arrived to find a tow truck starting to drag the suspects' vehicle away from a New York stoplight that had gone down hard in the line of duty. Erin saw all the usual SNEU folks scattered around the area. Logan and Firelli were standing over a pair of sullen-looking young men. The suspects were seated on the curb, hands cuffed behind them. Janovich was engaged in a heated discussion with a traffic cop in the middle of the intersection. The cop was making angry gestures at Janovich with one hand and trying to direct traffic with the other, with mixed results. Piekarski was next to the tow truck, signaling him to park the food truck curbside.

Erin approached the linked trucks. The wrecked vehicle had one wheel twisted at a grotesque angle, the wheel well smashed in. Erin shook her head. A well-executed PIT maneuver was actually a fairly gentle move, as far as car crashes went. The pursuer was supposed to come alongside, make light contact with the other vehicle, then steer sharply into the target to make it spin out.

"Evening, Piekarski," she said. "Janovich get a little enthusiastic?"

"Oh, hey, O'Reilly," Piekarski said. She was a petite blonde who didn't look tough until you got close and saw her eyes. "Yeah, we do mostly foot chases and I think he was out of practice. But he did stop them."

"I can see that. Anyone get hurt?"

Piekarski shook her head. "Jan banged his head on the steering wheel and bloodied up his nose. He's lucky the airbag didn't deploy or it actually could've been worse. But his ride will be in the shop for a while. What're you doing here? Did we step in another Major Crimes case?"

"No, I don't know these mopes," Erin said, cocking her head toward the prisoners. "I just needed to talk to Logan and he told me to come to him. His office, those were his words."

Piekarski chuckled. "Logan's office is wherever Logan parks his backside for more than five minutes," she said. "He's got a desk back at the Five, but I don't think he remembers where it is."

The tow truck driver leaned out his window. "Hey, ladies!" he yelled. "You want me to put this here, or what? You can swap recipes some other time!"

"You want a recipe?" Piekarski shot back. "I'll give you one. My boot, your ass, served up hot. Just leave it there and get the hell out of here if you're in such a hurry."

While the muttering truck driver climbed out of his vehicle and started uncoupling from the food truck, Piekarski turned back to Erin. "Swap recipes," she muttered. "Jesus! What decade are we living in? He knows I'm carrying two guns and a Taser, doesn't he?"

"Forget about it," Erin advised. "Let's go see Logan."

"Copy that," Piekarski said. "But can I catch you once you're done with your business, before you bounce?"

"Of course," Erin said, but she had the feeling Piekarski wanted to talk about Vic. And she wasn't looking forward to it.

"Glad you could join us, O'Reilly," Logan said, catching sight of her as she approached. "You missed the good stuff. All we're doing now is cleanup."

"That's okay," she said. "I'm not here to have fun."

"Change your mind about that meatball sub?"

She smiled. "I'm good, thanks. I was hoping to pick your brain about the Lucarellis."

He shrugged. "Which ones?"

"The *capos* that haven't already been popped."

Logan walked away from the handcuffed prisoners, motioning for Erin to follow. Once they were out of earshot, he turned back to face her.

"You working the hits?" he asked.

"Yeah," she said. "What do you know about them?"

"They've got the Lucarellis running around like a bunch of headless chickens," he said. "Word on the street is, everybody's scared. Acerbo getting nailed was bad enough, but with two of his top guys buying it the same day... that's no coincidence."

"What've you got on Rossi and Crea?" she asked. "Why would they have been targeted?"

"Cleaning house," Logan said. "Aside from the Oil Man, they were Acerbo's closest associates. Rossi in particular had to go."

"Why?"

"Because he was a muscle guy and he was tight with Acerbo. You can bet if he hadn't gone down, he'd be out for revenge right now."

"What about Crea?"

"He was more of an earner. He wasn't big on the narcotics side of things, so I don't know much about him. He was mostly involved with the labor rackets on Long Island."

"The Garbage Mafia?" Erin asked.

"You know about that?" Logan looked surprised. "Oh yeah, I guess you would. Your dad used to work that area back in the day, didn't he?"

"Yeah. He told me some stories." Erin decided not to tell Logan about her boyfriend's suspected involvement in a series of garbage-truck bombings in the '90s.

"All I know is, Crea was in good with Acerbo," Logan said. "The closest thing to friends you're likely to get in this business."

"What about heroin?" Erin was thinking about the agreement Vinnie had made with Evan O'Malley.

"What about it? It's terrible. It'll ruin your life. And it's everywhere, no matter what we do."

"Who's in charge of distribution for the Lucarellis?"

Logan looked at her like she was an idiot. "The Oil Man, of course," he said. "You know that. Not that we can prove it."

"Besides him."

"Material Mattie."

Erin gave him a look. "His real name, if you don't mind?"

"Matthew Madonna." Logan waited with an expectant look on his face.

Erin sighed. "I give up. What's the joke?"

"You know, Madonna? Like the singer?"

"Yes, I know who Madonna is." Erin had been on the opposite side of this pop-culture reference once before.

"*Material Girl*? So, Matthew Madonna, Material Mattie."

"Okay, okay, I get it."

"You're not laughing," Logan said.

"It's not funny. So, Matt Madonna is a heroin pusher for Vinnie Moreno?"

"I guess he is now. He used to work for Acerbo. The Oil Man just ran things in Acerbo's name. But I suppose Vinnie's in charge now, or he will be once they make it official. Why are you asking about heroin?"

"I heard a rumor about the Lucarellis expanding their narcotics operations," she said. "Great opportunity for you and your team to pick up a few more busts."

"And you think that has something to do with their leadership getting taken out?"

"Maybe. The timing is a little suspicious. Do you know where Madonna hangs out?"

Logan whistled sharply and waved. "Hey, Firelli! Come over here a minute!"

"What you want me to do with these losers?" Firelli asked, pointing to the prisoners.

"Just leave 'em there. They'll keep. Have Piekarski keep an eye on 'em."

Firelli trotted over. "What's up, Sarge?"

"O'Reilly here wants to find Material Mattie," Logan said.

The little Italian cop grinned. "Oh yeah, I know where he hangs out."

"We've got this," Logan said. "Why don't you take O'Reilly on a tour, show her the old neighborhood?"

"Copy that, Sarge."

"Do I need my car?" Erin asked.

"Nah, it's just down the street," Firelli said.

"Rain check," Erin said to Piekarski, trying to hide her relief.

The other woman scowled but said nothing.

Chapter 11

"Old neighborhood?" Erin asked as she, Rolf, and Firelli walked. She couldn't help looking around for Mafiosi. Rolf was sniffing at interesting lampposts and fire hydrants. Firelli ambled along, as relaxed as if they were just out for an evening stroll.

"Oh yeah, I grew up here," he said. "Spent most of my time on the street. Hung out with a lot of Mob guys. I was just like Ray Liotta in *Goodfellas*. Always wanted to be a gangster."

"I kind of hate to mention this," she said. "But you're wearing the opposing team's colors."

Firelli laughed. "Yeah, funny world, ain't it? I was just hitting my teen years when the Feds really cracked down on the Mob and threw all the Family bosses in prison. A bunch of guys I knew went away on account of that. It took a little of the glamor out of the Life." He stopped laughing. "And my best friend OD'd. Two weeks before his sixteenth birthday. I was fooling around with drugs a little myself. I was the one who bought the stuff he used. The problem with buying smack off the street is, you never know what's in it, or how much."

"You ended up with a bad batch?" Erin guessed.

"The opposite," Firelli said. "Apparently this dipshit dealer screwed up somehow, didn't cut his product enough. The shit you find on the street is usually between one and sixty percent pure."

"That's a pretty wide range," she said.

"Tell me about it," he said. "And with the different tolerances people build up if they've been using a while, it's like playing Russian roulette with a needle. But in my buddy's case, he got a shot that was seventy-five percent or more. The really good shit. Like taking a high dive into ice water. He went into a coma, never woke up."

"Sorry to hear it."

"Woke me up, though," Firelli said with a grim smile. "I got off the stuff, cold turkey. Haven't touched it since."

"Is that why you became a cop?" she asked. "Because of your friend?"

"Nah. I became a cop because I'm an adrenaline junkie. If I can't get high off China white, I can still get high off life."

"You got shot earlier this year," she reminded him.

"You think I'll forget something like that? You telling me you've never been shot?"

Erin blinked. "Well, yeah, but that's not exactly typical. Besides, my vest stopped mine. Most cops don't catch bullets."

"Just the lucky ones," he said. "Hey, here we are."

They'd stopped in front of a bar, Erin saw with no surprise whatsoever. An old neon sign proclaimed it to be Lucia's. The front windows were so stained with age and cigarette smoke that it was impossible to see anything through them. The brickwork was old and pitted.

"Nice joint," she observed.

"What do you expect?" Firelli replied. "Being a gangster ain't what it used to be."

He pushed open the door. A thick cloud of cigarette smoke boiled out to meet them.

"This looks like Lieutenant Webb's kind of place," Erin said, waving a hand in front of her face. "He wouldn't even need to buy his own smokes. Let's make this quick. I don't want to get lung cancer."

"That's the least of your worries in a place like this," Firelli said, but he didn't look concerned. "No sweat, O'Reilly. I've got your back."

It was dark outside, but even so, Erin's eyes needed a minute to adjust to the dim, smoky air in Lucia's Bar. It was like stepping back in time to the 1950s. She gradually made out the shapes of men sitting around tables with cigarettes in their hands and glasses of beer and wine in front of them. They were, for the most part, old Italian men with lined faces, wearing out-of-style suits. The bartender was a middle-aged, tough-looking woman. She and Erin were the only females in the place.

"Hey, Cindy," Firelli said, raising a hand in greeting as he walked up to the bar.

The bartender gave him a cool once-over. "If it ain't Bobby the Blade," she said. "How's tricks, kid?"

"Same shit, different day," Firelli said. "How's your mom?"

"She's doing all right, I guess," Cindy said. "She's got good days and bad ones. They got her on the oxygen now. Y'know, like out of a tank, with those little plugs that go up your nose. I tell you, that ain't no way to live. She got the cancer, y'know?"

Cindy paused to take a long drag on a cigarette. "Hell of a thing," she sighed.

Erin noted the big No Smoking sign on the wall, and considered informing the bartender that smoking was prohibited in New York bars; had been since 2002. She decided that would be undiplomatic, so she kept her mouth shut and let Firelli take the lead.

"Sorry to hear it," Firelli said. "Lucia's one hell of a woman. Tell her I said hi, will you?"

"Sure. Who's your girlfriend?" Cindy turned her eyes on Erin.

"Erin O'Reilly," Erin said.

"No kidding?" Cindy raised an eyebrow. "I heard of you. Ain't you the girl that took out Mickey Connor a couple months ago?"

"The same," Erin said, watching to see how the bartender took the news.

Cindy just shrugged a shoulder, dismissing the subject and Erin as she turned back to Firelli. "Get you anything?" she asked.

"Can't," Firelli said. "I'm on the clock."

"You follow the rules all the time now?" Cindy looked amused.

"Only the important ones," Firelli said. "I came here looking for Material Mattie. He in back?"

Cindy's eyes flickered and she glanced at Erin again. "How come you wanna find Mattie?" she asked. "And what's with the dog? We don't allow pets in here."

"You follow the rules all the time?" Erin shot back, letting her eyes travel to the No Smoking sign again.

"I don't want no trouble," Cindy said.

"Mattie's boss got clipped this morning," Firelli said.

"Yeah, I heard about that." Cindy sounded as unconcerned as if prison stabbings were just one of those everyday things, like taking out the trash or wiping down the bar.

"We think Mattie might be in danger, too," Firelli went on. "I need to talk to him."

"What makes you think he'll talk to you?" she retorted. "He don't like cops."

"Neither do you," Firelli said. "But you're talking to me."

"I ain't talking to no cop. I'm talking to my old pal Bobby the Blade, who just happens to wear a badge."

"We'll just step back and make sure he's okay," Firelli said. "No trouble."

"I don't think that's a good idea," Cindy said. She looked distinctly nervous now.

"Look, Cindy, I promise I'm not here to bust him," Firelli said. "You know me. My word's good."

"Yeah, course it is," she said.

"And O'Reilly's okay. She's with me."

"Sure," Cindy said.

"So what's the problem?"

"You ain't the first guy to come looking for him today."

Firelli tensed. "This other guy, he still here?"

Cindy nodded almost imperceptibly.

"You know this guy?" Firelli pressed.

She nodded again. Her lips were pressed tightly together now, so tightly they were turning pale.

"Thanks," Firelli said. "Appreciate it."

"Forget about it," Cindy said in classic Mob style.

Firelli turned and stepped a few feet away from the bar. Erin went with him, Rolf sticking close to her side.

"What's going on?" she asked in an undertone.

"Trouble, I think," Firelli said. "Cindy knows most of the players in this neighborhood. A guy came in to see Madonna. She didn't like the looks of him, but she won't tell me anything about him. That tells me he's connected and he's dangerous."

"So is Madonna," Erin said with a shrug. "What else is new?"

Firelli shook his head. "There's levels, O'Reilly. Cindy's a tough girl. Me and her go way back. If she's worried, something's not right."

"What do you want to do?" Erin asked.

"You tell me. You're the detective. How important is this guy to you?"

"I don't know yet. I have to talk to him to find out."

"Okay, then let's talk to him." Firelli set his jaw and started toward the back of the bar.

"Backup?" Erin suggested.

"You fancy downtown detectives always want backup," Firelli said. "Don't want to get your nice gold shields all dirty."

At the back of the room, beside the restrooms, was an unmarked door. Firelli knocked twice, paused a moment, and opened it.

The room beyond was like a seedier version of the Barley Corner's gambling room. Instead of Carlyle's polished wood and green baize was a plain metal card table surrounded by folding chairs. Two chairs were empty. The other two were occupied by a pair of Italian gentlemen. One was gray-haired, dignified, and well-dressed. The other, much younger, wore flashier clothes and had a gold chain around his neck. But the main thing that grabbed Erin's attention was the pair of pistols, one in each man's hand, pointed directly at her and Firelli.

"Shit! Gun!" Erin shouted, stepping behind the doorframe and going for her Glock.

Firelli flinched, but made no move for his own weapon. He held up both hands, palms out and empty.

There was a breathless moment. The Italians' fingers tightened on the triggers of their revolvers.

"Bobby?" the older man said in tones of surprise.

"Evening, Mattie," Firelli said. "You seem a little tense. Catch you at a bad time?"

"It's okay, Alfie," Mattie said, lowering his gun. "I know this guy. He's stand-up."

"Says who, Dad?" Alfie replied, keeping his weapon trained on Firelli. Erin drew a bead on him around the doorframe.

"Says me," Mattie said.

"How do you know he ain't one of them?" Alfie insisted.

"He's a cop," Mattie replied.

Alfie looked at him in disbelief, the gun wavering in his hand. "And that makes you trust him?"

"Like I said, he's stand-up," Mattie said. "He's got his rules and he lives by them. I knew him back when he was just a kid. How you doing, Bobby?"

"Getting by," Firelli said. "You mind if I come in?"

"Sure, sure. We got beers here. Grab one and have a seat. Stop waving that thing around and stick it back in your pocket, Alfie. You're embarrassing yourself."

The younger man sullenly tucked his pistol back into his coat and scowled at Firelli.

"That's a couple of felony weapons violations," Erin said very quietly into Firelli's ear.

"Let it slide," Firelli said out of the side of his mouth. "I know these guys."

Erin lowered her Glock but didn't holster it, leaving it pointed at the floor but ready for action. She cautiously stepped into the room, scanning it for other occupants. She saw only a big metal cooler against one wall, a six-pack of beer resting on top of it; a mop in a yellow plastic bucket; and a rack of shelves piled with cardboard liquor boxes. The floor was wet and stained and the air, like the bar outside, was redolent with smoke. She caught a faint whiff of metal, like copper, and a hint of what might have been gunpowder.

Something wasn't right. She tried to figure what was going on. The two men at the table had been facing the door. They'd already had their guns in hand when Firelli had opened the door. They'd been expecting trouble.

Firelli, apparently unconcerned, walked over to the cooler and pulled two cans of beer out of their plastic collars. He handed one to Erin and sat down in one of the vacant chairs. Erin set her back to the right-hand wall and remained standing. The beer can was lukewarm in her hand. She didn't bother to open it. She had no intention of drinking anything.

The old man half-rose and nodded politely to Erin. "Matthew Madonna, at your service," he said. "But please, call me Mattie. This is my son Alfredo. Alfie, this is Roberto Firelli. We called him Bobby the Blade in his younger days. And you are, ma'am?"

"Erin O'Reilly."

"Are you indeed?" A faint smile creased Mattie's face. "I am honored to meet you, Detective O'Reilly. I've heard so much about you."

Firelli glanced at Erin. "You're famous," he said with a wry smile.

"Now, what can I do for you?" Mattie asked.

"What do you know about Vittorio Acerbo's murder?" Erin asked bluntly.

Mattie's smile turned sad. "Enough," he said softly.

"Do you know who killed him?"

"It doesn't matter," Mattie said. "How's your beer?"

"Warm."

"My apologies," Mattie said. "We seem to be having a little trouble with our refrigeration. You know how finicky old appliances can be. If you'd like a cold beverage, I'm sure Cindy can get you one up front."

"You know the Oil Man and Valentino Vitelli went to see Evan O'Malley today?" Erin asked, looking for a reaction.

Mattie blinked, but didn't look surprised. If anything, he just looked tired. "That figures," he said.

"You know something, Mattie," she said.

"What does it matter what I know?" the old gangster replied.

"You handle heroin distribution for the Lucarellis," she said. "Don't bother denying it, we all know it's true. Evan agreed to shut down the O'Malley network, in exchange for the labor rackets on Long Island. Wonderboy Crea was in charge of those for the Lucarellis, but he didn't have anything to say about it because he's on a slab at the morgue. Was Crea a friend of yours?"

"I didn't kill him," Mattie said quietly.

"I know you didn't kill him," she said. "There's a big gap between killing a guy and being his friend."

"Not in my line of work."

"Dad, these are the cops!" Alfie said. "You can't just talk to them like—"

Mattie held up his hand. His son fell immediately silent.

"I apologize for my boy," Mattie said. "He don't understand. But I know the two of you. Bobby, I knew him from when he was ten. You was always a good boy, Bobby. You understood respect. You had your code. I never held it against you, what you decided to do with your life. And whenever you came at me or mine, you did it with respect, according to the rules of the game. Most of the young guys on the street, they don't do that no more. And Detective O'Reilly, I know what stake you've got in the game. You say they've made peace, Evan and my people? You give me your word?"

"That's right," she said. "The O'Malleys and the Lucarellis aren't at war anymore."

"Then we've got nothing to fight about, you and me," he said. "And I don't want to fight no more. I'm too old for the Life. Too tired. Maybe that's why this has gotta happen."

"What has to happen?" Erin asked.

Mattie shrugged. "Out with the old, in with the new," he said. "You gotta make room for the new blood. A guy lives too long, the world moves on. I didn't want things to go down like this. What happened to those guys, it wasn't right. But it's the life we chose, so what can you do? At least we got a choice."

"You thought we were somebody else when we came in," Firelli said. "Were you expecting guys with guns?"

"I ain't telling you nothing about nobody," Mattie said. "I ain't proud of what I am, but I ain't no goddamn rat. If a guy lives his life one way, he can't go changing his mind at the last minute just 'cause he don't like what's coming. Deathbed conversions don't mean nothing. That's just guys getting scared, and God hates a coward."

"You're not on your deathbed, Mattie," Firelli said.

"Wanna bet?" Mattie replied, deadpan.

"Dad, let's get out of here," Alfie said. "We got nothing to say to these jerks. And you know what's gonna happen."

"I told you to go, Alfie," Mattie said. "You're the one who's choosing not to. Me, I'm staying right here."

"Dad, please," Alfie said. "I'm not leaving you here alone." To Erin's surprise, she saw the pleading look in the kid's face, along with what might have been tears in his eyes.

"What's going on, Mattie?" she asked. "Why don't you want to leave?"

"I'm too old to run," he said. "Anyone ever wanted me, they always knew where to find me. I never hid from nobody, never backed down from a fight. When you boys in blue nabbed me, I stood up and took what I had coming. And that's what I taught my boy. I taught him too good, as you see. Now he won't do what's good for him. He wants to stand by his old man. And I'm proud of him. Because he got a cinderblock for a brain, but he ain't no coward."

"They're coming for you," Erin said softly. "To kill you."

"I ain't saying that," the old man said. "But if they do, they know where I am."

"Don't you have a bodyguard?" Firelli asked. "Besides Alfie, I mean."

"Not no more," Mattie said. "I had to let him go."

Erin nodded. "I think I understand," she said. "So, just to be clear. You didn't have Acerbo, Crea, or Rossi killed?"

"I had nothing to do with that," Mattie said flatly.

"And you won't tell us who did?"

"No way."

"So it was an inside job."

"I didn't say that."

"You didn't have to. We can protect you, you know." Erin said it without much hope.

Mattie smiled wearily. "No thanks, Detective. And good luck to you."

"Good luck," she said, not even quite sure why she said it.

Firelli stood up and offered his hand. Mattie got to his feet and took it, a brief, firm handshake.

"Be seeing you," Firelli said.

"One side or the other," Mattie replied.

Chapter 12

As the front door of Lucia's swung shut behind them, leaving them out in the Manhattan night, Erin and Firelli glanced at one another. Rolf kept his eyes on Erin, waiting for instructions.

"Well?" Firelli said. "What did you think?"

"I think there's a big pile of felonies in that room," she said.

"Yeah, I know," he said. "The weapons, for starters. Both of them are convicted felons, so there's parole violations for just being in the same room with each other, much less holding illegal handguns."

"What about the dead guy in the fridge?" Erin asked. "What are we going to do about him?"

Firelli blinked. "What dead guy?"

Erin counted off the points on her fingers. "One: nobody keeps warm beer on top of a cooler, whether it's running or not. Unless the cooler's full of something... or someone. Two: didn't you smell the gunsmoke and blood in the air? At least one of those guns was fired. Recently. Three: the floor was wet, but they didn't quite manage to wipe up all the blood. Four: Material Mattie doesn't have a bodyguard... anymore. Five:

Cindy saw another man go in that room, but nobody came out and we only saw two guys in there. Conclusion: the bodyguard flipped. But Mattie and his kid got the drop on the guy and nailed him. That room doesn't have a back door. They couldn't exactly carry a corpse out while people were around, so they took the beer out of the fridge and stuffed the dead guy inside to wait for closing time."

Firelli nodded. "Okay, that makes sense. But then why the hell are they just sitting there like nothing happened?"

"Mattie told you why," she said. "He's sticking around. He'll wait for the bar to close. Then he and Alfie will bundle the body out the back and dump it somewhere. Maybe they won't even bother taking it out of the fridge, just move the whole unit. But in the meantime, he's too proud or old to make a run for it. He told his son to leave him, but the kid won't go. Probably because he loves his dad and doesn't want to abandon him."

"It's kind of sweet," Firelli said. "If they hadn't just murdered a guy. So I guess we have to do something about that. We could let the small shit slide, but not a body."

"Right," Erin said. "Problem is, I don't think I can get a warrant on the basis of what I just told you."

"How about with the weapons and the parole violations?"

"Maybe. But it'll be better to get them in possession of the corpse."

"Okay," Firelli said. "So let's stake out the place and wait for them to move the body."

"Good idea," Erin said. "We better call Logan and see if I can borrow you for the rest of the night."

"You kidding?" Firelli grinned. "You think the rest of the guys would miss something like this? They'll all want to come play with us."

"It's going to be boring for a couple of hours," she warned.

"No big deal," he said. "We'll just get started on our DD-5s for the food truck bust while we wait."

* * *

As Firelli had predicted, Logan and the rest of his team jumped at the opportunity to sit in darkened cars and bitch at one another. Janovich drew the short straw and had to go back to the Precinct 5 station with the prisoners from their earlier arrest, but Piekarski and Logan linked up with Erin and Firelli. They agreed to station a pair of cops at each entrance to Lucia's, with Logan and Firelli in back and Piekarski and Erin out front.

The two guys in the back alley were on foot, hidden behind a dumpster. Piekarski and Erin ended up in Firelli's beat-up T-bird across the street from the bar. Despite Firelli's earlier suggestion that they do paperwork while they waited, the officers kept the dome light off and sat low in their seats, trying to give the impression of an empty car. Rolf lay at Erin's feet, curled up behind her legs, snoozing.

"Okay," Erin said. "You've got me all to yourself, which is what I assume you wanted. What's the deal?"

In the dark, it was hard to see Piekarski's face. The other woman swallowed and cleared her throat a couple of times.

"Is Vic okay?" Piekarski finally asked.

"Well... he's Vic," Erin said. "I mean, he's a grumpy son of a bitch, but that's pretty much his baseline."

"Yeah, he's not exactly the sensitive type," Piekarski said. "Has he said anything about me?"

"Look, Zofia, Vic's my partner. I don't want to get caught in the middle of whatever you've got going on."

"I'm not asking you to be some sort of go-between," Piekarski said hastily. "Geez, we're not in middle school. It's just... we don't talk about stuff, okay? So it's hard for me to know what he's thinking."

"Vic's smarter than he looks," Erin said. "You can talk to him."

"I think he's scared." Piekarski said in in a near-whisper.

"Scared?" Erin repeated incredulously. "Vic doesn't get scared. The only time I've ever seen him look scared was when he thought I was dead. What do you think he's scared of?"

"Me. Us. Commitment. The usual masculine bullshit."

"He did say you'd given him an ultimatum."

Piekarski laughed nervously. "Is that what he called it? I told him to get his shit together and figure things out."

"You gave him a time limit."

"Yeah. But that wasn't my idea. It's because... never mind why. I just need to know where he wants this thing to go."

"Are you in love with him?"

"What the hell kind of a question is that?" Piekarski bristled.

"An important one, under the circumstances. I don't need to know the answer, but I think maybe you need to know."

"I don't know. He's fun, sure. And you're right, he's smarter than he looks. I like that about him. He hides it, but he's a good guy. And he likes that I'm as tough as he is. You ever been in love?"

Erin smiled in the darkness. "Still am."

"What's your guy think about you being a badass policewoman?"

Erin almost succeeded in suppressing a laugh. "It was a stumbling block, but we got past it."

"He doesn't care you're in one of the most dangerous jobs in New York? Or is it a turn-on?"

"He thinks the world's a dangerous place," Erin said. "He likes that I can take care of myself. He was married once before, but his wife got murdered."

"Oh. Shit." Piekarski paused awkwardly. "Did you catch the killer?"

"No. It happened a long time ago, before I was a cop."

"Jesus, how old is this guy?"

"None of your damn business. Why do you want a commitment out of Vic?"

"None of yours."

"Hey, you wanted this conversation."

"O'Reilly?"

"Yeah?"

"I just realized something."

"What's that?"

"We're the only girls on this operation and we're sitting here on a stakeout, talking about boys and our love lives. We can't ever tell anyone on your squad or mine we did this. They'd never let us forget it."

"Not a word," Erin agreed.

They sat in silence for a few minutes.

"You should tell Vic," Erin said.

"Tell him what?"

"Whatever it is that's such a big deal. That way he'll be making an informed decision."

"I don't want him to feel trapped," Piekarski said. "Or pressured. He's stubborn, and if he thinks I'm manipulating him he'll get mad. Or maybe he'll just run."

The pieces clicked into place in Erin's head. She twisted around to face the other woman, trying to make out her features in the dark.

"Zofia? Are you *pregnant?*"

"You goddamn detectives," Piekarski spat. "Tell you anything, you're always trying to solve a damn puzzle, figure everything out. What the hell difference does it make if I am or not?"

"Sorry. You're right, it's none of my business. And it's a habit."

Piekarski sighed. "I don't know," she said. "I'm late, though."

"How late?" Erin knew Piekarski was talking about her monthly cycle.

"A couple weeks."

"Did you take a test?"

"No."

"Why not?"

"Because I'm already a little freaked out, okay?"

"Okay." Erin was trying to wrap her head around the idea of a baby version of Vic running around Manhattan. It was disconcerting.

"So I want to know, within the next month, if he's on board," Piekarski said. "I don't want to run off to Vegas and get married or anything. I just need to know if he's gonna be there. And you can't tell him, okay? Promise!"

"I..." Erin began. She was trying to sort out what the right thing to do was. Vic deserved to know, but he should hear it from his girlfriend, not his partner. Erin needed to have Vic's back, but what did that mean in this context?

"It's your news to tell," she said at last. "But I think you should tell him. Otherwise you're giving him a secret test, and once he figures it out, and he will, he'll be pissed. He'll feel blindsided."

"You're probably right," Piekarski said. "But he'll be pissed anyway. I was hoping—eyes front!"

The change in the woman's voice brought Erin's mind back to the business at hand. She spun to face forward just in time to see three men go into Lucia's. The last one paused in the doorway and gave a swift, searching look up and down the block before going inside.

Erin knew that face. It was Carlo, the Lucarelli gunman. And from the way he moved and the look in his eye, she knew what he was there to do. Piekarski's street-smart eyes had picked up on it immediately, too.

There was no need for discussion. Erin was already flinging open her door and springing out onto the street, drawing her Glock. Rolf scrambled to his paws and followed, instantly awake and alert. Piekarski was on the radio, talking very quickly to Logan.

"It's going down now!" Piekarski was saying as Erin and Rolf ran across the street. "Three shooters, front door!"

Erin hit the door with her shoulder and flung it open. Several patrons jumped to their feet. At the bar, Cindy dropped the glass she'd been cleaning. It shattered on the floor.

"Everybody stay down!" Erin barked. "NYPD!"

Then, from the back room, the shooting started.

Erin heard three pistol shots in rapid succession. She ducked and crouched, using the corner of the bar for cover. "Rolf! *Platz!*" she shouted. The K-9 immediately dropped flat on his belly, chin on the floor. Two more shots echoed, then another two almost overlapping them.

Piekarski rushed in, gun in hand.

"10-13!" Erin called over her shoulder, hoping the other woman still had her radio channel open. "Shots fired!"

"I'll cover you!" Piekarski shouted.

Erin scampered forward in a crouch, keeping the bar and stools between her and the door to the back room. That door was standing open, but no targets presented themselves.

"Rolf! *Fuss!*" Erin ordered. Rolf scrambled up and heeled, just as he'd been told. No more than an inch separated him from Erin's hip.

Two men burst out of the back hallway by the restrooms. Erin saw a small Italian man with a thin mustache and an automatic pistol. She started to swing her Glock to aim at him, but caught the white POLICE lettering on his vest and recognized Firelli. Logan was right behind him.

Erin pointed to the open door and held up three fingers, then two more, indicating how many men she thought were inside. Logan nodded. He and Firelli took up position to one side of the door, pistols raised.

Erin hurried toward the other side, getting out of the line of fire as fast as she could. As she approached, she saw why the door hadn't closed. A body was propping it open. It looked like one of the men who'd been with Carlo. He was lying on his stomach, not moving.

There was a brief moment of tense stillness. Sirens were Maseratible outside, closing fast. Their backup would be there in a minute, maybe less. But Erin also heard a wheezing, gurgling noise inside the back room. Someone was alive in there, but only barely by the sound of it. He might not have a minute.

"NYPD!" she shouted. "We're coming in! Show me your hands! If I see you holding a gun, I'm putting you down!"

"Get in here!" a man called. He sounded very young and very scared. "We need an ambulance!"

Erin glanced toward the front door and saw Piekarski resting her gun on the bar, still covering them.

"We'll go first," Logan said. "Follow us in."

Erin nodded and gripped her Glock tightly, taking deep breaths, getting psyched.

"Now!" Logan said. He led the way. The three officers and one dog rushed in over the body of the fallen man. Doorways were choke points, kill-zones. If you were going to get shot raiding a building, chances were you'd get it in a doorway.

The smoke in the back room was even thicker than before, the stink of gunsmoke and blood heavy in the air. Alfie Madonna was on his knees in the middle of the room. His father lay in front of him, blood soaking the older man's expensive silk shirt and tie. Two more men were sprawled on the concrete. One, flat on his back, stared at the ceiling with a frozen expression of stunned disbelief on his face. A bullet hole gaped just above the bridge of his nose, right between his startled eyes. The other lay in an awkward half-sitting posture against the wall, legs sticking out in front of him. That was Carlo. He was still alive, but his complexion had turned pale and waxy. His hands were clasped over the front of his suit coat. Blood pulsed through his fingers.

"Hands!" Logan snapped. His gun was pointed directly at the young mobster.

Alfie raised bloodstained, empty hands. "Help my dad," he said in a choking sob. "Please."

Erin spun to cover Carlo. A revolver lay on the concrete a few inches from the wounded man's leg. She kicked it into the corner. Then she holstered her gun. Alfie appeared to be the only man in the room capable of offering resistance, and he wasn't interested in fighting.

"Call two buses!" Firelli shouted to Piekarski. "We got four men down. One dead, one wounded, don't know about the others!"

Erin dropped to one knee next to Carlo. Firelli was examining Mattie, and Logan was checking the other two bodies. The Mafia hitman looked at her with a face straining against the pain and shock of his wound.

"O'Reilly," Carlo said through clenched teeth. "Might've known."

"How you doing, Carlo?" she said. "How bad are you hit?" Carlo might be a murderous thug, but right now, he was also a hurt human being and it was both Erin's job and moral imperative to take care of him.

"Forget about it," Carlo said. He coughed. Blood sprayed from his lips in a fine mist. His breath was coming in short gasps as his body desperately tried to get enough oxygen to his torn tissues. He'd been hit in the lung, Erin was sure of it.

"We've got an ambulance on the way," she said. "Hang in there. You're going to be fine."

"Bullshit," Carlo coughed.

"Who shot you?" she asked.

Carlo's bloodstained lips curled in a sardonic smile. "I ain't... no rat," he whispered. "Ain't nobody... shot me."

"Did Vinnie the Oil Man send you here?" she demanded.

"Nobody... sent me... nowhere. You got... a priest?"

"I'm a cop, Carlo," she said. "We don't have clergy on tap. You just hang in there, okay?"

In answer, he murmured something in Latin. Erin's church said Mass in English, but she recognized last rites when she heard them. A shudder ran through her as she remembered standing over another bloody man in another room, listening to what he'd thought would be his last prayer. She felt suddenly nauseated and claustrophobic. She willed herself to calm down, to do her job, but her heart was racing. She felt sweat on her forehead and goosebumps on her arms.

She peeled back Carlo's fingers. Her own hands were shaking. His clothing was saturated with blood. She tore open his shirt. Buttons hopped and bounced across the floor. He'd been hit twice that she could see. One shot had punched through him just under the ribs on his left side. That was serious, but probably not fatal if they got him to a hospital fast. But the other one was high up in his center of mass, just to the right of his sternum. It hadn't clipped his heart or he'd already be dead. But it had gone through his lung for sure. Pink froth bubbled in and out of the wound.

Erin clapped her hand over the hole. "Piekarski!" she yelled.

"What?" The other woman was in the doorway.

"I need tape! Duct tape, Scotch tape, whatever!"

"Copy that!" Piekarski ran out of the room again. A moment later she was back with a roll of duct tape and a pair of uniformed Patrol officers who'd arrived in the meantime.

Erin snatched the tape out of Piekarski's hands and slapped a piece of it over the sucking chest wound. The most important thing was to make an airtight seal, so Carlo didn't drown in his own blood. That was just about the only thing she could do. Maybe, if the ambulance was quick, he might make it.

Carlo's voice slurred and stopped in the middle of his prayer. His head tilted slowly forward and down. He slumped against the wall, unconscious or maybe dead. Erin wasn't sure which and wasn't sure how much it mattered. She leaned back and looked around the room.

Logan was kneeling beside the second of the two unidentified bodies. He caught Erin's eye and shook his head. That man was dead. Firelli was working feverishly on Mattie. He was alternating mouth-to-mouth and chest compressions. Alfie was on his feet, bloody to the elbows, looking dazed. Tears ran down the young man's cheeks.

"Dad?" he whispered, sounding for all the world like a frightened little boy, not a Mafia hard case who'd just survived a point-blank shootout.

Material Mattie Madonna didn't hear him, didn't answer. Logan kept at it, pounding his chest, trying to hold life in him until the paramedics arrived, but it was a losing battle and everyone knew it.

Chapter 13

Erin had spent way too much time in ambulances, even not counting the previous incident she couldn't remember. But someone needed to ride along with the EMTs on the way to Bellevue Hospital, both to provide security and to listen if the patients said anything. Erin was in the bus that had Mattie in back, while Piekarski was riding with Carlo. The rest of the SNEU team had stayed at the bar to secure the scene. Rolf got to ride up front with the driver, which kept the K-9 both entertained and out of the way.

The two ambulances were moving fast, sirens blaring, which told Erin everything she needed to know about the condition of the men in them. A modern ambulance had just about everything you'd find in an emergency room, so you only rushed to the hospital with the patient if they were going to die without immediate surgical attention. As she watched, the medic checked the feed on Mattie's oxygen mask.

"Is he going to make it?" she asked.

"Don't know," the EMT replied. "He's got two GSW in the chest, through and through. Hell of a lot of blood loss. Put pressure here, could you?"

Erin obeyed, trying not to think of the memories that bubbled up whenever she had her hands dipped in fresh, hot blood.

Mattie shifted and groaned. His eyelids fluttered.

"Don't move," the medic cautioned. "We'll be at the hospital soon."

Mattie's eyes opened. He looked blearily around the jolting interior of the ambulance and saw Erin. Recognition came into his face. Laboriously, as though it weighed a hundred pounds, he raised a hand and beckoned to her.

She leaned over him and took hold of his hand with one of hers, keeping the other where the EMT had told her to put it. "It's okay, Mattie," she said.

The wounded man worked his mouth. It was hard to talk while wearing an oxygen mask. The mask made a tight seal around the lower part of the face. He very carefully shaped words Erin could barely hear over the siren and the road noise.

"Alfie. Where's Alfie?"

"He's fine," she assured him. "He wasn't hit."

"He didn't... didn't shoot..." Mattie said.

"You say he didn't shoot anyone?" she asked.

He nodded slightly. "Was me. Just me."

Erin didn't believe a word of it, but she nodded. "Okay, I hear you," she said. "Did you know the guys who came after you?"

He nodded again. "Carlo," he murmured. "Little prick. Glad... it was him. Didn't mind... putting one... in his... lousy... guts."

"Why'd you do it?" she asked. "You survived one hit attempt and then you just waited for the next guys to show up? What were you thinking?"

Mattie's smile was a tight grimace under the clear plastic mask. "Thinking I'd... take some of them... with me. Bastards."

"Who sent them?"

He didn't answer.

"Who sent them, Mattie?"

"Detective, please," the EMT said. "Don't make him exert himself."

Erin disregarded the paramedic's words. She'd been around a lot of death and she'd learned to recognize it. She saw the shadow creeping into Mattie's eyes and knew there was very little the doctors would be able to do for him.

"If you've got anything important to say," she said quietly, giving his hand a gentle squeeze, "this would be a good time to say it."

"Can't... prove it," he whispered. "But I know... Vinnie... did it. Won't... testify. Not... a rat."

"I know you won't," she said. "That's okay, Mattie. How do you know it was him?"

"Old Man... Acerbo... told me."

"What?" Erin hadn't expected that. "When?"

"Talked to him... last week. Visited. Told me he'd said... no. To the Oil Man. Expected... trouble. Look after... my boy. You know... the game. You're... player. Know what... we call you?"

"What?" Erin bent closer. Mattie's voice was growing fainter.

"Junkyard. Junkyard... O'Reilly." He smiled again. "Not... bad... nickname. Better... than mine. Alfie's... a good boy. Don't let him... do nothing... stupid. Don't tell him... about..."

"I won't," she promised, not sure what he was asking.

"Money," Mattie sighed. "With... lawyer. Schultz. For Alfie. Tell him... I said... ten percent. For you."

"I can't take your money, Mattie," she said gently. "I'm a cop."

"Not... asking... a cop," Mattie murmured. "Asking... Junkyard. Take care... of... Oil Man..."

Erin rocked back on her heels, stunned. She'd known something like that might happen ever since Evan O'Malley had given her a heft cash bonus for taking care of his Mickey Connor problem. Apparently word was out on the street that hitwoman Erin O'Reilly was open for business.

The ambulance made a hard turn and slowed down. The siren cut out. They'd arrived at the hospital.

"Don't worry about that right now, Mattie," she said diplomatically. "We're going to get you fixed up. Then we can talk about what happens next."

"Knew... they were..." Mattie gasped. "Not... my boy... not... Alfie. Don't... let... bastards..."

"I'll protect him as well as I can," she promised.

She stopped talking. The hand she held had gone limp and the chest on which her other hand rested was no longer rising and falling. Matthew Madonna was still looking at her, but his eyes were staring straight through her into whatever was waiting for him on the other side.

The EMT shouldered Erin aside and started chest compressions as the ambulance halted. A few seconds later, the back door swung open to reveal the driver and the Bellevue trauma team. She stood back and let them work. If anyone could save Mattie, they could. Her brother was one of the best emergency surgeons in New York and the rest of the hospital crew was right up there with him. But she didn't think they'd manage this one.

She went around to the front of the ambulance and opened the passenger door. Rolf was sitting in the car seat, tongue hanging out. He loved car rides and almost never got to be up front. He cocked his head at her, picking up on her serious mood. The Shepherd ducked his head and nosed at her cheek. His snout was cold and damp.

She rubbed his shoulder, remembering a little too late that her hands had fresh blood on them. Rolf had just earned himself a bath. The K-9 didn't care at the moment. He was watching Erin, trying to figure out what was going on.

The other ambulance pulled up seconds later. It, too, unloaded in a hurry. Apparently the EMTs thought there was still a chance to save Carlo.

"Not that he's worth it," she muttered. But then, if she thought he was a lousy human being because he was a hitman for the Mafia, what did it say about her? Because Erin was a hitter herself, if rumor was to be believed.

"That was a mess," Piekarski said, walking over to join Erin and Rolf.

"Yeah," Erin said.

"Did you know more shooters were on their way?" Piekarski asked.

Erin shook her head. "I thought we were just waiting to grab the Madonna boys on the way out. I should've thought. We knew more hitmen might be coming. We were too damned slow. We should've been on those jerks the moment they walked up. They should've never got as far as the back room. We should've had them without a shot fired. Damn it, this is my fault!"

"You know better than that," Piekarski said, but there was no real conviction in her voice. She looked down at her own feet and scuffed a shoe across the pavement. "Sorry."

"Sorry? For what?"

"I hung back. Let you go first."

"You had to call the others," Erin said.

"Yeah, but..." Piekarski hesitated. The moment stretched out uncomfortably.

"I usually get jazzed on the action," she finally went on. "I love mixing it up. But ever since I started wondering, you know... about what we talked about, I feel like I've been holding back. Like it's not just about me. Is that crazy?"

Erin started to put a hand on the other woman's shoulder, saw the blood on her fingers, and stopped herself. "No," she said. "That's a saner reaction than we usually have. It's the Job that's crazy."

Piekarski laughed. "Copy that," she said. "You think these guys are gonna pull through? Mine looked pretty rough."

"I think Material Mattie's already gone," Erin said. "But we'll just have to wait and see."

* * *

Erin, Piekarski, and Rolf set up camp in the hospital waiting room. While they waited to find out who was going to live through surgery, Erin and Piekarski checked in with their respective commanding officers. It was almost eleven when Erin called Webb.

"Start talking," he said, sounding only a little groggy.

"O'Reilly here, sir," she said.

"What did you get from Carlyle?" he asked.

It took Erin a second to remember Webb's last orders before she'd left the Eightball that afternoon. It felt like days had passed.

"I actually ended up talking to SNEU," she said.

"Okay, what did they get you?"

"I got a line on Matthew Madonna. Firelli knew him, so the two of us went to have a chat with him."

"How'd it go?"

"Not great."

"What do you mean?"

"I'm at the hospital. Madonna's in the ER. Not sure if he's going to pull through."

"Christ on the cross." Erin could imagine the look on Webb's face. "You shot him?"

"No!" she exclaimed, her voice loud enough that Piekarski turned toward her and raised an eyebrow. "A Mafia hit squad shot him," she went on in a quieter voice, turning her back on the room and facing the window.

"You were in *another* shootout?"

"No, sir. The shooting happened while we were outside. It was all over by the time we got in. We've got two dead at the scene, two critically wounded, and Madonna's son in custody. The kid's not hurt."

"Do you have positive ID on the shooters?"

"One of them. Remember Carlo, that foot soldier who was hanging around Vinnie Moreno during the Bianchi case?"

"Yeah. Didn't we like him for Paulie Bianchi's shooting?"

"That's the guy," Erin confirmed. "But we couldn't prove anything. Besides, we handed that one off to the Feds."

"Want to bet a certain Italian FBI agent is working that case?" Webb asked sourly.

"No bet, sir." That thought had already crossed Erin's mind. She took a deep breath and went on. "There's some complications on this one. I can't talk about them."

"Not over the phone?"

"Not at all, sir."

"I see." Webb paused. Erin imagined him rubbing his temples the way he did when he was tired and frustrated. "Then I guess you've got another call to make, one I don't need to know about."

"Yes, sir."

"Vic or I will get to the hospital as soon as possible. You at Bellevue?"

"Yes, sir."

"Where was the shooting?"

"A bar in Little Italy called Lucia's."

"I assume the scene is secured?"

"Yes, sir. And make sure they check the fridge in the back room. I think there's a dead guy in it."

"Dead guy in the fridge. Copy that." To Webb's credit, he didn't even sound surprised.

Then Erin stepped out of the waiting room. She needed a little more privacy for this next call. She couldn't risk even Piekarski overhearing it. She took out her other phone, a prepaid burner cell with only one contact in it, and called the number.

It took three rings, but the man who answered sounded awake and alert. "Everything okay?" he asked with no preamble.

"Yeah," she said. "I'm fine. But we need to talk. I hope I didn't wake you."

"Don't worry about that," Phil Stachowski said. "I told you, you can call any time, day or night. Do you want to do this over the phone, or do we need to meet in person?"

"It's late. Are you working the dog watch?"

"No, I'm home. Cam and the kids are asleep. I can duck out if I need to."

"I've got relief coming to spell me at Bellevue Hospital," she said. "If it's convenient, we can meet after that. Maybe forty minutes or an hour?"

"I can swing that. The Coffee Express on East 28th, midnight?"

"Copy that. See you there." Erin hung up and went back inside to wait for reinforcements.

Half an hour later, Vic walked in. He looked reasonably chipper and completely sober, which was a pleasant surprise. He started toward her, raising a hand in greeting.

"What were you thinking, Erin?" he asked. "Having a shootout without me? Are you *trying* to hurt my feelings? You're just lucky—"

He stopped mid-sentence. His face froze.

"Hey, Vic," Piekarski said.

Vic's mouth worked as if he was chewing a big bite of something gristly.

"Cat got your tongue?" Piekarski asked. "Or did you just hit your head and lose the power of speech?"

"Well," Erin said with artificial cheerfulness. "I've got a thing I need to get to. So now that you're here, Vic, I'll take off. I assume Webb's at the bar?"

"Yeah." Vic bit the word off and spit it into the air.

"Okay," Erin said. "Let him know what happens here. Piekarski can fill you in on what happened."

"Thanks," he said, dripping sarcasm.

Erin got out of there. It would be interesting to see how those two handled one another, but it was safer to be somewhere else. Besides, Phil would be waiting for her, and Rolf would appreciate a walk down the block.

The coffee express wasn't a building. It was a trailer, lit up by a word ticker around the top that advertised donuts, coffee, and pastries. A pair of multicolored umbrellas festooned the roof. A few late-night customers stood around sipping coffee out of paper cups.

Phil Stachowski was leaning against a wrought-iron fence a few feet away. He had a pair of coffees in hand. Erin reflected, not for the first time, that he looked less like a police officer than any man she'd ever met. He was balding, slightly overweight, and sporting wire-rimmed glasses that made him look like a professor at a community college. He had soft, gentle eyes and a genuinely warm smile.

"Cream, no sugar, right?" he said.

"You pay attention," she said.

"Details are important," he said, handing her the coffee and leading her away from the trailer, out of earshot of the other patrons. "What's the situation?"

She explained, starting with the assassinations, working through the meeting between Evan and Vinnie, and ending with the shooting at Lucia's and the odd conversation she'd had with Mattie in the ambulance.

"So that's where we stand," she finished. "The O'Malleys now have an alliance with Vinnie. And I'm a gun for hire who's been asked to take Vinnie out."

"Did the EMT hear what Madonna told you?" Phil asked.

"I don't think so. There was a lot of road noise, plus the life-support machines, and Mattie was whispering. I could hardly hear him."

"Good. And you don't think Madonna is likely to make it?"

She shook her head. "I'd give him hundred to one odds. He was already coding when they got him out of the ambulance."

Phil sighed. "Then I don't think you need to worry about his offer. It sounds like you're the only person who knows about it."

"But if he thinks I'm open to that kind of work, he won't be the only one," she said.

"Right," Phil said. "So you need to keep your wire on you whenever you can. If you get the chance, record any contract you get. We can use that. And remember, we're not going to actually have you kill anyone. We'll shut down the op if it gets to that point. You'll be fine."

"But Carlyle won't," she said. "What if we're not ready to take down all the O'Malleys when that happens? And now we've got the Lucarellis to worry about, too. Are we expanding the operation? Do you want to move on a Mafia family, too? How big is this going to get?"

He laid a hand on her arm. "Erin, relax," he said. "You're borrowing trouble. Obviously we want as many fish as we can land, but we're not trying to clear out the whole ocean. The O'Malleys are still your main concern. If we can get Vinnie or any of his people, so much the better. You're sure he's the one calling the shots now?"

"Mattie was sure," she said. "And Vinnie was definitely talking to Evan like he's the one in charge. He's got Valentino Vitelli in his corner, too. There's only a few of the Lucarelli senior leadership still breathing. I assume either they're on his side or they're scared of him. But Evan wants me to take pressure off the Lucarellis."

"That's an awkward spot to be in," he said. "Your primary goal is to keep in good standing with Evan."

"So I let Vinnie skate? Even if he just had three men killed?" Erin shook her head. "I can't do that, Phil. That's not who I am."

"Then you have to prioritize," he said quietly. "How much damage will it do your relationship with Evan if you come down hard on Vinnie?"

"I don't know. They were enemies yesterday. Now they're friends, but I don't know how close they are."

"I can tell you that," Phil said. "They're never going to trust each other and they probably don't even like each other. That's how these guys work. As long as it's convenient, they'll pretend to be buddies, but it's all on the surface. These men are all psychopaths, Erin."

"Carlyle isn't," she said.

He smiled sadly. "I hope he realizes how lucky he is to have you in his corner."

"I want to take Vinnie down," she said. "Because you're right, he's a stone-cold psychopath. But I don't know if we can, unless Carlo survives and we can flip him."

"From the sound of it, you've got Carlo cold on murder," Phil said. "I'm guessing Madonna's kid won't testify, though."

"He knows his dad wouldn't like it," she agreed. "And he thinks the world of Mattie."

"But you've still got leverage on Carlo," he said. "And you've got Rossi's killer in custody, too. Play them against one another. You know how that game works. This is assuming Carlo survives and recovers enough to talk. If the hitmen don't flip, you don't have to worry about appearances. You won't have a choice."

"Because we won't have a case against Vinnie," Erin said. "You're right. Sorry to drag you out of bed and all the way down here."

Phil smiled again. "Don't sweat it. Cam understands. She knew she was marrying the Job along with me."

"Sounds like you've got one of the good ones."

"She's my rock," he said. "How are you holding up?"

"I've got this," she said with a little more confidence than she felt at that moment.

"It'll be over soon," he promised.

Erin nodded, but she wondered.

Chapter 14

The September night air was cool, but Erin stepped into the hospital waiting room and felt an immediate drop in the temperature. Vic was standing at one end of the room, arms crossed, glaring at the floor. Piekarski was sitting in a chair at the other end, pretending to read a magazine. It was possible the SNEU officer was actually reading it, but Piekarski had never struck Erin as a *Cosmopolitan* fan, so it struck Erin as unlikely.

"Any news?" Erin asked, trying to keep her tone neutral.

"Your guy didn't make it," Piekarski said without looking up. "Mine's still in surgery."

Erin nodded, feeling a mix of emotions. From what she'd seen on the way in, Matthew Madonna had needed a miracle, and those were in short supply in New York.

"Any word from Webb?" she asked Vic.

"Nothing yet," he said.

Feeling like an awkward third wheel, Erin picked a magazine at random off a nearby table and sat down. Rolf settled beside her and rested his chin on his paws. The Shepherd went immediately to sleep.

"What's this guy Carlo know anyway?" Vic asked after a moment.

"I assume he can give us the guy who sent him," Erin said.

"He's not gonna talk," Vic scoffed. "He's more scared of the Mafia than of us."

"Yeah," Erin said. "But he still might say something we can use. *Omerta* isn't what it used to be."

"We should just stand back and let the Lucarellis clear themselves off the street," he said. "Save us the trouble."

"Tempting," she said.

"We could abandon the hospital," he suggested. "Just let things take their course. Like in *The Godfather*. You remember when Pacino goes to visit his dad and the place is deserted?"

"Yes, Vic, I've seen *The Godfather*," she said, rolling her eyes. "Remember what happens to the cop who does that?"

"Pacino shoots him in the face," Vic said.

"Is that your ambition, Vic? To have Al Pacino shoot you in the face?"

"If somebody's gotta do it, might as well be him. The man's a legend."

Erin's phone buzzed. "That'll be Webb," she said, pulling it out. But the number was unidentified. It was probably a scam robo-call, but on the off-chance it wasn't, she thumbed open her apps and found one she'd installed a while back, just in case. It would record the call. Tapping a phone without a warrant was illegal, but not if it was your own phone. New York was a one-party consent state, which meant if she wanted to make a recording of her own telephone, it was her business.

"O'Reilly," she said.

"Heard you got a couple guys in the hospital," a rough male voice said.

"Erin?" Vic said. He'd seen the sudden change in her expression. She waved him back, signaling him to be quiet.

"What about it?" she replied. "Who is this?"

"Who I am don't matter," the man said. "What matters is, you gotta take care of 'em. Both of 'em. It'll be worth your while."

Erin clenched her hand, feeling the hard plastic of her phone case dig into her fingers. She was getting tired of this. "I don't know who you think you are," she said. "But I don't take orders from strangers."

"It's just a job," the man said. "And it oughta be easy. Things happen in hospitals. Accidents. You can get in there. It'll make one of our friends real happy."

"Yeah? What friend is that?" Erin asked. She silently prayed, *say his name. Just say his name.*

"I don't gotta tell you that," the man said. "Cause you already know. You don't want the job? You don't want the bread? Then forget about it. He'll find someone else. But I heard you could make this happen. He'll know when it's done. Then you'll get a little something."

"How'd you get this number?" Erin demanded. "Listen..."

But she was talking to herself. Her caller had hung up. She gritted her teeth and stopped the recording. Tracing the call was pointless. It would be a burner or one of the few remaining pay phones in the world.

"What the hell was that all about?" Vic asked, coming to stand next to her. Piekarski, setting aside her anger with Vic in favor of professional interest, hurried to Erin's other side.

"That was interesting," she said. "But I can't tell you. Sorry."

"You're a real tease sometimes, you know that?" Vic said.

"Top-secret spy shit, is that it?" Piekarski asked.

"Something like that," Erin said. "Look, I need to report this. And we need to make sure Carlo stays safe. Vic, this is important. You need to get in where he is and stick to him like glue."

"Carlo?" Vic repeated. "The hitman? Erin, you're not making any sense. Madonna was the guy they wanted to kill. And he's dead! Nobody gives a shit about the hitman!"

She put a hand on his arm. "Trust me, okay?"

He snorted. "Okay, whatever. I'll babysit. But a couple uniforms could do the same job. I've got valuable skills. I'm a detective, remember?"

"I'll try to throw a security detail together," she said. "But for now, I need someone I can trust looking after him."

"I don't care about the hitman either," he said. "I kinda hope he dies on the table. Save us a lot of trouble. Riker's Island is overcrowded enough."

Erin shook her head, knowing Vic didn't really mean it. He'd do his best to protect the Mafioso. "One other thing," she said.

"What's that?"

"I need a car. I rode here in an ambulance."

"I got a couple fillings in my back teeth," Vic said. "You want those, while I'm at it?" But he fished out his keys and tossed them to her. "Just don't leave me stranded here."

"Where are you going?" Piekarski asked.

"Back to the bar to check in with my boss," Erin said.

"Give me a lift?"

"Sure, why not."

* * *

"I feel a little weird driving you around in Vic's car," Erin said as they put Bellevue Hospital in the rearview mirror.

"It'd be weirder if I was driving," Piekarski replied. "But then I might decide to run it into something."

"This is his official ride," Erin said. "If it gets trashed, they don't take it out of his paycheck. Hell, his insurance premiums don't even go up. You'd only be hurting the Department."

"It's the thought that counts," Piekarski said.

"That bad, huh?"

"That friggin' guy," Piekarski growled in true Brooklyn style.

"Did you tell him?"

"No. He was being such a jackass already."

Rolf, in the back seat, thrust his muzzle against the mesh screen that separated him from his partner. He panted and wagged his tail.

"Want to switch?" Piekarski asked.

"Switch what?" Erin asked.

"Sleeping partners. You can have the big Russian and I'll take the dog."

"Hell no."

"Afraid you might like it?"

"No. I'm pretty sure Vic snores."

"Yeah, he does. How did you know?"

"When a guy's nose has been broken as many times as his, he'll snore," Erin said. "The worst Rolf ever does is this make these cute little yipping sounds when he's dreaming."

Rolf turned serious brown eyes on his partner, as if to deny he had ever in his life made a cute little yipping sound.

They arrived back at Lucia's Bar to find the building cordoned off and two NYPD blue-and-whites parked out front, along with the CSU van. Erin and Piekarski showed their shields to the four officers working the perimeter and were allowed in.

"I guess now I go back to the street narcotics grind," Piekarski said.

"Zofia?" Erin said.

"Yeah?"

Erin had been thinking about what she wanted to say. "If you and Vic are done, I get it," she said. "No judgment. But don't throw a good thing away for nothing."

Piekarski nodded once and turned away.

Erin found Webb in the back room. The Lieutenant was watching the CSU techs collect evidence. He was twirling an unlit cigarette, making the thin white stick dance around his fingers.

"You could've been a street magician, sir," she said. "I bet you could do some pretty good card tricks."

"O'Reilly," Webb said. "Welcome back. You were right about the fridge. Nice fresh corpse, hadn't even gotten all the way cold yet."

"You got an ID on him?"

"Yeah. He still had his wallet in his pocket. Diego Beneventi. Lucarelli muscle, known associate of Matthew Madonna. But you knew that already."

"I figured," Erin said. "Madonna's former bodyguard?"

"The very same." Webb sighed. "If he didn't already have a Mob nickname, ten bucks says they'd call him Iceman after this."

Erin couldn't help smiling at that. "Probably."

"Neshenko told me Madonna didn't make it."

"That's right, sir."

"What about Peralta?"

"Who?"

"Carlo Peralta? The other survivor?"

"Oh, him." Erin hadn't known Carlo's last name until that moment. "He's on the table. Might make it, might not. He was banged up pretty bad."

"Can you tell me what happened here and why?"

She stepped away from the evidence techs, motioning Webb with her head to follow. Once they were out of earshot of the other cops, she started talking quietly.

"Mattie Madonna was tight with Acerbo," she said. "Vinnie Moreno is cleaning out the old guard, getting rid of everyone who was loyal to the old man."

"So it's a palace coup," Webb said. "I guess that makes sense. The Oil Man's been running the Lucarellis long enough to get a taste for it. You know all the fairy tales where the evil advisor tries to replace the king."

"That's about the shape of it," she said. "Vinnie wanted to make a deal with Evan O'Malley about drug distribution and labor rackets. Acerbo wasn't going for it, so it was a good time for Vinnie to get him out of the picture."

"What do the Lucarellis get?"

"Narcotics distribution. Evan's out of that game."

"Really?" Webb raised his eyebrows. "That's a lot of money he's leaving on the table."

"That business has been getting more dangerous," she said. "Remember that thing with the Colombians, and what happened to Evan's head narcotics guy?"

"Liam McIntyre, wasn't that his name?"

"That's him. Evan decided he didn't need the headache, as long as he could get something in exchange."

"Which was?"

"Garbage."

"Labor rackets," Webb said. "That figures. Wasn't Carlyle involved in something with that, back in the day?"

"He's suspected of blowing up some garbage trucks," Erin said dryly. "Never enough evidence to charge him. Nobody died, or was even hurt. The statute of limitations ran out a while back, so does it really matter?"

"I suppose that depends on your point of view," Webb said just as dryly. "So the O'Malleys get full control of the garbage rackets on Long Island?"

"That's what I heard."

"And the Lucarellis go over almost exclusively to the drug trade?"

"I don't know what else they're into, but that's their main line, yeah."

"That explains the victims," Webb said. "The Lucarellis lost their top narcotics man and their top labor guy."

"I can understand killing the guy who ran the labor rackets," Erin said. "He might object to being downsized. But why kill your drug boss? Wouldn't Vinnie need him?"

"It'll be a lucrative and important position," Webb said. "The sort of position you'd want to make sure was occupied by a guy loyal to you."

"Right." Erin felt foolish.

"How did you get all this inside info on the deal?" Webb asked.

"I can't talk about that, sir."

Webb nodded. "Forget I asked. It's been a long day and we're both tired."

"I need to talk to the Captain," she said. "But he's probably asleep."

"I should hope so," Webb said. "I'll set up a meeting for you tomorrow. Can we make any of this stick? On Vinnie?"

"That's what I need to talk to Holliday about," she said slowly.

Webb was confused. "What does the Oil Man have to do with you?"

"Again, sir, I can't talk about it."

He wasn't happy with that answer. He fidgeted with his cigarette, actually taking out his lighter and flipping it open before realizing what he was doing and putting it away again.

"You know, sir, you could probably light that up," she said. "This bar was full of smoking violations when I got here. Can't you smell it?"

"That's not the point, O'Reilly. Just because everybody's doing it doesn't mean we shouldn't set a better example." But Webb gave his cigarette a wistful look.

"You know, sir, those things are going to kill you," she said.

"I should live so long," he replied. "You and Neshenko are going to give me a heart attack long before lung cancer does me in. Being your boss is a constant cardiac disaster."

Erin didn't know what to say to that.

"Well, if you can't tell me anything useful about the Lucarellis, there's no reason for you to be here," he said after a moment. "Go home, get some sleep, and come back when you're ready to do some work."

"Copy that, sir." Erin wanted to go home, but she didn't think sleep was on the cards. Not until she'd talked to her boyfriend. "Oh, here's Vic's keys. Somebody needs to relieve him at the hospital. He's babysitting Peralta. And he's not happy about it."

Chapter 15

Erin and Rolf arrived at the Barley Corner at an hour when any reasonable person would be in bed and asleep. The pub was humming with the activity of unreasonable people. On the biggest TV screen was some sort of sporting event. At a glance it looked like soccer, but the players seemed to be wearing helmets and carrying sticks. Lacrosse, maybe, Erin thought without much interest. She was too tired to pay attention to sports.

She scanned the crowded room, looking for Carlyle's slender form amid the broad-shouldered Irishmen. She didn't see him. An empty spot at the bar gaped like a missing tooth. Even when Carlyle wasn't around, nobody sat on his barstool.

Cursing inwardly, she went to the bar and sat down in Carlyle's place of honor. Being the boss's girl had some perks, after all. If she couldn't get her boyfriend's advice about Mob politics, the next best thing was to steal his seat while she had a stiff drink. She signaled the bartender.

"Evening, Erin," he said, working toward her and handing out pints to three big guys along the way. "Long day?"

"Danny, you have no idea," she said. "Give me a Glen D, straight."

"Coming up." Danny poured the drink with the speed and skill of long practice and slid it across to her.

"Where's Carlyle?" she asked.

"At some sort of meeting, I think," Danny said. "That guy from Jersey picked him up about an hour ago."

"Which guy from Jersey?"

"The raspy guy with the scars. The one everyone calls Snake."

"Oh." Erin decided the whiskey was an even better idea than she'd thought. She knocked back half the shot. If Carlyle had gone off with Gordon Pritchard, either he'd been called away on Evan O'Malley's business or he'd probably already been murdered. Dating a mobster was a hell of a thing.

"He's gone to Long Island," Corky said from just to Erin's left.

Erin spun on her stool. She hadn't noticed him when she'd come in; Corky was much smaller than most of the Corner's clientele, but he usually made up for his modest size through force of immodest personality. Now, however, he was hunched over his drink in an uncharacteristically subdued posture. He had some sort of ghastly yellow concoction in a glass in front of him and several empty glasses of various shapes and sizes lined up on the bar.

She glowered at him, weighing her need for information against her residual anger. But she was a professional detective and knew how to set her emotions aside. She'd pretended to let a serial killer seduce her once, just to get him talking.

She stood up and moved over to Corky's shoulder. He didn't so much as glance at her. Instead, he picked up his drink, studied it for a moment, and drained it in one long draught.

Then he set the empty glass down next to the others and held up a finger for Danny.

"What're you drinking?" she asked.

He did look at her then. His eyes were red-rimmed and watery, but his speech was clear and he didn't seem particularly impaired. "That was a bossa nova," he said.

"That's not your usual," she observed. Like Carlyle, Corky tended toward Guinness and whiskey. "What's in it?"

"I've no idea." Corky raised his voice. "Danny, what's in that drink you just gave me?"

"Bacardi, Galliano, apricot brandy, and fruit juice," Danny said. "Get you anything else?"

"A brass monkey, I think," Corky said.

"One brass monkey, coming right up," Danny said with a hint of doubt.

"Brass monkey?" Erin asked. "What's in that?"

"Danny, what's the brass monkey?" Corky asked.

"Bacardi, vodka, and OJ," Danny said.

"You don't know what these things are, but you're ordering them anyway?" Erin asked Corky.

He shrugged. "That's the next one on the menu."

"You're ordering every cocktail *in alphabetical order*?"

"Working my way down the list."

"That's one way to get drunk, I guess. I suppose I should be glad you've only reached the Bs. You'll be dead of liver disease before you hit the middle of the alphabet. You said Carlyle went to Long Island?"

"Aye," Corky said. "Evan wants him to have a look at the dustman business."

Erin nodded her understanding. She knew "dustman" was the Irish term for a garbage collector. "Checking out the new territory?" she asked.

"Aye," he said again.

"Why didn't you go with him? You work with the Teamsters. I thought you'd be involved if the O'Malleys were dealing with truckers."

"No doubt I'll be down one of these days. Everything's moving a mite quickly at the moment. I think there's a wee bit of a scramble. Nature abhors a vacuum, or so I'm told. Are you needing Cars for something I can provide?"

"In your dreams," she said automatically, but Corky had said it without his usual flirtatious spark. He really was feeling deflated. Erin knew she'd been hard on him, but the man dealt with gangsters every day. She'd thought he had a thicker skin.

"Look, Corky," she said wearily. "I'm not going to apologize for chewing your head off. You had it coming."

"Erin, no disrespect, but I'm in the middle of something here." Corky took up the brass monkey cocktail Danny had left for him and gulped it down.

"You're not even tasting that," she said. "What's the point of ordering different drinks if that's what you're going to do with them?"

"You're thinking taste is the point of alcohol?" Corky countered. "For an Irishwoman, you surely know nothing at all about the science of drinking. Danny, I'll have a breakfast club next."

"No he won't," Erin said, holding up a hand to forestall Danny. "He's eighty-sixed."

"Erin, he's a paying customer..." Danny began.

"Back off, lass," Corky said sullenly.

"I can arrest you for public intoxication," she said. "If that's what you'd prefer. But you're coming with me, either by choice or in handcuffs."

She almost hoped he'd take the opening to deliver more of his trademark innuendo, but he let it slide by. "What the devil are you doing?" he said instead.

In answer, Erin got hold of his shoulder and propelled him away from the bar. She steered him to the stairs, keyed in, and shoved him through. Rolf watched with interest. The K-9 wasn't quite sure what was going on. It looked like an arrest, but not exactly. The Shepherd kept an eye on Corky just in case he needed to bite him.

"I thought you didn't want me around you," Corky said as the door clicked shut. "You've a curious way of avoiding a lad."

"Shut up and listen," Erin said. "You know what's at stake here. Your best friend is playing both sides and trying not to get killed. You're working with us, because he'd rather go down himself than hang you out to dry. If even one word of what we're doing gets out to Evan, Carlyle's going to die. Maybe you and I will, too. Now I know you don't give a shit about your own life, but I'd think you'd spare at least a little thought for his."

"What is it I've done now?" Corky asked. "How, exactly, am I not measuring up?"

"You need to shut down your goddamn pity party!" she snapped. "We both almost got her killed. And we both know how badly you stepped out of line. So you screwed up. It wasn't the first time, it won't be the last. Deal with it. Do what those guys do out on the field, playing... whatever the hell game it is they're playing on the TV in there."

"Hurling," he said. "Fine Irish sport. Don't tell me you've not heard of it?"

"Heard the name," she said. "Never played it. I grew up in Queens, not Belfast. That's not the point. The point is, I need you on your game, because this is the semifinals and we can't afford any more errors. You're acting weird. People will notice, if they haven't already. And the last thing we want is suspicion. Besides, the more hammered you get, the more chance there is that you'll let something slip."

"I'm not going to betray you," Corky said, and Erin was gratified to see a spark of defiance in his eyes. "And I'm certainly not going to rat out Cars. I don't understand you, Erin. I thought you hated me because I didn't take things seriously. Now that I'm feeling truly bad about something, something that's important to you, you're hating me for that. I can't bloody win with you!"

"If you're trying to win with me, hitting on my sister-in-law wasn't the best way to do it," she said. "Just tell me what you were thinking. Help me understand what goes on in that head of yours. Because from where I'm standing, you look completely crazy."

"I've always had a soft spot for the colleens," he said. "And Shelley's a right fine one, no doubt."

"That's all there was to it?"

Corky's eyes slid away from hers. "I suppose a wee part of me might have wanted to do something risky," he admitted. "I've a certain tendency that way, you'll not deny."

"Deny it? I'm amazed you're still alive."

"You've noticed, haven't you, how folk tend to become what others expect them to be?"

Erin nodded. "Yeah, I guess it's one of the reasons I became a cop."

"Because of your da?"

"Yeah. Are you telling me you do stupid shit because people expect you to? That's sort of a chicken-and-egg thing, isn't it?"

"I'm thinking it goes back to my own da, come to that."

"What did he do?"

Corky smiled bitterly. "Nothing worth doing. At least, that's what my mum always told me, after he'd run off. She said he'd never amounted to anything, no Corcoran ever had, and I'd not manage it either."

"How old were you when she told you this?"

"I don't remember precisely. Just a wee lad."

"That's a lousy thing to tell a kid."

"Here in America, they tell you to follow your dreams," he said. "I don't recall hearing that when I was growing up. Most of the adults I met just told me I was headed for a bad end. And I'd hate to disappoint them."

"Do you know what a self-fulfilling prophecy is?" she asked.

"Isn't that one of those things that makes a lad murder his da and marry his mum? Freudian, I think is the word for it?"

"That's one example, yeah."

"Well, I've no desire whatever to marry my mum," he said. "But I might stick a knife in my da, given the chance. Does that make you feel better?"

Erin shook her head. "I don't hate you, Corky. I'm pissed at you, but I don't hate you. I thought I wanted you to be sorry, but I mostly want you to be better instead. What happens if I expect you to improve?"

She was rewarded with a slight but genuine smile. "Then I'll do what you're needing," he said. "It'll be my pleasure."

"Good. What I want right now is for you to keep your shit together. Can you do that?"

"Aye. But I'll admit I was hoping for something more along the lines of sexual favors. If nothing of that sort is wanting, I'll be on my way before the lads outside get to whispering about us."

With that, he was gone. Erin watched the door swing shut behind him. She was feeling better about Corky. He might still be a crazy, reckless son of a bitch, but she thought she could handle him. And at least he'd sounded more like himself.

Chapter 16

Despite her fatigue, Erin was still awake when Carlyle came in a little after two in the morning. She was in bed, hands behind her head, staring at the ceiling by the light of the bedside lamp. Rolf was curled in a furry ball at her feet, snout tucked under his tail. He, at least, was sleeping soundly, making adorable little yips with each exhalation.

She heard Carlyle go into the bathroom, listened to the sound of the faucet as he brushed his teeth. Then the bedroom door swung open and there he stood, coat draped over one arm, necktie hanging loose.

"I'm glad I didn't wake you," he said, smiling at her. "Darling, you're a finer sight in an old T-shirt, hair all helter-skelter, than many a colleen who's dolled herself up at the salon."

"You're sweet," she said, sitting up. "Everything go okay on Long Island?"

"Aye, all's well," he said, hanging up his coat and swiping his tie out from under his collar. He placed it carefully on the rack and began unbuttoning his shirt. Erin recognized the tie as one of the ones with a hidden recording device. "Evan's inspecting his new domain."

"Why'd he take you with him? He already knows the territory."

"He'd a few things on his mind. It seems our lad's a mite concerned about internal politics. He wanted to discuss the matter of Miss Blackburn."

"Veronica? What's she got to do with anything?"

Carlyle stepped out of his trousers and pulled back the comforter, sliding into bed beside her. "You'll recall she was put in charge of the O'Malley narcotics operation after Liam's unpleasantness," he said.

"Does Evan think she'll be upset at losing the spot?" Erin asked.

"It's a great deal of money she won't be seeing. Added to that, she was rather sweet on the late, unlamented Mr. Connor."

"If she misses him, she's the only person on Earth who does," Erin muttered.

"Nonetheless, you'll concede she's suffered a number of personal disappointments of late," he said.

"Does Evan think she'll try anything?"

Carlyle shook his head. "Nay. Miss Blackburn can be a nasty piece of work, but she's no killer. He simply wanted to discuss how we might soften the blow to her. He's thinking to expand her particular operations in Brooklyn and Queens."

Carlyle's face showed what he thought of that. He'd never approved of prostitution. Erin laid a hand on his arm.

"Don't worry," she said. "I don't like it either. But this whole thing will be over before anything much happens on those lines."

"I'm sure you're right, darling." He kissed her cheek. "But tell me about your evening. It's not like a veteran copper such as yourself to be missing valuable sleep. Something's troubling you."

"Matthew Madonna's dead," she said. "Along with three guys who tried to kill him, with a fourth hanging by a thread."

"I wasn't expecting more casualties," Carlyle said. "Was it a retaliatory attack? Payback for the earlier assassinations?"

"I don't think so," she said. "Looks more like tying off a loose end. But that's not the problem."

Carlyle touched her lightly under the chin, turning her face so they were eye to eye. "What's the matter, darling?" he asked softly.

"Madonna asked me to kill the Oil Man," she said. "He offered me ten percent of whatever's in this account run by some guy called Schultz. Whoever the hell that is."

Carlyle blinked. Then he began to laugh quietly.

"Stop it!" Erin said, shaking her head free and pulling back. "It's not funny!"

"And just how much might ten percent be?" he asked.

"I have no idea! Why does that matter?"

"Darling, I'm not certain you ought to be taking contracts if you don't even know what you're being paid. That should have been your first question."

"Those were practically his last words," she said. "He was dead minutes later."

"Then it definitely should've been your first question." He was still smiling.

"It gets better," she said bitterly. "While I was at the hospital I got a call from some mook who must have been speaking for the Oil Man. Vinnie hadn't heard about Madonna yet, so he wanted me to arrange a little hospital accident. And get this. He wants me to kill his own gunman, too."

Carlyle was laughing harder now. "Congratulations, darling," he said. "You've won your place in the game at last.

There's a regular bidding war for your services. You're in great demand."

"There's an actual war," she retorted. "With bullets and bodies. And it doesn't matter, because Madonna's dead. I'm not working for him and I'm sure as hell not working for Vinnie."

"It matters to the wounded shooter," Carlyle said. "Do you know the lad?"

"Yeah, I ran into him once before. He's a spear-carrier for Vinnie; this loser named Carlo Peralta."

"The Hyena?" Carlyle said, surprised.

"Is that his nickname?"

"Aye. It's a bad joke, like many such titles. You've heard of Carlos the Jackal, surely?"

"The terrorist? Of course I have." Erin, like every cop, had heard of the Venezuelan communist. She knew he'd done a bunch of terrible things, but she also knew him from his appearances in spy novels, so she wasn't quite sure what crimes he'd actually committed.

"Well, Carlo sounds a bit like Carlos," he explained. "And hyenas, like jackals, are scavenger dogs, so..."

"Right, I get it. He and Vinnie go way back, don't they?"

"Far enough. Carlo's done some killing for Vinnie. I can think of three or four lads he's thought to have done for, including one you'd know."

"Paulie Bianchi," she said, feeling a pang of residual guilt. "We should've protected him better. His mom made a deal to get him out of jail."

"I remember," he said. "She's still imprisoned, aye?"

"Yeah. She confessed to first-degree murder. Of course she's in prison."

"You've been playing the part of a rogue copper who's willing to kill," Carlyle said. "Are you complaining now that you've done such a fine job of it? You've convinced not just Evan, but the rest of the underworld. I should think you'd be proud."

"Something Corky said stuck with me," she said.

"You've spoken to the lad?"

"Yeah. Don't worry, Rolf didn't bite him and neither did I."

"What did he say?"

"He said people turn into what you expect them to be." She swallowed and forced herself to look him directly in the eye. "I killed Mickey Connor, and he wasn't my first. Sure, he was coming at me, but I went there wanting to kill him. Hell, I told Vic I was going to kill him. What if I'd had the choice? Would I have just gunned him down? I don't know, and that scares the hell out of me! What if I'm turning into a killer? A murderer?"

Carlyle shook his head. He clasped her hand and held it, speaking softly but earnestly. "Darling, you're a lovely lass, with a bright shining spirit. You're too good for this terrible world. You've pulled my soul out of the darkness and given me hope. I believe in you. We all get stained and battered, but you'll not break. I'd bet my life on it. And I'm a gambler, darling. I know a winning bet when I see one."

Erin started to laugh, then choked as a sob surprised her. The next thing she knew, to her acute embarrassment, she was crying. She wasn't even entirely sure why. Carlyle was startled too, but he put his arms around her and held her. It was only a momentary weakness, one that soon passed.

"Sorry," she said, wiping her eyes. "Thanks. I guess I just needed to let out some emotion. God, I feel like such a cliché."

"Nay, darling. You're the furthest thing from a fainting damsel." He kissed her lightly on the lips.

"I know what to do," Erin said suddenly.

"Oh? Grand. Though I was thinking we might want a bit of sleep, if you've a better notion, I'm all ears."

"I know who to talk to," she said. "To get the dirt on Vinnie."

Carlyle was baffled, but he smiled. "Grand," he said again. "Is it something you're needing to do right at this moment?"

"No, it can wait till tomorrow," she said. "That's good, because I'm tired. I feel like I've been up for two or three days. But now that I think about it, even though I'm feeling better, maybe I don't want to go to sleep just yet."

He raised an eyebrow. "And why's that?"

"I'm really tired," she said, giving him a sly smile and sliding closer to him, laying one leg over his. "But not too tired, if you're not."

His hands were warm against her skin as he slipped them up under her shirt, caressing her back. "I'll find the energy, never fear," he said. "And just what—"

She stopped his words with her lips.

* * *

Morning came too soon. Rolf was up, bright eyed, tail wagging, ready to go for their run. Erin wished she could siphon off some of his energy. She made do with coffee, dragging herself out of bed and starting the machine as quietly as she could. Carlyle didn't need to get up early, so she wanted to let him sleep. She put Rolf on his leash, slipped out of the apartment, and made for Central Park.

The coffee and the cool early-fall air snapped her more or less awake. For the first mile, she just concentrated on her own breathing and the feel of the ground under her feet. The steady, familiar rhythm of her sneakers on the footpath made a backdrop to her thoughts.

She missed Ian. They'd gotten accustomed to running together, but his leg was acting up and he'd been sidelined on this particular morning. At least she had Rolf for company.

When she got to the Eightball, hair still wet from her quick post-workout shower, the first thing she did was power up the coffee machine in the break room and get herself another cup. The other members of the squad hadn't come in yet, so she had the place to herself.

She was planning to take a trip to Riker's Island, to follow up the idea she'd had while talking to Carlyle, but visiting hours didn't start until one o'clock. She logged into the prison database and registered her request to meet with an inmate. Then, with a few hours to kill, she had a lawyer to look up.

Unsurprisingly, with almost two hundred thousand lawyers in New York State, there were dozens with the last name Schultz. But that didn't bother Erin, because Matthew Madonna and his son both had criminal records. It was a simple matter to find the paperwork of their most recent criminal charges, which included the names of their legal representation. Sure enough, Alfredo Madonna's last bout of legal troubles, which had resulted in a plea bargain, had been handled by one Kingston Schultz, a senior partner in the firm of Schultz and Becker.

Erin thought about calling the law firm, but decided to take the advantage of surprise instead. The law office was in Midtown. She left a Post-It on Webb's desk to let him know she was following up a lead. Then she and Rolf went to see a lawyer.

Schultz and Becker was a typical Manhattan law office, on the twenty-sixth floor of a high rise. Figuring Ian's concerns about elevators didn't apply to quite so many flights of stairs, she and her K-9 rode up, emerging to find a clean, modern office suite with lots of glass and polished marble.

The receptionist, a dark-skinned brunette, turned an incandescent smile on them. "Good morning, ma'am," she said with a distinctively Jamaican accent which made Erin do a slight double-take. It wasn't what she expected from someone working for the Mafia. "How may I help you?"

Erin showed her shield. "Detective O'Reilly, NYPD Major Crimes," she said. "I need to talk to Mr. Schultz."

To the receptionist's credit, her smile didn't even flicker. "Of course, Detective," she said. "He's in, but he may be on a call. If you'd be so kind as to take a seat, I'll see if he's available."

Erin stayed standing, examining the office. It certainly didn't look like a Mob attorney's office, but then, lawyers were just lawyers. They didn't wear color-coded suits so you could tell the good ones from the bad ones. While pretending to study a framed photo of a Caribbean island that hung on the wall, she activated the recording wire that was sewn into the lining of her leather jacket.

"Detective?" the receptionist said. "Mr. Schultz will see you in his office. If you'll go to the first door on your right?"

Erin knocked on the indicated door. The man who opened it was definitely not Italian. His skin definitely showed his African heritage and his hair, going gray at the temples, was close-cropped and curly. He grinned and held out a hand.

"Detective O'Reilly," he said with the same West Indies accent as his receptionist. "Kingston Schultz. It's a pleasure to meet you."

She shook the offered hand. "Thank you for seeing me, Mr. Schultz."

"Please, madam, call me Kingston, or just King, if you'd rather. Would you care for coffee? I have an excellent Colombian blend here, fresh-brewed."

"Thank you," she said. She could already smell the coffee and it made her mouth water. "Cream, no sugar, please. Kingston's an interesting name."

"My family came from Jamaica," Schultz explained. "I was named after the city in which my grandfather was born. During Prohibition, they ran rum up the coast to New York and Atlantic City. I hope that doesn't bother you, Detective."

"I'm Irish," she said with a smile. "And Prohibition's a long time gone, thank God." So that was how a Jamaican lawyer ended up working for the Mob, she thought. His family was probably connected all the way back to 1919.

Schultz handed her the cup of coffee. He motioned to a chair in front of his desk. "Please, sit down."

Erin sat. "Rolf, *sitz*," she said. The K-9 took a seat next to her chair and awaited further instructions.

"Now," Schultz said, sinking into his leather swivel chair on the opposite side of the desk and crossing his legs, clasping his hands on his knee. "What can I do for you?"

"You represent the Madonna family," she said.

"Indeed I do," he said, giving her that infectious smile again. "Among many other clients. Perhaps I should thank you and your department for providing me with such lucrative legal opportunities."

"You're welcome," she said dryly. "I assume you've heard what happened last night?"

"It appears I will be representing the younger Mr. Madonna once more," Schultz said. "He requested my presence at your police station. In fact, I will be traveling there upon conclusion of our unexpected meeting."

"Then I assume Alfie also told you about his dad?"

Schultz nodded and his smile faded. "Yes. I heard he was badly injured. Can you tell me his condition?"

"I'm afraid he won't be throwing any more business your way." She said it with deliberate, calculated callousness, mainly to judge his reaction.

To her surprise, Schultz's face fell with what appeared to be genuine shock and sadness. "I am sorry to hear that," he said. "Matthew Madonna was a good client and a fine man."

"He was a drug dealer and a Mafioso," she said.

"And you are a hired killer for the New York Police Department," he said.

The words hung in the air between them. Erin couldn't believe he'd actually said it to her face.

After a moment of tense silence, Schultz went on in a gentler tone. "Does that mean you are a bad woman? I think not. I think we live in a bad world that does bad things to us, and sometimes we must do bad things to survive. That is why we have police officers, lawyers, and churches, too. I knew Matthew my whole life. He was my father's friend and client before he was mine, and I have been in this business a very long time. And I tell you that while he may have been in a bad business, he was not a bad man. He loved his family, he went to church every week. He was generous."

"I was with him when he died," she said. "He told me to find you."

Schultz looked mildly surprised. "Really? And what did he say?"

"He wanted his accounts made over to Alfie."

"I knew this already. His affairs were in good order. He knew he was not a young man, and he was in a dangerous occupation. He was not, I think, surprised by what happened."

"And he said to give me ten percent."

Erin watched Schultz's face closely as she said it. The lawyer had put on his poker face, but she caught a hint of surprise and something else, a flash of intense interest.

"Did he say for what this commission was intended to pay?"

"Yes sir, he did." Her wire was recording every word of the conversation. She wanted Schultz to implicate himself, but she also knew that if she came right out and said Madonna had offered her a contract, the attorney was too canny to nibble the bait.

"Do you know how much money is being discussed?" Schultz asked.

"No."

He smiled again, more thinly this time. "But you trust me to provide the proper amount?"

"I trust you wouldn't screw over your friend Matthew Madonna, even dead," she said.

He nodded and his smile widened. "Very good, Detective. May I call you Erin?"

"Sure." The moment the word was out of her mouth, it struck her that she hadn't introduced herself by first name. Schultz already knew who she was, had probably known the moment she'd walked in the door.

"Erin, the late Mr. Madonna was my client. As such, we held many conversations which contained privileged information. You understand I could not discuss this information with you, even if you were not a police officer."

"Of course."

"I will say, however, that I received a telephone call from him only a short while before his misfortune. He indicated he had certain concerns regarding a member of the organization to which he allegedly belonged."

Erin hated talking to lawyers. She resisted the urge to roll her eyes and nodded instead, waiting for more.

"He said that, in the contingency of an accident befalling him, a situation might arise in which certain steps, shall we say, might need to be taken. If those actions were performed, a gratuity might be given to the one who performed them."

"In the amount of, say, ten percent of an undisclosed amount?" Erin guessed.

Schultz nodded. "However, since those steps have not been taken, at the present time, we find ourselves at an impasse. Should that impasse be resolved, of course, funds might then be released as requested."

"How much is that ten percent?"

"Approximately eighty thousand dollars."

Erin repressed the desire to whistle. She just nodded.

Schultz stood up. "My apologies, Erin, but I really must be on my way to my next appointment. You understand?"

"Of course." Erin got to her feet. She and Schultz shook hands again. "One other question, King."

"Yes?"

"I'm just curious. The young woman out front. Is she...?"

"My daughter Aayla," he said proudly. "Learning the business. It has been a pleasure meeting you, Erin. I hope to see you again, quite soon."

Chapter 17

Erin wasn't exactly thrilled to go straight from one proud gangster parent to another. She had until one o'clock to get to Riker's Island, so she went back to the Eightball first. Vic and Webb had arrived in the meantime. They were at their desks. Vic's desk was decorated with a matched pair of two-liter Mountain Dew bottles. One of them was almost half-empty.

"Everything okay at the hospital?" Erin asked.

"Peralta isn't dead yet, if that's what you're asking," Vic said. "He's on the edge, but the doc says he's maybe gonna make it."

"Then why are you back here?"

"Relax," he said. "He's got a protection detail."

"There's a contract out on him," she said.

Vic grinned nastily. "I'm not talking your average donut-pushers here. I called in a favor, got a couple guys I know from ESU hanging out by his room. Anyone tries to get past them, the poor bastard who tries is gonna end up staying at the hospital a lot longer than he planned."

"Are they solid? Reliable?"

Vic's grin vanished. "I trust these guys. If you're asking if any of them are dating mob bosses, the answer is no."

She wrinkled her nose at him. She figured she'd deserved that one.

"Did you get anything useful?" Webb asked her.

She shook her head. "I was just looking up an associate of Madonna's. It's probably a dead end."

"Who is it?"

"His lawyer. How much trouble is his son in?"

"Parole violation at absolute minimum," Webb said. "And a weapons charge. One of the guns we recovered from the scene has his prints on it. We don't have the ballistics yet, but I'm guessing he put a couple of bullets in at least one of the dead guys."

"His dad said his son didn't do any of the killing."

"Yeah, he'd say that," Vic said.

"So we've got three Lucarelli bosses dead in New York," Webb said. "And their chief. Plus three goons."

"Lucky seven," Vic said. "But we don't have to worry about Acerbo. He's way out of our jurisdiction."

"But he's the reason this all happened," Erin said. "Without his murder, none of the rest of this makes any sense."

"You're probably right," Webb said. "But that's a Federal case. And if everything else stems from that, it's RICO, which is definitely Federal."

"You saying we should just kick this over to the Feebies and call it a day?" Vic wasn't happy with the idea.

"That might be the only thing to do," Webb said. "Except for..."

"Agent Freddy Giusto," Erin said. "Which means..."

"Precisely," Webb said.

"You two aren't having a conversation," Vic said. "You're just finishing each other's sentences. I can't read minds. What about this punk?"

"He's in with the Lucarellis," Erin said. "Like John Connelly with Whitey Bulger up in Boston." She was referring to the infamous former FBI agent who had gotten involved with organized crime and shielded Bulger under the guise of running him as an informant.

"Which we can't prove," Webb sighed. "I can report it to the local FBI office, but after that, it's up to them what to do about him."

"I hate investigating cops," Vic growled. "Even Feds."

"Somebody needs to," Erin said.

"That's why we have Internal Affairs," he said.

"I never thought I'd see the day you'd like having IAB around," Webb said.

"I don't think we should report this to the Feds," Erin said.

"Why not?" Webb asked sharply.

"No proof, like you said," she replied. "And it might jeopardize an ongoing investigation."

All three of them were silent for a moment. Erin knew they were thinking the same thing.

"So this is tied in with your other thing," Vic said.

"I'm afraid so," she said.

"So, what does that mean?" he demanded. "We can't arrest anybody?"

"It means if we dig deeper we need to be careful about it," Webb said. "Don't rush anything. But it also means there's a connection between two mobs here. The Lucarellis and the Irish."

Erin nodded.

"I'm not going to ask how you know that," Webb said. "I'm just going to ask if you're sure."

"Yes, sir. I am."

"So why are you still digging?"

"Just because I'm loading bullets doesn't mean I'm about to fire them," she said.

"Can you at least tell us who you think is behind all these bodies?" Vic asked.

"Vinnie Moreno," she said.

Vic rolled his eyes. "I should've guessed. I hate that greasy bastard."

"He's the one who benefits most," she said. "With Acerbo and the old man's strongest supporters out of the picture, Vinnie's in charge of the Lucarellis."

"He was already in charge of the Lucarellis," Webb said. "Acerbo was never getting out of prison."

"They had a difference of opinion about the family's direction," Erin said. "Acerbo still had influence, even behind bars. Vinnie needed to clean out the old guard."

"So now he's the new boss," Vic said. "And he can do whatever he wants. We're gonna have to take him down sooner or later, especially if he's got Feds on his payroll."

"I agree," Webb said. "Do you have enough to go after him, O'Reilly?"

"Not yet," Erin said. "Not unless one of his hitmen talks."

"And we've got two in custody," Webb said. "Assuming Peralta doesn't die. That's what Moreno is afraid of. Which is why you two have ESU officers guarding Peralta. God, I feel like the slow kid in class right now."

"What's our next play?" Vic asked. "Peralta won't be able to talk for a while, even if he pulls through."

"I'm going to Riker's Island after lunch," she said.

"Visiting an inmate?" Webb asked. "Which one?"

"Nina Bianchi."

Vic whistled. "You better take me with you."

"You think she'll talk to you?" Erin asked, surprised.

"No, I think she may try to strangle you," he answered. "And if she does, you might need an extra pair of hands to pull her off you. She's a sizable lady, as I recall."

* * *

Erin left Rolf in the Major Crimes office with Webb, the dog's leash tied around the leg of her desk. The Shepherd gave her a look of deep betrayal, but she couldn't take a K-9 into a prison visiting area, especially if she was trying to get information. She would have preferred to leave Vic behind, too, but he insisted on coming, so they rode north in Erin's Charger.

Most of the drive was silent. Vic apparently had a lot on his mind, as did Erin. She was trying to find a way to fulfill all her obligations. She couldn't think of a way. If she took down Vinnie, it would get her in trouble with Evan O'Malley. If she let him skate, she'd be letting down the NYPD and failing as a cop. And if she killed him, she'd be doing what Matthew Madonna had wanted, but she'd be a murderer. And why was she even thinking about that last option? She gritted her teeth, clutched the steering wheel tighter, and kept driving.

Vic finally broke the silence as they were parking just outside the prison. "You remember the deal we had with this lady," he said conversationally.

"Yeah, I remember," she said.

"She confessed to murder in exchange for her son getting off the hook," he went on. "But then the little loser got himself killed right after we let him out of jail."

"I said, I remember."

"I'm just reminding you that this lady is capable of killing and she's got an excellent reason to hate us."

"You're the one who wanted to come along," she said. "What's the matter, are you afraid you can't take an overweight, middle-aged woman?"

"Of course I can," he said. "But who'd want to? I just hope she's worth it."

Inside the prison, they presented their shields, signed in, and handed over all their weapons. Then a female guard escorted them down a cold concrete hallway to a steel door. She opened the door. In the room, at a metal table, sat a large Italian woman in a prison jumpsuit.

The guard started to follow them in. Erin held up a hand.

"Ma'am, this is a private interview," she said. "And please make sure any recording devices are turned off." She didn't add that her own personal wire was merrily recording away.

"If you say so, Detective," the guard said doubtfully. "We'll have video running. I can't do anything about that. Regulations. But no Maseratio."

"That's fine," Erin said. The guard nodded reluctantly and departed, closing the door behind her. Erin and Vic walked over to the table and sat down opposite the prisoner, who glared at them.

"Detective O'Reilly," the prisoner said. "And that other copper. The meathead. You got a lotta nerve coming here."

"Mrs. Bianchi," Erin said. "Please accept our sympathies for the loss of your son."

"Well, I don't accept them!" Nina Bianchi snapped. "You got my Paulie killed! He was just a kid, and you staked him out like a goddamn sacrificial lamb and he got killed! My boy!"

"I understand that you're angry," Erin said.

"I only talked to you to keep him safe!" Nina went on. "To get him outta prison!"

"We kept our deal," Erin said, keeping her tone calm and conciliatory.

"I oughta break your damn nose!" Nina said.

"Now that I'd like to see," Vic said.

Erin shot him a look and turned back to Nina. "You know who had Paulie killed," she said. "And it wasn't the NYPD. It was Vinnie the Oil Man."

"What's it matter who gave the order?" Nina raged. "You're as much to blame as he is! I'm stuck in here and my sweet boy's dead!"

"Do you really think Paulie would've been safer behind bars?" Erin asked gently. "In gen-pop with other Lucarelli associates? You know what would've happened. It wouldn't have been a bullet. It would've been a sharpened toothbrush handle in the bathroom or a scrap-metal shiv in the lunch line, just like happened to Vittorio Acerbo yesterday."

"What're you talking about?" Nina demanded.

"Acerbo's dead," Erin said. "Stabbed at breakfast by a Lucarelli assassin."

"Jesus, Mary, and Joseph," Nina said. "What's this damn world coming to?"

"Vinnie sent Carlo Peralta to kill Paulie," Erin said. "Because Paulie knew too much and Vinnie thought he'd been flipped. Now Vinnie's at it again, killing his own guys. Do you know Wonderboy Crea? Stefano Rossi? Material Mattie Madonna?"

"What about them?" Nina asked suspiciously.

"They're all dead," Vic said. "Rossi got his throat slit in a restaurant, Crea got shot fetching the morning paper, and Madonna's full of holes after a gunfight."

Nina's face sagged. She still looked angry, but she also looked suddenly old and tired. "Wonderboy's got kids," she said. "I know his family. Mattie, too. Wonderboy sent me stuff in here. Money, clothes, food. He really dead?"

"I'm afraid so," Erin said. "I'm sorry."

"Like hell you are," Nina said bitterly. "You don't care how many Mafia hoods pop each other. You never liked us."

"I didn't know any of these guys," she said. "But I liked what I saw of Mattie Madonna. I was with him when he died. He was trying to protect his son. He asked me to do two things for him: look after Alfie and take Vinnie down. That's why I'm here."

"What're you selling this time?" Nina demanded. "I got nothing left. My husband and my son are dead and I'm in here for twenty to life, which comes to the same thing. I'm gonna die in here."

Erin diplomatically refrained from pointing out that the reason Nina's husband was dead was that Nina herself had killed him. "I'm offering you the chance to settle the score with Vinnie," she said.

"And what makes you think I know anything that'll hurt him?"

"You were married to one of the higher-ups in the Lucarellis for decades," she said. "You heard things. You know where some of the bodies are buried."

"And if I tell you any of that, I'm dead," Nina said. "Rats get killed, and I ain't no rat."

"He doesn't deserve your loyalty," Erin said. "He killed your son. And Paulie hadn't turned. Vinnie was wrong about him. Paulie died for nothing."

"What's in it for me? Revenge don't put meat on the table."

"What if I can get you a deal with the DA?" Erin asked, speaking slowly and carefully. She had to be very cautious in what she promised.

"What sort of deal?"

"Witness protection."

"Meaning what?"

"You could get out of prison," Erin said. "You'd get a new life, somewhere else. Away from New York."

"New York's my home," Nina said stubbornly.

"Not anymore," Erin replied. "You said it yourself. Your family is gone. You've got nothing here."

"Think about it," Vic said. "This place is pretty friggin' bleak. A change of scenery might do you good."

"Okay," Nina said. "I'll think about it. You put the deal in front of me, in writing, and then we'll talk."

"You give us what we need to burn the Oil Man," Erin countered.

"When I see the deal," Nina said. "I ain't taking you on faith, and I don't trust none of you bastards."

"Fair enough," Erin said. She stood up and offered her hand.

Nina pretended not to see it. "You got kids?" she asked Erin.

"No," Erin said.

"Then you don't know what I've been through."

Erin's mind went back to a terrible moment three months ago, to a desperate search of her brother's house, calling her niece and nephew's names, sure they'd been taken by a psychopath. She'd relived that moment over and over in nightmares.

"No, ma'am, I don't," she said quietly. "But I do respect it. And I am sorry."

"I don't need your damn pity," Nina said. "Now get outta here and let me get back to what's left of my life."

Chapter 18

"You think she's got the goods on Vinnie?" Vic asked once they were back in the car.

"She knows something," Erin said. "Maybe not enough by itself, but sometimes all you need to do is pry the door a couple inches open."

"So, how does this square with that other thing you've got going on?"

"I don't want to talk about it," she said. Then she put a finger to her lips and shook her head.

"Seriously?" he said, startled. But he nodded. "Okay, how do you like the Yankees for next year?"

"Can't be worse than this year. What do you think they need?" The Yankees were far enough behind the rival Red Sox that they couldn't possibly hope to make the playoffs.

"A priest," Vic said sourly. "Or maybe one of those faith healers you see on late-night TV. Besides that? Another decent starting pitcher. Hey, can we stop at that coffee shop? I need a drink, and they won't let me have vodka on duty."

"Sure." Erin pulled off the road into the parking lot. They climbed out of the car. She glanced at him as she closed her door.

"You don't really want a cup of coffee," she said. It wasn't a question.

"How do you know?" he retorted.

"You never drink coffee. Liquor and soda are your drinks. You just wanted to talk outside my car." She glanced around the lot out of habit, making sure nobody was paying attention to them.

"And that's why you're a detective," he said. "Who do you think is bugging your ride?"

"I don't *think* anybody is."

"But you're afraid someone is. Who?"

She shrugged. "IAB, probably."

Vic blinked. "I thought Keane was in on this."

"He is."

"Then... then what the hell are you worried about?"

"Vic, you're not even supposed to know I'm undercover," she said quietly. "Nobody's supposed to know. The more I talk about it, the more chance it gets to somebody it shouldn't. And I don't trust Keane."

"Nobody trusts Keane. Bloodhound? They oughta call him the Bloodsucker. I swear, he's gotta be a vampire. He's that cold-blooded. But you don't think he's dirty, do you?"

"No... but for all I know, someone in the Eightball may be on Evan's payroll. Or Vinnie's. And someone in the O'Malleys is out to get Carlyle and me."

"I know. You blew his head off three months ago."

"I don't mean Mickey. Mickey hated me, but someone else set me up. That car bombing was meant to make Mickey think Carlyle and I were trying to kill him."

"And this mysterious mastermind is still at large?" Vic sounded skeptical and Erin couldn't blame him. It did sound a little far-fetched.

"Yeah," she said.

"How do you know I'm not working for the bad guys?" he asked.

"Vic, you're an asshole, but you're a clean one."

He laughed. "I want a bumper sticker that says that. Or maybe you can just put it in my personnel file. You should tell Zofia. Maybe she won't be pissed at me anymore."

"Did you talk with her?"

"Not really. She just kept acting like I should already know what was going on. I hate when girls do that. Do you know why she's mad at me?"

"I think this is a conversation you should be having with her."

"Not gonna betray the sisterhood, huh?"

"I don't want to betray anybody, Vic." She rubbed her forehead. "But it's getting hard."

"Undercover thing getting to you?"

"Maybe. They think I'm one of them now."

"Isn't that the point?"

"Yeah, but you don't know what it's like."

"Of course not," he deadpanned. "A cop would never know what it's like for people to assume he's a bad guy."

"I just hope it ends soon," she said.

"That reminds me of a joke," Vic said. "A wise man once said, there's only two things wrong with life. Know what they are?"

"Enlighten me."

"It's a horrible experience, and it's over too soon."

"Thank you for that pep talk. It's a real morale-booster."

"So what's this whole thing got to do with you? This is the Italian Mafia, not the Irish Mob." He gave her a shrewd look. "But you knew about that deal between Vinnie and the O'Malleys. So now you're in with the Mafia, too?"

"I don't know."

"What do they want you to do?"

Her jaw tightened. "They want me not to look too close, for starters."

"They can kiss my ass!" Vic snapped.

"It's not that simple," she said. "I can build the case quietly, behind the scenes. For later."

"They don't expect you to get their triggermen off, do they?"

Erin smiled bitterly. "No, they expect me to kill Carlo Peralta."

"You're joking."

"Do I look like I'm joking?"

"Holy shit."

"Yeah, pretty much."

"Because they're afraid he might talk?"

"I assume so."

"But you told me to guard Peralta."

"Of course I did! I'm not actually going to kill him!"

"Right." But Vic did look slightly relieved. "In case there's other interested parties?"

"Yeah. If Vinnie wants Carlo dead, it must be that Carlo can pin the murders on him."

"We've gotta get back to Bellevue," Vic said. "Like, right now."

"I thought you trusted your ESU guys," she said.

"I do, but they're more muscles than brains."

"I don't know anybody like that," she said with a straight face.

"Real funny, Erin. Bite me. What I'm saying is, if the Lucarellis want Peralta dead, maybe he's the key to the whole thing. So we get down there, you and me, 'cause we're the only ones I trust a hundred percent right now."

"That's sweet. So I've made you paranoid, too?"

"It's contagious," he said. "Let's go see what that loser has to say."

"He might have a breathing tube."

"Then I'll rip it out of his throat."

"I'm pretty sure you can't do that, Vic."

"Have you seen these biceps? I'm pretty sure I can."

* * *

Vic's description of his ESU buddies as "more muscles than brains" was accurate. The two officers outside Carlo's room had one head of hair and no necks between them, and outweighed Erin by a total of at least three to one. The cop with the shaved head was leaning against the wall. His buzz-cut buddy was in a chair across the hall from him. Both looked bored, but when they saw Erin and Vic, they came instantly alert. When they recognized Vic, they relaxed again.

"Hey guys," Vic said. "You know Erin O'Reilly?"

"Heard of her," said Buzz-cut. "How ya doin', Detective?"

"This is Five Cent and Chunky," Vic said.

Erin raised an eyebrow. "We're not actually a street gang, Vic," she said. "We just act like one sometimes."

He sighed. "Nichols and Campbell, if you'd prefer."

"Copy that," Erin said. "Anything happening, guys?"

"Nah," Campbell said. "Our boy's been resting. He's been so quiet I thought maybe he was dead, but the machines say no. How come you got us riding this loser, Toothpick?"

"Toothpick?" Erin repeated quietly. She reminded herself to give Vic some crap about that later.

"Material witness," Vic said, ignoring her

"You could have a couple boots doing the same job," Campbell said. "Cost the taxpayers less."

"Someplace you'd rather be?" Vic asked.

"No way," Campbell said. "I love sitting in hospital hallways doing nothing. Reminds me of waiting for my kids to be born, only without the fear and pure joy."

Erin peered through the pane of glass in the door. "He's awake," she said. "At least, he's moving."

"Let's talk to him," Vic said.

"Maybe I should do it alone," she suggested.

He didn't like it. "I oughta be with you," he said.

"The more cops, the less chance he talks," she argued.

"You said you weren't gonna..." he said, trailing off meaningfully.

"And I'm not," she said, giving him a hard look. "I promise, I'll leave him in the same shape I found him."

Vic shook his head. "Somebody else has to be in that room. For your sake. Suppose he kicks off all on his own?"

She hadn't thought of that. But it didn't change things. "Vic, what I've got to say to this guy, I have to be the only one there."

"You sure?" He looked at her closely.

She nodded and went in, closing the door behind her. The familiar rhythmic beep of the heart monitor brought back a cluster of unpleasant memories. Too many friends and family had lain in rooms just like this one, fighting for their lives. Erin had to pause a moment and collect herself. Then she took a breath, squared her shoulders, and walked to the bed.

Carlo Peralta looked like warmed-over death. His complexion was waxy, his eyes dull with pain, fatigue, and blood loss. He had a saline drip snaking out of one arm, the heart monitor clipped to a fingertip, and a few yards of fresh, white bandages swathed around his upper chest. He stared at her and said nothing.

"How you feeling, Carlo?" she asked, pulling over a chair and taking a seat.

"So it's you," he said quietly. "The junkyard dog. Cars Carlyle's attack mutt."

"I guess we've both got reputations, Hyena," she said. "But I'm not your biggest problem right now."

His mouth twitched in what might have been an attempt at a smile, but pain made it more of a grimace. "From where I'm sitting, looks like you are."

"Madonna got you good," she said. "You're lucky to be alive."

"I got nothing to say about that," Carlo said.

"Who told you to kill Madonna and his son?"

"I told you, I got nothing to say. You know that."

"Yeah, I thought you might say that. But you want to think."

"What about?"

"About how useful you are to the Oil Man right now," she said. "I said I'm not your biggest problem and I meant it. You're looking at Murder One. That's life in prison. We've got the gun you used to kill Matthew Madonna, with your prints on it, and we've got you at the scene. That's plenty to burn you right there. But that's not your biggest problem either."

"Then tell me," he said. "What's my biggest problem, since you care so very much?"

"Vinnie the Oil Man," she said. "He knows you can link him to the killing, and he knows you're looking at a whole lot of years. You may think he trusts you, but I think you know better. Vinnie doesn't trust anybody and he doesn't take chances. Word on the street is, whoever clips you is looking at a big payday."

"Okay, I don't want any misunderstandings," Carlo said. "So listen carefully. Bite me, bitch."

"Push me hard enough, I just might," she said. "You're looking at the woman who took down Mickey Connor and Hans Rüdel. Do you really want to find out how sharp my teeth can be?"

"You threatening me?" He meant it to sound defiant, but Erin saw the fear in his eyes. He was thinking she might just be there to kill him.

"If I was threatening you, I'd be talking about how easy it is to make it look like an accident in a hospital," she said, looking him square in the eye. She felt a twinge of nausea, but she forced herself to say the words, trying to make them convincing. It was easier than she thought. "There's so many things that can go wrong when a guy's lying there helpless. An air bubble in an IV line, the wrong medication, a morphine overdose... these things happen."

"You wouldn't," Carlo said, but his voice cracked slightly. He genuinely believed she would.

"You're worth more dead than alive right now," she said. "You want to think about that. Now, who gave the word to kill Madonna? Was it Vinnie?"

"I tell you that, I'm a dead man," he said.

"Haven't you been listening, Carlo?" she retorted. "Vinnie's going to kill you either way. Your only chance is to make a deal with the NYPD, one that keeps you out of Riker's Island and away from the other Lucarellis."

He hesitated. She could tell he was right on the edge, wanting to reach for the desperate hope she was offering. She held her breath and waited.

"This is a test," he said, his eyes hardening. "You tell Vinnie I'm no goddamn rat."

"This is a test all right," she said grimly. "It's your final exam, Carlo. You flunk this and you're done. Think what you're doing."

"I'm done talking," he said, turning his head away. "You want to come back, you do it with my lawyer. I'm on pain pills and you threatened me. None of this is admissible. So screw you and get the hell out of here."

Erin was torn between frustration and reluctant admiration for the wounded man. Even helpless, faced with a person he thought might have come to kill him, he wasn't backing down. He'd called her bluff.

If it was a bluff. Erin looked at the IV in Carlo's arm, tracing it up to the bag of clear fluid that dangled above the bed. An air bubble injected into a vein could kill a man, in a way that could never be proved as homicide. Then Vinnie and Evan would trust her that much more, she'd be even further inside, and better able to take all these bastards down.

Her head spun. Vic had been right to want to be here with her. Carlo wasn't the only person in danger. She had to get out of there.

"I'll come back if I can," she said, standing up a little too quickly. "And if you're still alive. Be careful, Carlo."

* * *

Out in the hallway, Erin looked at Nichols and Campbell. "This man's in serious trouble," she said. "The Mob has a contract out on him. You don't let anybody but Vic or me in to see him. Even a doctor or nurse, you check their credentials and you stay right beside them. You copy?"

"We copy," Nichols said.

"How long we gotta stay here?" Campbell asked.

"We'll get relief for you as soon as we can," Vic said. "But we gotta make sure it's guys we can trust."

Campbell sighed. "Okay. It beats raiding meth labs, I guess. Healthier."

Vic followed Erin down the hall. "What'd he say?" the Russian asked.

"I thought I had him," she said, shaking her head. "He's more scared of Vinnie, though."

"Damn," Vic said.

"So, Five Cent, Chunky, and Toothpick, huh?" she said.

"Old squad nicknames," he explained. "Nichols is Five Cent, obviously. Campbell goes by Chunky, as in chunky soup, like the kind out of a can."

"And Toothpick?"

"That's me," he said, smiling. "I used to smoke once upon a time, but I heard those things'll kill you. So when I switched to ESU and started playing with assault rifles, I found out having something in my mouth made it easier not to start sucking a cig. I don't like gum, so I chewed toothpicks. Somebody started calling me 'Toothpick Vic' and it stuck."

"Gotcha. It's not a bad nickname. You want me to call you that?"

"I got a choice?"

"Depends on if you stay on my good side."

"Now what?" he asked.

"Now we try Alphonse Luna. Is he still here?"

"No, they kept him overnight but they discharged him this morning. We've got him in Holding back at the Eightball."

"Then that's where we're going. We just need to play the hitmen against each other, tell Luna the first one to crack gets a good deal, and Carlo's ready to talk. I'm guessing he'll break."

"You better hope so," Vic said. "Because otherwise we've got nothing."

Chapter 19

"Home sweet home," Vic said as they started up the stairs from the basement garage at Precinct 8. "You think we oughta get welcome mats?"

"I think it might send perps the wrong message," Erin said. "What would you put on them, anyway?"

"Abandon hope, all ye who enter?"

"Isn't that what's posted over the gates of Hell?"

He grinned. "Your point being...?"

Webb was in the office, filling out paperwork. "Oh, good," he said when he saw them. "We've got some reports from the Madonna shooting that need to be filed."

Vic made an unsuccessful effort to take cover behind Erin. Rolf, who had been lying morosely beside Erin's desk, looked up. His ears perked when he saw his partner, the rest of him springing up right behind. His tail started going so vigorously the whole back half of him went into motion.

Erin hurried to the K-9 and knelt down, rubbing the base of his ears. "How's my good boy?" she said. "You've been good, haven't you?"

Rolf poked her with his snout, telling her what a very good boy he was.

"I think he's bored," Webb said. "I know how he feels. What'd you get?"

Erin took a reflexive glance around the room. Nobody else was present. Captain Holliday's door was closed and no light showed under it. "Nina Bianchi might roll over on Vinnie if she gets a good deal," she said quietly.

"She hates us, but she hates him worse," Vic agreed. "Think the DA will bite?"

"I'll take it to him," Webb said doubtfully. "She's a convicted murderer."

"If it means taking down the head of the Lucarellis, I bet he'll go for it," Erin said. "And we'll need either her or Luna. Peralta turned us down."

Webb sighed and got heavily to his feet. "Okay, let's go downstairs and see what our guest has to say for himself," he said. "You and me, O'Reilly. Neshenko, you've got dog duty."

"What am I, a babysitter?" Vic said indignantly.

"Nobody's saying that," Erin said. "Rolf's a dog. That makes you a pet-sitter."

"Maybe I should sit on him," he grumbled.

"Try it," she said. "You'll wind up missing a chunk of your ass. He's done it before."

"You can come down to Interrogation with us," Webb said. "Just don't bring the dog into the room. Stay in the gallery while we talk to him."

"Let's fetch Luna from Holding," Erin said. "Can he walk?"

"He was a little shaky when they brought him in," Webb said. "But he's well enough to be discharged from Bellevue. After they stitched him up and pumped a couple units of blood in him, the doc said he improved a lot."

"Did he ask for a lawyer yet?" she asked.

"Not yet. He went to sleep right away. That's why I haven't taken a serious crack at him yet."

They took the elevator down to the lockup. All three detectives paused at the outer security door and put their guns in the little lockers outside. Webb got the keys for the holding cells and opened the security door.

"Pretty quiet in here," Vic observed as they started down the hall between empty holding cells.

"The cupboard's always bare on a Monday," Webb said.

"Not as many drunks after Sunday night," Erin said.

"Hey, Mr. Luna," Webb said loudly. "Wake up. We need to talk to you. We've just got a few—"

Webb cut himself off mid-sentence, as abruptly as if he'd just taken a bullet to the forehead. Erin saw her commanding officer standing frozen, staring into the holding cell. She followed his look and saw Alphonse Luna.

The wounded Mafia hitman was leaning against the bars of his cell. His body was at an awkward angle, his feet splayed out in front of him. He was still wearing the clothes he'd had on when he'd been arrested; prisoners weren't given orange jumpsuits until they landed at Riker's Island. But the NYPD had confiscated Luna's belt and shoelaces, just in case he'd been thinking of using them as an alternate exit from police custody. That was why Luna's shirt had been taken off. One sleeve had been tied around a steel crossbar. The other was knotted around the man's throat. His head was down, chin resting on his chest. He wasn't moving.

"Call a bus!" Webb snapped, breaking out of his momentary paralysis. He shoved one of the keys into the lock, hands moving so fast he nearly fumbled them.

Erin was moving too, snatching out the Swiss Army knife she kept in her hip pocket. She unfolded its largest blade and started sawing at the shirt fabric. The strands of cloth ripped and parted. Luna's body hit the floor with a muffled thud. He slumped over sideways, landing in a boneless heap on the concrete.

Webb got the cell door open and rushed inside. Erin was right behind him. She could hear Vic on the phone, getting an ambulance. Webb pulled at the shirt, trying to loosen it. He and Erin got Luna straightened out on the floor, tilting his head back to clear his airway. Erin grabbed the man's wrist.

"No pulse," she said.

"No respiration," Webb said grimly, bending close over Luna's face. "Start CPR."

"I'll do the compressions," she said, positioning herself over the downed man. She traced his bottom rib with a fingertip to find the xiphoid process, the little bone that stuck out at the bottom of the sternum. She put a hand just above that, over Luna's heart and interlaced the fingers of her other hand with it. She locked her wrists and elbows and started pushing and counting aloud, finding a rhythm.

"One and two and three and four and..."

It wasn't the first time she'd done CPR. It was common for Patrol cops to be first on the scene of heart attacks. But Erin knew, from unhappy experience, that it didn't work like it did on TV. The dark joke was that in Hollywood CPR stood for "Clean, Pretty, Reliable." The real thing was none of the above. She'd performed compressions on half a dozen people over her years on the Job, five men and one woman. Not one of them had bounced back from the brink on the basis of her efforts alone. Only one, a middle-aged man, had been revived by the paramedics. The other five had died. CPR was a stopgap at best, a way to keep the victim going just long enough for the EMTs to arrive with their defibrillators and modern medicines.

But without it, Luna was a goner for sure. So Erin kept going, counting to thirty, keeping the compressions firm, hard, and consistent. You had to go at least two inches into a guy's chest to do any good. Sometimes you broke ribs. That was just part of the deal.

She hit thirty and took her hands off Luna's chest. She pulled his mouth open, stooped, and gave him two breaths from her own lungs in the weirdly intimate way of first aid. Then it was back to the chest again for thirty more compressions.

And so it went. Once you started CPR, you kept doing it until a trained professional told you to stop, or your arms gave out. So Erin kept going.

She worked on Luna for almost five minutes, though it felt longer. Vic and Webb stood over her, unable to contribute anything useful. Vic was ready to step in when Erin wore out. Rolf whined anxiously and wagged his tail. He knew his partner was upset, but in the absence of bad guys to bite, all he could do was hover.

Then a pair of EMTs rushed in, accompanied by a handful of uniformed cops. One of the medics knelt down opposite Erin, medical bag in hand.

"I'll take over, ma'am," he said.

She sat back, rubbing her aching wrists. "Thanks," she said.

"You guys got here quick," Vic said to the other medic, who was prepping a stretcher.

"We were in the neighborhood," the EMT said. "Just lucky."

He got down and joined his partner, checking Luna's vitals while the other man kept up what Erin had started. They worked with calm professionalism, going through all the usual resuscitation protocols, doing everything they knew. Minutes passed. Two of the uniforms lingered. The others, recognizing they weren't needed, returned to their duties.

After about fifteen long minutes, one of the EMTs rocked back on his heels and said what they were all thinking.

"Call it."

"Time of death, 1413," the other medic said, using the twenty-four hour military clock terminology for 2:13 PM.

"Shit," Vic said.

That one syllable pretty much summed up the situation.

"Suicide," Webb muttered, rubbing his temples.

"Not a chance, sir," Erin said.

"What do you mean, O'Reilly?" he asked.

She turned to the uniforms who were still loitering. "Don't you guys have work to do?" she demanded.

Red-faced, the two Patrolmen made themselves scarce. Erin turned back to Webb, speaking more softly.

"Luna was glad to be arrested," she said. "He was happy to see us. He'd been wounded, but he wanted to live. If he hadn't been shot in the shoulder, I think he would've given me a hug when I busted him. He didn't want to die."

"He was locked in a holding cell," Webb reminded her. "In our own police station. Are you saying what I think you're saying?"

She nodded.

"Sounds like you guys need to examine the body," one of the EMTs said.

"We'll take care of it," Webb said. "Thanks for your help."

"Sorry it came out wrong," the medic said. "This is a crap job sometimes."

"All day every day," Vic said. "Try wearing a shield sometime. At least people are always glad when you guys show up."

"But not always when we leave," the EMT replied.

Webb pulled out his phone while the paramedics started packing up their equipment. He dialed and held it up to his ear.

"Hello, Dr. Levine?" he said. "Are you in the morgue? Okay, great. I've got a body for you to take a look at. No, we're already here. Just come up to Holding. We're in the third cell on the right."

He hung up and turned back to his detectives. "She's on her way up," he said. "We'll know if this was suicide soon enough."

"And if it wasn't..." Erin began.

"Then we've got a big goddamn problem," Vic said.

* * *

Levine was already wearing her lab coat and gloves when she walked into the holding cell. She completely ignored all the living people, going straight to the body and kneeling beside it. She got out a temperature probe and checked the core temp.

"Just one degree below normal," she said to no one in particular. "Time of death approximately forty minutes ago."

"Just a few minutes before we showed up," Erin said quietly to Vic.

"Initial cause of death appears to be asphyxia resulting from strangulation," Levine went on.

"Suicide?" Webb asked. "Or homicide?"

"I see no defensive wounds on the hands or arms," Levine said without looking at Webb. "Ligature marks appear consistent with some sort of fabric. However, it appears the body has been disturbed. Who moved it?"

"O'Reilly and I did," Webb said.

"Why?" Levine asked.

"Because we weren't sure he was dead," Webb said, annoyed. "Sorry if that makes your job harder."

Levine drew back one of Luna's eyelids and checked his pupil. "I'll need to do bloodwork to check for chemical agents," she said. Then she paused and looked more closely at Luna's neck. "It appears there are two sets of ligature marks here."

"So he was strangled and then strung up?" Vic asked. "Kinda hard to do that to yourself."

"He had an injured shoulder," Erin said. "He was shot yesterday."

"I can see that." It was Levine's turn to be irritated. "But that wound did not contribute to death. It wasn't life-threatening and has been cleaned, sutured, and dressed by a professional."

"But could he have rigged a noose one-handed?" Erin asked.

"He would have had partial use of the injured limb," Levine said. "It would have been relatively easy. How was he suspended?"

"Seated," Erin said. "Against the bars. Like this." She leaned against them and demonstrated, putting a hand to her throat to simulate a noose.

"Easy," Levine repeated. "However, this bullet wound appears fresh. You said it happened yesterday?"

"Around noon," Erin confirmed. "Why?"

"The clavicle is fractured," Levine said. "If he was treated by a professional, they should have given him a sling."

"So where is it?" Erin asked.

"He must've taken it off," Vic said. "He couldn't have gotten out of his shirt with it on."

"There," she said, pointing to the bed against the wall. On the floor next to it lay an ordinary hospital sling.

Vic shrugged. "I guess he could've taken it off, then come over and rigged the noose."

"Have you ever broken your collarbone?" Erin asked him.

"Hell yeah. Twice. Hurts like a son of a bitch when it happens."

"Would you take off your sling?"

He shrugged again. "Not while I was awake. But I wouldn't off myself either, so how do I know what was going through this mope's head?"

"If he was going to hang himself, why leave his medical support over there?" Erin wondered. "I think he took it off to sleep. Then someone entered the cell and choked him unconscious. He was off guard, sleepy, weak, and injured, so he could hardly put up a fight. Then the killer pulled him over here and strung him up with his own shirt."

"Are you saying there's been a murder inside a police station, Detective? That sounds like a job for my people."

Erin spun around at the sound of the familiar voice. She hadn't heard Andrew Keane come in, but the Internal Affairs Lieutenant was standing a little behind Webb. His suit was slightly rumpled, something Erin had never seen on him before, and the normally put-together man was looking uncharacteristically disheveled. He must have come down in one hell of a hurry.

"Lieutenant Keane," Webb said in a carefully neutral tone.

"Lieutenant Webb," Keane replied with just a hint of amusement. "Would someone like to tell me what's going on here?"

"I'm examining a corpse," Levine said. "Not having a conversation." Then she dismissed Keane from her thoughts and went back to looking at Luna's body.

"We've got a suspect who died in custody," Webb said.

"In that case, we'll need to bring in an outside forensic pathologist," Keane said. "Meaning no disparagement, Doctor. It's standard procedure."

"I'm aware of proper procedure," Levine said. "I'm also working. Be quiet."

Vic put a hand to his mouth to stifle a snicker. Levine was the only person at the Eightball with the guts and lack of social awareness to talk to Keane that way.

"Who found the body?" Keane asked.

"My squad," Webb said. "All three of us were together, along with O'Reilly's K-9."

Rolf, sitting quietly to one side, cocked his head when everyone looked at him. He wagged his tail at Erin.

"And he was dead when you found him?" Keane asked.

"He was nonresponsive," Webb said, choosing his words carefully. "O'Reilly performed CPR until the bus crew showed up to take over. The EMTs called time of death several minutes after they arrived."

"I'll have my people take pictures of the scene," Keane said. "Nobody touch or move anything."

"We already moved the body," Erin said. "To render first aid."

"I understand that, Detective," Keane said. "But don't do anything further. This is now an IAB case. I'll be needing statements from all three of you. Please report to separate interview rooms. I, or one of my team, will be with you shortly."

Chapter 20

"Jones and Clayborn are talking to Lieutenant Webb and Detective Neshenko," Keane said, sliding into the chair across the table from Erin. "Looks like it's you and me."

"Lucky me," Erin said sourly. She laid a hand on Rolf's head for moral support, hardly aware she was doing it. This was an interview, she reminded herself, not an interrogation, and the K-9's presence was proof of that.

"This is routine," Keane said. "It's fortunate all three of you were together. Assuming your stories corroborate one another, you can go about your business."

"You're saying I'd be a suspect if I'd gone to talk to Luna on my own?" she shot back.

"I'm implying nothing," Keane said calmly. "Now, you have the right to a Police Union attorney. Would you like to exercise that right?"

Erin considered telling him what he could do with the departmental lawyer. "I don't think we need him," she said instead.

"The record will show Detective O'Reilly has waived her legal representation," Keane said. "Now, Detective, in your own words, please describe the incident with Alphonse Luna."

Erin laid it out, briefly and truthfully. She kept to the straight facts, avoiding speculation. She should have told him about her suspicion that Luna had been murdered. He was an Internal Affairs cop, after all. The only people who'd had access to Luna had been cops. Therefore, if Luna had been killed, one of the officers at the Eightball had done it.

But she didn't. Maybe it was because she didn't like Keane on a personal level. She didn't know a single person who did. He was an ambitious jerk, probably a sociopath; the sort of guy who'd have been an amoral CEO if he'd gone into the private sector. Or maybe it was the sort of paranoia that came from working an extended undercover assignment with a bunch of murderous street thugs. Whatever the reason, she wasn't interested in baring her inner thoughts to the man in the too-expensive suit on the other side of the table.

"Did you know the deceased?" Keane asked.

"No," she said. "The first time I saw him was at Andolini's Restaurant on Sunday. I only spoke to him when the ESU squad and I arrested him at the veterinarian's office."

"How did you know to look for him there?"

"We leaned on his girlfriend. She tipped us off."

Keane nodded. "Good police work, Detective."

Your approval means so very much to me, she thought of saying. "It did the job," she said.

"And you've made an arrest in the shooting of Matthew Madonna," Keane said.

"Yes, sir."

"The alleged shooter is at Bellevue Hospital, I understand?"

"There's nothing alleged about it," Erin said. "He's the guy. We watched him go in with his buddies. We found him next to his gun. He may not have been the one who shot Madonna, but he's the only one of the hit squad still breathing."

"How close are you to clearing the Crea shooting?"

"I don't see how that's pertinent to the current interview, sir."

Keane smiled faintly. "I'm just trying to construct an accurate picture of the situation, Detective. I know mob hits are difficult to solve. The shooter can be very hard to ID. You may get the assassin, if you're lucky, or you may know who wanted the target killed, but connecting the two can be effectively impossible. Was Luna murdered?"

The suddenness of the question, and the sharp glance Keane threw her way, startled Erin. "I didn't see it happen," she said, trying to maintain a poker face. "The Medical Examiner hasn't given a cause of death yet. And as I understand it, you'll be using someone other than Levine to make that determination. So I don't see how I can answer that question at this time."

"Of course not," Keane said. "But what's your opinion?"

"My opinions would only matter if I was the officer investigating the death," she said. "Since your office is doing the investigating, and you're the OIC, I'd say your opinion carries more weight than mine."

"You're right, I'm Officer in Command," Keane said. "But you've proven yourself to be highly skilled at finding solutions to mysteries. I value your input. This can be off the record. What do you think?"

"I think nothing's ever off the record with you, sir," she said, looking him in the eye.

Keane stood up. "Thank you, Detective O'Reilly, for your time and cooperation. My office will contact you with any follow-up questions. This interview is concluded." He offered his hand.

Erin got to her feet and accepted the offered hand. She'd shaken with worse men than Keane. The Internal Affairs Lieutenant politely held the door for her. As she and Rolf walked past him, the Shepherd gave the man a baleful look. Rolf could tell his partner didn't like Keane and he wanted the Lieutenant to know that one wrong move would result in teeth.

* * *

Erin's interview had been perfunctory. She cooled her heels up in Major Crimes for a quarter of an hour waiting for the other two to finish giving their statements. Vic was the next one out of the box. He arrived with a scowl on his face and a Mountain Dew from the downstairs vending machine in his hand.

"Kira was a lot nicer when she was one of us," he growled.

"Aw, did she hurt your feelings?" Erin asked in saccharine tones.

"I don't want to talk about it."

"Good," she said. "I don't think we're supposed to."

Webb was only a moment behind. He came up the elevator and disappeared into the break room, emerging with a cup of coffee and a slightly stale donut.

"Everything okay, sir?" Erin asked.

"Reminded me of my last colonoscopy," Webb said. His punchline timing was perfect, catching Vic mid-swallow. The Russian snorted yellow soda out of both nostrils, clapping a hand to his face with a gurgled curse.

"You all right, Neshenko?" Webb asked mildly.

Vic, busy blowing his nose into a leftover fast food napkin, didn't answer.

"Good analogy, sir," Erin interjected. "IA cops are just like proctologists. They have a dirty job, no one likes to talk to them..."

"...and you're walking funny when you come back from an appointment with them," Vic managed to say. "God, that stings!"

"You're the one drinking it," Webb reminded him. "So, that's over with. I think it's safe to say we won't be getting anything useful out of Alphonse Luna. So forget him. That leaves us two possible avenues."

"Carlo Peralta might decide to talk," Erin said. "But he might not. He's scared, but he's old school."

"Let's let him soften overnight," Webb said. "He may want to play ball in the morning."

"Assuming he's still alive," Erin said.

"Five Cent and Chunky are solid," Vic objected. "Nobody's getting past them."

"Carlo got shot," Erin said. "He might still die of that, even if nobody touches him."

"You've got a point," Webb said. "But you already tried talking to him once. Even assuming the doctors let you question him again, I think it's a good idea to let him sit for a bit. In my experience, if you try to interview the same suspect twice in the same afternoon, it tells him you're desperate."

"We are desperate," Vic said. He'd gotten his nose under control, but his eyes were still streaming.

"I know," Webb said. "But it's not smart to let your target know that."

"So what do we do now?" Erin asked.

"I don't know what we can do," he replied, spreading his hands. "The only thing I can think of we haven't tried is Alfredo Madonna."

"Why isn't he in our holding cells right now?" Vic asked.

"Because Precinct 5 has him," Erin said. "The shooting happened in their backyard, remember?"

"Oh, yeah," Vic said.

"Okay," Webb said. "I want the two of you to go over and find out what he's got to say for himself."

"Sir—" Vic began.

"I don't want to hear it, Neshenko. Your problems are your problems, not mine. This isn't a volunteer organization. It's a hierarchy and I outrank you. That means I give the orders, you carry them out. Put on your big boy pants and get your ass to the Five."

* * *

"Relax, Vic," Erin said. "Zofia won't even be on duty. She works the dog watch."

"It's not that," Vic grumbled. "I can't dodge her forever. I just wish I knew why she was pissed at me. If I'm gonna get a girl mad, I should at least have the fun of doing something. I mean, I haven't been sleeping around. I never hit her. I didn't cash in my retirement fund to buy a motorcycle. Hell, we haven't even had an anniversary for me to forget yet!"

Erin bit her lip and reminded herself it wasn't her secret to tell. Fortunately, they were just about at the Precinct 5 house and she didn't have to say anything. She parked and unloaded Rolf. Vic followed them, still grumbling.

She presented her shield at the front desk and told the duty sergeant their errand. She was gratified to see him double-check her credentials in his computer. They probably hadn't heard about Luna's misfortune yet, but were taking no chances with their prisoner regardless.

The sergeant checked Vic's ID even more closely, probably because Vic looked like a hitman. But after a couple of minutes he cleared them and got a uniform to escort them to Holding. Erin left Rolf in the gallery with instructions to stay, which the Shepherd did, though not without giving her a reproachful look.

Alfie Madonna looked like hell. The NYPD's holding facilities weren't the Ritz, but they weren't as bad as all that. Still, from the look of him, he might've spent the night in a medieval dungeon. He had dark shadows under his bloodshot eyes, his hair was uncombed, and his clothes were rumpled. He made no protest when Vic cuffed him and steered him down the hall to the interrogation room.

"Nobody comes in there," Erin told the uniform, pointing to the observation gallery. "I left my K-9, and without me to tell him what to do, we wouldn't want anyone getting bitten."

This was absurd. Rolf would never bite a random cop who just happened to be in the same place he was. But Erin didn't want officers she didn't know eavesdropping on the interrogation.

Alfie slumped in the metal chair and stared at his hands. Erin took a calculated risk and unfastened his cuffs. She didn't think a skinny, unarmed Italian guy was any match for her, let alone Vic. And she was playing "good cop." Removing the restraints was a good first step toward establishing rapport.

"How're you feeling, Alfie?" she asked.

"Dad's dead, isn't he," the younger Madonna said dully. It was more statement than question.

"I'm afraid so," she said. "We got him to the hospital as fast as we could, but he was too badly hurt. The docs did everything they could."

"I told him to get out," Alfie said, still looking at his hands. "I said we had time. We could run for it. He told me to go."

"Why didn't you?" she asked.

Now looked up. "Would you? If it was your dad?"

Erin shook her head. "Not a chance."

"What do you want?" he asked.

"Your father made a dying confession," she said. "He told us everything that happened; how you wanted to protect him, but how he made you give him your gun, so he shot them when they came for him."

"Erin!" Vic hissed, shooting her a look that asked what the hell she thought she was doing. In Vic's book, one of the reasons they were there was to get a confession out of Alfie. Everyone in the room knew perfectly well he'd had a gun and had done at least some of the shooting.

She kicked Vic's leg under the table, hoping Alfie didn't notice the movement. The kid seemed wrapped up in his own thoughts and made no reaction.

"Do you know who sent Carlo the Hyena and his buddies?" she asked.

"Yeah, but it don't matter none," Alfie said bitterly.

"Why doesn't it matter? They killed your dad!"

"I know that!" he snapped. His red-rimmed eyes were shining with unshed tears. He clenched his hands into fists and pressed the knuckles against the tabletop. "I was there! I watched it happen! Why didn't you arrest Dad, dammit?"

"If we'd taken him in, we'd have had to take you in, too," Erin said gently. "He didn't want that. He was trying to look out for you."

"He was trying to follow his goddamn code!" Alfie said, getting the words out with difficulty. "He always thought he was some character in some friggin' gangster movie. Like rules mattered. Rules don't mean shit on the street! Sure, he followed 'em, but the other guys didn't, and now he's dead!"

"You want to get the guy who did this?" Erin asked.

"Goddamn right I do! But I'm in here, he's out there. And I can't touch him nohow!"

"It's Vinnie the Oil Man," Erin said. "We know that."

"Then what the hell do you need me for?" Alfie shot back. "Bust his ass! Throw him in jail! Just do me one favor. Put him in the same cell block as me. I guarantee you won't need no room and board for him. Forty-eight hours, tops. Won't be no trial, neither."

"I'll be happy to throw him behind bars," Erin said. "But to do that, I need to link him to the shootings. For that, I need your help, Alfie."

He shook his head. "I can't do that, lady."

"You talk about your dad's stupid code," Vic broke in. "Now what? You gonna follow the same damn rules that got him killed?"

"That's not what I mean," Alfie said. "I can't give you nothing on Vinnie, 'cause I got nothing! I've met him, sure, plenty of times, but I ain't never seen him do nothing illegal. Sure, we all know what he's got going on, but that's just words. I can't prove none of it. I been doing some thinking, and yeah, if I could give him to you, I'd do it. But I can't. I'm just a little guy, you think I don't know that? Dad was the big man in the Family. He coulda got you Vinnie. But he wouldn't."

"Because of his code?" Erin asked.

"Yeah, his damn stupid code." A tear overflowed Alfie's left eye and ran down his cheek. "You think he was some sorta scumbag, just 'cause he sold drugs. Who the hell's fault is that? People sell worse shit all the time, it's just legal for them. How many people die 'cause of cigarettes? Booze? Dad was the best man I ever knew. He was always tryin' to keep me outta trouble, get me doin' the right thing, especially since Mom died. Now what am I gonna do?"

The young gangster buried his face in his hands. His shoulders shook with suppressed sobs. Erin broke protocol by putting out a hand and resting it gently on his shoulder. You weren't supposed to ever touch a suspect in interrogation. A good defense lawyer could get a whole case thrown out if he could prove you'd laid a hand on his client. But she took the chance.

"It'll be okay, Alfie," she said. "We're going to get Vinnie, I promise. Can you give us anything? Do you know where he likes to hang out? Where would he be on a Monday night?"

"He'll be watching football at his place," Alfie sniffled.

"Alone?" Erin asked.

"Sometimes he has some guys over. And he's got a couple guards, of course. He ain't stupid." Alfie swiped his sleeve across his eyes. "Sorry. I didn't mean to lose my shit like that. Dad would kick my ass if he knew."

"Forget about it," Erin said. "This is your dad we were talking about. I know he meant a lot to you."

"Tell you what," Alfie said. He stared at Erin, his eyes burning. "Just let me outta here. You won't have to worry about the Oil Man."

"That's a new one," Vic said. "Trying to make the NYPD an accessory to murder? Not gonna happen, pal. You're going to jail."

"You just take it easy, Alfie," Erin said, motioning with her hand for Vic to back down. "Did you ever see Vinnie with Carlo Peralta?"

"All the time," Alfie said. "Carlo's his go-to guy for muscle work. Tell me that asshole's dead too."

"He got hit pretty bad," Erin said truthfully. "We don't know if he's going to pull through."

"Good," Alfie said savagely. "Look, lady. I'm sorry about my mouth, and I'm sorry I can't give you more. I hate that son of a bitch Vinnie worse than you do, okay? But you take him down, I promise I'll do what I can for you."

"I'll keep it in mind, Alfie," she said.

* * *

After returning Alfie to his holding cell, Erin and Vic went back to the observation room to collect Rolf. The K-9 let Erin know, with the motion of his tail, that she was forgiven for abandoning him. But he hoped she'd never do it again.

"Waste of our goddamn time," Vic muttered. "The kid doesn't know anything. I bet we could've got him to cop to Murder Two at least, if you hadn't cut me off. What were you thinking?"

"I was thinking we're after bigger fish," Erin said. "Besides, that was self-defense."

"You're nuts!" Vic snapped. "Alfie Madonna's a convicted felon with an illegal handgun! There's no such thing as self-defense if he shoots a guy, because he's committing a crime holding the damn gun in the first place! Don't tell me you buy into that bullshit about his dad getting both guns!"

"Of course not," Erin said. "But there's the law, and then there's the street. You know what happened there. His dad was set on making a last stand. His personal code wouldn't let him run away from Vinnie's guys. And Alfie wouldn't leave his dad to face the music alone. I think it's kind of admirable."

Vic stared at her. "This guy's a crook!" he burst out. "And he killed a guy! Maybe more than one!"

"Maybe not," she said. "We won't know who killed whom until we get the ballistics report on the guns that were used. He might've missed."

"Now you're just splitting hairs!" he said. "Jesus! I didn't think Carlyle had gotten to you this badly. I thought he was on our side!"

"Quiet!" she snapped with such sudden ferocity that Vic stopped short, swallowing whatever else he'd been about to say.

"Don't ever say a word about that!" she went on in a near-whisper. "Not here, not anywhere. Are you *trying* to get me killed? You and I both know there's a mole at the Eightball now. That's the only way Luna could've been killed. And that's probably not the only one. The Five is Lucarelli territory. If he's got a guy at the Eightball, he's probably got half a dozen here."

"Holy shit," Vic said. "You're paranoid as hell, Erin. You'll be making tinfoil hats next. We're the cops, not the goddamn Mob!"

"And we're pretty sure Freddy Giusto is with Vinnie," Erin went on, still keeping her voice low. "So the Feds are compromised. We don't know who we can trust, Vic. So keep your voice down!"

"Okay, okay. Sheesh. But if you're right about that, what are we gonna do?"

"We're going to get that bastard," Erin said grimly, gritting her teeth. "I don't know how. But I swear, he's going down."

Chapter 21

Erin, Vic, and Rolf left the Five and started across the street. Erin hadn't been able to find a close parking space; unsurprisingly, all the police spaces near the station were occupied. The afternoon was wearing away. Erin's stomach growled.

"You want to maybe grab a sandwich on the way back to the Eightball?" she asked.

"I could go for a BLT," Vic said. "And then, I think maybe we oughta—"

"Don't you walk away from me, Vic Neshenko!"

Vic froze at the shout that came from behind. Erin saw his face go rigid and his shoulders tense up. Then he sagged and turned with a resigned sigh.

Zofia Piekarski stalked out into the street. One hand was extended, the index finger pointing directly at Vic.

"How can I walk away from you if I didn't know you were there?" Vic asked. "Or are you just looking for another reason to be pissed?"

"That depends," Piekarski said. "You make up your mind yet? I know it takes you a while, but it's not a hard choice."

"What do you want from me?" Vic demanded. "What the hell did I ever do to you?"

"Plenty," Piekarski said. She was close now, staring up at Vic. He was more than a foot taller than she was, but she made up for it with fierce energy. He backed up a step.

"I don't know what you think you know," he said. "But I've got no idea what you're talking about. Did I forget your birthday or something?"

Piekarski snorted. "I didn't think you were such a goddamn coward," she said.

"The hell I am!" Vic retorted. "I'm telling you, I had no idea you were here! You're not on the clock right now! Erin and I were interviewing a suspect, for Christ's sake! Not everything's about you!"

"I was pulling a double shift!" she shouted back. "And that's not what I'm talking about!"

Erin and Rolf stood on the sidelines, their eyes following the exchange as if they were watching a tennis match. Rolf's head was cocked quizzically, his ears slanted off to the side. He, like Vic, had no idea what was going on.

"You keep running away!" Piekarski went on. "You've been dodging me because you're scared!"

"I've been busy," Vic said defensively. "Working."

"Bullshit!" Piekarski said, echoing Erin's unspoken thought. It was a weak excuse and all of them knew it.

"Okay, fine!" Vic snapped. "I've been steering clear of you. Because you're acting really weird, and it seems like you don't want me around. Look, you came after me in the first place, okay?"

"So now I'm crazy *and* desperate?" Piekarski said. She'd sounded angry before. Now she sounded dangerous. Out of twelve years' street instincts, Erin watched the other woman's hands, making sure they didn't move toward a weapon. It was unlikely, but every cop knew domestic disputes were some of the nastiest conflicts. They could turn violent surprisingly fast.

"That's not what I meant!" Vic said. "Jesus! Will you just tell me what's got you all wound up? If I did something outta line, tell me! I'll buy you flowers or a new Smith and Wesson or something!"

Piekarski had been opening her mouth to say something else, but Vic's final words startled a laugh out of her. It caught her mid-speech and she almost choked on it.

"I'm sorry," Vic said. "Seriously. I've got no idea what I'm apologizing for, but I swear, I'll make it up to you, whatever it is."

Piekarski had her breathing under control now. "I just need to know," she said. "Are you in or out?"

"Is that, like, a proposal or something?" Vic asked. He looked confused and a little scared.

"Hell no!" Piekarski said. "If it was, it was the shittiest one I've ever heard."

"Me, too," he said, but he was relieved. "It kinda sounded like..."

"If you're going to bail on me," she said, "you better get out right the hell now."

"Why would I do that?"

"I can't tell you," she said. "Not until I get your answer."

"That makes no damn sense at all," he said. But Erin could see the wheels turning in Vic's head. Under the rough exterior and all the macho bullshit he had the brain of a detective, a damn good one. He was considering possibilities, figuring things out.

Piekarski saw it too. It was her turn to look suddenly scared. "Look," she said, taking a couple of steps back. "I don't need your answer right this second. And maybe I came on a little strong, gave you the wrong idea."

Vic was staring at her. Erin saw it hit him, the look in his eyes like headlights that had just been switched on.

"Holy fuck," he whispered.

Piekarski's face froze in an expression midway between hope and fear. She was holding her breath. So was Erin.

"That's what this is?" Vic asked. His voice was much quieter than usual. "Are you sure?"

"I wasn't till today," Piekarski said. "I didn't take the test until this morning."

"When were you gonna tell me?"

"When I knew. About you and me."

Vic swallowed. "And you didn't tell me before, because you thought I'd run out on you? Christ on crutches, what kind of loser do you think I am?"

"That's not why," she said. Her face crumpled a little. "I wanted you to choose. I didn't want you to feel, you know, *obligated*. I thought if you knew, you'd feel like you had to do the right thing. I don't want to be some sympathy date, and I sure as hell don't want a man marrying me because he feels like he screwed up. I don't want you to feel sorry for me!"

"Sorry?" Vic was bewildered. He looked helplessly at Erin. "Do you know what she's talking about? I don't understand chicks."

Erin held up her hands. "You're on your own for this one, buddy," she said. "I'm not getting in the middle of it. Tell you what. You two obviously have a lot to talk about. Zofia, can you see that this big guy gets home okay?"

"Yeah," Piekarski said, recovering herself a little. "I think I can get him where he needs to go."

"I'll tell Webb you're following up a lead," Erin said. "See you tomorrow."

"Thanks," Vic said. He looked stunned, like he'd just taken a lead pipe to the forehead, but he didn't look unhappy. Erin thought he'd probably be okay by morning. If not, he might never be okay again. But in either case, it was none of her damn business. She flicked Rolf's leash and walked away, the K-9 trotting beside her.

* * *

Back behind the wheel of her Charger, Erin turned the key. The 8-cylinder engine rumbled to life with its familiar throaty roar. Rolf poked his head through the hatch from his rear compartment. His ears were fully upright, his tongue hanging out, his tail wagging. He was ready for whatever came next, hopefully involving chasing someone.

Erin knew how he felt. She wanted to go out and get Vinnie. She knew, beyond any doubt, he was responsible for every death she'd been investigating. But she couldn't prove it. The best she could do was catch the shooters, and even then, there was no guarantee they'd survive to face trial. Her last hope was either that Carlo Peralta would decide to flip, or Nina Bianchi would decide she wanted to hurt Vinnie more than she didn't want to help Erin. And that was assuming Nina even had anything on the Oil Man.

"What do we do?" she asked Rolf.

The K-9 cocked his head at her and kept wagging. He thought it would be a good idea to find a bad guy and bite him. He trusted Erin to point him the right direction.

"Monday night football," she muttered, putting the car in gear. She could try leaning on Nina again in the morning. Carlo, too, assuming he lived through the night. She knew, at least, where Vinnie would be. It was as good a time as any to swing down to Brooklyn and see what the Lucarelli chieftain was up to.

She pulled out her phone and hit Webb's number as she drove away from the Five. It rang twice. Then his familiar, weary voice came on the line.

"Tell me you've got good news," he said.

"No dice, sir. Alfie Madonna doesn't know anything. He's small fry. He's sure Vinnie had his dad whacked, and he hates him for it, but he can't give us what we need."

"Damn," Webb said. "Well, it was worth a try. When you've got seconds left on the clock, there's no harm in doing a Hail Mary."

"Seconds left, sir? What do you mean?"

"We're shut down. The Captain just passed me the word. I was about to call you."

"Shut down?" Erin wasn't sure she'd heard him right. "Why?"

"RICO," Webb said. "The Feds are taking this one over. Just like they did with the Bianchi case last year."

"I bet I know why," Erin said bitterly. "And I bet I know who's in charge of the 'investigation.'"

"I'm not taking that bet," he replied. "I've got little enough saved for retirement without giving you my hard-earned dollars."

"So that's it? Vinnie walks?" She didn't try to hide the disgust in her voice.

"This is out of my hands, O'Reilly. Yours, too. This is how the game works sometimes."

"It's not a game!" she burst out. "Seven people are dead!"

"That many?" Webb said. "I've lost count."

"Rossi at the restaurant," she said. "And Crea in his front lawn. Then there's Matthew Madonna and the two shooters that went after him, plus the guy in the fridge, Beneventi. And Luna in his jail cell makes seven. Did I miss anyone?"

"No. But they're all Mafia guys. No civilians."

"Murder is murder, sir!"

"You're not wrong, O'Reilly. But there's nothing we can do."

The thought struck Erin that by giving up leaning on the Lucarelli organization, they were doing exactly what Evan O'Malley had asked her to do. It would help her standing with the Irish Mob. It would enhance her street cred. And right then and there, it made her feel even worse.

"Orders, sir?" she asked, forcing the words out between clenched teeth.

"Is Neshenko with you?"

"No, sir. He had some stuff to take care of at the Five."

"Copy that. Don't bother coming back here. It's close to quitting time and the only thing left to do is box up what we've got and send it to the Feebies. I can take care of that."

"We're keeping copies, aren't we?" she asked.

"Why would we—" Webb began, then stopped himself. "Yeah, that's not a bad idea."

"Not on the departmental database," Erin said. Her paranoia was really humming. "Maybe hard copies?"

"They'll be somewhere safe," he agreed. "Just in case. You know this goes against normal protocol, right?"

"I won't tell anyone, sir."

"Of course not. Stay out of trouble, O'Reilly."

"Doing my best, sir."

Webb hung up. Erin drove for a few seconds in silence, gripping the steering wheel. Then she banged her fist on the dashboard, three times, hard. It hurt, but it felt good, too.

"God damn it!" she shouted.

Rolf thrust his nose against her ear and whined softly, anxiously. Erin took a deep breath and tried to let it out slowly.

She felt like a red-hot vise was squeezing her head. Her temples pounded. She wanted to hit something else, something more satisfying.

The right thing to do was to give it up, go home for the night. A good hot meal at the Barley Corner, a glass of Guinness with a Glen D whiskey chaser, and some time with Carlyle ought to calm her down. Webb was right. They couldn't win every day. Sometimes the bad guys got away. That was just part of the Job.

But Erin didn't want to calm down and she wasn't ready to go home, not yet.

"We're still going to Brooklyn," she told Rolf.

He wagged his tail and stared over her shoulder at the road. It sounded like a great plan to him.

Chapter 22

"Crime doesn't pay" was one of the lies people told kids. It was right up there with "sticks and stones may break my bones, but words will never hurt me," and "you can do anything you want to if you set your mind to it." Erin knew why people told kids those things, but she also knew why parents talked about the Easter Bunny and Santa Claus.

The truth was, if crime didn't pay, nobody would steal. Crime paid just fine for Vincenzo Moreno, and she was looking at the proof. Vinnie the Oil Man lived in a classy brownstone in Carroll Gardens that overlooked Carroll Park. It wasn't exactly a gated mansion like in *The Godfather*, but Erin knew enough about New York real estate to guess the price tag on that place probably ran two and a half million.

She parked on President Street, three houses down from Vinnie's front door. Her Charger was unmarked, but any criminal with one good eye and half a brain would make it as a police vehicle. She adjusted her coat to cover her holster and shield. Then she clipped Rolf's leash on and unloaded him. She went into the park, acting the part of an ordinary New York woman walking her dog.

The park was pleasant, a low iron fence surrounding a mix of trees, rocks, shrubbery, and a playground full of kids. It was getting close to suppertime and the children were running off their post-school energy. The weather was cool, but not yet cold enough to keep them off the jungle gym. Erin watched the kids for a few minutes, trying to capture a sense of normality. But their proximity to the Mafia chieftain only made her angrier. She remembered how her own niece and nephew had been pulled into the crossfire in a Mob civil war. She thought of Anna hiding under the bed with Patrick, scared out of her wits, the little girl acting out what they'd taught her in active-shooter drills at school.

Vinnie's house looked the same as those on either side: a respectable New York row house with steps leading up to a fine hardwood front door. No armed thugs stood outside. It wasn't ringed with razorwire. Vinnie was subtle enough to keep a low profile, especially on his home ground. But Erin was completely sure the man had alarms on his doors and windows, a couple of guys with guns inside, and more within reach of an easy phone call. The house looked ordinary, but it was a fortress.

And she couldn't get in. Not without a warrant, and good luck getting one, especially now. Vinnie was called the Oil Man because his slipperiness was legendary. Word on the street was that he could weasel out of any jam, get out of any trouble. He'd done a little time in jail as a youngster; nearly every Mafia associate did, sooner or later. But since then, his skin had been pure Teflon. And no wonder, considering what was happening to all his enemies.

Erin tried not to focus her attention on the house. The key to good low-key surveillance was to appear not to be paying attention. She took Rolf on a slow circuit of the park, letting him sniff whatever he wanted for as long as he wanted. He took the opportunity to lay claim to half the trees in the park. She'd have to remember to fill up his water dish when she got him home.

A couple of adorable little girls ran up giggling, asking if they could pet Rolf. Erin, smiling, agreed. It helped sell the illusion. The K-9 accepted the attention with his usual quiet dignity. The girls patted him briefly, then ran back to their games.

Erin didn't know what she was waiting for. She had no real hope of getting anything on Vinnie; the man was too careful, too canny. But she couldn't make herself leave. She lingered until almost six. Then, with the autumn sun getting low, she finally turned back to her car. It was time to cut her losses and go home. Weariness and hunger had almost overwhelmed her earlier frustration. She opened the back of the Charger. Rolf hopped in. At least he was happy. The outing hadn't been a total waste.

As Erin slid into the driver's seat, she glanced at Vinnie's house once more. The front door was open.

She narrowed her eyes and watched. A pair of serious-looking guys in black topcoats came down the stairs. They stopped at the bottom, hands clasped at their waists, looking around. After a moment, Vinnie himself emerged.

Erin knew him at once by the slicked-back black hair and the expensive clothes. Vincenzo Moreno was every inch the Mafia don, all smooth polish and polite manners over psychopathic violence. He walked calmly, showing no hint of fear. And why should he be afraid? He was the biggest, baddest lion in the urban jungle. Other people were afraid of him; predators knew no fear.

Vinnie must have arranged for his car in advance. A black Maserati sedan that had been idling up the street pulled forward and stopped in front of the house. One of Vinnie's wingmen got the door for him and he climbed in. The thug got in behind him. The other goon watched as the car started to drive away. Then he turned and went back up the stairs, presumably to mind the house while his boss was away.

Erin started her own engine. With no clear plan in mind, she followed the Maserati into the Brooklyn streets.

* * *

The best way to follow a suspect vehicle was to use a revolving tail, where you frequently swapped out cars. That way the target wouldn't notice a particular follower. But that required preparation, organization, and most importantly, a team of officers and cars. Erin had none of these. All she had was an unmarked black Charger with low-profile flashers. She could only keep as far back as she dared and balance the possibilities of losing the other car versus arousing the target's suspicions.

She'd expected Vinnie to head north toward Manhattan, but the Maserati got on South 278 instead. Traffic was standard for New York, which meant it was terrible. Rush hour was more of a four-hour slog from four to eight, and it was impossible to escape the knowledge that New York was a series of islands connected by too few bridges and tunnels.

"You're going to miss your football game," Erin said aloud, watching as the Maserati moved as quickly as it could. If not for using the E-ZPass lane, it would hardly have been moving at all. Erin also had a transponder in her car for the express lane, so they left countless stingy commuters behind. She kept a buffer of three cars between her and the Maserati and hoped for the best.

Erin followed Vinnie across the Verrazzano Narrows Bridge into Staten Island, growing more confused as they went. Where the hell was he going? She didn't know of any Lucarelli business interests there. Had he decided to get out of town for a while?

That didn't seem likely; he'd had no luggage with him, not even an overnight bag. A meeting, then. But with whom? A business associate? A girlfriend or mistress?

She took advantage of a slowdown in traffic to bring up Vinnie's file on her car's computer. He was married, had been for over twenty years, but that didn't mean anything. Plenty of married guys, particularly gangsters, had something going on the side. But she would've expected any girl of Vinnie's to be either in Brooklyn or Little Italy, somewhere close and convenient.

The Maserati kept going on 278, straight across Staten Island. It was almost seven o'clock when they crossed Goethals Bridge into Jersey. The sun was nearly down by the time Vinnie's driver worked his way through the complicated interchange between 278, 95, and the New Jersey Turnpike. As he abruptly turned off onto a smaller street in Elizabeth, Erin dropped back further. The gathering twilight helped a little, but she was nervous. It would be too easy to get made now.

Vinnie's car went around the block, doubled back onto a one-way street, and swung into the parking lot of a Dunkin' Donuts. The safe thing would have been to drive on past, but if Erin did, she'd lose them. She'd be back on 278 with nowhere to park and no good way to loop back around.

So she did the bold thing and turned into the restaurant too. The sky was nearly dark now and it would be very hard to see into her car. She saw the Maserati in a parking space, next to a black Lincoln Town Car. To Erin's astonishment, she saw a police antenna protruding from the roof of the Town Car. It was an unmarked law-enforcement vehicle like hers.

Erin kept going, rolling around the corner of the Dunkin' Donuts and finding a parking place just barely in line of sight of Vinnie's car. She came to a stop and considered her options.

The only thing to do, she decided, was to wait and watch. She turned off the car and adjusted her rear-view mirror. The mirror showed a very close image of a furry, inquisitive face.

"Rolf, *platz!*" she ordered.

The K-9 sank down onto his belly, clearing her field of view.

Erin watched as Vinnie's bodyguard got out, followed by Vinnie himself. The two men crossed the lot and went into the donut shop.

"A guy drives clear to Jersey to buy donuts?" Erin said to Rolf. "No freaking way. He's up to something."

Rolf wagged his tail. He agreed with her.

She didn't have a view inside the restaurant. On this side was only a plain wall and the drive-thru window. Erin gritted her teeth and got out of the car.

"*Bleib*," she told Rolf, who put his snout between his paws and reproached her with his eyes, just like he did every time she left him behind. She tugged down her jacket to make sure her gun and shield were out of sight and walked around the building.

It was a small facility and she didn't dare go in. Vinnie knew her, had just seen her in Evan's company, and would never believe it was a coincidental encounter. But she needed to see what he was doing. She glanced at the Lincoln and Maserati and cursed inwardly. In her interest to see what Vinnie was up to, she'd forgotten about his driver. There the guy was, standing against the side of his car, smoking a cigarette.

Erin was glad of the cigarette. Cancer sticks, in addition to wrecking your lungs, also ruined your night vision. A glowing light right in front of your nose made it very hard to make out details in the dark. She brazened it out, walking right past him. He saw her and pegged her as female, to judge from the way he gave her legs an appreciative once-over, but that was good. It meant he didn't see her as a potential threat.

Vinnie and his goon were at a table with a third man. The new guy was also obviously Italian, from his slicked-back black hair to his expensive-looking leather shoes. He had on a long dark coat and a red scarf. And he was familiar. He was in the middle of saying something to Vinnie, his face earnest. He had his hands out in front of him, making gestures to emphasize his words.

Erin pulled out her phone, thumbed it, and raised it to her ear as if she were talking. What she was really doing was taking pictures through the window. She took three shots on her way around the building. That was all she dared, what with Vinnie's driver checking out her ass.

She made a full circuit of the donut shop and circled back to her Charger, getting in and closing the door. Rolf looked at her curiously, wondering what was happening. She rubbed his head in greeting. Then she took out her phone again and made a call.

"Webb," the Lieutenant said. His voice sounded a little funny, but it was hard to tell from the one word.

"Sorry to bother you, sir," she said. "Are you still at the office?"

"Yes, but—" he began.

"I'm sending you a picture," she said. "It's the Oil Man. He's meeting another guy. You're going to know him."

"Of course. But—"

"We've got problems," she said grimly. "Big ones. But with these pics, maybe we can—"

"Erin!"

That brought her up short. Webb almost never used her first name. "What is it, sir?" she asked.

"Nina Bianchi is dead."

The bottom dropped out of Erin's stomach. "How?" she managed to ask. "When?"

"In the prison showers," Webb said. "She hit her head on a steel knob. Cracked her skull open."

"That wasn't an accident," Erin said. Her pulse was thundering in her ears and she felt that red-hot vise starting to squeeze her brain again.

"Of course not," Webb said. "Not unless she beat her own head against it five or six times."

"Who?" Erin demanded.

"Nobody saw nothing," Webb said, doing a deadpan gangster impression. "It could've been any of a dozen other inmates. The guard didn't see a thing. I guess Bianchi did know something after all."

"But..." Erin said. "But she's been locked up for months! What gives?"

"It could've been a prison fight," Webb said. "It might have nothing to do with us."

"That's bullshit, sir, and you know it."

"It's a possibility," he insisted. "People get killed in prisons sometimes. It's not always some big conspiracy."

"No, this was Vinnie," Erin said in tones of absolute certainty. She put her free hand against her face and rubbed her temples, trying to massage the headache away. "Just one more goddamn loose end for him to snip off. He'll get Carlo, too, somehow. We can't guard him forever. And even if he doesn't, what does it matter? Carlo won't flip on him. And that means we've got nothing. Jack shit."

"You don't know that, O'Reilly," Webb said.

"I do know that!" she exploded. "Every move we make on this asshole, he's one step ahead! He's got cops on his payroll, cops who'll kill for him! He's got everything he wanted and he's getting away clean! And the Feds won't do a damn thing to him, because he's got them in his pocket too! Don't you get it, sir? He wins! He always wins! He left Nina alone until we went to see her, and then, because she just might be a threat, he took care of her."

"That's nonsense," he said. "Vinnie didn't know you were going to see her. I guess he might've heard something from Riker's Island, but it would've been hard to set up a hit that fast. Besides, he wouldn't have even known what you were talking to her about."

"Not unless he heard us talking about it," Erin said. Her mind was whirling. "Sir, where are you? Right now?"

"I'm at my desk, boxing up files, just like I told you I was doing." He sounded confused and a little irritated. "What's that got to do with anything?"

"Sir," she said more quietly. "We talked about my visit to Riker's in the Major Crimes office. Nobody was there but you, Vic, and me. So one of two things happened. Either one of the three of us is Vinnie's mole, or—"

"I see what you're saying," Webb said. "Just a second."

After a few moments, he came back on the line. "I'm outside the station," he said. "You seriously think there's a bug in our office?"

"It would explain some things," she said grimly.

"Okay, I'll contact IAB and ask them to make a sweep," he said.

"No!" Erin exclaimed.

"That's what they're for, O'Reilly."

"We don't know who's compromised."

"You think Internal Affairs might be... Christ," Webb muttered. "You're crazy, O'Reilly. You're jumping at shadows. Look, you're upset, I get that. We'll talk about this tomorrow."

"Don't brush me off," she said angrily.

"I'm not," he replied. "But we'll come at this with clear heads in the morning. Then we can decide if the Oil Man's got the entire NYPD in his pocket or not. Good night."

Before Erin could say any of the half dozen things that were trying to climb out of her mouth all at the same time, Webb hung up.

Chapter 23

Erin sat behind the wheel of her Charger and looked for a way out. There had to be one; there always was. The bad guys always made a mistake, left enough dangling thread to hang them with. Vinnie was smart, but he wasn't some all-powerful super-genius. She'd taken down worse guys than him.

Her knuckles ached. She looked down at her hands and saw she was gripping the steering wheel so tightly her hands were trembling. She hadn't even known she was holding on to it.

She kept thinking of Matthew Madonna's face, hearing his dying words. He'd asked her to take care of the Oil Man. And she thought of Nina Bianchi. The woman had lost everything to the Mafia. They'd taken her son, her liberty, and finally her life.

"And I helped him do it," she muttered. She'd signed Nina's death warrant without even knowing it.

Erin was no stranger to anger. It motivated her, kept her going, gave her the edge she needed in order to deal with murderers and psychopaths. But this anger felt different. It was unreasonable, enormous, consuming. She felt like she was standing outside her own head, looking in, unable to clear her mind.

How could they get Vinnie Moreno? They couldn't tie him to any of the murders, not strongly enough to get him charged, let alone convicted. How had the Feds gotten Al Capone, back in the Thirties?

"Tax evasion," she said. "But that took *years.*" And in the meantime he'd killed hundreds, maybe thousands, of people. And the bad guys had gotten better at laundering money since then. Besides, the Feds were compromised. As long as Freddy Giusto was in charge of the Lucarelli investigation, the Oil Man was safe. Because she'd just followed Vinnie to a secret meeting over the New Jersey border with Special Agent Giusto himself. She had the pictures to prove it.

What were they discussing? How to kill the FBI investigation, obviously. And there wasn't a damn thing she could do about it. They'd already stopped the NYPD. She was outside her jurisdiction as it was. That was probably why they'd picked a donut shop in Jersey for their meeting, just in case any nosy New York cops were still hanging on.

What the hell, she thought. This wasn't her case anymore, if it ever really had been. So what if Vinnie stayed out of prison? She was doing her job, taking down the O'Malleys, and laying off Vinnie made that job a little easier. It would make Evan trust her that tiny bit more, and that might be the margin between success and disaster.

"No."

Rolf looked quizzically at her. He hadn't been doing anything, so he knew he wasn't being scolded, but there was nobody else in the car. He watched her carefully, looking for some signal that would tell him what he ought to do.

"No," she said again. "Not in my house." Vinnie didn't get to do this. He was not going to walk away, not if Sean O'Reilly's daughter had anything to say about it. So she couldn't get him playing by the rules? Every officer stepped over the lines sometimes. You couldn't help it. There were just too many regs in the Patrol Guide, some of which conflicted with each other. The best you could hope for was not to get caught doing anything too terrible.

Her hand came down on the butt of her Glock. Not really thinking about it, she slid the black pistol out of its holster and held it in her lap, turning it over in her hands, feeling its familiar weight. A full magazine was slotted into the grip, seventeen nine-millimeter hollow-points ready and waiting. Just one of those could solve all her problems if she aimed it right. One bullet in the Oil Man's head. That would be one jam he couldn't weasel his way out of.

Ballistics would trace the bullet, though. CSU could match it to her sidearm. She'd have to use a different gun. Maybe get one out of Evidence? No, that could also leave a trail. Better to just retrieve the bullet afterward, dig it out. Then there'd be no proof, no way to trace it back to her. Or she could just make the whole body disappear. Carlyle could help with that. He knew people. He'd do it if she asked.

This might be the best time, while Vinnie was away from New York with only a pair of bodyguards. She might have to take them down, too, but what did that matter? They were gangsters too, hired muscle. She'd taken down Mickey Connor. These men were as bad as he was, pretty much.

The thing to do was to let Vinnie finish his meeting with Agent Giusto and start back toward New York. She'd pull them over with her flashers. It was dark now. They wouldn't recognize her until she was close enough for clean shots. Put two in each of them, starting with the driver and the bodyguard. Vinnie was the real target, but he was less physically dangerous. Retrieve the bullets and shell casings, make sure she left no evidence at the scene, and get back to Manhattan.

Erin was liking the plan more and more. She could see Vinnie's face in her mind's eye, the sudden realization and fear as he knew she'd come for him. Would he try to bargain with her, buy her off? That was a delicious thought. She could cut him off mid-sentence, shut that slick bastard's mouth. And nobody else would ever know. Who'd question just another in the current string of gangland hits? They'd all assume it was payback for Rossi or Crea or Madonna. It'd give Special Agent Giusto fits, his meal ticket getting punched.

Something cold and wet poked Erin's ear. She jumped in her seat and fumbled the Glock, almost dropping it on the floor of the car. Heart thundering, she whirled and got a face full of Rolf's snout. He licked her nose and whined softly.

She stared at the dog, hardly able to make out his dark brown eyes in the Charger's dim interior. What was he thinking? She'd had years of experience learning to read the K-9's features. His ears were tilted back, his mouth hanging slightly open. He was panting. He was anxious, worried. And that meant, of course, that he was worried about her.

As Erin looked at her partner, the creature whose loyalty and love went far beyond anything she'd ever known from a human being, her hands started to shake. Her eyes blurred. She blinked away the moisture, but they filled again.

"Oh my God," she whispered. "Oh my God."

Rolf, not understanding, nosed her again. His tail was tucked low. Its tip swept from side to side in slow, worried wags.

"I have to get out of here," she said. She felt something in her hand and looked down, surprised to find her Glock resting there, heavy and dangerous. She had to fight the sudden urge to hurl it away, as if she'd found herself clutching a rattlesnake. Hand still trembling, she pushed the gun back into its holster. It took three tries before she got the wavering barrel lined up properly and slid it home.

She started the engine and drove out of the parking lot as fast as she dared. She kept just enough situational awareness to check her rear-view and make sure she hadn't been made. She pointed the Charger's nose toward Staten Island and drove into the gathering night, wiping at her eyes as she went.

Erin took the Gulf Avenue exit off 278 and hooked under the highway on Forest Avenue. Graniteville Swamp Park stretched out in front of her, dark and silent. She pulled over to the side of the road and got out of the car, opening the back for Rolf. The K-9 hopped down to join her, looking up at her. His ears had perked up a little and his tail wagged more eagerly. She knelt down beside him and wrapped her arms around him, just holding him. He let her do it, though he wasn't much of a cuddler by nature.

After a few moments, she reached into her pocket and pulled out her burner cell. She saw her hand still hadn't stopped shaking. That pissed her off a little, but it scared her too. She brought up the number filed under "Leo" and called.

"Are you safe?" Phil Stachowski said by way of greeting.

"Yeah," she said.

"Is everything okay?"

"It... I..." she said, fighting back more tears. "I don't know."

"Where are you?" he asked, his voice taking on sudden concern. "I'll come to you, if you can't get local backup."

"No," she said. "You don't have to do that. I'm... Phil, I was going to kill a guy this evening. Three of them."

He took a slow breath. "Okay, Erin," he said quietly. "I'm listening. I'm right here, don't worry. I'm not going anywhere. Take your time."

"This asshole Vinnie Moreno," she said, and she started talking faster and faster as the words spilled out of her. "The son of a bitch who's taken over the Lucarellis. We can't get him, Phil. He wrecked our whole case. He's killing all the witnesses. He just had a woman murdered. In prison, in the showers. And I know he's got a Fed in his pocket, and he got the agent to pull the case out from under us, and there's seven people dead, *seven*, and we've got no case anymore! We've got *nothing*, and I followed him to a goddamn donut shop in New freaking Jersey. He's right there right now, talking to this dirty fucking agent and drinking goddamn fast-food coffee, and I started thinking how the only way to stop him is to put one in his head, and... Shit, Phil, I almost did it. I *wanted* to do it!"

"Erin." His voice was gentle. "Wanting to do something bad isn't a crime."

"You don't get it," she said. "I was making plans! I knew exactly how I was going to do it, how I'd get away with it."

"But you called me instead," he said. "That was the brave choice, the right one. I'm proud of you."

"Proud?" she echoed in disbelief. "My... my dad spent his whole life as a cop. He never would've even thought something like this! How am I supposed to look him in the face now? I don't... I don't deserve this shield."

Her voice broke as she finished the sentence. The tears she'd been holding back were finally too much. They started running down her cheeks. She tasted salt on her lips.

"You're living between worlds, Erin," Phil said. "This happens to a lot of Undercovers. It's understandable to start seeing the street solution as the right one. It's quick and it's easy. But you're not one of them, Erin. And you know that. What changed your mind?"

"Huh? What do you mean?"

"Why didn't you kill that lousy son of a bitch? Doesn't he deserve it?"

"Of course he does! I wanted to watch him die. I still do."

"So why aren't you doing it right now?"

"Rolf."

There was a brief, baffled pause. "Your dog?" Phil asked.

"Yeah. He told me not to."

"I see." She heard neither laughter nor disbelief in his voice. "That's good. You keep him close, Erin. And you listen to him."

"I plan to."

"And you need to forgive yourself for bad thoughts. Everyone has moments of weakness. What matters isn't what we think, it's what we do."

"But I can't *do* anything! I told you that! I know who's behind all this and I can't stop him!"

"Maybe not," he said. "But you can save yourself."

"That's not enough," she said bitterly.

"Sometimes it's the best we can do," he said. "If you're drowning, don't be too hard on yourself if you're only able to keep your own head above water. Because you won't always be drowning. You'll get out of the water. You've had a close call tonight, Erin. Think of it like being in a gunfight where a bullet grazed you. It could've killed you, but it didn't. So you survived, and for right now, that's good enough. That's a win. Tomorrow, or maybe the day after, or next week, or whenever, you'll find your feet on firm ground again. And then you'll be able to look outside yourself. Then you'll get Vinnie Moreno."

Erin snuffled and swiped her sleeve across her nose. "What are you, some kind of Zen Buddhist or what?"

He laughed. "No, I'm Roman Catholic, same as you. I'm just used to looking at the long term. I find it useful, when I'm making tough choices, to think how I'm likely to feel about them the next morning. You might find it helps, too, if you lean on your faith."

"Mob guys go to church too," she said.

"If it helps them be at peace with themselves, why wouldn't it help you?"

"Stop being logical. You're making my head spin."

"Are you still having doubts? About whether you're doing the right thing?"

"I guess not." She sighed. "But what if Vinnie kills someone else? Before we can get him the right way?"

"Then that's on him, not on you." Phil's voice was firmer now. "You're not responsible for him, or for anyone but yourself. You copy?"

"I copy," she said, only a little sulkily. "Thanks, Phil."

"Forget about it," he said, doing such a good gangster impression that both of them laughed. "I was serious. I can meet if you need to talk in person."

"No, I'm good," she said. "I'm going to go home. I'm tired."

"Call me anytime. Any reason."

"Copy that. Goodnight."

"Goodnight, Erin. And good work. You're a fine cop."

She almost believed it.

Chapter 24

"Rough day, darling?"

"You don't know the half of it."

Erin leaned into Carlyle's shoulder as they sat on his couch. They'd gone upstairs on her arrival to the Barley Corner. Erin had ordered a shepherd's pie from the kitchen and a pint of Guinness. She'd brought the food up with her. Rolf had finished his own supper and now lay at Erin's feet, making himself available just in case she didn't want all the pie.

"Are you wanting to talk about it?" Carlyle asked.

"Not really."

She'd had the drive from Staten Island to think about what she wanted to tell him. Mostly she was thinking about Mickey Connor. When Mickey had first become a problem, both Carlyle and Ian had wanted to take care of him their own way—a bullet in the head from Ian, a car bomb from Carlyle—and she'd had to talk them out of it. Then Mickey had gone for them again. The resulting mayhem had nearly torn Erin's family apart and left her, Ian, and Rolf seriously injured. What if she started talking to Carlyle about another mobster who was causing trouble? What would he do?

She had the feeling if she said what she'd been planning, Carlyle would tell her she'd done the right thing not murdering Vinnie. He'd be calm, quiet, and supportive. Then, in a few days' time, Vinnie Moreno would climb into his nice black Maserati and it would explode. Or maybe Vinnie would step out of his front door and a rifle bullet, fired from a respectable distance, would go in his ear and blow out the far side of his skull. And Ian Thompson would have an ironclad alibi, prepared in advance.

In spite of her own conscience and her conversation with Phil, Erin still wasn't completely convinced they'd be wrong to do it, either. The world would be a better place without Vinnie the Oil Man leaving his slimy trail in it.

"The Feds took over the case," she said, deciding that much would do no harm.

"Ah," Carlyle said. "So that's why the sour face. Not to fret, darling. That serves our purposes. I'll pass the word to Evan that the investigation's been stalled, just as he wanted."

"Yeah," Erin said without enthusiasm. "You'd better do that."

"You've put a couple of lads behind bars," he said. "And that's a fine day's work for you, aye?"

"Alphonse Luna is dead," she said. "And Carlo Peralta's hanging by a thread." Then her own word choice struck her with its unintentional dark humor and she laughed bitterly.

"From their wounds?" he asked.

"We found Luna on a noose in his cell."

Carlyle whistled softly. "Suicide?"

"That's what IAB's forensics guy is going to determine," she said. "But yeah, he'll rule it a suicide."

"And that's troubling you? That a couple of lads in the Life came out on the short end of it?"

"No, but it should," she said, straightening up and turning to face him. "Sure, they're assholes, and they murder people, but they are human beings. I can't forget that, no matter what, or I'll turn into one of them."

"Never," he said with a smile, touching her cheek. "I'll not believe it of you."

Seeing the trust and love in his eyes, Erin knew she couldn't tell him. She couldn't break his faith in her. It was his lifeline. If she lost herself, she'd lose him, too. He'd slide back into his personal darkness.

"Thanks," she said.

"And just what is it you're thanking me for?"

"For taking me to church this week. I think I needed it. I'll go next time, too."

He smiled. "Are you thinking on your sins, darling?"

"Maybe. Or maybe I just want to make sure God's in my corner."

"Set your mind at rest. I've told you before, you're on the side of the angels."

"Just tell me something."

"Anything, darling."

She put her arms around him and rested her head against his shoulder. "Tell me this will be over. This whole mess with Evan and Vinnie and all the rest of them."

He kissed the top of her head. "I promise," he said. "It'll end someday. Soon"

* * *

That night was bad. Erin kept turning over, trying to get comfortable. She adjusted the covers. She tried sleeping on her left, then her right, then her back. None of it was any good. She was used to bad dreams, but insomnia was worse.

Carlyle was downstairs, dealing with mobsters. He wouldn't come up to bed until after two, if then. She invited Rolf to climb onto the mattress with her and wrapped her arms around him. That helped a little, but she was still awake when she heard the security door open and Carlyle's familiar footfalls on the stairs at two-thirty.

She didn't feel much like talking, so she rolled over and put her back to the bedroom door. She heard the swish of Rolf's fur as the K-9 hopped down from the bed to make sure everything was on the up-and-up. Then came the sounds of Carlyle's bedtime routine; the rustle of clothing, the running water in the bathroom. Finally, she felt a breath of cool air against her back as he picked up the comforter and then the warmth of his body as he slid in beside her.

They lay there for a minute, maybe two. Erin breathed slowly and deeply, but with each moment she felt wider awake.

"Not sleeping, darling?" Carlyle asked gently.

There was no point denying it. She rolled over to face him. He was a black silhouette in the darkened room.

"Sorry," she said.

"No need for apologies," he said. "But while I'd flatter myself you're waiting up for me, feigning sleep's a curious way to go about greeting a lad. Are you angry with me?"

"No," she said quickly. "It's nothing like that. I'm just sorting through some stuff. Work."

"Anything I can be helping with?"

"No."

"As you wish, darling."

He lay back on his pillow, folding his hands behind his head. The two of them lay that way, both of them thinking.

"Did you ever do something really bad?" she asked suddenly.

His laugh was soft but heartfelt. "Just what sort of a question is that? You do know who's sharing your bed, aye?"

"Yeah," she said. "I know you've done things you knew were against the law. That isn't what I meant. I meant, have you ever done anything that went completely against who you were? But you still did it, because it was the only thing *to* do?"

"I'm not certain I follow."

"I guess I'm asking, what's the worst thing you've ever done? According to you?"

He let out a breath in a long, slow whistle. "You don't ask for much in the wee hours, do you, darling? Are you asking for a full catalogue of my various sins?"

"No. Just the worst one."

His silhouette shifted and she saw the glint of a faint reflection in his eyes. "Erin, why are you asking me this? Have you done something?"

"Please don't ask," she said. "Not right now."

"You're asking me to bare my inner soul, but not to pry into yours? That's scarcely fair, darling."

"I know it's not. But I'm still asking."

"You do know I've a blanket immunity for all my previous transgressions, aye? Signed and witnessed by your District Attorney."

She swatted irritably at his arm. "I'm not trying to trick you into confessing to a crime. I know what your deal says. I've read it."

"I'm still not certain I ought to tell you this."

Erin felt a twinge of apprehension. "How bad is it?"

"Bad enough. And the worst of it is, it's not like you say."

"You're going to need to explain that."

"What I did was a sin," he said softly. "But to this day, I'm not certain it was wrong."

Erin waited. She could be very patient when an interviewee was about to tell her something. She had a theory that many criminals, even most, wanted to tell someone what they'd done.

The whole trick of interrogation was to make yourself into the person they wanted to tell.

"It's almost twenty years since I came to this country," he said. "You know why I left Ireland."

"Your wife was murdered," she said.

"My sweet Rosie," he said. "And our unborn bairn with her. I ran away, aye, like a great bloody coward. It was either that or go mad. I'd a fair idea who'd done for her, and a heart burning with anger, but even then, I knew revenge was a path leading nowhere. Look what it did to Ireland."

"The UVF killed her," she said, naming the Ulster Volunteer Front, one of the many paramilitary terror groups that had plagued Northern Ireland during the Troubles.

"True enough. I knew it then and I'm even surer of it now. The bloody bastards. But I knew Rosie wouldn't be wanting me to kill in her name. She never liked me fighting with the Brigades in the first place, even though her sympathies lay with the Cause. How could I take vengeance on behalf of a lass who'd hate and fear me for doing it?"

Erin put out a hand in the darkness and found his shoulder. "I'm sorry," she said again.

"I was tearing myself apart," he said. "So I got away from bloody Belfast, took ship to the New World like so many millions of my countrymen."

"Like my family," she said. "Mom and Dad were born here, but their people came over near the start of the last century."

"Aye," he said. "And I landed in New York, the city the Irish built. I'd only just arrived. I was getting my bearings, starting to think about finding work. Just a lad still, younger than you are now."

"I'm not that young."

"I needed to think, so I did what any self-respecting Irishman would."

"You went to a bar?"

"I went to a bar. A fine Irish place by the name of MacKenzie's, by LaGuardia Airport, and bought myself the tallest glass of whiskey they had."

"I've heard of worse ideas," she said. "But drinking alone can be risky, especially if you're upset."

"I'd have been a sight safer if I'd been alone," he replied. "But another lad was drinking just down the bar from me. I'd paid him no mind, being busy with my own thoughts. But then I heard him say the name of my hometown and that pricked my ears up."

"Belfast's a big city," she said.

"Just as I told myself," he said. "Still, I thought it a fine thing to hear, seeing as how I'd just come thousands of miles and was already feeling a mite homesick. I started listening. This lad was full of himself and he'd already had a few too many. He was talking too loudly, particularly given the subject matter."

Erin listened, her own inner conflict momentarily forgotten. "What was he saying?" she asked.

"He was just in from Ireland himself," Carlyle said. "And he made no secret of the fact he was lying low in America for a while, letting the heat die down."

"Was he with the IRA too?"

"Farthest thing from it," he said grimly. "He was UVF. A fellow by the name of Doyle. Art Doyle. I'd heard of him, you ken, during the Troubles. Nasty piece of work."

The name sounded oddly familiar to Erin, though she couldn't immediately place it. She said nothing.

"I'd just decided to take myself elsewhere," Carlyle continued. "I was in no mood to be listening to that gobshite's prattling. But then he said something about knocking over a flat with some dozy Catholic floozy cooking her dinner. Those were his words. I remember them like it was yesterday. And I remember him saying something about the look of surprise on her face. Then he laughed and made a motion with his hands, like he was firing a machine gun."

Carlyle sighed heavily. "It was the laughter that did for me," he said. "I don't rightly recall what happened after. It was like the sort of dream you have when you're in hospital running a dangerous temperature. I've flashes of recollection. I remember standing, and picking up my stool. And I remember after, in the loo, washing blood off my hands and picking out wood slivers. It splintered in my hands, I think."

"Jesus Christ," Erin said. "That was you."

"What was?" Carlyle asked, confused. "Erin, I don't remember doing it, exactly, but I know just what I did. And the coppers never found the lad who'd done it, but that was well before your time on the Force. I can't imagine it was the sort of incident that finds its way into Department legend."

"No," she agreed. "But it's a crazy coincidence. I knew that guy's name was familiar! I heard about him from an old friend of my dad's. He was the responding officer. The bartender covered for you. So did everyone else in the place."

"That doesn't surprise me," Carlyle said dryly. "The lad was in Evan O'Malley's pocket. So were half the customers. Evan himself was there. He saw the whole bloody thing. Then he came to see me later that evening. He'd had one of his lads tail me to my hotel, naturally, so he knew where to find me. He said I was just the sort of lad he was looking for."

"He recruited you?"

"Of course he did. In five minutes' time I'd shown I was proper gangster material and I'd given him a firm hold over me. If I didn't play ball with him, he'd tip off the coppers and I'd be done for."

"That son of a bitch." Erin said it quietly, almost wonderingly.

"Erin," Carlyle said. "I've just told you I murdered a lad, beat him to death with a bloody barstool, hit him so hard it drove the splinters into my hands, and you're angry at someone else?"

"Art Doyle killed your wife," she said.

"He was one of them, aye. And it was a strange act of God putting me in the same damned bar with him on the opposite side of the Atlantic. But that's the sort of action your lads normally frown on. If your DA hadn't signed that slip of paper, you'd be doing your duty hauling me down to your station in irons this very night."

"It was two decades ago," she said weakly.

"No statute of limitations on murder, darling. I needn't tell you that."

"God damn it, why are you telling me this?"

"You asked me to."

"Yeah, but..." Erin found she had no idea what to say next. "Are... are you telling me that's the worst thing you've done?"

"Aye. He's the only lad I know for certain I've killed. I built bombs for the IRA, sure enough, and they killed men, but others made use of them. As well blame a gunsmith when some lad guns another down in the street. And I don't regret Doyle's departure, but I do fear for my own soul. Murder's a mortal sin, darling."

"Is that why you go to church every Sunday?"

"It's one reason, aye. But I've plenty to atone for, and more than one soul I'm praying for."

"Rosie?"

"And the child I never knew. And Siobhan Finneran, and her da, and so many others. Every death is a weight on my soul, Erin, whether I killed them or no. How do you feel over the lads you've put down?"

"It depends," she said. "I don't lose too much sleep over Mickey. Or that Russian slave-trader at the airport. Those were necessary. But I wish..."

"What?"

"I wish they hadn't been. I wish they hadn't made me do it."

"Erin?"

"Yeah?"

"Don't ever kill a lad in revenge. It's not worth it. When I'd done with Doyle, and he was lying on the floor, Rosie was just as dead as before and my heart just as broken as that bastard's bloody head. So if there's something you're contemplating... don't."

"Don't worry about me," she said.

"Truly, Erin," he said. "You're not angry with me? I'm a murderer."

"We've both killed," she said.

"It was legal for you."

"And you've got your deal with the DA," she retorted, almost angrily. "One of the things I've learned from you is that the world isn't black and white."

"Did you truly think that, once on a time?"

"Yeah," she said ruefully. "I did. So thank you."

"For what?"

"For trusting me. And helping me learn. And loving me."

"Erin, you needn't thank me for loving you. I've no choice at all in the matter."

"You're sweet." She kissed him. "Now we should both get some sleep."

But sleep still didn't come easy for Erin. She wasn't mad at Carlyle, and that by itself was worrying. What kind of woman could shrug off her lover being a murderer? Why could she forgive him, but not Vinnie? Was it just because she was close to him? And what did that say about her?

She opened her eyes. It was amazing how much you could see once you got accustomed to the dark. There was an old saying that if you were walking at night, a blind man was your best guide. Maybe Carlyle, who'd been living in the dark for so many years, could help her find her way until the sun came up.

She was still thinking about that when she finally drifted into an uneasy sleep.

Chapter 25

The Major Crimes office had a depressing look to it. Webb had brought in several cardboard file boxes and had packed up all the information from the Lucarelli murders. The whiteboard was clean and empty. The room reminded Erin of a store that had gone out of business. Now all that was left was for the staff to clean out their desks and turn off the lights on their way out.

Webb sat at his computer, drumming his fingers on his desk and clearly wishing he had a smoke. Even Rolf was subdued. The Shepherd stood up, walked in a tight circle, and curled up again, tucking his snout under his tail with a heavy sigh.

"What've we got going on, sir?" Erin asked.

"Nothing," Webb said. "Carlo Peralta's going to be in the hospital for a couple of weeks yet, but even if we still had the case, we couldn't talk to him. He's lawyered up."

"The Lucarellis will kill him if a secondary infection doesn't get him first," she predicted gloomily.

"Maybe," Webb said. "But if he keeps his mouth shut, who knows? He may get to enjoy the next twenty to life on an all-expenses-paid staycation, courtesy of the great state of New

York. A guy from the FBI should be coming to pick up this junk around ten. Where's Neshenko?"

Erin spread her hands. "Got me, sir. Last I saw of him was at the Five yesterday afternoon."

At that moment, like an answer to a drunkard's prayers, Vic Neshenko stumbled in. He was bleary-eyed and visibly weaving as he made his way unsteadily to his chair.

"Are you hung over, Neshenko?" Webb asked.

"Huh?" Vic asked. He managed to locate his chair and plopped down.

"Hung over," Webb repeated. "As in, suffering a headache as an aftereffect of excessive alcohol consumption?"

"Maybe."

Webb shook his head. "It's a good thing we don't have an active investigation right now. Sober up."

"I'm plenty sober," he said. "That's the problem. You can't have a hangover while you're still drunk."

"He's got a point, sir," Erin said.

"Both of you look like crap," Webb said in disgust. "I can't believe the city's paying your salaries. You know what? Screw it. Take a day. Take a sick day. You could use it, from what I'm seeing. It's not like you'll be missing much."

"I'm fine, sir," Erin said.

Webb gave her a hard, searching look. He shook his head ever so slightly. Erin knew her eyes were bloodshot, dark smudges under them. She wasn't young enough to shake off a mostly sleepless night anymore. She could've forced herself to bear down and do her job if there was anything to be done. But Webb was right; there wasn't anything to do right now. Someone would get murdered, sooner or later. It was inevitable. Then they'd go back to work. But here and now, the Eightball's Major Crimes office was the only thing that was dead.

"I'll give Rolf a training day," she suggested. "The fresh air will do us both some good."

"That's a fine idea," Webb said. "Neshenko? Get out of here."

"Is that an order, sir?" Vic asked.

"Yes."

"I don't think you can order a guy to take a sick day," Vic said.

"I think you'll find I can," Webb said. "I could always shoot you in the leg if you'd prefer. Then I'd have something to do for the rest of the day, filling out use-of-force forms, and you'd be able to take temporary disability."

* * *

"Somebody's in a bad mood this morning," Vic said to Erin as they walked downstairs, Rolf at Erin's hip.

"He didn't like the Feebies swiping our case," Erin said. "Are you okay?"

"Me? Sure."

"How'd things go? With Piekarski?"

Vic chewed the inside of his cheek for a moment. "I think it's gonna be okay," he said at last.

"How do you feel about it?"

"I dunno. This wasn't something we did on purpose, y'know? We were taking precautions."

Erin made a face. "I don't think I need quite that much information, Vic."

"She thought it was gonna spook me, I guess. And she got scared. But I don't spook easy."

"I've noticed. So what are you going to do?"

"I'm gonna do my job," he said. "But geez, the thought of a little Vic running around..."

"Yeah, that scares all of us," she said. "But it could be worse."

"How?"

"It could be a girl. Could be a little Piekarski."

"Shit," Vic said. "I hadn't thought of that."

"Relax," she said, patting him on the shoulder. "You'll do fine."

"It's not me I'm worried about," he said. "It's this crazy damn world. You see the heinous shit we deal with all day long. And it's only gonna get worse."

"No wonder you got drunk last night."

"Seemed like a good idea at the time. What's your excuse?"

"I wasn't drunk."

They went into the parking garage. Vic angled toward his Taurus.

"It feels weird," he said. "I know I screwed up, but maybe it'll come out fine. Maybe it's even a good thing. Guess I'll find out. I got a couple months, at least."

"I guess so. Catch you on the flip-side." Erin got back into her Charger with a confused but obedient K-9. She drove out of the garage and aimed toward Central Park. She'd do some search drills with Rolf, have him find some explosives. She had scent packets with her to hide under the bushes. It was good for the dog to brush up on his training whenever possible.

Erin wished she had something more important to work on, for her own peace of mind. She couldn't stop thinking about sitting in that dark car, a gun in her lap, plotting murder. She'd wanted to kill people before, but this had been different. What was scary was how easy it had been to fall into that mindset. She had no guarantee it wouldn't happen again. Would Rolf be able to jolt her back to herself? What if he wasn't there? What if there was no time for second thoughts? Would she have killed Vinnie if he'd been standing right in front of her?

She had no answers. The Manhattan streets rolled by under her wheels. She passed people all around; civilians, mostly, but a few cops and doubtless some perps among them. She knew, in spite of the FBI taking over the case, that she wasn't done with the Lucarellis. They'd have a reckoning, and before that happened, she needed to get her head right. Otherwise she'd be risking more than her life. She'd be putting her soul on the line.

She was on 8th Avenue, a few blocks south of the park, when she saw the church on 49th Street. It was a one-way and she was on the wrong end of the block, but on impulse, she circled around and came back to it. She parked in the police spot near the corner and got out.

"*Bleib*," she told Rolf. It was a cool morning; he'd be fine waiting in the car for a little while. She walked up to the church and studied the façade. It was St. Malachy's. She'd passed it before but had never gone in.

Erin climbed the concrete steps and opened the door. She went into the sanctuary, pausing to dip her fingers in the font and cross herself. Childhood habits died hard. Still not entirely sure why she was there, she walked down the aisle toward the altar. The daily mass had ended and the parishioners had left. The room was empty except for the priest, a white-haired man who was wiping one of the pews with a cloth. He glanced up and saw her.

"Good morning," he said. "How can I help you?"

"I... I don't know," she said. "You don't know me, Father."

"That's all right," he said. "God knows you. Are you a Christian, my child?"

"Raised Catholic," she said.

"I'm afraid we've already said Mass," he said. "It's at eight on weekdays. But if you'd like to pray, you're more than welcome here."

Erin nodded. The priest started to turn back to his chores, but something in her look caught his attention.

"Is there something you need to talk about, my child?" he asked.

The weight of all her secrets pressed down on Erin. She knew it was dangerous to tell anyone, particularly a stranger, but she'd been brought up in the Church. She knew how seriously the clergy took their jobs. And she was worried she might fall completely apart.

"Can we?" she asked, pointing to the confessional booth.

"Of course," he said, understanding immediately. He picked up his stole and draped it around his shoulders, indicating that he'd gone on duty. He went through one of the little doors into the booth. Erin straightened her back and opened the other door.

The confessional booth was small, smelling of old wood and leather. She sat down, remembering doing the same thing as a little girl, back when the worst sins she'd committed were sneaking candy between meals or punching a boy at recess.

"Whatever I say here, you can't repeat," she said. She knew that already, but she needed to say it anyway.

"We are under the seal of the confessional," he said. "What you say here is between you and God. I'm just an intermediary."

There were exceptions, she knew. If she told the priest she was about to rob a bank, for instance, he'd be obligated to inform the cops. But that wasn't the problem. She didn't know if this would help. Phil Stachowski and Carlyle both seemed to think it might, and right now she trusted them at least as much as she trusted herself. When things got too tough on the street, you called for backup. There was no shame in that.

Erin took a deep breath.

"Bless me, Father, for I have sinned..."

Here's a sneak peek from Book 17: Blackout

Coming 9/26/22

There was pain, a heavy throbbing behind closed eyelids. With every beat of her pulse, more pain swelled in her head. That was all; no thoughts, no sense of time or space.

She lay where she was, reluctant to move. There was a dull sense, an impression that movement might make the pain worse. So she stayed still. But gradually, in increments, she started to wake up. The head was the worst pain, but her shoulder hurt, too. The sensation was almost like a burn. The whole shoulder felt flushed and raw, rubbing against her blouse.

She became aware of a strange buzzing sensation at her hip. It was insistent, annoying. And something cold and wet was rubbing against her hand. The cold damp was what brought her back to full consciousness. She curled her hand around the furry head that belonged to the wet nose. She felt a pair of very large, perky ears.

"Okay," she muttered. Her tongue felt swollen and the word came out mumbled. That buzzing was still going at her hip. She opened her eyes.

She stared into a pair of intense brown eyes only a few inches from her own. A rhythmic panting was audible. Then her vision was momentarily blocked by a pink, slobbery tongue that swept up across her face.

The thing at her hip kept buzzing. She muttered an oath and fumbled it out of her hip pocket. Swiping her thumb across the screen, she brought the phone up to her ear.

"O'Reilly," she said thickly.

"Where the hell are you?" a voice demanded. It was at least thirty decibels too loud.

Erin O'Reilly blinked and tried to focus her eyes on her surroundings. Where was she? She couldn't remember getting here. The events of the last few hours were a blank.

"I don't know," she said after a moment.

There was a brief pause. "Okay, that's my mistake," said the voice on the phone. "I didn't ask the right question. Fact is, I don't actually care where you are. What I want to know, well, what the Lieutenant wants to know, is why you're not where you're supposed to be. Wanna know how I know you're not there? Because I'm there and you're not."

"Vic?" she guessed.

"You okay, Erin?" Vic Neshenko asked. "You sound kinda funny."

"Yeah. I'm fine. I think."

"Color me unconvinced. Do a vitals check for me. I already know you're breathing, or you wouldn't be talking. You got a pulse?"

Erin forced herself to a sitting position. Her headache spiked. She put a hand to her forehead and felt the blood rushing under her fingertips. "Yeah," she said. "Unfortunately."

"Okay. That means you're alive. And that means you need to, and I quote, 'Get your ass behind your desk before I plant my boot up it.' That's Lieutenant Webb's boot, and your ass he'll be planting it up. If you're confused."

"Thanks for clearing that up, Vic." Erin felt another nudge at her elbow and looked down at Rolf, her German Shepherd K-9. The dog was obviously worried about her.

"Care to give me an ETA I can give Webb?" Vic asked.

"Just a sec." Erin glanced around. She was sitting up on a sofa, a blanket wrapped around her legs. The couch looked vaguely familiar, but the living room wasn't one she knew well. Maybe she'd been there before, but she couldn't be sure. Where on Earth was she? And why couldn't she remember? She saw a glass coffee table in front of her. On it lay a gold detective's shield with the numbers 4640 emblazoned on it. Next to the shield rested a pair of holstered handguns; a Glock automatic and a snub-nosed revolver. She also saw a couple of candles, burned down to stubs. A faint aroma of perfume lingered in the air.

"Erin?" Vic had sounded amused. Now he sounded a little worried. "You sure you're okay?"

"I think so," she said. "I just need to figure out what happened." Her shoulder really felt funny. She rubbed it gingerly.

"Yeah, it was kind of a crazy night for all of us," he said. "I was handling a big pileup on Fifth Avenue half the night. You run into any serious trouble?"

"That's a really good question." There was a sudden silence, and in that silence she realized there'd been a background noise that had been going on since she'd woken up. Running water. It had just stopped.

Erin turned her head toward the hallway and saw a door standing ajar. Little curls of steam were wafting out around it.

"I'll get back to you, Vic," she said quietly. "Somebody's here."

"Erin? What do you mean?" Vic's worry had turned to alarm. "You need backup?"

"Call you back," she said and hung up. She got off the couch, letting the blanket fall to the floor. She'd slept in her clothes, apparently. Her bare feet sank into deep, comfortable carpet. She reached down and picked up her Glock, sliding it out of its holster. Out of habit and training, she pulled back the slide and checked the chamber. It was loaded, a nine-millimeter hollow-point poised and ready to fire.

"*Fuss*," she murmured, giving Rolf his "heel" command in his native German. Then she advanced across the living room, pistol held in a two-handed grip. The dog stayed at her hip, watching her. He'd picked up on the tension in her voice. His hackles had risen. Though his tail was wagging, it was the furthest thing from friendliness. It was the anticipation of violence.

Erin reached the door. She heard a male voice, a pleasant tenor, somewhat familiar, softly singing. It had a distinctive Irish lilt.

"In a neat little town they call Belfast,
Apprentice to trade I was bound,
And many an hour's sweet happiness
I spent in that neat little town.
'Til a great misfortune came o'er me,
And caused me to stray from the land,
Far away from my friends and relations
To follow the black velvet band."

She put out a foot and shoved the door open, leveling her Glock. "NYPD," she said. "Hands in the air!"

The bathroom air was hot and heavy with clouds of steam. Through the mist, Erin saw a slender man, pale-skinned and red-headed, a spray of freckles across his shoulders. On one shoulder was an intricate Celtic tattoo. He was staring at her with very bright green eyes that showed no fear at all, just a mixture of surprise and mischief. His hands were down at his waist, holding a bath towel. Not counting the towel, he was completely naked.

"And a good morning to you too, love," he said, breaking off his song. "I hope the gun in your hand means you're pleased to see me. I'd love to do as you ask, but if I put my hands up, you'll be getting quite the eyeful."

Erin's aching head spun. "Corky?" she exclaimed. "What in God's name are you doing?"

James Corcoran gave Erin a megawatt smile. "I'm taking a shower, love. In the washroom, which is the customary place, so I'm told."

"Not that!" she snapped, trying to ignore the man's nudity. "I mean, what are you doing here?"

He blinked. "This is my flat, love. I live here."

"Oh. What am I doing here?"

"Would you mind pointing your revolver elsewhere?" he said, tying the towel around his waist. "You can clearly see I'm unarmed. Though if you'd care to pat me down...?"

"No, thanks." She lowered the Glock. "So, I'm at your apartment. No wonder it looked familiar."

"I don't recall bringing you home with me before," Corky said. "Sadly, our affair never got so far. Besides, I'd have taken you to my other flat in that case."

"I came here last year," she reminded him. "When Carlyle was hiding out from that German hitman."

"Oh, of course! I'd forgotten."

Now Erin knew where she was. But she still didn't know why. "Look, Corky," she said. "I have to go. I guess I overslept and I'm late for work. Just tell me what happened last night and I'll get out of your hair."

"You truly don't know, love? Some lads might find that a mite insulting. I'd hoped I was more memorable than that."

Erin fought down a jolt of pure horror. "You don't mean... we didn't..."

Corky held his poker face as long as he could, but it dissolved into laughter. "Nay, love. Your virtue's as intact as it was before crossing my threshold, and there's not many lasses can say that. But I had to see the look on your face. You should've seen yourself. Eyes like great saucer plates, they were."

Annoyance and relief rushed through her in equal parts. "I'm in a hurry," she said.

"Very well." He took a bathrobe off its hook and swept it around his shoulders. "We were at the Corner, having a few drinks."

"We?" she prompted.

"You, myself, and a few of the lads."

"Carlyle?"

He gave her an odd look. "Nay, love. He's in Chicago with Kyle Finnegan, seeing to business. Don't you recall?"

"Oh. Right." Now that he said it, Erin did remember. Her boyfriend had gone out of town for a few days.

"I was looking after you," Corky went on. "And you did want looking after. I don't know what got into you, but you were drinking the lads right under the table. I don't mind telling you, I was impressed. Not many can match me shot for shot. And then there was the tattoo."

"The *what?*"

He blinked. "Are you feeling quite all right, love? The whole thing was your idea. Though I'll admit you'd a fair few drinks in you by then. I know a lad down the way, a right wizard with the ink, and I'm not one to deny a lass, so I took you there. You were under the needle quite some time."

Erin touched her shoulder again. "Dear Lord," she muttered. "What was the design?"

"You went for a fine, traditional pattern," he said. "Rather like my own, come to that. A Celtic knot, about the size of a golf ball."

"It feels bigger," she said. Her shoulder felt inflamed.

"The lad did fine work," Corky said. "Though I'll admit he was painting on a grand canvas to begin with. It's fortunate he was nearly done when the lights went out."

"I passed out?"

He shook his head. "I'm not being metaphorical, love. The power went down. Not just in the Corner, either. All over Manhattan. Worst blackout I've seen."

"So how did we end up here?"

He grinned. "I took you back to your flat first. Carlyle's got a lovely security system. State of the bloody art. Only one wee problem with it. His door's electrically locked, and there's no sense in it opening if the power goes down. In that case, if a lad wanted to break in, all he'd have to do would be cut the cable. So that fine steel door to his flat won't open for love nor money once the current stops flowing."

Erin put a hand to her face. "I couldn't get my door open," she sighed.

"We waited a wee spell, to see if the power came back," he said. "But after a few minutes, some of the lads downstairs started getting a mite restless. And I did promise Cars you'd be in good hands while he was away, so I thought the best thing was to bring you back here till it all blew over."

"Through the middle of a New York blackout? Was that safe?"

"Of course not," he said cheerfully. "It's a pity you don't remember the adventures we had on the darkened streets. You thought you'd best be going in to work, as your lads would be needing all hands on deck, but I could tell you were sailing a few sheets to the wind, so I talked you out of it."

"Thanks," she said, meaning it. Showing up for work blind drunk wouldn't have done anyone any good.

"In the end, we got here," he said. "I'll have to take my car into the shop to take care of that wee fender-bender, and it's lucky my head was harder than that lad's outside, but no real harm done. I lit some candles, fetched a bottle from my private supply, and we shared it between us. Then your personal lights went out. I'd have given you the bed and slept on the couch myself, but you were already laid out on it and... well, love, there's no way to put this delicately. My back's not what it was, so I thought it best to leave you here."

"Are you making a crack about my weight?" Erin bristled. She was five-foot-six and kept herself in excellent shape. Corky wasn't particularly large or muscular, however, so he might have a point. Dead-weight human bodies were surprisingly hard to shift.

He held up his hands. "Cars would have my head if he heard I was taking liberties with his lass," he said. "Better all 'round not to be manhandling you."

"And that was all that happened?" she pressed, giving him a hard stare.

"What is it you're wanting me to say? You woke up fully clothed, in a separate room from me. And I'm not keen on your implication if you're suggesting I'd take advantage of an unconscious lass. I've never had a girl who wasn't ready and willing."

"I'll bet," she muttered. "Thanks, I guess. But it sounds like we took your car here."

"You were in no condition to drive."

"Why was I drinking so much?" she asked.

He shrugged. "That's between you, your liver, and the Almighty, love. If you don't recall, how can you expect it of me? I'll give you a lift back to the Corner."

"Didn't you just say your car needed to go into the shop?"

"Aye, but it's mostly cosmetic. We only caught a wee piece of that other scunner going through the intersection. The traffic lights went out, too, you ken, so it was a mite exciting."

Erin raised an eyebrow, waiting for details that didn't come. After a beat, she said, "I'll call a cab."

Ready for more?

Join Steven Henry's author email list
for the latest on new releases, upcoming books and
series, behind-the-scenes details, events, and more.

Be the first to know about new releases in the Erin
O'Reilly Mysteries by signing up at
tinyurl.com/StevenHenryEmail

Now keep reading to enjoy

Saline Solution

An Ian Thompson Story

Saline Solution

An Ian Thompson Story

Steven Henry

Clickworks Press • Baltimore, MD

First publication: Clickworks Press, 2022
Release: CWP-EORIT2-INT-P.IS-1.0

Sign up for updates, deals, and exclusive sneak peeks at clickworkspress.com/join.

Saline Solution

A mixture of water and sodium chloride (table salt). Used in medicine to clean wounds and can be injected into a vein to treat dehydration.

Chapter 1

"You're late, Jordan."

"None of your crap today, Larry. I mean it." Cassie paused just long enough on her way across the lobby to throw a glare at the guy behind the counter.

Larry grinned. "Let me guess. Hot date? Slept over, had to run home to shower and change?"

"I wish." She talked fast, over her shoulder, while she swiped her ID card and pulled open the clinic's inner door. "Ben was supposed to be out the door at seven-thirty to get to daycare. Then he spilled orange juice all down his front, broke the glass, and cut his foot."

"Oh, no!" Larry's face fell almost comically. "Poor little guy. Is he okay?"

"Don't worry, we won't be seeing him here," she said, coming over to stand next to him and look at the computer screen. "A couple Band-Aids fixed him right up. But between that and changing his clothes, we lost some time, and now here I am. So yes, I'm late. And no, I'm not taking any shit from you this morning."

He held up his hands. "Sorry, Jordan. Seriously. I don't know how you single moms do it. You got your job, your boy, and you have to take care of yourself, too. Beats me how you keep it together."

"You'd be surprised what you can do when you don't have a choice," Cassie said. "What's my first appointment?"

Larry called up the schedule. "He's already here. Showed up right on time. We got a new one for you. First rehab appointment, recovering from multiple GSW."

"We get his DoD file?" The New York Harbor Healthcare System was part of the Veterans Administration, so they got the service records of their patients as a matter of course. Within the military's bureaucracy, however, things had a tendency to get delayed or even lost.

"Yeah. Have a look."

Cassie quickly scanned the record. She knew her patient was waiting, but she also knew it was best to go into a first meeting knowing what sort of person, and injury, to expect. Veterans were often sensitive about their wounds. Better not to stare or ask stupid questions.

Larry was reading along with her. He whistled. "Dang. This guy's a genuine, grade-A hero."

"They're all heroes, Larry," she said absently.

"No, I mean it. Silver Star, Purple Heart, Scout Sniper training... holy crap."

"You're working for the US military," she said. "You really need to pick up some better swear words. This is weird."

"What?"

"According to his service record, he was discharged four years ago. Combination medical/psychological. Just a few weeks before the end of his tour."

"That's not so strange," Larry said. "Lots of guys get hit right before they rotate home. It's ironic, but not unusual."

"That's not what irony means," she said.

"Blame Alanis Morrissette. She's the one who taught me the word with that damn song."

"I mean, what's weird is, he was discharged four years back. Why are we only seeing him now?"

"Maybe his wounds reopened," Larry suggested. "There was this one guy, Joshua Chamberlain, who died of wounds he got in the Civil War. In *1914*. You believe that? Fifty years after he got hit."

"I guess stranger things have happened," Cassie said. "Where's my guy now?"

"Room One."

* * *

Cassie was used to dealing with tough, broken young men. That was her job. She wasn't always sure it was wise, but she couldn't stay away from the rehab clinic. After what had happened to her family, a world full of damaged people seemed entirely appropriate to her. This patient wasn't too badly torn up, according to his medical records. A bullet could do a hell of a lot of damage, but she'd seen men with limbs blown completely off, bodies torn practically apart. His charts from Bellevue didn't indicate any spinal damage, there was no cerebral trauma, and he had the use of his arms and legs. It was a good starting place, all things considered.

She still paused just outside the room and checked herself. A rehab nurse couldn't bring her own trauma or drama with her. She had to leave that shit at the door. She took several deep, calming breaths, centering herself. Then she opened the door.

"Sergeant Thompson?" she said, keeping her tone brisk but pleasant. No fake bubbly cheerfulness. A wounded man might resent it.

She saw a guy in his mid-twenties, a little old compared to most of the combat casualties she handled. He might have been out of the service for a few years, but he'd kept the military-style buzz cut. He was wearing a dark gray T-shirt, khaki cargo shorts, and a pair of tough-looking, comfortable shoes. An intricate tattoo ran all the way down his left arm to his wrist, but the look was spoiled by a bandage around the upper arm. His neck had another bandage and there was a cast on his right thigh. A pair of crutches leaned against the examining couch beside him.

He looked at her, straight into her eyes, and she was aware of an intense stillness that didn't quite cover a nervous energy. His hands were perfectly still, but she knew, with a nurse's eye, that he was jumping all over the place on the inside.

"Thompson, Ian," he said. "Reporting, ma'am."

"I'm Cassie Jordan," she said. "I'm going to be working with you. What would you like me to call you, Sergeant?"

"Ian's fine. Haven't worn stripes for a while."

"Okay. You can call me Cassie, or Nurse Jordan, whichever you'd prefer."

"I know the drill, ma'am. Not my first time."

"I see that. Looks like you caught a couple in Afghanistan a few years back."

"Yes, ma'am." His politeness was almost a verbal tic.

"And a couple more just recently?"

"Affirmative, ma'am. Five rounds, small caliber. Nine-millimeter."

"How'd you manage that?"

His expression didn't change. "Saw a crime happening, got in the way. Local law didn't have good intel, figured I was one of the bad guys."

"You got shot by cops?"

"Yes, ma'am. Wasn't their fault. Got tunnel vision, lost my situational awareness. Didn't hear them tell me to give up."

"You don't seem like a guy who gives up easy," she said, smiling at him. She'd learned her smile had a good effect on the men she treated, though it often led to misunderstandings and abortive flirtations. Being a young, good-looking nurse was a two-edged weapon when dealing with hormone-addled young men, many of whom hadn't seen an American woman in civilian clothes for months. That was why she still wore her wedding ring when she was working. One of the reasons.

"Don't know if I am," Ian said. "Never tried it. What do you need from me here, ma'am?"

Not even a flicker of interest, no response to her smile. Cassie could think of plenty of reasons for that. She internally filed the information for her initial diagnosis. The more closed-off a patient was, the harder she'd have to work to break through to him so they could get down to the business of healing.

"Let's start with a basic physical exam," she said. "What's your current pain level? On a scale of one to ten, one being totally fine, ten being the worst pain you've ever had."

He considered. "Three."

"How long ago did you get hit?"

"Twelve days, ma'am. Just got released from the hospital yesterday."

"According to your chart, you were wounded in the left arm, right leg, neck, and twice in the torso. Is that right?"

"Yes, ma'am."

"I'll need to take your shirt off. Would you like me to help with that?" This was another opportunity for him to make some snappy remark or to make a pass at her, but he let it go by.

"I can do it," he said, peeling off the garment to reveal a lean, well-muscled chest. Some guys let themselves go once they were out of the military. They were used to a high-calorie diet, but without someone kicking their ass and making them do PT, they got thick around the middle. Not this man. The only physical problem he seemed to have was the extra holes the NYPD had put in him.

"What was the crime you tried to stop?" she asked as she examined the sites of his various wounds.

"Kidnapping, ma'am. Some bad guys grabbed a lady out of her house."

"You took on a gang of kidnappers?"

"Seemed like the right thing to do."

She probed around the wounds. Ian didn't flinch, though she knew he had to feel some of it. He was clearly no stranger to pain. There was an old saying that went, "Every Marine always knows he's the toughest guy in the room." Her husband had loved quoting that.

"Sucks that you were just trying to help and the cops shot you," she said.

He shrugged ever so slightly. "They were doing their job. Not the first time I've been shot at by guys who weren't so bad, personally."

"I guess that's true. Did your doc talk to you about this gut shot?"

"Yes, ma'am. Won't be a problem long-term. Same with the one in the chest. Neck shot was nothing, just grazed me."

"What about the arm and leg?"

"Arm's fine, missed the bone and went through the meat. Leg's worse. Cracked the femur and the doc says there might be some nerve damage."

"Anything feel funny lower down?"

"Foot goes numb sometimes."

"Okay, Ian. Looks like the doc who patched you up did a pretty good job. No plates or screws?"

"No, ma'am. All original equipment."

She caught the flicker of dry humor, though he didn't crack even a hint of a smile. That was a good sign. It was the depressed ones you had to watch out for.

"I think we should be able to get you fixed up just fine," she said. "Assuming you follow instructions and don't try any stupid macho bullshit."

"Wouldn't think of it, ma'am."

Chapter 2

Ian was a good patient. He listened, didn't argue, and did what she told him. He was unfailingly polite. To the average observer, he was a pleasant, calm, well-adjusted young man.

Cassie didn't believe it for a second. She'd treated dozens of veterans and she was used to seeing through them. Post-traumatic stress manifested in all kinds of ways. Some guys went to pieces. They got the shakes, cried, screamed. She'd seen a man try to dig a hole in a tile floor with his fingernails, ripping one of them clean off. Some lost the ability to speak, or to form complex words. Some started wetting the bed, giving them yet another reason to feel ashamed of themselves.

Then there were the ones who used chemicals to cope. Alcohol was the most common, but Cassie had seen all sorts of addicts. Narcotics, barbiturates, cocaine, heroin, meth. You name it, someone had tried it. And those weren't the only addictions. Some guys chased the adrenaline high they remembered from combat and became thrill-seekers: driving too fast, skydiving, picking fights.

But there were other, less obvious indicators. Some vets tried to deal with their demons by locking themselves down tight, shutting down their emotions. It was a kind of numbing behavior, the same as alcohol, but without chemical assistance.

Combat, Cassie had learned, was an incredibly intense experience. She'd heard men compare it to sex. The first time she'd heard that, she'd thought the guy was crazy. Now she just figured she hadn't felt it herself, so what did she know? She was a combat virgin. The young men who passed through her clinic weren't crazy. They were having a normal, reasonable response to the abnormal conditions of battle.

She'd learned to look at the eyes. Those were the only part of the body, in her experience, that didn't lie. You had to look below the surface, seek out whatever was hiding at the back.

Some men couldn't take Cassie's stare. Ian looked straight back, unflinching. What she saw was a pain that went deeper than wounds. The understated description a soldier might use seemed appropriate. Ian Thompson had seen some shit.

Her job was to heal his body. But Cassie wasn't sure you could heal a body without tending to its spirit. She didn't have a psych degree, wasn't a counselor. Not that soldiers liked to talk to therapists anyway. They were too determined to prove they were tough. The trick was to forge some sort of meaningful human connection, crack open the protective shell. Easier said than done, but Cassie Jordan could be persistent.

"Where are you from?" she asked. She had him down on his back and was doing manual therapy, helping him manipulate his leg.

"New York, ma'am. Queens."

She'd known that, of course, just as she knew the answer to the next question. "You still have family around here?"

"No."

He didn't say "ma'am" that time, Cassie thought. Just a short, sharp answer. Either it was a lie or an uncomfortable truth. The best way to deal with a lie wasn't to call it out. That just made the liar defensive. Better to work around it.

"You have a place you're staying?"

"Yes, ma'am. Got an apartment. Lower Manhattan."

"Any roommates?"

"No, ma'am."

She pressed gently on his leg and felt his flesh flinch, but his face didn't change. He didn't even blink.

"Sorry," she said. "Some of this is going to hurt, I'm afraid."

"Not a problem, ma'am."

"Tell me something about yourself," she said.

"What for?"

"It helps the process."

"How?" He didn't sound particularly hostile. He just looked steadily at her.

"It distracts you from the pain," she said. "And it builds rapport."

"What do you want to know, ma'am?"

"Whatever you'd like to tell me. Doesn't have to be about the war."

Ian thought about it while he went through the exercises mechanically. Cassie knew some of them hurt, but he didn't seem to care, or even notice. This man's self-control was beyond anything she'd seen. It made her curious about him, more determined to break through his façade.

"Everything's about the war," he said quietly, after five minutes of silence.

Cassie nodded. "It's hard coming back," she said.

"I wouldn't know, ma'am."

That gave her pause. His mask had slipped, just a little. That was a good thing, but it made her heart hurt. Even so, it was an opportunity to build rapport, to find common ground.

"Okay," she said. "Tell me something about the war."

"Why? You work with veterans all the time. Must get boring hearing about it."

She smiled. "Most of you don't talk much. I pretty much need a crowbar to pry anything out."

"That's because you're a civilian, ma'am."

"I work for the US government, same as you."

"So does my congressman. Doesn't mean he's not a civilian."

"My husband was a Marine."

"Was, ma'am?" Now she had Ian's full attention. His voice was gentler than she expected.

"Roadside bomb," she said. "Iraq."

"Sorry, ma'am."

"Everybody says that," she said, knowing her smile was sad now. "Not sure anybody back here understands, except guys who've been over there. And their wives."

"Not what I meant, ma'am. Sorry for calling you a civilian. No excuse."

Cassie surprised both of them by laughing. Ian gave her a funny look. That was good, too. It was a genuine human reaction, unguarded. She'd gotten through to him for a second.

"Don't get it, ma'am," he said.

"You sounded just like Dean when you said that. He'd always say it when we were fighting. 'No excuse.' I swear, Marines just use that line to get out of trouble."

"Nobody likes excuses, ma'am."

"No mother likes them, that's for sure."

"You got a kid?"

"A son."

"How old?"

"Six."

Then Cassie saw a miracle. Ian smiled, faint but genuine. It transformed his whole face, brought it to life.

"That's a good age," he said. "What's his name?"

"Ben."

"Thanks for sharing, ma'am." Then he was all business again. "What's next?"

"For the leg, you'll want to do these exercises daily. A little ache is fine, we expect that, but if you feel any sudden sharp pain, stop what you're doing right away and give us a call. Don't be that macho idiot who tries to tough it out, not if you want the bone to heal. We'll do some gentle electrical stimulation and then send you home. You have meds?"

"More than I need. Don't like drugs."

"There's nothing wrong with taking your pain medication," she said with a touch of severity. "What did I just say about being a macho idiot?"

"It's not that," he said. "Like to keep my head clear. Need to for my job."

"What sort of work do you do, Ian?"

"Driver and bodyguard, ma'am."

"For the government?" She hadn't seen that in his service record.

"No, ma'am. Private."

"Well, I hope your boss has a substitute until you're back on your feet," she said. "They wouldn't put you in the front lines with your injuries if you were still in the Corps."

"Understood, ma'am. But he needs me."

"What's this boss of yours do?" she asked. "Is he some sort of celebrity or something?"

It was like shutters slammed down behind Ian's eyes. "That's classified, ma'am," he said, sitting up. "We done here?"

"For now," Cassie said, mystified. "If you'll just come over to the Electrical Stimulator, we'll get you all set."

And just like that, the rapport was broken again. Cassie didn't know what she'd said wrong. But Ian had piqued her curiosity. What sort of man would need a former Marine so badly that five bullets wouldn't stop his bodyguard coming back on duty?

And was it really a coincidence, she asked herself, that Ian had just happened to be on the scene of an attempted kidnapping?

When she got home from work, Cassie promised herself, she was going to do a little digging.

* * *

Cassie left the clinic in a better mood than she'd arrived in. Her last patient of the day, Chuck Steiner, always cheered her up. An Army veteran who'd left both legs behind in Iraq, he was relentlessly upbeat and a natural comedian. Chuck had a wonderful, supportive wife and two adorable daughters who always came to pick him up. He put the girls on the stumps of his thighs and let them ride on his wheelchair, which gave them the giggles.

Cassie still had a smile on her face as she pulled up to the curb at the daycare center. The kids were out on the playground, supervised by one of the center's workers. The playground had a fence that separated it from the sidewalk, with a gate that opened only outward. In these modern days of child abductions and rampage shooters, it was a depressing necessity.

Ben was sitting on a swing, going back and forth, kicking his legs for extra height. On his way forward, almost at the high point of his arc, he caught sight of her. His face lit up and he waved with both hands, letting go of the swing chains.

Cassie felt her smile freeze in place. She watched in slow motion, knowing suddenly exactly what was going to happen and unable to do anything about it. She saw Ben start his descent, saw his eyes widen as he lost his balance and started to fall. He gave a cry of surprise and fear as he tumbled toward the ground.

Cassie, forgetting the gate couldn't be opened from her side, snatched at it and pulled. It swung open, which shouldn't have happened, but she didn't notice. She sprinted toward her son. But not even an Olympic runner could outrun gravity. Ben hit the ground with a jarring thud. He looked at her, more in surprise than pain. Then his face scrunched up and, with no hint of self-consciousness, he started wailing.

She was there a second later, before the daycare attendant was more than halfway, scooping up her boy in her arms. The ground was made of shredded recycled rubber and she supposed it was the safest thing they could make it out of, but that had been a long fall. She felt real panic as she feverishly examined him for injuries.

The attendant, a heavyset woman, puffed her way to Cassie and Ben. "Oh my heavens," she said. "That was some tumble you took, young man."

Ben, muffled in his mother's arms and sobbing, took no notice.

"He'll be all right, I think," the woman went on, talking to Cassie now. "Land sakes, when I think of the things I played on when I was his age, it's a wonder any of us lived to adulthood. Why, I remember Bobby Beaufort, two doors down, broke both his ankles trying to use his mother's bedsheet as a parachute off the back of the bleachers at the high school. And another time—"

"Thanks, Pauline," Cassie said through tight lips. "I get the idea. I'll take it from here."

"Well, no harm done, praise the Lord," Pauline said. She reached into her purse for a cigarette and actually had the pack in her hand before remembering that smoking was prohibited at daycare. Clearly wishing she could light it up, she returned the pack to its place.

Cassie stood up, holding Ben against her hip, and turned for the gate. Then she realized what had happened with the gate and looked at Pauline.

"That thing's supposed to be locked," she said.

"Oh, yes," Pauline said. "But the lock rusted and froze in place. We're going to have someone fix it as soon as we can. In the meantime, of course, one of us is always out whenever any of the kids are. Don't worry."

Cassie nodded absently, thinking there were plenty of moms in New York who'd be happy to sue the daycare for that breach of safety rules. She was glad she wasn't one of them. She knew, better than most, how dangerous the world could be, but she also knew that expecting everyone else to take responsibility for it was a surefire way to screw up your life. So she let it go and carried Ben back to her car.

"That was an awesome jump, kiddo," she said, trying to cheer him up. "Just like they do it in the Airborne."

Ben sniffled. "Really?" he blurted out.

"Yeah," she said. "Before they go up in planes with parachutes, they practice jumping off things about that high. That way they learn how to land so they don't get hurt."

"Wow," he said. "So, that's like training?"

"Just like boot camp," she said. "But you shouldn't do it until you're older. Your bones are still developing and you could hurt them. Then you wouldn't grow tall like you want to."

"Did Daddy jump out of planes?" he asked as Cassie opened the back door of her Dodge Neon and set him in the seat.

Cassie felt a sudden pang. Dean had been gone three years, and most days she only felt a hollow, empty ache, like poking her tongue into the gap where a tooth had been, but the grief was always there. It could jump up and bite with no warning. She had a sudden, intense memory of his grin, the sparkle in his eyes, the easy strength in his arms.

She blinked and cleared her throat, trying not to show what she was feeling. "He went up in helicopters sometimes," she said. "But he didn't parachute."

"Can I go in a helicopter?"

"Maybe someday. But for practice, make sure you know how to ride in a car first," she said, pointing to his waist. "Seatbelt, young man."

Ben clicked the belt into place and smiled at her, his tears forgotten. "When I grow up, I'm going to be a Marine and ride around in helicopters just like Daddy," he said with a six-year-old's certainty.

"We'll see about that," she said, closing the door and walking around to the driver's side. She hoped he hadn't seen or guessed the flash of pure panic his words sparked in her.

No, dear God, no, she thought as she fished out her keys and got behind the wheel. *Not my son. Not after Dean.*

Chapter 3

Cassie had more or less recovered from her shock by the time she got home, but she knew sleep would be hard to come by that night. Adrenaline didn't leave the system nearly as quickly as it arrived. The effects of a bad scare could take up to eight hours to dissipate, or so the literature told her. She distracted herself cooking dinner, but that was no major undertaking. When you had a six-year-old, you got used to what the kid liked to eat. Tonight it was mac and cheese with frozen broccoli on the side, chocolate milk for a beverage.

She really would have liked something stronger, but she'd promised herself, that first awful week after getting the news about Dean, she'd never take a drink while Ben was around. No matter how bad she felt, and it really had felt like the world was ending, she couldn't hide in a bottle. Her son needed her, and that meant all of her, present and sober. She'd thrown out all the alcohol in the apartment: Dean's beer, which she didn't like anyway; the champagne they'd only drunk to celebrate New Year; the bottle of red they'd gotten on their honeymoon to

California; even the cooking wine. Drinking any of those would only have reminded her of him anyway.

She could still remember every detail of the CACO. That stood for "Casualty Assistance Calls Officer," because the Corps had acronyms for literally everything. They also had regulations for everything. Dean Jordan had been a Lance Corporal, which meant the Marine doing the notification needed to be at least a Sergeant, one rank above. This one had been a Staff Sergeant, a grizzled Marine twice Dean's age. He'd been polite, courteous, even kind, as he'd torn her world to pieces.

Dean had been blown up by a suicide bomber while manning a roadside checkpoint in Iraq, on the edge of some town she'd never heard of. The bomber had driven a car full of explosives right into the middle of the checkpoint and triggered the bomb, taking three Marines and Dean with him to Paradise and wounding five others.

A coffin had been flown into Dover Air Force Base, but she'd had to take their word it was Dean inside. They wouldn't open it, and she wouldn't have recognized him if they had. He'd been less than ten feet from the bomb when it had blown. There hadn't been much left of him. Nothing, really. Just memories. And Ben.

Cassie's eyes strayed to the triangular-folded American flag in its place of honor in the living room on the middle bookshelf. On one side of it was a photo of Dean in his dress blues, trying to look stern and noble but not quite able to hide a smile. On the other was a picture of the two of them on their wedding day. Dean was wearing his dress uniform for that, too, but he was grinning his head off. So was Cassie as the two of them, arm in arm, stared at the photographer with all the bright anticipation of a young couple who had no idea their happy marriage would last all of four years, two months, and thirteen days.

Cassie tried to shake loose of the memories, determined not to spend another evening mooning over photos and sad recollections. She hated crying and she'd done too much of it, holding it in until Ben was asleep, then trying to keep the sobs quiet so he wouldn't wake up. *Not tonight*, she told herself with all the firmness she could muster.

She played Go Fish with Ben on the living room carpet after dinner. Then they went through the usual evening rituals of bathing, brushing teeth, and putting on pajamas. She tucked him in bed and sat next to him, propped against the headboard, and read him his bedtime story. Tonight it was "The Giving Tree" by Shel Silverstein, about a tree that loves a boy so much that it gives him everything it has. In the end, all that's left of it is a stump, which it offers to the boy, now an old man, as a place to rest his weary bones.

Kids liked that story more than adults. They didn't fully understand the implications. They looked at it from the perspective of the boy; mothers tended to relate to the tree's position.

Once Ben was cozy and sleeping, Cassie went to the living room with a cup of hot cocoa and her laptop. It was time to find out what Ian Thompson's deal was.

She started with the *New York Times*. She knew the date he'd been shot and guessed, correctly, that the gunfight had made the news. When she found the first article about it, she remembered reading the story when it had happened. It had made the front page, and she could see why. A gang of thugs had snatched a woman right out of her own house in Midtown in broad daylight. A pair of police officers and a concerned citizen had intervened. Details were sketchy, but one of the officers and two kidnappers had been killed in a chaotic shootout. The other officer and the citizen had been seriously wounded. Two other criminals had escaped with the woman, identified as Michelle

O'Reilly, wife of a Manhattan trauma surgeon and mother of two. The children had hidden in the house and escaped harm.

Cassie kept looking and found the follow-up articles. The police had tracked the kidnappers to an abandoned factory where, in another shootout, two suspects had been captured and the ringleader killed. Ms. O'Reilly had been rescued and, according to the statement from the NYPD, she was uninjured. Another police officer, Erin O'Reilly, had also been wounded. The *Times* noted the detective was the sister-in-law of the abducted woman.

"Wow," Cassie said quietly. That had been the top law-enforcement story of the week, probably the month, and Ian had been right in the middle of it. She dug a little deeper and found a smaller article under the fold a couple of days later. That piece stated that the District Attorney had declined to bring charges against Ian Thompson, considering his actions entirely appropriate under the circumstances. He had apparently killed the two men outside the O'Reilly house, but the City of New York wasn't about to bust him for that, since he'd done the shooting with a legally-registered handgun while trying to save an innocent woman and her family. Ian had not returned calls asking for comment.

None of that answered her main question, which concerned Ian himself. What had he been doing there? The coincidences were piling up too high to ignore. An abducted woman rescued by her husband's sister? A former Marine who just happened to be in exactly the right place to shoot it out with a gang of hardened criminals? He'd said he was a bodyguard. Had the O'Reilly family hired him? That would make sense. She'd seen a movie about a bodyguard whose charge, a young girl, got kidnapped. Then the bodyguard started killing all the kidnappers. Dean had liked it, but it had been a little dark and violent for Cassie's taste, even if it did have Denzel Washington in it. She'd watch Denzel no matter what he was doing.

But why would a cop's family need to employ private security? More to the point, why on Earth was Ian doing the bodyguard gig? He had the skills, no doubt about that. But it was the very last thing a man with PTSD should be doing.

She shut down her laptop and leaned back on the couch. She was out of ideas for the moment. Maybe her next meeting with Ian would give her the chance to figure him out.

* * *

Cassie was on time for Ian's next PT appointment. She was waiting when he came into the lobby. He was alone, moving on crutches under his own power. Crutches could be tricky until the patient got the hang of them, but Ian just moved forward one halting step at a time, his broken leg swinging underneath him.

She got the door for him, ushering him into the exercise room. "How are you feeling, Ian?" she asked with her customary bright smile.

"Been worse, ma'am." He didn't return the smile, but he didn't seem angry, either.

"We're going to do the same exercises as last time," she said. "We'll try for a little more range of motion, to make sure you recover your mobility as much as we can. A little electrical stimulation and we'll see how we go from there."

"Suits me, ma'am."

Cassie waited until she had him down on the mat on his back, flexing his leg. Then she hit him with her first question.

"So," she said with deliberate casualness. "How do you know Michelle O'Reilly?"

"You were right," Ian said. He stopped moving his leg and looked steadily into her eyes. "You're no civilian."

"What do you mean?"

"You've been doing recon."

"Isn't recon something you do with enemies? I'm not your enemy, Ian. I'm on your side."

"If you say so, ma'am."

She bristled, but contained it. "You're my patient," she said calmly. "I'm just trying to help you recover."

"Don't see what this has to do with my leg, ma'am."

"I'm not talking about your leg." She let him see her earnestness. After all, she was telling the truth. "Have you been diagnosed with PTSD?"

"You've got the medical file, ma'am," he said, not giving anything away. "You know what's in it."

"What do you think?"

"How do you mean, ma'am?"

"Do you think you've got post-traumatic stress?"

He shrugged. "Plenty of guys had it worse over there. Still do."

"It's not something to be ashamed of, Ian. And it's got nothing to do with how tough you are. Everybody breaks in combat eventually. It's mathematical. The military's done studies. The human psyche isn't meant to handle that level of stress indefinitely."

"But they keep sending us out there," he said. She thought she caught the briefest flicker of dark humor in his voice.

"And you keep volunteering," she agreed. "If they'd send you back now, would you go?"

"Can't anymore."

"Really?" That hadn't been the answer she expected. "Why not?"

"Got responsibilities here, ma'am."

"The O'Reilly family?" she guessed.

"Them too."

"So you do know them."

"You work with cops, ma'am?" he asked suddenly.

"Cops? No. Military veterans. Some MPs, I guess. Why?"

"Starting to feel like an interrogation, ma'am. Maybe ought to have a lawyer present."

"Think of it more as an unofficial counseling session," she said.

"You got psych training?"

"Only what I've gotten on the job," she said. "I spend a lot of time with veterans. Why did you become a bodyguard after coming home?"

He shrugged again. "Good at it. Knew a guy who offered me the job. Got a good eye for when something's about to go down."

"From your combat experience?"

He nodded.

"Have you ever heard of hypervigilance?" she asked.

"Yes, ma'am."

"What is it?"

"Means I can't turn myself off. See everything, all the time, really sharp. Tips me off to trouble."

"And it tells you when danger is nearby," she said. "The problem is, a lot of the time, the danger is in your head."

"You going to say these are imaginary bullet holes, ma'am?"

She smiled. "Of course not. But being a bodyguard makes you give in to your hypervigilance. It encourages you to stay in a state of high sensitivity. That isn't good for you long-term. It wears you down."

"Going to teach me how to be a civilian again, ma'am?" There was that hint of dark humor again.

"Somebody needs to," she said. "The Marines do a great job programming you to go out and fight. They haven't figured out how to bring you home."

"So that's your plan? Bring me home?"

"That's my plan," she agreed. "Don't you want to come home?"

His eyes went distant with remembered pain. "Don't know about that, ma'am."

"Ian," she said gently. "Your bad stuff didn't start with the war, did it?"

"World's full of it, ma'am."

Cassie was thinking of what he'd said at their last encounter. "You went through something when you were a kid," she guessed. "What was it?"

"Can't complain. Other guys got it worse."

"That's the second time you've said that. Are you trying to impress me, or yourself?"

He was startled. "Not trying to impress anyone, ma'am."

"You're a hard guy to get close to," she said. "Even for a Marine."

"Trying to get close to me?" he asked. "Not sure that's appropriate."

Cassie felt her cheeks burning. "That wasn't what I meant and you know it."

"My mistake, ma'am. No excuse."

"I'm not trying to flirt with you and I'm not trying to make friends. I'm not your friend, Ian. I'm your rehab nurse. A friend won't hurt you. I'll hurt you if I have to, because sometimes to get well, you have to hurt. They kicked your ass in boot camp, I've heard the stories, and combat kicked it worse. But if I have to, I'll wear out my boot on your backside. You hear me, Marine?"

There it was. A genuine smile. "Oorah, ma'am. But you don't wear boots."

"Of course not. I'm a nurse. We wear comfy sneakers." But he hadn't so much as glanced at her feet. "You noticed my shoes?"

"You're the one who talking about hypervigilance," he said. "Notice everything. Can't help it."

"I see," she said. "What else did you notice about me?"

"You're not combat-trained," he said at once.

"How can you tell?"

"You don't walk that way. You move with a purpose, but you're thinking about where you're going. You lean forward a little, you're not balanced like a warrior. Guessing you've never taken martial arts. You wear makeup, but only a little. Not trying to attract attention. Probably use it to cover up."

Cassie felt a little shiver run down her spine. "Cover what up?"

"Bags under your eyes. You're tired."

"I'm a single mom. It's a tiring lifestyle." She recognized the defensiveness in her own voice.

"You don't sleep well," he went on relentlessly. "You've got good hands, you know what to do with them, but when you're not doing something, you fiddle with your ring."

Cassie looked down at her hands. She was doing exactly that. She made herself stop.

"Okay," she said. "What's your conclusion?"

"About what, ma'am?"

"About me. What do you see?"

"Pain. Strength. Grit. You're not a Marine, but you'd be a good one with the right training. Except..."

"Except what?"

"You're a fighter, ma'am, but not a killer. No disrespect."

"None taken," she said automatically. "And you're right. I'm not. Now it's my turn."

He waited and watched her.

"You trust yourself," she said. "You came here alone. You make a point of doing things for yourself. You don't trust other people easily, not because you don't think they're worthy of it, but because you've learned you can lose them. You've lost friends, people you counted on, too many times. You're hurting, but you don't want to show pain, because you think that's the same as weakness. You like kids because you see innocence in them, something you don't see in yourself. You want to protect people, you want them to count on you, but it's a one-way street for you.

"You're a guardian," she finished. "But you keep yourself separate because you think that way you'll be safe. But you're wrong about that. Being alone isn't safe. It's just lonely."

"Maybe not," he said. "But aren't you the same way?"

Cassie flinched as if he'd slapped her. "Of course not," she retorted. "I've got my kid."

"And you need to take care of him," he agreed. "So who's got time for anything else?"

They stared at one another. The pause for breath turned into ten seconds of silence. Fifteen. Twenty.

Then Cassie laughed. She couldn't help it. The tension had become ridiculous. Ian didn't join in, but he wasn't a man who laughed easily. His eyes twinkled in a way that reminded her of Dean, but for some reason, the memory didn't hurt quite as badly just then.

"We're just a couple of people who got screwed by life, huh?" she said.

"Affirmative, ma'am. Lot of that going around."

"Let's get you hooked up for your electrotherapy," she said. "Enough of this psychobabble bullshit."

"This is your show, ma'am."

Cassie was glad to drop the conversation. She'd meant to get inside his head, not let him in hers. They'd both let their guard down for a moment. She'd been shaken by the experience. Ian was sharp all right, no doubt about that. But this wasn't about her. It wasn't fair to expect her patients to heal her. She'd have to be more careful about that in the future. Boundaries were important.

Chapter 4

The human body had an amazing ability to heal, but it worked slowly. The human spirit healed even more slowly, in Cassie's experience. If it healed at all. Physical pain was a problem for the present, requiring instant attention, but soon fading into memory. Psychic pain had its roots in memory and was hard to get rid of.

Ian's physical recovery was relatively rapid. He was in good shape and he did every exercise she told him to, efficiently and without complaint. A broken femur could take twelve weeks to completely heal, but Cassie was confident he'd be walking normally in more like ten.

But she remained troubled by the weight he was carrying on his heart. She'd seen plenty of veterans who were engulfed by the darkness of past trauma, but Ian was different than most. He channeled that darkness, kept it under pressure. In her experience, that was never a permanent coping mechanism. It always found a way out, usually unpredictably and violently.

In their fifth weekly meeting, she had him on a weight machine, doing a few reps with his legs. She kept the weights light, making sure not to put too much strain on the bone.

"You're doing well," she said. "I don't think you'll have any long-term effects."

"Good to hear, ma'am."

"Do you have any close friends, Ian? People you can talk to?"

"A few."

"Buddies from the Corps?"

"A couple. Got a cop I go running with sometimes."

Cassie made the connection. "This cop wouldn't be named O'Reilly by any chance, would she?"

Ian paused with his legs flexed. "Didn't say that, ma'am."

"Lucky guess," she said. "She your girlfriend?"

A very odd expression crossed Ian's face. "No, ma'am," he said slowly. "She is not my girlfriend."

"Sorry. I just thought—"

"She's seeing someone else," he said, cutting her sentence short.

He'd never interrupted her before. That was interesting. "Who?" Cassie asked.

"My boss."

"But she's your friend?"

"Yes, ma'am."

"Do you have a girlfriend?" She paused. "Or boyfriend?"

He shook his head. "Why do you care?"

"I'd like to know what sort of support network you've got. There's people you can talk to, if there's anything bothering you. You told me you didn't have family around, so I was wondering about friends. There's also professionals—"

"Don't need professional help." He cut her off again.

Cassie nodded. She'd seen that response more than once from vets. "You could get a dog," she said.

"A dog? Why?"

"Animals are good for therapy. Having someone to care for will help you, too."

He was staring at her. "What makes you think I need help, ma'am?"

"I've been working with veterans for years," she said. "What do you think? Are you really going to tell me you feel totally fine? You're happy?"

"Can't complain."

"And you think that's the same thing as happiness?"

"Wouldn't know, ma'am."

"Ian? Have you ever been really happy?"

"Have you?"

"Yeah, smartass," she said. "I have."

"Are you now?"

She thought of Dean's photo, sitting on the shelf next to the flag that had draped his coffin. She remembered, vaguely, the sound she'd made when the Marine at the door had told her he was dead. It had been something between a wail and a groan. Her legs had given out and she'd gone down, right there on her living room floor. If it wasn't for Ben, knowing he needed her, she wondered if she'd ever have been able to stand up again.

"I'm working on it," she said. "At least I'm trying. Are you?"

"Don't know how. You know any exercises for that?"

She smiled. "We don't have the equipment for it," she admitted. "But it's like a muscle. You find out what works and you keep flexing it. Then you grow stronger. You have to go toward what you want. What's the happiest you've been in the last six months?"

"Got invited to dinner," Ian said. "Sat next to this kid. His mom made me feel... like I belonged. Like one of them. Felt good."

"You felt like part of their family?"

He nodded. "For a little while, felt like... like home, I guess. But wasn't mine. Was just visiting. Still liked it."

"That mother... was that Michelle O'Reilly?" Cassie guessed.

"You sure you don't hang with cops, ma'am?"

She laughed. "No. I just listen when people talk. It's less common than you'd think. So you were near her house when she got grabbed?"

He nodded again. "Wasn't going to let them take her. Not on my watch. But wasn't good enough, wasn't fast enough."

"You got shot," she reminded him. "Five times."

"If I'd been quicker, could've had them before they got away," he argued. "Before the cops engaged me. Tried. Kept the kids safe, at least. They wanted the kids, too."

"How do you know that?"

"They were trying to get to Detective O'Reilly. Wanted to hurt her, take out her family."

"That's horrible," Cassie said, shuddering. She thought of Ben, and suddenly she wanted very much to have him in her arms, to know he was safe.

"Knew the guy who took her," Ian added. "Nasty piece of work."

"Wait a second," Cassie said. "You *knew* the kidnapper?"

Ian seemed to realize he'd said too much. "Not a friend," he said. "Enemy. Guy was on bad terms with my boss."

"This whole thing seems pretty complicated," she said.

"Affirmative, ma'am. Pretty simple for me, though."

"You saw people you cared about in danger," she said. "And you took action."

"Only wish I'd done a better job."

"What does Michelle O'Reilly think about the job you did?"

Ian's gaze slid away from Cassie and he looked down. "Came to see me in the hospital," he said quietly. "She cried. Said she felt lousy about what happened, wished I hadn't got hurt on her behalf. Said I was welcome anytime, wherever they were."

"Sounds to me like you've got a family," Cassie said with a smile. "And they'd love to see you again."

"Not mine," he said. "But they're good people. Glad to know them."

"You have to open yourself up, Ian," she said. "Let people in. I know it's scary. But it's important."

"Think I'm scared?"

"I know you are. But it's okay to be scared. Everyone gets scared." She put a hand on his shoulder and gave it a squeeze. "I still think a dog might be a good starting place for you."

"Detective O'Reilly would agree," Ian said.

"Oh? Why's that?"

"She's got a K-9," he said. "Thinks a dog is the answer to everything."

* * *

Have you ever been really happy?

The question bounced around Cassie's head that night, after she'd read Ben his bedtime story and gotten him tucked in. She'd said yes, but had that been true? The good years, between her marriage and Dean's death, hadn't always seemed so good. They'd had money problems; living in New York was never cheap, and she'd still been going to nursing school, which was a strain on their budget and on her schedule. Then Ben had come, which was a blessing, absolutely, but the timing had been lousy. Cassie was stretched way too thin already, between school and her part-time job.

Then Dean had gotten his orders for Iraq. Cassie remembered crying that whole night. She'd tried not to, had known it would only make things harder, but she couldn't help it. Had she known, even then, that he wouldn't be coming home?

Of course not. Her name might be Cassandra, like the seer in the Greek myth, but she had no power to see the future. All she'd had was fear, and fear was more than enough.

Still, those had been the good years, the happy years. Was happiness something you could only see in the rearview mirror, after it was over? Was it only grief that made the past look good by comparison?

"I'm not unhappy," she said quietly, talking to Dean's military photo. "Really, Dean, I'm not. I've got Ben, I've got my job, and I got to have you. Not as long as I wanted, but hey, I'm the one who married a Marine."

Dean looked back at her with his almost-serious expression, the hidden smile peeking through.

"Three years," she said. How many minutes was that? Something like one and a half million. That was, what, ninety million heartbeats? Give or take? Maybe her math was wrong. She'd never been great with numbers.

She put a hand over her own heart. It was broken, but it kept beating. Grief could be such a selfish emotion. It blinded her to everyone else, everything else. Dean wouldn't want her to waste away grieving for him. He'd never been one to dwell on the past.

How could a man with his heart so much in the present, his eyes fixed on the future, be nothing but past? How could he just be *gone*?

Angry tears pooled in Cassie's eyes. She knew the stages of grief, they'd talked about them in nursing school. Denial led to anger, bargaining, depression, and finally acceptance. What they hadn't told her was that it wasn't a linear process. Some days she went all the way back to denial and genuinely expected Dean to walk in the door. Other days, she thought she'd finally worked through it all and was ready to move on. But then she'd be back to anger, and so on.

"It's a damn roller coaster," she muttered. Except she didn't know when the ride would end. Maybe it would just keep going up and down, tossing her all over the place forever.

"Maybe I need a dog, too," she said. "What do you think, Dean? Maybe a nice puppy for Ben to play with?"

Dean looked back, eyes sparkling in a face she'd never touch again.

Chapter 5

"Do you like music?" Cassie asked Ian at the start of their exercises.

"Like it fine, ma'am," he said.

The room had a pretty decent sound system and an eclectic collection of CDs, many donated by previous patients. She gestured to it.

"What kind?"

He shrugged. "The Boss. Classic rock. That sort of thing."

"No heavy metal?" she joked. "I thought you jarheads were all about the loud stuff."

"That's because most of us like getting amped up when we go into action," he said. "Like football players hitting the field. Plus, a lot of the guys have hearing loss. Too much time shooting guns and blowing things up. Start losing some decibels. Need to crank up the volume to compensate."

"Not you?"

"Was a sniper. No point going crazy out there. Better to stay calm, keep focused."

"You're all about control, aren't you?"

"Beats being out of control, ma'am."

"It's an illusion, you know," she said, scanning the CD collection for something Ian might like.

"What is? Control?"

"Yeah."

Cassie found a copy of the Bruce Springsteen album *The Rising*. She hadn't heard much of The Boss, except for the occasional radio hit, so she didn't know quite what to expect. She slipped the CD in and pressed Play. Springsteen started singing about a lonesome day.

"Sure you want that album, ma'am?" Ian asked.

"Something wrong with it?" she retorted. "I thought you liked this guy."

"This disc's one of my favorites. You might not like it."

"Why not?"

"It's about losing people. Might hurt to hear it."

"Then why are you fond of it?"

"He gets it," Ian said. "*Devils and Dust* is even better. Some of those songs got me out of Kandahar."

"You want to tell me about it?"

"Aren't we supposed to be doing PT?"

"This is part of your therapy." She leaned against the wall and crossed her arms.

"Used the songs," he said. "Kept me going. On my own. Robbins was there, too, but hurt. He was hardly conscious most of the time. Talked to myself, too. Thought maybe I was going crazy."

"It's pretty common," she said.

"Going crazy? No kidding."

She laughed. "No. Well, maybe, but that's not what I meant. A lot of people talk to themselves in survival situations. They set up a dialogue. It helps them make choices. And it helps them feel like they're not alone."

He nodded. "Makes sense. Have to lie to yourself a lot out there."

"Was that how you made it back?"

"Want to know how I made it out of that chopper crash?" He sat up and gave her a hard, penetrating look. "Should've died, you know. Plenty of times. Don't know how many. Wasn't that I was the best. Maybe just lucky. Sometimes that's all it is, luck. Fate. Whatever. Rest of it's training and grit. When it gets bad, you dig deep, find more, keep going. Don't worry about everything else. Sometimes you make it, sometimes you don't."

"And that's your lie," Cassie said softly. "You have to tell yourself you're in control, because otherwise you go crazy. That's why you don't take your pain meds."

He nodded. "It's more important to keep control. Even when it hurts."

"So you're voluntarily going through more pain?"

Ian actually smiled slightly. "That's the tradeoff, ma'am. Know what's funny, though?"

"What?"

"Know that stuff they give you when you're dehydrated? When they stick the needle in your arm and hang the bag over your bed?"

"Saline solution?"

"That's it. They don't just put pure water into you, because you've been sweating out all this other stuff, too. Salt mostly, I think."

"Electrolytes," Cassie said.

"Right," Ian said. "The whole point is to get fluid back in you. Because you'll die without it. But I remember, lying in the hospital, while they were pumping me full of that saline solution, didn't make me feel better. Made me thirsty."

“That’s because of the salt in it,” she said.

“I figured. But it’s weird. Thing that makes you better makes you feel worse. Good thing I trusted the docs. Might’ve pulled the needle otherwise.”

Cassie smiled. “Healing hurts sometimes. Our bodies don’t always know what’s best for us. Neither do our minds. If we only did what felt good or safe, we’d never grow and we’d never get better. Speaking of which, it’s time for your leg mobility exercises. Let’s get on it, Marine.”

“Yes, ma’am.”

* * *

Ian swung his crutches toward the door. He was already moving a lot better than he had when Cassie had first met him. He’d learned to use the crutches, but he was also putting more weight on his leg. He leaned on his right-hand crutch while he opened the door with that hand. Then he was out and on his way.

Cassie turned to see Larry watching her with a grin on his face.

“Okay,” she said, hands on her hips. “What?”

“Good-looking guy,” he said. “If you like that sort of thing.”

“What are you talking about?”

“Young, strong, cut bod,” he said, still grinning. “And they say chicks dig scars.”

“They say wrong,” she said. “Besides, every guy who comes in here has scars.”

“Not the ones with closed-head injuries.”

“Them too. They just carry theirs on the inside. Did you have a point?”

“I’m just saying, a girl might want a piece of that.”

“I can’t date a patient,” she said. “That’d be unethical.”

"Who said anything about dating?" Larry retorted. "I said a girl might want a piece."

"You're a pig."

"You can't tell me you've never thought about it," he said, unperturbed by her low opinion. "Plenty of hot young guys come through here, mostly intact." He winked. "The important parts, at least."

She shook her head and rolled her eyes. "It doesn't matter," she said. "I'm not ready for anything."

"How long has it been?" he asked.

"Are you seriously asking me when I last got laid? Because there's no way I'm telling you that."

"No." The smile slid off his face. "I mean, since... you know."

"Three years."

"You going to mourn him forever?"

"Yes."

"That wasn't quite what I meant. I meant..."

"I know what you meant. And I'm not sure. I thought Dean was it, you know? I'd never want to be with anyone else. Ever."

Larry nodded. "But it wasn't up to you. And you're what, twenty-eight?"

"Yeah."

"You've got a long lonely road you're looking at. You sure you want to do that to yourself?"

Cassie shook her head again. "I'm not lonely."

Larry was grinning again. "I call bullshit."

"I've got my kid."

"Not the same thing and you know it."

"And you're missing the point," she insisted. "Ian... Sergeant Thompson is a patient. I'd get fired if I put the moves on him."

"Meaning you want to?"

"I didn't say that!"

"And you didn't say you didn't, either."

"You're a younger brother, aren't you, Larry?"

"Well, yeah, but what's that got to do with anything?"

"I could tell. You're so good at being a pest, I knew you had years of practice."

"Does he like you?" Larry asked.

Cassie snorted. "Hard to say."

"No it isn't. Has he checked you out? Made a pass? Got a little handsy in the middle of PT?"

"No. He's polite. A perfect gentleman."

"Do I detect a hint of disappointment?"

"Stop playing matchmaker."

"Are you familiar with the Florence Nightingale Effect?" Larry waggled his eyebrows suggestively.

"I'm a female healthcare worker," she said. "Of course I'm familiar with it. I have patients hoping I'll fall hopelessly in love with them once a week. Sometimes more."

"But not Thompson?"

"No."

He shrugged. "In that case, you won't mind if I take a shot with him."

"Larry!"

"It's not unethical for me. He's not my patient."

"I don't think he swings your way."

"You sure about that?"

Now that he mentioned it, she wasn't. "I don't think he's that interested in anyone," she said. "Male or female."

"What a waste," he said sadly, turning back to his computer. "Both of you."

* * *

That evening, Cassie was sitting next to Ben in his bed. She had his bedtime story in her lap, that old favorite, *Goodnight*

Moon, but she hadn't opened it yet. Ben was snuggled up next to her and she was just enjoying the feeling of sitting with her son, an arm around him, holding him close.

"Can I ask you a question, kiddo?" she asked.

"Okay," he said.

"Does... does it bother you that it's just the two of us?"

He looked up at her. "You want to know if I miss Daddy," he said.

"Well... sort of," she said. "I miss him too, you know."

"I know."

"But sometimes, when a mommy loses a daddy, she finds another man," she said.

"A new daddy?" Ben sounded doubtful.

"You understand, no one will ever replace you," she said, giving him a squeeze. "I will always, always love you, no matter what, forever."

"I know," he said.

"But if, someday, Mommy found a man and they... and they fell in love, would that be okay? With you?"

She couldn't tell if Ben really understood. He was a sharp kid, but that sort of situation could be complicated for adults, let alone children. She let him think about it.

"Would he be nice?" he asked.

"Of course he would," she said. "Otherwise I wouldn't fall in love with him, right?"

"Would he take me to ball games?"

"I'm sure he would."

"And play blocks with me?"

"Absolutely." Cassie was fighting back tears again and losing the battle.

"And would he be my daddy?"

"He'd never replace Daddy," she said, managing not to choke on the words. "But he'd be a new Daddy. So you'd have two, the old one and the new one."

"Oh." Ben nodded. "Okay. Can we read now?"

"Of course." She opened the book, though she had every word memorized. That was good. The moisture in her eyes made it hard to see the print. "In the great green room there was a telephone..."

By the time she got to the end, Ben was asleep. Cassie eased herself out of his bed, gently lowering his head to his pillow. She bent over him, whispered "Good night noises everywhere," kissed his forehead, and stood up. She paused in the doorway, looking at the sleeping boy.

He deserved a father, she thought. Hell, he deserved *everything*. But that wasn't the way the world worked. You didn't get what you deserved.

Cassie flipped the switch. The room went dark, except for the little nightlight in the wall socket. It was shaped like a puppy's head and gave a faint golden gleam. She closed the door very slowly, being careful to twist the knob so the latch didn't make a noise.

Chapter 6

"I think this will be our last appointment," Cassie said.

"Typical," Ian said.

"What do you mean?"

"Typical government response. Do half the job, then declare victory."

Cassie burst out laughing. "You know, we've been doing this for two months, and I still don't know when you're joking."

"Haven't got a sense of humor, ma'am. The Corps forgot to issue me one."

"See, that's what I'm talking about. You've got a sense of humor, it's just dry as dust."

"Comes from my tour in the Sandbox."

"Seriously, though," she said. "You've made good progress. If you stick to your exercises, I think you can do the rest of the healing yourself. Just don't go jumping in front of any more bullets."

"Can you write me a prescription for that? So I can show it if someone pulls a gun on me?"

"You're in a good mood," she observed.

"Feeling pretty good today."

"How's your pain level?"

"Hardly registers."

"By your standards, or by a normal guy's?"

"Don't know many normal guys, ma'am."

She smiled. "Not many normal guys in the Corps, do you mean?"

"Or on the street," he said. "Had kind of a rough childhood. Not complaining."

"Of course not. Marines never complain. So, why are you feeling good?"

"Told Detective O'Reilly about your medical advice."

"What advice is that?"

"The dog."

"Were you right? About her?"

"Affirmative. Next thing I knew, was at the animal shelter looking at strays. Not really sure how I got there."

Cassie laughed again. "Pushy woman, Detective O'Reilly?"

"You've got no idea."

"So? Did you find a dog?"

"Saw plenty I'd get along with. Nothing special, until..."

"Until what?"

Ian's smile held a hint of wistfulness. "A stray in a pen at the end of the hallway. Don't know what kind. Scruffy mutt, medium-sized. Hair all over the place. Female. Couple years old. Not the kind of dog most people want. Lady said she'd been there a couple months. They were going to put her down. Asked them not to."

"So you've got a dog?" Cassie grinned.

"Sorting things out with my landlord," he said. "Dog's a little too big. Rules say nothing over twenty-five pounds. She's forty-five. Shelter's holding her while I get things straight. Should have her in a couple days."

"That's great, Ian! What was it about her?"

He looked away, uncharacteristically shy. "You know," he said quietly. "Look in a man's eyes, you can tell how much he's seen."

"Yeah," Cassie said. "I know."

"Dogs are the same," he said. "She's been through it. We understand each other."

Cassie nodded. They were silent for a few moments. Then Ian stirred himself and stood up.

"Guess we're done here, then?" he asked.

"I guess so."

He braced himself on one of his crutches and held out his hand. "Thanks, ma'am."

She took his hand. "My pleasure," she said. "Do me a favor, okay? We've put a lot of work into putting you back together. Don't waste it. Take care of yourself."

"Affirmative, ma'am."

He turned to go. Cassie watched him. The feeling hit her that she needed to say something else, to do something else, before this moment slipped away from her.

"Hey, Ian?"

He stopped and pivoted on his crutches to face her. "Yes, ma'am?"

"You're not my patient anymore," she said.

"Yes, ma'am. I know."

She took a breath and plunged onward, not even sure what answer she was hoping for. "Do you want to get dinner sometime?"

He stared at her with an unreadable expression on his face, studying her. Cassie felt blood tingling in her cheeks. The moment became awkward, then uncomfortable.

"What for?" he asked at last.

She felt a flash of irritation. "You know what for."

"Is this what you do with former patients?"

That stung. "No, it isn't," she snapped. "Not that it's any of your business."

He seemed surprised. "Sorry, ma'am. Didn't mean to offend you. No—"

"If you say 'no excuse,' I'll break your other leg," she interrupted. "Then you'll be my patient again. Would that make you happy?"

She'd never seen him taken completely aback before. It made him look younger, less tough. She felt a little of her anger drain away, but her face still burned with embarrassment.

"Didn't mean it like that," he said softly. "Just trying to figure what you want from me. Not sure I can give you what you need."

"Don't you like me?" Cassie asked. It sounded cheaply pathetic as the words left her mouth and she immediately wished she could take them back and think of something better.

"Impossible not to," he said. "That's not the problem."

"Are you... seeing someone?" she asked.

"No, ma'am. Not sure I'm ready."

"Oh." Cassie wondered if this could get any more awkward. "I'm not sure I am either. I just thought maybe we could find out. If we were ready. Together."

He nodded. "Understood. Sorry, ma'am. Caught me a little off guard."

"I don't think you've ever been caught off guard in your life," she said.

"First time for everything, ma'am."

"So, you're turning me down?"

"Not how I'd say it," he said. "Could be the timing's just bad. Don't know if it'd be good if it happened now."

"Okay," she said. "Message received. Take care of yourself, Ian. And good luck with the dog."

"I'll let you know how it goes," he said. "In case you want to meet her. No hard feelings?"

"None," she said, feeling an odd mix of relief and disappointment.

Cassie watched the door swing shut. What had she been thinking? It had been a crazy impulse, nothing more. Now he was gone and things could get back to normal.

We lie to ourselves, she thought. *That's how we keep going.*

* * *

Cassie thought Ian might call, but he didn't. She could call him, of course. His contact info was in the computer at work. But she held back. Was it pride? She didn't think so. She wasn't even sure she wanted to get in touch. The whole idea of going out with him had been a crazy spur-of-the-moment plan, at least partially inspired by Larry's teasing. Ian had been right to turn her down. It couldn't possibly have ended well.

Still, she was disappointed. What was it about Ian? Dean had been so lively, so cheerful. Ian was quiet, intense. The only thing they had in common was that they were both Marines. And she'd decided it'd been crazy to marry a Marine in the first place.

So she put Ian out of her mind. There was plenty to keep her busy. The really crazy thing, she decided, was ever having thought she could juggle a young boy, a full-time job, and a relationship.

Two weeks after her last appointment with Ian, she said a pleasant goodbye to Chuck Steiner and headed to Ben's daycare. Chuck was upbeat as always. She wondered what he'd been like before he'd been wounded. Losing a limb changed a man, but it was hard to guess how. Brushing up against your own mortality, especially when you were still young, was always a significant emotional event.

Cassie wondered whether her work had skewed her perspective. Most of the people she met had experienced terrible trauma. Did it make her less inclined to take risks? She didn't need anyone to tell her the world was a dangerous place, but was it really as bad as it looked from the veterans' hospital? She'd heard cops were pessimistic about human nature for the same reason. Dealing with criminals all the time tended to make you view people in the worst possible light.

She resolved to be better, more optimistic. She had a six-year-old son, all his life in front of him. She had the chance to watch him grow and learn, experiencing everything the world had to offer. She wouldn't be one of those worrywart mothers who always thought something awful was going to happen to their kids.

Traffic was heavy in front of the daycare and cars were bumper-to-bumper on that side of the street. Cassie parked on the opposite side and climbed out of the car. She could see the kids on the playground, running around and squealing gleefully.

She started down the block to the crosswalk. Halfway there, she heard Ben's voice.

"Mommy!"

Cassie turned and raised her hand to wave, smiling a greeting. There was no fear in his voice, only glad excitement. He was running to meet her at the gate, eager to see her. Cassie felt the same thrill, the same joy she knew every time she saw her son.

She'd forgotten all about the broken latch on the gate.

Ben hit the metal bars at a dead run. The gate flew open and he spilled out onto the sidewalk. He kept going, straight on toward his mother, into the middle of the busy Manhattan street.

A pedestrian made a lunge for the boy but missed. Cassie's hand still hung in the air, totally forgotten. Her smile froze into a grimace. She was screaming on the inside, but no sound came out of her mouth. Car horns blared. Tires squealed.

A man tumbled into the street after the boy. He'd been walking his dog and had dropped the leash and rushed right into the mass of swerving, screeching cars, no hesitation at all. He grabbed Ben from behind and wrapped his arms around the kid just as a big old Chevrolet clipped him.

The fender caught the man at knee height and he fell back onto the hood. The driver stood up on his brakes and the car jerked to a stop. Man and child rolled off the hood onto the asphalt and lay there in a jumbled heap.

For just a second there was dead silence. Then a chorus of horns and voices erupted on all sides. Cassie ignored them. She threaded between the cars, heart pounding. The man's dog, abandoned on the sidewalk, barked a couple of times. A stranger bent to pick up the leash but the dog scuttled away from him and cowered against the playground fence.

Cassie saw the back of the man who'd grabbed her son. He was lying in the street, arms still protectively enclosing the little boy.

"Ben?" she called anxiously. "Ben!"

"Mommy!" a muffled voice cried from under his rescuer.

Cassie sank to her knees beside them. "Oh thank God," she said. "Are you okay?"

The man slowly rolled on his side and released the boy. Ben was starting to cry, more from fear than pain. He appeared unhurt.

"Thank you," Cassie said to Ben's rescuer. "Thank you so—"

She stopped short. She knew him.

"No thanks needed, ma'am," Ian Thompson said. His voice was tight, breathless.

"Holy shit," the driver of the Chevy said. He'd gotten out of his car and was staring at them. "You okay, buddy?"

Horns continued to sound from New Yorkers more concerned with their schedules than with the drama playing out in the street. In fairness, most of them probably couldn't see what was going on.

Ian thrust Ben up toward Cassie, who scooped him into her arms and held on tight. The driver gave Ian a hand up. The former Marine got slowly to his feet.

"Thanks, sir," he said to the driver.

"Hey, buddy, I couldn't stop in time," the driver said. "There was no way I could stop in time. You gotta believe me."

Ian nodded. "Affirmative, sir," he said. "No harm done."

Cassie retreated to the sidewalk, Ian just behind her. She held Ben close against her chest, his head on her shoulder. She felt for wounds and found none. She was crying now, too, mostly from relief.

Ian got down on his heels in front of the dog. "Hey, Miri," he said quietly. "It's okay. It's fine. I got you."

The dog slunk forward, head low, tail tucked. But when she got close to Ian, the tip of her tail wagged hesitantly. She lay down at his feet and went over on her side, staring up at him. He laid a hand on her and gently stroked her, making soft, soothing sounds.

"Ben," Cassie said. "Don't you ever, *ever* run out in the street like that! You hear me?"

"I'm sorry, Mommy," Ben sniffled. "I didn't mean to."

Cassie caught motion out of the corner of her eye and saw the daycare attendant. "And you," she said, keeping her voice steady with great difficulty, "fix that damn gate."

The woman nodded wordlessly and fled back indoors, probably afraid Cassie would throw something at her, or maybe bite her.

Ian had hold of the dog's leash again. He straightened up. The dog rolled back onto her paws and looked up at him, wagging her tail more vigorously.

"Looks like you're squared away, ma'am," he said.

"Ian, what are you doing here?" Cassie demanded.

"Live just around the corner," he said, pointing. "Was just walking the dog."

"So, this is your dog?" she asked, blinking to clear her eyes and looking at the creature at Ian's side. She saw a mutt, its colors a mix of black and various browns. The dog's fur was incredibly disheveled, sticking out in odd tufts and clumps. If she'd had to guess, Cassie would have thought it was a cross between a German Shepherd and a Shih-Tzu, or maybe a Yorkie.

"This is Miri," Ian confirmed. "Short for Miriam. Had her about a week. Can't take her for long walks yet. Leg's not a hundred percent."

"And you just got hit by a car!" Cassie exclaimed. "We need to get you to a doctor and get you checked out!"

"I'm fine, ma'am." He shook his head. "Had enough doctors for a while."

"Then at least let me take a look at you," she argued. "I'm a trained nurse, remember?"

"Said I'm fine."

"It's the least I can do. We don't have to go to the hospital. You said your place is just around the corner. Let's go there. I'll have a look, just to be on the safe side."

Ian yielded. "If you insist, ma'am. Just a couple minutes this way."

Chapter 7

Ian lived in an old brick apartment, worn but well-kept. He keyed them into the lobby and started up the stairs. Miri trotted beside him, looking up at him the whole way.

"You don't want to take the elevator?" Cassie asked. She was still carrying Ben, though her arms were getting very tired. She might be able to put him down. Eventually.

"Don't like elevators," Ian said. "That's why I'm just on the third floor." He took the stairs slow and careful. Despite his protestations, it was obvious his leg was still causing him some problems.

"Why not?"

"Can't maneuver, no cover, they know you're coming. Ready-made killboxes."

"Who know you're coming?"

"Everyone."

Cassie couldn't help noticing how Ian scanned the hallway when they got to his floor, giving everything a quick once-over. He used his left hand, the one with Miri's leash in it, to handle the doorknob. His right was always empty, always poised. She could feel the nervous tension radiating from him.

He fished out his key, still with his left hand, and unlocked his door. He opened it and stepped quickly through the doorway, sidestepping to clear the entry. Cassie, not knowing whether to be amused or concerned, followed. Her heart was still pounding from Ben's close call. She found herself looking at dark corners, as if somebody might be hiding in one of them.

Ian closed the door behind them and clicked the bolt. He relaxed slightly and turned to Cassie.

"Okay, ma'am," he said. "Where do you want to do this?"

"You should sit down," she said. "Either the living room or the bedroom, I guess. Wherever you're comfortable."

"Living room is fine," he said.

Cassie looked around. It was one of the least furnished apartments she'd ever seen. A cheap love seat, a plain wooden coffee table, one bookshelf, a TV, and a lamp were the only furniture in the living room. There wasn't even a rug on the floor.

"How you doing, honey?" she asked Ben.

Ben didn't answer. He just buried his head against her neck.

"Hey there, lad," Ian said to him. "How'd you like to meet Miri? She's a nice dog. She's a little shy, but she likes kids."

Ben turned his head and glanced down at the dog. Miri looked back with big, soulful brown eyes.

"Miri, sit," Ian said. The dog sat. Her tail swished back and forth on the floorboards.

Cassie gave Ian a look. "Are you sure?" she asked. "If she's been abused, she might be fearful." *And fearful dogs bite*, she added silently.

"She's fond of children," Ian said. "She's met the O'Reilly kids already. Anna was all over her and she didn't so much as growl."

"Okay," Cassie said doubtfully, lowering Ben to the floor but keeping one hand on him, ready to snatch him back out of danger.

Ben looked at Miri with interest. The dog looked back. After a moment, Miri nudged him with her muzzle and wagged her tail faster. He patted her on the head. She licked him under the chin and nudged him again.

"I think they'll be fine, ma'am," Ian said.

"Okay," she said again and made herself let go of her son. Ben put his arms out and encircled Miri's neck. The dog leaned sideways against him.

"She knows he's not a threat," Ian said. "She doesn't like men much, but women are okay, and kids are great."

"She seems to like you," Cassie observed.

He nodded. "Not sure why. But she does. First night I had her, she climbed in bed with me. Curled right up. When she tries to sleep by herself, she has bad dreams."

"How can you tell?"

"She cries in her sleep."

Ian sat down at one end of the two-seater couch. Cassie took the other. She carefully felt around his thigh, checking for swelling or tenderness. This would normally be a very businesslike contact, but it felt more personal this time. She tried to shove the thought away and keep her mind on what she was doing.

"There doesn't seem to be any new injury," she said. "I think the bone has healed. What about the rest of your wounds?"

"Not a problem," he said. "The one in the gut still hurts, but they used those self-absorbent stitches and the incision sealed up a while ago. Just muscle damage underneath, takes some time. Been doing crunches to build back the tone."

"I'll bet you have," she said dryly. "That's why you're still hurting. You know, some of my patients, I have to really lean on them to get them to exercise. You've got the opposite problem."

"Sorry, ma'am. No—"

"I know, I know. No excuse." She smiled. Then she caught sight of his left arm with its intricate tattoo. It was streaked with blood.

He saw where she was looking. "Just a scrape," he said. "Caught a little road rash when I hit the pavement. It's nothing."

"Do you have disinfectant in your bathroom?"

"Yes, ma'am. Got a full aid kid behind the mirror."

She stood up. "I'll be right back. You stay there. And take off your shirt." Realizing how that might sound, she quickly went on, "So I can see if you've got any other scrapes."

Ian's bathroom was as Spartan and tidy as the rest of his place. She found the first-aid kit easily. While she was there, she couldn't help taking a quick look at his medications. Opioid addiction was all too common with veterans, whatever he said. She saw a bottle of Vicodin. The prescription date matched his surgery. She quickly popped the top and looked inside. It appeared that not a single pill was missing.

Cassie came back out into the living room. Ben was still holding Miri, who seemed content to stay there as long as he wanted. They were lying on the floor now, cuddled up in an absolutely adorable pile. Ian was on the couch, his T-shirt lying on the armrest. In addition to his scraped elbow, he'd lost a little skin on his other arm and the backs of his hands. She opened the disinfectant and poured some on a piece of gauze. Then she started dabbing it on the scrapes.

Disinfectant stung on contact with broken skin, but that apparently didn't even register on Ian's personal pain scale. He sat quietly, watching Ben and Miri. To Cassie's surprise, a thin but unmistakable smile was on his face.

"You said you'd let me know when you got your dog," Cassie reminded him.

"Sorry, ma'am," he said. "Didn't have your number."

"You what? Oh. Right. I'm in the phone book. Or you could've called the clinic," she finished lamely.

"They in the habit of giving out their nurses' personal info?"

"Larry might have," she said, taking a big Band-Aid out of the kit and applying it to his elbow. "He's trying to jump-start my love life."

"Is that what we're doing?" Ian asked.

Cassie inwardly cursed herself for the slip of the tongue. "I don't know," she admitted. "I thought, after the way we left things, you weren't interested."

He turned to face her. "Didn't think it mattered, ma'am. You don't want a guy like me."

"I don't know if I want any guy," she retorted. "Ian, my husband died. One day I was married, the next I was a widow. And I'm not even thirty! This isn't what's supposed to happen."

"No. It's not."

"So how do I know what to do? That damned war—" she began, her voice rising angrily. She cut herself short and glanced at Ben. He appeared to have fallen asleep, the way kids sometimes did after a fright had worn off. He had one arm across Miri's back. The dog's eyes were also closed.

"I don't know how to leave it behind," she finished in a quieter tone.

"Me neither," Ian said. "Most nights I'm back there. Used to like the night."

"How come?"

"Got in a lot of fights during the day," he said. "When I was a kid. And my dad was a drunk. Got mean when he got hammered. Beat on me when he could catch me. Easier to hide in the dark."

Cassie shuddered. "I'm sorry," she murmured. She held his hand gently, sponging his scraped knuckles as if she could wash away the past.

He shrugged. "Not complaining," he said. "Taught me some stuff. Might've kept me alive over there."

She traced a line of the tattoo on his left arm. "Did you get this done over there?"

He pulled his arm away, almost reflexively. "Yeah," he said.

"I'm sorry," she repeated. "I didn't mean—"

"It's fine," he said. "Just not used to... you know. Being touched. Got most of it done my second tour, the rest when I got back."

"I've seen a lot of military tattoos," she said.

"Wondering why mine's a Christmas scene? Instead of skulls, dragons, stuff like that?"

She nodded.

He touched his arm, his fingertip brushing against face after face. "One for each sniper kill," he said.

"Oh," Cassie said. She didn't know what she'd been expecting, but it wasn't that.

"Thirty-six," he said. He hesitated. Then he touched the central figure, Mother Mary with Baby Jesus in her arms. "Thirty-eight, counting these."

The face of Mary was gone, replaced by puckered scar tissue. The bullet that had hit Ian's bicep had neatly wiped the features away.

"Ian," Cassie said very quietly. "Do you mean...?"

"I shot a mom," he said, looking straight into her eyes. "And her baby."

She made herself look back, forced herself not to recoil. "Why?"

"Thought she was carrying a bomb. Screwed up." The muscles in his jaw clenched tight. "See why you don't want me?"

"Ian, that's got nothing to do with me," she said. "You did the best you could. You were in combat. You couldn't have known."

"Could've. Should've. They trained me better than that."

"They trained you to kill," she said sharply. "No one could blame you for that."

His eyes went soft and she saw all the way in, to the pain he cradled deep inside. "I can," he whispered.

"You saved my son's life," she said. "You saved that woman, Mrs. O'Reilly."

"Do you believe in God, Cassie Jordan?" he asked.

She was so startled by his use of her name that it took her a second to figure out he'd asked her a question. "Yes," she said. "I do."

"I don't," he said. "Least, I didn't. Still hope He doesn't exist. But now I'm afraid He does."

She reached out and rested her hand on his arm. "You're one of the good guys, Ian. No matter how you feel. I wish I could convince you of that. But God knows. And so do I."

"I want to come home," he whispered, so quietly she had to read the meaning on his lips. "I don't know how."

"Are you scared, Ian?"

He nodded. His eyes were shining with tears he refused to turn loose.

"So am I," she said. "But you know what's funny? I can't be brave for myself. But I can be brave for Ben. And maybe I can be brave for you, too. Can you be brave for me? For us?"

Then Cassie saw one of the most beautiful things she'd ever seen. Way down deep in Ian's intense, wounded eyes, she saw a glimmer of hope, like the flicker of a match flaring in the night.

"Yes," he said.

Chapter 8

"This is the first date I've ever been on where the guy wanted to have a kid along," Cassie said, three days later.

Ian nodded. "Most guys are looking to get laid, ma'am. A kid cramps their style."

"What's 'laid,' Mommy?" Ben asked, looking up from his placemat. He'd been tracing the Zodiac animal figures that were laid out around the edge.

Cassie looked around the restaurant, hoping to find inspiration, or at least a distraction. They were at a Chinese place, one of her favorites. Not that she ate out very often these days. She didn't find any help around her.

"It's a grownup thing," she said desperately. "It's like hugging and kissing."

"Like when you tuck me in?"

"Yeah. Kind of like that."

"Okay." Ben went back to looking at the Oriental dragon in front of him. "What's this?"

"That's a dragon," Ian said. "A big lizard. It breathes fire."

"Did you ever see a dragon?"

"Called in fire support from one once," Ian said. "Puff the Magic Dragon. Took out some Talibs that were engaging us."

"Wow," Ben said.

Cassie shot Ian a questioning glance.

"Nickname for a Spectre gunship, ma'am," Ian explained. "The one we got had a dragon painted on the side. Really was named Puff. Like in the song."

Cassie smiled. She wasn't quite sure what to expect from this evening. Having Ben with her did remove some of the pressure, and she was grateful for that, but it also left her confused. Was she supposed to act like a mother, or a young woman out on a date? Was it even possible to be both at the same time?

That confusion had extended to her choice of clothing. Guys had it easy. Ian was wearing a dark green button-down shirt, black slacks and sport coat, and a black necktie. A man could get away with that ensemble in almost any setting. But women sent messages with their clothes. It hadn't been until Cassie was staring into her closet, getting ready for this date, that she'd realized she hadn't worn anything deliberately sexy in years. Now her old spaghetti-strap tops, low-cut blouses, and lingerie just didn't feel like her anymore.

And was she even trying to be sexy? What did she want out of this date, anyway? Was *she* trying to get laid? Cassie didn't feel sexy. What was the difference between a widow and a woman?

She'd compromised on a blouse that was form-fitting but didn't show too much skin. She did, however, wear a skirt and high heels, both of which felt unfamiliar on her. Nurses opted for practical footwear, like the sneakers Ian had noticed during his rehab, and Cassie usually wore pants. The skirt wasn't exactly revealing, stopping just above her knees, but it did make her feel more feminine.

The waitress came to take their order. Cassie asked for sweet-and-sour chicken with a spare plate for Ben. Ian ordered chicken fried rice.

"So," Cassie said. "What *are* you looking for?"

"Ma'am?"

"You don't want... this?" She cocked her head downward, indicating herself.

To her astonishment, Ian actually looked embarrassed. He wasn't a blusher, but he couldn't meet her eyes for a moment.

"So what do you want?" she pressed.

He looked up at her, recovering. "This is your op, ma'am. Question is, what are *you* looking for?"

"I don't know."

"Why me?" he asked. "Dozens of guys like me come through the VA. Younger, better-looking. Better prospects."

"I don't know," she repeated. "Right place, right time, maybe. And Larry..."

"Who's Larry?"

"A guy I work with."

"Front desk?"

She nodded. "He picked up on something. Said I should give you a chance."

"Don't know I have much to offer," Ian said.

"Would you take Ben to a ball game?"

"Don't follow, ma'am."

"It's a simple question."

"Of course I will, ma'am. You got a day in mind?"

"It was a hypothetical question, Ian."

"Was it?"

Ben glanced up from his placemat. "Can I go to a ball game, Mommy?"

"Of course," she said. "Would you like Mr. Thompson to come with us?"

"Okay."

"Guess it wasn't hypothetical," Ian said. "Look, ma'am, you need something, I'll do what I can."

Cassie felt a surge of irrational irritation. "This isn't a business transaction," she said. "It's a relationship."

"Isn't that what relationships are?" he shot back. "The people I know, everything's a transaction."

"What sort of people do you know?"

"Not your kind of people, ma'am."

"Former Marines?"

"Not exactly."

"Kidnappers?"

Cassie hadn't meant to say it. It just slipped out and hung there in the air, a sharp-edged word dividing them. Ian's face went stony. The warmth seeped out of his eyes. They looked like glacial ice.

She suppressed a shiver. *Thirty-six confirmed kills*, she thought. *Thirty-eight, counting the woman and baby*.

"Think this was a mistake, ma'am," he said, pushing his chair back and starting to stand up.

Cassie felt a moment of sudden, blind panic. "Wait," she said. "I'm sorry. I didn't mean that. I don't... I don't know you. I'm trying to. Don't shut me out. I know you're hurting, Ian. And I can help. But don't fight me. I'm not your enemy."

Ian froze, halfway to his feet, staring at her. Ben looked at him with wide, confused eyes. A long moment passed.

"Sorry, ma'am," he said, settling back into his chair. "I overreacted. No excuse. You're right, anyway. More or less. Did know Mickey Connor. Never liked him, never trusted him. He and Mr. Carlyle had some contact."

"Mr. Carlyle?" she repeated. "Who's he?"

"My boss."

"What does Mr. Carlyle do?"

"Runs a pub. The Barley Corner in South Manhattan."

"Oh." Cassie was vaguely relieved. For a moment, she'd had a vision of Ian working for some sort of shady underworld figure. A bar owner was reassuringly normal.

"Know some... people," Ian said, flicking a sidelong glance Ben's direction. "People who've done some things. But I'm not one of them."

"I never thought you were."

The waitress arrived then, plates of food in her hands. Cassie dished some sweet-and-sour chicken for Ben, along with some rice. Then they started in on the meal.

"When we'd meet with tribal elders, we always tried to do it over dinner," Ian said.

"What'd you think of Afghan food?" she asked.

"Can't complain. Don't much care for goat. Too stringy. But made a nice change from MREs."

"I'll bet." Dean had once described what went into an MRE, or Meal Ready to Eat. It had made her lose her appetite.

"Always helped negotiations," Ian explained. "Eating together makes people friendlier."

"That must be why people eat out on dates," Cassie said.

"Running's the same way," he added. "Go on a five, ten-mile run with another guy, you get close."

"Any shared physical activity," she said. Then her thoughts slid sideways, thinking of the sorts of physical activities that often accompanied dating, and she swallowed hastily. "Sorry if I made you mad."

He shook his head. "Don't apologize, ma'am. My mistake."

Cassie thought about what had just happened. Both of them were sensitive, tender like fresh-healed skin over deep wounds.

They'd have to be gentle with each other, or somebody was going to get hurt.

"How's your fried rice?" she asked, reaching for a change of subject.

A thin but genuine smile creased Ian's face. "Beats goat."

* * *

After dinner, they walked down the block to an ice cream parlor. That had been Ben's idea. As they walked, the kid slipped easily between Cassie and Ian, holding her right hand and Ian's left. Cassie gave a sidelong glance. Ian was moving well, hardly any hitch in his stride.

They got their cones—plain vanilla for Ian, chocolate fudge for Cassie, strawberry for Ben—and sat outside to eat them. Cassie could feel Ian relaxing, though he still had that constant, low-level tension. She'd bet he noticed every car, every pedestrian, evaluating them as possible threats.

"Are you going to be my new daddy?" Ben abruptly asked.

Cassie, mortified, could only stare at her son, mouth hanging open.

Ian turned to Ben and gave him a long, serious look.

"Depends," he said.

"On what?" Ben asked.

"If all three of us want it to happen, that's the way it's going to be," Ian replied. "Mostly it's up to your mom and me, but you'll get a vote, too."

"Mommy misses Daddy," Ben said. "She cries sometimes, when I'm not looking."

Cassie was starting to wish the sidewalk would open under her and swallow her whole. She hoped she wasn't turning as red as she felt.

"If you're not looking, how do you know?" Ian asked.

"Her eyes get red and she sniffles after."

"You're a sharp kid. You notice things." Ian smiled at him. "But it's not polite to talk about other peoples' feelings in front of them. It embarrasses them."

"Oh. Sorry."

Cassie ruffled her son's hair. "That's okay," she said. "I'm not mad."

"Can I see your dog again?" Ben asked Ian.

"Absolutely."

"Now?"

Ian glanced at Cassie. "If your mom says it's okay. We can swing by my place and pick up Miri. Then I'll walk you home."

"You don't need to do that," Cassie said.

"I'll sleep better if I know you got back okay," he said.

"This isn't Baghdad," she said.

"I know that, ma'am. Also know a lady who got kidnapped a couple months ago, not too far from here."

Cassie didn't have a good answer to that, so she just nodded. "Okay, then we can walk while we finish our ice cream."

She was surprised at how much she enjoyed walking with Ben and Ian, how comfortable it felt, despite Ian's hypervigilance. She felt more complete than she had in a very long time. But a little guilt nagged at her. Was it so easy to replace Dean? Just slot another Marine into his place? What sort of wife did that?

The lonely kind, she answered herself. *And not a wife; a widow.*

They'd finished their cones by the time they got to Ian's apartment. Miri was quietly glad to see them, vigorously wagging her tail and leaning against Ian's leg. After the obligatory petting session between Ben and the dog, they set out for Cassie's apartment.

It was about a twenty-minute walk through the gathering dusk. Streetlights and headlights were starting to come on. Ian did move more easily as the sky darkened, just as he'd told her. He felt more at home in the nighttime.

She tried to think what to do, how to finish the evening. Was a simple "goodnight" enough? What about a kiss? She hadn't kissed a man in three years. What if he expected it? What if he kissed her?

No, he wouldn't. If anyone was going to make a move, it would be her. She'd forgotten how awkward a first date could be. Why couldn't they just skip the first couple of dates and jump ahead to a place where nobody was nervous anymore? She had butterflies in her stomach. Nerves, or guilt, or fear? She didn't know.

Too soon, before she'd finished fretting, they got to her building. Cassie fished out her keys.

"Thanks for seeing us home," she said. "Did you have a good time?"

"Yes, ma'am. Thank you." His expression was unreadable, but she saw him tense up. He was nervous, too.

"Do you want to come upstairs?" she blurted out.

He raised his eyebrows. "Ma'am?"

"Just to talk. For a few minutes. I'll put Ben to bed. And then we can sit. And talk." She felt herself starting to babble and stopped.

"Kind of you to offer, ma'am." He hesitated and she saw him almost refuse.

Then he said "Thanks," and fell in step behind her.

She left him in the living room while she got Ben tucked in. When she came out, he was standing in front of the bookshelf, looking at her wedding picture. Miri was lying on the rug, nose between her paws, watching him.

"That's Dean and me," she said quietly, coming up behind him. He didn't so much as twitch. Of course he'd heard her approach. It was probably impossible to sneak up on him.

"Looks like a good guy," Ian said.

"He was."

Ian turned slowly to face her. "Not sure what comes next, ma'am," he said.

"I know why you do that," she said.

"Do what, ma'am?"

"That. I've got a name."

"I know your name, ma'am."

"But you don't like to use it."

"Wouldn't be appropriate."

She laughed quietly. "Ian, we just went on a date," she said. "If that's not an appropriate time to call a girl by her name, what is? I don't buy it."

He watched her and waited for more.

"You try to keep people away from you," she said. "That's just one method you use. You try not to let anyone in. Why?"

"You work with plenty of vets," he said. "Guessing you've got a pretty good idea."

She put a hand on his arm, conscious of how close she was standing to him. "It's better if you say it."

"What do you want from me?" he asked.

"Just you," she said. "The real you. The truth."

"No. You don't."

Cassie knew what Ian was doing. He was still pushing back, still trying to protect himself. She had to show him she wouldn't be moved. She put a gentle smile on her face and stayed right where she was.

"It's okay, Ian. It's okay to be afraid. It's okay to be hurt. But if you stop yourself from feeling, you won't let yourself feel anything good. You'll just be numb. Anesthetic is fine. It's necessary sometimes. But after surgery, you have to wake up. Otherwise you'll never really be alive."

"I'm supposed to be dead," he said. "Too many times. Plenty of other guys didn't make it. When I was a kid, learned I couldn't count on anybody. Learned it well. Then I met a guy who showed me different. Learned to trust him. Wanted more. Went into the Corps when I got out of school. Taught me to trust my buddies. My brothers. Left some of them in the Sandbox, first tour. Second tour, most of the rest died in the 'Stan. And the Corps threw me out."

"I've seen your service record," she reminded him. "They didn't throw you out. The Marines just thought more combat would be bad for you."

"Combat's bad for everybody," he retorted. "Thing they didn't teach me was how to come home."

"What is home, Ian?" She curled her fingers around his, squeezing his hands lightly.

He shook his head. "Don't know. Why are you doing this, ma'am?"

"Doing what?"

"Picking me open. Like a scab."

"Remember what you said about saline solution?" she said. "Sometimes when you start getting better, it feels worse for a while. The fluids make you thirstier."

"Why are you doing this?" he asked again. The look in his eyes was softer than before, but more frightened, too. More vulnerable.

Cassie owed him the truth, owed him her own vulnerability. She'd asked him to be brave. She could do nothing less.

"Because I'm scared too," she said. "I'm trying to find my way back. I thought helping other people, wounded men, would help me, and it does. A little. But I need to do something for myself, too. And for Ben. He needs me to be whole, to be healed.

To have a life. I'm trying to fix me along with you. Does that make any sense?"

"Don't know, ma'am. You're the nurse."

"Are you jerking me around, Marine?"

He shook his head. "Not on purpose. Easy to hide behind protocol sometimes. Corps taught me the importance of taking cover."

"Semper fi," she said with a wry smile. "I need to know if I can move on. Neither one of us can just live in the past. It's part of us, sure, but it's over."

"Nothing's over," he said.

"But we can move on," she insisted, squeezing his hands tighter. "I need somebody, someone who understands. Someone who's broken, not quite like me, maybe, but close enough so we speak the same language. You understand if I start crying all of a sudden, for no damn reason. You know what that folded flag on the shelf means. You know pain."

"Lots of guys do," he said. "Why me?"

"I don't know. Why is it ever anybody? You think I know what the hell I'm doing?" She had tears in her eyes, the drops quivering on her lashes. "I don't know if you're the one for me, Ian. But I know there's only one way to find out. You ever jump out of an airplane?"

"Got thrown out of a chopper once."

"There's no in-between," she said. "You can't halfway jump. You have to just take the leap. On faith."

"Haven't got much faith."

"Feelings are like muscles," she said. "You need to work them. Let yourself feel. Take a chance. *Let me in, Ian.*"

His jaw clenched and unclenched. Defensiveness and loneliness fought across the terrain of his face. Cassie watched his internal battle, holding her breath.

"I'm trying, ma'am," he said in a tight voice. "Don't know how."

"Say my name," she said. "Just close your eyes and say it."

He took a deep, shuddering breath. "Cassie," he whispered. "Cassie Jordan."

She leaned in, closed her own eyes, and kissed him.

It wasn't a grand, passionate kiss, the kind that got a big musical fanfare at the movies. It was hesitant, gentle, coaxing. Ian's lips were like the rest of him: strong, quiet, slow to trust. That was okay. Cassie let herself feel, left herself open to whatever might come after.

She felt his startled reaction, felt him start to pull away. She held him there with nothing but the light sensation of her lips on his. Then, slowly, so slowly, she felt him yield to her. He softened and pressed close to her. The kiss was tender and so soft.

Cassie tasted salt on her lips. She drew back at last. Slowly, she opened her eyes.

Ian was crying. Tears chased each other down the wet trails on his cheeks.

She put up a hand and wiped his face with her thumb, brushing away the tears. "It's okay," she said.

"I'm sorry," he said. "Cassie, I'm so sorry."

She felt his legs start to buckle. Her nurses' reflexes kicked in and she pulled him to the couch, just in time. He sank down onto the cushions. She sat beside him and held him while he cried. After a few minutes, he put his arms around her. She was crying quietly too, not even sure quite why. They sat together, arms entwined, their inner scars open for the whole world to see. But nobody else was in that room, so nobody saw them.

After a while, Ian stopped crying. His breathing slowed. His head rested against Cassie's shoulder. Miri nosed at his knee, then lay down with a sigh and rested her snout across his feet. Cassie, more tired than she'd known, fell asleep there beside him.

Chapter 9

Cassie woke up with an awful, furry feeling in her mouth, like a mouse had crawled in there and died. Her neck was stiff and her right arm was completely numb. She forced her eyelids opened and groggily wondered where she was.

She was sitting on her couch, in her own living room. Ian Thompson lay against her, still asleep. His body had forced her arm back into the cushions and cut off her circulation.

Cassie tried to guess what time it was. The sky was a very dark blue, but with a hint of brightness in the air. Early morning, she figured. Very early morning. No wonder her mouth had that nasty taste in it. She'd gone to sleep without brushing her teeth.

She felt ridiculous. She'd invited her date up to her place, her son had gone to sleep, it had been just the two of them, they'd kissed, and then... they'd started crying and fallen asleep. "Anticlimax" was both a terrible pun and the simple truth. And she wasn't even unhappy about it. That was the weirdest thing.

Moving very slowly, so as not to disturb him, she started to ease her arm out from behind Ian. Almost immediately, the numbness was replaced by pins and needles all the way up to her shoulder. She drew in her breath in a tight hiss and held still until the feeling started to subside. Then she continued working her way free.

Her hand struck something at the back of his belt, a hard object. She explored it with her fingertips, tracing the outline. It was a pistol grip. He had a gun holstered in the small of his back, hidden under his sport coat.

"Ma'am?"

She jumped in surprise. Ian sat up, straightening his back. He was one of those guys who woke all at once, going from fast asleep to wide awake at one go. He looked around with a quick, searching stare.

"Good morning," she said, running a hand self-consciously through her hair. It was a tousled mess.

"Didn't mean to nod off there, ma'am." He started to stand up, then realized Miri was still lying on one of his feet. The dog was sound asleep, the tip of her tongue protruding slightly from her mouth. He sank back and stayed where he was.

"It's fine," she said. "I'm glad."

"Hope I didn't do or say anything inappropriate, ma'am."

"The only inappropriate thing you're saying is that word," she said.

The corners of his mouth quirked slightly in a hint of a smile. "Sorry, ma—Cassie. Force of habit. Surprised I went down. Usually better at staying awake. In the 'Stan one time, stayed awake for—"

"Five days," she said. "I know. I read your citation."

"They gave me a medal," he said in disgust. "Called me a damn hero. Do me a favor, ma'am. Don't ever call me that."

"Don't call me 'ma'am' again and you've got a deal."

His smile sheepishly reappeared. “Oops.”

“Maybe you couldn’t sleep out there because you didn’t feel safe,” she said.

“No maybe about it,” he said. “Wasn’t safe. Talibs trying to kill me all the time.”

“Do you feel safe here?”

He considered. “Don’t know,” he said, holding up both hands, palms up as if balancing a scale. “Feel a couple different things. Safer than I’ve been in a long time, but more exposed, too. Naked.”

“Naked?” She raised an eyebrow and looked at him. For a man who’d slept in his clothes, he still looked pretty put-together. Even his tie was still neatly knotted.

“Not what I meant, ma—Cassie. Didn’t mean to suggest—”

“It might be a little soon for that,” she said, giving him a soft smile, one she’d previously reserved for Dean. “But maybe somewhere down the line.”

He licked his lips, looking suddenly nervous. “Look, Cassie,” he said. “I hope you’re not expecting me to be... you know. Experienced.”

“Oh my God,” she blurted, flustered and fighting an inappropriate case of the giggles. “Are you a... I mean, it’s fine if you are. I just didn’t think... I assumed...”

He shook his head. “Not a virgin, if that’s what you’re asking. Ten years too late. High school sweetheart. Amanda. First time was after the district championship soccer game.”

Cassie grinned. “You don’t need to give me all the details. Unless you want to, of course. In which case, I’m all ears.”

“Was team captain,” he said. “Been going with her for a while. She played in the pep band. Clarinet. When I got out of the shower, she was waiting outside the gym.” He smiled at the memory. “Her dad didn’t like me. Thought I was a bad influence.”

"You? How could you possibly be a bad influence? Besides screwing around with his daughter, of course."

"Got in some trouble when I was younger. Running with a gang. Fights, skipping school, that sort of thing. Mr. Carlyle helped me clean up my act. By senior year I was solid, and Mr. Carlyle got my juvie record scrubbed, but Amanda's dad was a lawyer and gathered some intel, so..." He shrugged. "I joined up after graduation, and that was the end of it. Amanda went to college. Vassar. I went to Iraq. Haven't seen her since."

"Are you telling me you haven't slept with a girl in ten years?" she asked, half-joking.

He shrugged again. "Been busy."

"Do you miss it?"

"Do you?"

Cassie blinked. "Well, of course I do... I mean, sometimes. Mostly I miss the closeness. The connection. It wouldn't be the same with some guy I picked up at a bar or something, so the one-night things never really tempted me."

"Me neither."

"You know, Ian, for such a physical guy, you seem awfully reluctant to let yourself feel good."

"Morning after a date seems like a strange time to be talking about this."

She laughed quietly. "You're saying we should've talked about this last night?"

"Don't have to talk about it at all. Don't have to do anything if you don't want, either."

"Ian, you are completely missing the point," she said. "But it's sweet of you. It's funny. I've met a lot of tough guys in my line of work, and you might be the toughest one yet. You think you're a dangerous man, don't you?"

"Don't think," he said. "Know it. Killed people. Lots of them."

"I know," she said. "Thirty-eight."

"That's just confirmed sniper shots," he said. "Probably got double that many, give or take."

"And you're still carrying a gun."

"Sorry," he said. "Never feel right without it. Got a license to carry. Won't ever just leave one lying around, if that's what you're worried about. Not where a kid could get his hands on it. All my guns are locked up whenever I'm not carrying."

"Okay, you've got *lots* of guns," she corrected herself. "My point is, some people might think you're a little scary, but I'm not scared of you, no matter what you say."

"I'm not going to hurt you," he said. "Or your kid. No matter what."

"I know," she said. "What I'm trying to say is, I feel safe with you. I feel like I can trust you."

"Thanks," he said. "Won't let you down."

"I know that, too. Hell, you jumped in front of a car to protect Ben."

"Didn't know he was your son when I did it. Just saw a kid in trouble. Would've done the same for any kid. Only did what anybody would've done."

She smiled. "That's not true and we both know it. There must have been two dozen people on that sidewalk. Only one of them jumped out there."

"Always had good reflexes."

"And a recently-broken leg," she reminded him. "You know what some people would call a guy who does things like that, but I promised not to say it, so I won't."

"Thanks."

"But I have to warn you."

"What about?"

"If you really want to be a part of my life, Ben's going to look up to you. You'll need to be his role model, like it or not. And whatever anybody else thinks, you'll be his hero. There, I said it. Can you handle that?"

He returned the smile. "Absolutely... Cassie." He pulled up his sleeve and glanced at his wristwatch. It was a heavy, solid, military-style watch that looked not only waterproof but bulletproof, too. It would probably survive a nuclear explosion. The hands read half-past four.

"Sorry to run out on you," he said. "Got a couple things to take care of. Wasn't expecting this to be such a late night. Correction; morning."

"What could you possibly have to do at four-thirty?"

"Mr. Carlyle runs a pub. I keep unusual hours."

"Oh, right." She stood up. "Well, if you need to go..."

He nudged Miri, who stared sleepily up at him and wagged her tail once. The dog shifted to a sitting position, waiting to see what would happen.

"I'd like to see you again," he said. "If that's okay."

"We'll make sure of it," she said. She leaned in, uncomfortably conscious of her morning breath, and kissed him lightly on the cheek.

* * *

"You got laid," were the first words out of Larry's mouth when Cassie got to work.

"I did not!" she retorted.

"Oh." He was temporarily crestfallen, but recovered quickly. "Why not?"

"I hate to destroy your illusions about hot single moms," she said. "But we happen to spend most of our time working and taking care of our kids, not cruising for one-night stands."

"Sucks to be you," Larry said. "Go on, ask me."

"Ask you what?"

"Did I get laid last night?"

"I don't ask questions like that."

"Personal questions?"

"Questions I don't want the answers to."

"Fair enough. Did you at least call him?"

"Call who?"

He grinned. "You know perfectly well who. You're a crummy liar."

"Not exactly."

"Aha!" he said triumphantly. "He called you?"

"He saved my son's life."

Larry blinked. That wasn't in the script. "Wait, what?"

"The idiots at daycare have a broken latch on the playground gate. Ben saw me coming to pick him up, ran straight out into the street, and nearly got run over. Ian—Sergeant Thompson, I mean—was walking his dog and saw the whole thing. He jumped into the middle of traffic, bad leg and all."

"Wow. And you didn't even give him a gratitude screw?"

Cassie slapped his shoulder. "You're a pig."

"I prefer to think of myself as the obnoxious kid brother you never had."

"Same thing."

"So... details?" Larry said, resting his chin on his hands and leaning forward.

"Nothing to tell. We had a date last night. He slept over."

"And you told me you didn't get laid!"

"I didn't. We fell asleep. On the couch. And now my neck is stiff and my virtue unspoiled."

"So why didn't you get some?"

Cassie shrugged uncomfortably. "My son was asleep in the next room!"

"If that stopped people, we'd all be only children."

"Why do you care, anyway? What's it to you?"

"I think the morale of my coworkers is important," he said. "And maybe you ought to think about why you and that handsome, chiseled war hero didn't have sweet, patriotic, all-American sex when you had the chance."

"I swear," she said. "If you say one word about 'standing to attention,' I'm going to brain you with this clipboard."

Larry just smiled. The situation was defused by the arrival of the first patient of the day. Cassie was able to retreat into her normal workday routine. But she kept thinking about Larry's words. Why hadn't she and Ian made love? Because it was a first date? Because of Ben? Because they were both instinctively shy people?

Maybe all those things were a little bit true. But Cassie thought it was probably something else. She thought it was the war.

* * *

Cassie got off work and started out of the clinic. Her phone chimed before she'd made it to the front door.

"Hello?" she said.

"Hello, ma'am—Cassie."

"Ian," she said. "What's going on?"

"Hope I'm not interrupting," he said. "My intel said you'd be going off duty a few minutes ago."

"You're very... precise," she said. "You know, some girls might think that was a little creepy."

"No excuse."

She couldn't help smiling. "None needed. You're right. I'm on the way to fetch Ben."

"Got a line on three tickets for the Saturday ballgame," he said. "Yankee Stadium, against Cleveland. Afternoon game. You Ben want to go?"

"That's sweet of you to think of us," she said. "We'd love to."

"I can come by your place," he said. "When should I be there?"

"Maybe noon?" she said. "We can catch the subway and grab something to eat beforehand."

"Affirmative."

"See you then. And thank you. Ben will be over the moon."

Chapter 10

Saturday morning crawled. Ben was tremendously excited about the upcoming ballgame, and like most six-year-olds, he wasn't good at waiting. It was just like being on a long car trip with the kid in the back seat asking every five minutes if they were there yet. They'd been to baseball games before, but not often. Dean had loved baseball, and even though Ben had been too young to play when Dean had died, some of that love had apparently been handed down. Whenever Cassie had taken Ben to a game, she'd always been terribly conscious of an empty space on the opposite side of the boy, the space where his dad should've been. She'd shied away from ballparks as a result, which wasn't fair to her son.

If you were going to exorcise your personal demons, Cassie could think of better places to do it than Yankee Stadium, but she wasn't about to shoot Ian down, especially since he'd paid attention to what her son had wanted. So she dug around in the back of her dresser and found an old Yankees jersey Dean had bought for her. It said SABATHIA across the back, the name of the team's top starter when the shirt had been printed. He was still pitching for the Yanks, though he wouldn't be on the mound this particular afternoon.

She got her baseball cap from the top shelf of the closet and dusted it off. She set it out alongside Ben's matching hat and little first-baseman's glove. Ben announced that he was going to catch a foul ball. Cassie hoped one wouldn't come too close. After the day-care incident, she wasn't sure she could handle a scare like that.

The living room clock's hands hovered at 11:58 when the lobby buzzer went off. Cassie unlocked the entrance. About a minute later, Ian was knocking on the apartment's door. He was wearing a black button-down shirt and slacks. His face was stoic as ever, but she saw the nervousness behind his eyes.

"You're early," she teased, pointing to the clock, which now read 11:59.

"Figured on a few seconds to give you a positive ID in the lobby," he said, unsmiling. "You shouldn't open the door without checking who it is. Could've been anybody."

"Or it could've been the guy who said he'd be here at noon," she said. "Do you want to go back outside and come in again? I can do one of those computer voice-pattern checks."

"Not necessary," he said, either not getting the joke or not finding it funny. "You squared away?"

"Hi Mr. Thompson," Ben said, bouncing into the living room. "Can we go to the game now?"

"Pretty soon, lad," Ian said. "I think we're going to get some food first."

"I want a hamburger," Ben announced.

Ian looked at Cassie and raised his eyebrows. "Your call, Ma'am."

"And ice cream," Ben added.

“Fine with me,” she said, winking at Ian. “I know a place that does great goat-burgers.”

“Ewww!” Ben said.

“You ever had goat?” Ian asked him.

Ben had to think about it. “No,” he said. “But I bet it’s gross.”

“Depends,” Ian said.

“On how it’s cooked?” Cassie asked.

“How hungry you are,” Ian said. “Two days without food, goat starts to sound pretty good.”

* * *

They went to a burger place just down the block from Cassie’s apartment, one of those little hole-in-the-wall restaurants that tourists didn’t know about, that looked awful and served fantastic food. It was a beautiful late-summer day, the temperature a sunny eighty-six degrees. Ian had his head on a swivel all the way there, but Cassie could tell he was trying to relax. He was limping slightly. However, he gave no other sign of pain.

“How’s the leg?” she asked.

“Can’t complain,” was his predictable reply. “A little better every day.”

“I don’t see a holster,” she said quietly.

“Not carrying today.”

“You’re not?”

“Of course not. Ballpark has metal detectors.”

“Oh. Right. Silly me.” She paused. “Does it bother you? Not packing?”

He nodded. “Trying to get used to it,” he said. “Going to try to be a civilian today.”

She slipped her hand into his and squeezed. “That’s brave of you,” she said. “I appreciate what you’re doing. And if you say you're just doing your job, or it's what any guy would do, I'm going to re-break that leg of yours."

Ian opened his mouth, closed it without a sound, then opened it again. "Doesn't that violate your Hippocratic Oath?"

"I'm not a doctor," she said with a sweet smile. "I'm a registered nurse. We don't take the Oath. I can do whatever I want to you."

"I'll keep that in mind," he said, and though he didn't smile, she caught the slight twinkle in his eye. The rush of warmth she felt from the touch of his hand and the look in his eye surprised her with its strength. Disconcerted, she looked the other way to where Ben, attached to her left hand, was skipping along the sidewalk, swinging her arm as far as he could get it to go.

The restaurant had a handful of tables behind an iron railing out front. It was a little warm to eat indoors, so they took their burgers and fries outside. Cassie had a chocolate malt, Ian drank a Sprite, and Ben had a strawberry ice cream cone for dessert. They ate and talked, enjoying the sunshine. Ian's nervousness had melted away and he was openly smiling now, chatting with Ben about baseball. As she watched the two of them, Cassie felt something tight inside her coming slowly unknotted.

"Daddy took me to a game a long time ago," Ben said to Ian. "But I don't remember it."

"That was two days before he deployed," Cassie said. Her throat tightened up again, almost in reflex. "Ben was just three."

"Did you go to games with your daddy?" Ben asked.

"No," Ian said.

"Did your daddy die in the war too?" Ben asked solemnly.

Ian blinked, but gave no other sign of being surprised. His smile faded. "He's still alive," he said. "But I don't see him these days."

"Why not?"

Cassie marveled at the ability of small children to ask the really awkward questions with no self-consciousness at all. Ian took a moment to reply, sipping his Sprite.

"My dad's not a very nice guy," he said at last. "We don't get along."

"Oh," Ben said. He licked the edge of his cone where a small avalanche of melted strawberry was threatening to overflow. "He should've taken you to a game."

"Yeah," Ian said. "He probably should've."

"You're a nice guy," Ben said in tones of absolute certainty.

Cassie saw the denial in Ian's face, the equal certainty that he was not, in fact, a nice guy. She reached across the table for his hand and gave it another squeeze. He looked at her and she shook her head very slightly. He nodded in acknowledgment and said nothing.

* * *

On the subway to the stadium, Cassie could see Ian fighting with himself, trying and failing to relax. Post-traumatic stress was a constant struggle, just as grief was. Even if it wasn't in the front of your mind, it was always hovering in the background. Just dealing with the emotion was exhausting. She wondered if either of them would ever be truly free of it. She knew, from her training and experience, that the best way to move on from trauma wasn't to forget about it. It became a part of you. What you needed to do was accept it and make peace with it.

Of course, knowing what to do was only half the battle, the easy half.

The stadium was humming with people, exactly the sort of place to make a traumatized, hypervigilant veteran especially edgy. Cassie watched Ian with concern, but he seemed to have himself under control. She wondered again just what it cost him to maintain that façade of calm strength. It was strange. Usually, being around tense people made her nervous, but Ian made her feel safe. She was completely confident he'd do everything in his power to protect her and Ben.

She thought they'd go to the ticket window, but Ian already had the tickets. He pulled them out of his pocket as they neared the gate, dropping down on one knee to hand Ben his.

"Don't lose this," he said. "I'm counting on you."

"I won't," Ben said.

Cassie glanced at her ticket. Her eyes widened. She'd been expecting something in the family section, way in the upper decks somewhere. These were in Section 17B, in the fourth row, just a little to one side of home plate.

"Ian," she said in a low voice, catching him by the arm.

"Problem?" he asked.

She shook her head. "There must be some mistake. These tickets..."

"No mistake," he said. "I double-checked."

"But these cost hundreds of dollars," she said. She'd looked up home plate seats the last time she'd gone to a game, on a whim, and had taken the rest of the day getting over the sticker shock. "I can't afford these."

"No charge," he said.

"You can't do this," she said. "You're not a rich guy, Ian. I don't think you can afford these either. We can... I don't know, can't we sell them to a scalper or something and get some less expensive seats?"

"If that's what you want," he said. He looked confused, and maybe a little hurt. "Didn't pay hundreds of dollars, if that's what you're worried about. One of Mr. Carlyle's associates knows a guy, who knows another guy who has season tickets. That guy's out of town, so he wasn't using them today. It's just a favor, already paid for."

"That's quite a favor," she said. "Who is this guy, anyway?"

Ian shrugged. "Don't know the guy with the tickets, but Mr. Carlyle went through his friend Mr. Corcoran. Mr. Corcoran knows pretty much everybody, and if he doesn't know the right guy, he knows the guy who knows the guy."

"Okay," she said doubtfully.

"Look," he said. "If you're not comfortable, we can find something else..."

"Mommy, can we go in?" Ben asked. He was hopping with impatience, bored with the grown-up talk.

"Game's starting in a few minutes," Ian said.

"Okay," Cassie said again, conceding defeat. "I guess this is all right. I'm just not used to being so well-connected."

They handed over their tickets, walked through the metal detectors just as Ian had foreseen, and went down to find their seats. The sun was high overhead, the sky a spectacular blue, the grass a green so vibrant it was almost unreal. They settled into their appointed places, so close that they could practically reach out and touch the field. The players were just finishing their warmup. A cluster of fans lined the railing, hoping for autographs.

"Mommy," Ben said. "Can I go down closer?"

"Okay," she said. "Let's go."

The Yankees filed past the stands on their way into the dugout. A few of them angled toward the fans and shook some hands, signing balls and T-shirts that were thrust toward them. With an odd shock, Cassie realized she was standing right in front of a group of multi-millionaires, star athletes who commanded the loyalty of legions of enthusiastic fans.

One of them caught her eye and, to her astonishment, winked at her. Ben, at her side, waved wildly to the man, who jogged over to them.

"Hey there, little guy," the player said. Cassie saw a face she'd seen on TV dozens of times, a face as familiar to Yankees fans as the faces of their own close family. He was smiling broadly. "What've you got?"

Ben looked at his mother in sudden panic. They hadn't anticipated this, and had neither baseball nor pen.

The player, still grinning, produced a baseball. Taking a pen from another autograph-seeker, he scrawled his signature on it and handed it to Ben, who clutched it to his chest like it was the Hope Diamond.

"There you go," he said. "Enjoy the game."

"Say thank you to Mr. Jeter, Ben," Cassie managed to say.

"Thank you, Mr. Jeter," Ben obediently parroted to the Yankees shortstop, who nodded pleasantly and turned to the next fan.

Feeling slightly dazed, Cassie returned to her seat. Ben sat next to her, staring raptly at the baseball with Derek Jeter's autograph.

"Guess that's why the seats cost so much," Ian said.

* * *

The weather was fine, the seats were fantastic, and Ben was enthralled by his autographed ball, but the Yankees let them down. Cleveland got two runs in the second inning and an insurance run in the eighth, while the home team flailed ineffectually with their bats. By the time it was all over, the Yanks had gone down 3-0, having scattered a pathetic five hits over nine innings.

It didn't matter. Ben was happy, Ian was smiling, and Cassie was conscious only of a very slight tug at her heartstrings. Being there together just felt *right*.

They trooped out of the stands at the end warm, cheerful, and slightly sunburnt. Ben chattered all the way to the subway, showing off his baseball to anyone he thought might want to see it. Then, as soon as they climbed aboard the train, he crawled up between Ian and Cassie, leaned against Ian's leg, and went to sleep, hand still clutching his treasure.

Ian looked down at the boy with an expression of complete, open tenderness that melted Cassie's heart. She had a lump in her throat.

Dear God, she thought. *I'm in love with this man*. And that was all wrong. She wasn't ready for this. She was too tender, too broken. She had her son to take care of, her life to live. She couldn't let Ian in. He was as broken as she was; more, even. And what if he didn't want it, didn't want her?

Cassie tried to wrestle down the dark thoughts. She was feeling good, damn it, and wasn't going to let her grief ruin a good day. She smiled at Ian and rested her hand on his arm. He returned the smile and she saw his eyes were shining.

"It's nice, isn't it," she said. It was a terribly inadequate thing to say, but it was all she could think of.

He nodded. "Too bad Miri couldn't come with," he said.

"How's she treating you?"

"She's amazing. Can't explain it. Needing someone and being needed at the same time. I guess you get it." He nodded to Ben.

"Yeah," Cassie said. "I get it."

"She trusts me," Ian said. "So much, it makes me trust myself more. Keeps me here with her instead of over there. Told you about her bad dreams."

"You did," she said.

"She can tell when I've got bad ones, too. Lies down next to me, lays her head on me. Helps."

At their stop, Ian scooped Ben up in his arms. The boy nestled against his shoulder and made a sleepy sound, but didn't even open his eyes.

"He's all used up," Cassie said softly. "Is your leg bothering you? Is he too heavy to carry back to my place?"

"Carried a Marine through Kandahar for five days once," Ian said.

"You could've just said no, it's fine," she teased. "You don't have to always be the toughest guy in the world."

"Of course I do," he replied, stepping off the train. "I'm a Marine."

"Being tough isn't enough, you know," she said quietly.

"Starting to figure that out, ma'am," he said. "Sorry. Cassie."

She keyed in to the apartment. Ian kept carrying Ben, showing no sign of weariness. When she reached for the elevator call button, he cleared his throat.

"Rather take the stairs," he said.

"Even with your leg?" she asked.

"You know how I feel about elevators."

"Yeah, I know," she said. "But I bet more New Yorkers die falling on the stairs than die in elevators."

"Good point," he said. "Fine, we'll take the elevator."

As the elevator hummed up to her floor, Cassie watched Ian thoughtfully. He was unarmed, his hands full with a sleeping little boy, and he was trapped in what he'd described as a ready-made kill-box. He was voluntarily making himself helpless and vulnerable. She felt ashamed of her own fears.

She unlocked her apartment and eased open the door. "Just lay him in bed," she said in a low voice. "I'll wake him up for supper."

"Affirmative," Ian replied. He carried Ben into the boy's room and very gently laid him down. He picked up one of Ben's stuffed animals, a plush dog, and tucked it in next to him. Then he drew the sheet over him and walked out of the room with all the stealth a Scout Sniper could muster.

Cassie muffled a giggle at the sight of Ian tiptoeing out of the room and closing the door behind him as gingerly as if it was strapped to a live grenade. He paused, took a deep breath, and stretched his shoulders.

"A little stiff?" she asked.

"A little," he said. "Once you stop running in full kit, you get out of practice. Won't be able to carry him like that too much longer."

"I guess we'll see about that," she said, and just like that, it was out in the open. She wanted him to stick around, to watch Ben get older.

"Guess so," he said. "Hope you had a good time today."

In answer, she took off her baseball cap, pulling it free of her ponytail, and tossed it onto the coffee table. She stepped in close, tilted her face up to his, and kissed him.

She felt his surprise, the ever-present tension in his body. She fought down the urge to pull back, to protect herself. Instead, she leaned in closer, letting herself feel him, molding herself to him.

He hesitated, and the fear flared up in Cassie again. What if he really didn't want her? But then he put his arms around her and he was kissing her back. His mouth, like all of him, was cautious and wary at first, but strong and competent. He was all lean muscle, the closeness of his body awakening an incredible thirst in Cassie that she hadn't known was there. She had denied so much to herself for so long that this taste of desire fed on itself, making her want more, need more.

He was the one who drew back, the look on his face mirroring Cassie's own private fears.

"I'm sorry," she said. "I didn't realize—"

"Sorry," he said simultaneously. "Didn't mean to get carried away. You don't owe me—"

"Ian," she said, cutting him off.

"What?"

Their faces were very close together. Cassie's cheeks were flushed with sunburn and the blood that was pounding in her veins. She felt like her whole body was going warm and melty, like ice cream under the summer sun.

"Let's go to my room."

He looked at her for a long moment. "You sure?" he asked.

"I want you," she said. "Maybe you're not used to girls telling you that. I know I'm not used to saying it. I'm scared, Ian, and I know you are, too. But we can't wait till we're not, because we'll be dead by the time that happens."

"I can't be him," Ian said. "The man you lost."

"I'm not asking you to be. All I'm asking you to be is you. I'm never not going to miss Dean. I'm not looking for his replacement. I wasn't even looking for anybody, but I found you and you found me."

A tear overflowed Ian's left eye and left a glistening trail down his cheek. "What if I can't, Cassie?" he whispered. "What if I can't be what you need? What if I'm... What if I'm broken?"

"Of course you're broken, Ian. So am I. This is how we heal. Together."

"You think it'll make everything better?" he asked, his eyebrows crinkling in the middle.

"No," she said. "But it'll bring us closer."

His jaw worked as if he was chewing on the thought.

"What's the problem?" she asked, saying it lightly to cover her ever-present fear. "You're not even a little tempted? I'm not pretty enough for you?"

"Cassie Jordan," he said, putting his hands on both her shoulders. "You're the most beautiful woman I think I've ever seen. I'm no good with words, can't say it right."

She knew it was an exaggeration. Her hair was a mess, sweaty and clumpy from being under a baseball cap all afternoon. Her cheeks were flushed pink and she was wearing old jeans and a baseball jersey. But she also knew he meant it.

"Then you'd better take me in there," she said slowly, "and show me."

She had just enough presence of mind to turn the lock on the bedroom doorknob in case Ben woke up and tried to wander in. Then she stripped off her tattered, worn-out grief like an old shirt and concentrated on the man in front of her.

They went slowly, tenderly; no mad tearing-off of clothing. Both of them were too wounded to be reckless. She undressed him one button at a time, peeling away layers of protective fabric. His body was a patchwork of scars over hard muscle, marred by years of war, broken and beautiful. The tattoo on his arm, the monument he'd carved in his own flesh to the people he'd killed, was a roadmap of old pain. But his strong, skillful hands were gentle.

After she had removed his shirt, it was his turn. Her jersey went awkwardly over her head, Cassie wishing for something she could unbutton or slide off her shoulders. The jersey got tangled in her hair for a second, but that was all right. Both of them laughed at the minor mishap. He had a little trouble with the hooks on her bra, since he didn't have much experience with that type of fastener, but he got it open in the end.

Cassie felt a moment of intense self-consciousness as she was laid bare to him. But Ian was looking mostly into her face. He saw her nervousness and smiled slightly.

"Don't worry," he whispered. "I've got you."

She opened her arms and melted into his embrace.

Chapter 11

"Cassie? You okay?"

Ian's question was so absurd, so cliché, that Cassie grabbed her pillow and clamped it over her mouth to muffle her giggles. After a moment, when she got herself under control, she removed the pillow to find him staring thoughtfully at her. He was propped up on his elbow, lying beside her in the queen bed that had always seemed to have too much room in it since Dean had gone. Now it felt almost crowded. The apartment's air conditioning was only so-so and in spite of kicking the sheets off, they were both bathed in sweat. Summer, Cassie thought, wasn't the best time to start a physical relationship.

"Sorry," she said. "It's just... this whole thing. It's a little funny, isn't it?"

He didn't see the humor. He was worrying that she was laughing at him, maybe. Male egos were so fragile. She reached out and ran a hand down his chest.

"I'm fine," she said.

"Don't want to screw things up," he said. "Don't ever want to hurt you."

"You didn't," she said. "Just the opposite. It's just been... God, it's been *years*. I forgot what it's like. That was... it was great. Honestly."

"You want me to go?"

The question stopped her short, wiped the smile off her face. "Go?" she repeated. "What are you talking about? Why would you think that?"

"Don't want to get in your way."

Cassie didn't know whether to kiss him or slap him in the face, so she did neither. "Ian, what do you think we're doing here?" she demanded.

"Think that's pretty obvious," he said.

"Of course we were making love," she said. "But that's not what I'm talking about. I'm talking about all of it. You. Me. Ben. This."

His eyes were serious, thoughtful. "Don't really know," he said. "All I know is, when I'm here, don't want to be anywhere else. You feel like... can't say what. Like when you're out pounding the sand in the Sandbox, three days in the field. Sleeping in the open. Water in the canteen is a hundred degrees plus, tastes like it's boiling in your mouth. Sand gets under your collar, in your skivvies, everywhere. Blisters, heat rash, flies. Whole world smells awful: sweat, bad breath, trash, rotting meat, burning shit from the cans off the base. Not even counting when the bad guys shoot at you. Then you come back to base, strip off your battle rattle, right down to the skin. Step in the shower, feel that clean water rain down. And know you're safe. You're that shower, Cassie. You make me feel clean. Wash all the war off me. I want to get clean, stay clean. More than anything."

Cassie swallowed. She tried to say something, but couldn't. She blinked several times, trying to clear her eyes, but the waterworks were really flowing. She fell back on the mattress and started crying.

"Shit," Ian said. "I'm sorry. Cassie, I didn't mean... what's the matter?" His hand was on her upper arm. He was leaning over her, his face a blurry mask of concern.

She shook her head, trying to form words and failing. His words kept echoing in her, over and over. *Wash all the war off me. I want to get clean, stay clean. More than anything*. She started to sob, hiccupping and gulping for air. Ian watched her helplessly, the man of action unsure for once what to do.

"Hold me," she finally managed to choke out.

"Roger that," he said, gathering her into his arms. He held her close, heedless of the heat, as if he could shield her with his body.

After a while, her sobs quieted and her tears diminished to a slow trickle. She sniffled loudly. Ian, always practical, reached for the box of tissues she kept by the bedside and handed it to her. She sat up and blew her nose with a loud, unladylike honk.

"Thanks," she said. "Sorry."

"No apology needed," he said. "Sorry I said the wrong thing. Said I wasn't good with words."

Cassie gave him a look. "You said exactly the right thing," she said. "I just... it all came out. I think I needed that, maybe as much as the other thing. So thank you."

"You're welcome."

"And I don't want you to leave. Not now, not..." She let it trail off. The enormity of what she'd almost said was suddenly very large and overwhelming.

"Okay," he said. "I'm on duty tonight, but I can stay another hour or two."

"You're so damn literal," she said. "Of course you can leave. But I want you to come back."

"Oh." The look of relief in his face was so comical that she felt another bout of giggles coming on. Cassie had never been hysterical before. She wondered if this was what it felt like. She smothered the laughter as ruthlessly as she could. This was no time for it.

"Listen to me, Ian," she said. "I'm pretty sure I'm falling in love with you. You get that?"

He was looking straight into her eyes. "Yes," he said. "I get that."

"I'm still hurting," she said. "And a little sex isn't going to fix that. It doesn't work that way."

"I know."

"But I want to get better," she went on. "With you. And I want you to get better, too. It's something we have to work on. I'm going to keep crying. And you're going to keep going back to the war. This isn't a miracle cure. It's more like doing physical rehab. Small steps, little improvements, one day at a time."

"Like being on a saline drip," he said.

"Maybe, yeah," she said. "But my life's better with you in it, Ian. You made me... you *make* me want to take a chance again."

"Glad you took the chance on me," he said. "Think maybe I love you too, Cassie."

He put his arms around her and kissed her. The kiss tasted salty, tinged with sadness, but it was sweet, too. Cassie felt that melty, warm feeling again. She let herself feel it, let herself hope. The image of Dean flitted in front of her mind's eye, and for a moment she felt guilty, but she knew he wouldn't have wanted her to. He would've wanted her to be happy. She wasn't betraying him; she was honoring his memory by going on, moving forward. Like a Marine.

"I'd better grab a shower," he said, after.

"Me, too," she said. Then, "Would you like to join me?"

"Be glad to," he said with a smile that warmed her right to her toes.

Ben's door was still closed. They tiptoed past it to the bathroom, feeling furtive and adventurous. They set the water cooler than Cassie usually showered, letting it wash the sweat away. She soaped up her hands and let them roam over Ian's body, exploring him, learning him, and he did the same for her.

"You want to stay for supper?" she murmured into his ear.

"If you'll have me," he said. "Want me to cook something?"

"What can you cook?"

"Learned something you can make with canned pineapple and Spam," he said. "What you do is, you fry the Spam and then you add the pineapples, let the juice get into the meat. Just takes a few minutes. Goes okay with rice, or whatever else you got."

"Marine field cooking?" she guessed.

"Affirmative. Learned it from an old Gunnery Sergeant who picked it up when he was in Hawaii. Gunny said fresh pineapple's better than canned, but you can't usually get it fresh on deployment."

"I'll try it sometime," she said. "But I don't think I've got any Spam."

"I know how to cook goat, too," he said.

"You know, I didn't think you had much sense of humor when we first met. How about we just call in for pizza?"

"Works for me."

"Are you doing anything tomorrow?" she asked suddenly, not wanting to leave the future completely to chance.

"Going to church."

That startled her. "You told me you didn't believe in God," she said.

"Mr. Carlyle goes to Mass every Sunday," he replied. "Never misses one, except the time he was in the hospital. You go to church?"

"Not very much lately," she admitted. "I probably should. Got kind of out of the habit after... you know."

"Why don't you come with us?" he suggested. "I'll double-check with Mr. Carlyle, but he'll be okay with it."

"I'm Methodist," she said.

"Don't see the problem. Same God, right?"

She smiled. "Okay. I'd be happy to come."

* * *

After supper, after a game of Uno which Ben won, after Ben's bedtime story, after Ian had gone home to walk Miri and go to work, Cassie Jordan sat on her couch, alone, thinking.

She ought to feel happy, and for the most part, she did. She replayed the day in her mind, treasuring each moment. The way Ian's eyes had shone when he looked at her and her child. Ben licking the melting ice cream from his cone. The autographed baseball. The little boy asleep in the arms of the man he scarcely knew, but instinctively trusted. The taste of Ian's lips, salty-sweet. His hands, so gentle but so strong.

Cassie sighed and wrapped her arms around her elbows. How could she feel so good and still hurt? Because she did. She still felt the hollow place in her where Dean had been. Amputees were often surprised by "phantom pain," the ache in a limb that was long gone. But what was grief if not the ache in a part of her that was missing?

What had she expected? That Ian could just slide into her heart and shove the remnants of Dean out? Was that even what she wanted?

"It's not fair," she whispered. None of it was. It wasn't fair that Dean had never gotten to see his son grow up, would never grow old alongside his wife. It wasn't fair that Ben hardly remembered his father and might have to learn about manhood from a broken, traumatized stranger. It wasn't fair that Cassie was crying out her grief again when she'd been crying happy tears just a couple of hours before. And it wasn't fair to Ian that his lover was carrying a blackened, burnt-out torch for a comrade three years in his grave. But that was the way it was.

Back when she'd first been dating Dean, they'd gone to a karaoke bar and Dean had sung that one Marvin Gaye song from the '80s. Cassie remembered him looking her straight in the eye and singing about getting that feeling and needing sexual healing. He'd said it would make him feel so fine.

Marvin Gaye had gotten it wrong. Or else he hadn't gotten it all the way right. For Cassie, it felt more like surgery. She felt uniquely vulnerable and tender. Ian was her saline drip, sending a little stream of life into her withered heart, coaxing the dried-out organ back to life. He couldn't heal her; Cassie was too experienced a nurse to believe that. The patient was always ultimately responsible for her own healing. But he could give her a lifeline.

Maybe that would be enough. Cassie didn't know. But she wanted to find out.

About the Author

Steven Henry learned how to read almost before he learned how to walk. Ever since he began reading stories, he wanted to put his own on the page. He lives a very quiet and ordinary life in Minnesota with his wife and dog.

Also by Steven Henry

Ember of Dreams

The Clarion Chronicles, Book One

When magic awakens a long-forgotten folk, a noble lady, a young apprentice, and a solitary blacksmith band together to prevent war and seek understanding between humans and elves.

Lady Kristyn Tremayne – An otherwise unremarkable young lady's open heart and inquisitive mind reveal a hidden world of magic.

Robert Blackford – A humble harp maker's apprentice dreams of being a hero.

Master Gabriel Zane – A master blacksmith's pursuit of perfection leads him to craft an enchanted sword, drawing him out of his isolation and far from his cozy home.

Lord Luthor Carnarvon – A lonely nobleman with a dark past has won the heart of Kristyn's mother, but at what cost?

Readers love *Ember of Dreams*

"The more I got to know the characters, the more I liked them. The female lead in particular is a treat to accompany on her journey from ordinary to extraordinary."

"The author's deep understanding of his protagonists' motivations and keen eye for psychological detail make Robert and his companions a likable and memorable cast."

Learn more at tinyurl.com/emberofdreams.

Death's Dream Kingdom
Gabriel Blanchard

A young woman of Victorian London has been transformed into a vampire. Can she survive the world of the immortal dead—or perhaps, escape it?

"The wit and humor are as Victorian as the setting... a winsomely vulnerable and tremendously crafted work of art."

"A dramatic, engaging novel which explores themes of death, love, damnation, and redemption."

Learn more at clickworkspress.com/ddk.

Share the love!

Join our microlending team at
kiva.org/team/clickworkspress.

Keep in touch!

Join the Clickworks Press email list
and get freebies, production updates, special deals,
behind-the-scenes sneak peeks, and more.

Sign up today at clickworkspress.com/join.

CPSIA information can be obtained
at www.ICGtesting.com
Printed in the USA
BVHW071043050722
641279BV00006B/147